THE NEW WIFE

BOOKS BY SUE WATSON

Psychological Thrillers

The New Wife

The Forever Home

First Date

The Sister-in-Law

The Empty Nest

The Woman Next Door

Our Little Lies

Romantic Comedies

THE LOVE AND LIES SERIES

Love, Lies and Lemon Cake

Love, Lies and Wedding Cake

THE ICE-CREAM CAFE SERIES

Ella's Ice Cream Summer

Curves, Kisses and Chocolate Ice Cream

Snowflakes, Iced Cakes and Second Chances

The Christmas Cake Cafe

Bella's Christmas Bake Off

Summer Flings and Dancing Dreams

Snow Angels, Secrets and Christmas Cake

We'll Always Have Paris

THE NEW WIFE

SUE WATSON

bookouture

Published by Bookouture in 2021

An imprint of Storyfire Ltd.
Carmelite House
50 Victoria Embankment
London EC4Y 0DZ

www.bookouture.com

ISBN: 978-1-80019-282-9
eBook ISBN: 978-1-80019-281-2

For you, the reader, thank you so much for choosing this book. I hope it takes you somewhere special and that at the end of the journey, you're glad you came with me.

PROLOGUE

I'll never forget the way she looked – the sun behind her like a halo, the fitted, ivory satin gown, long, glossy blonde hair coiled and twisted down her back.

It was spring, fresh and warm for May, but we knew the weather would be perfect, because the sun always seemed to shine on Sam and Lauren. My son was marrying his childhood sweetheart, the daughter I'd never had. I think I was almost as happy as the bride and groom. In a moment both families had dreamed of, our children exchanged vows and gold rings, bringing us all together. And as a single parent, I wasn't just gaining a daughter, I was becoming family with people I loved – Lauren's parents, my best friends. Like all fairy stories, there'd been dragons to slay along the way, but on that warm afternoon, the smiles said it all. Their fairy tale had finally reached its happy ending.

Later, we jostled for position, our phone cameras on, clicking away, outside the church. The froth of spring blossom filling the air with the sweetest perfume. I remember the details so clearly; Sam awkward in a suit, the tiny freshwater pearls dotting Lauren's veil, the way they looked at each other, like a lifetime wouldn't be long enough. But, most of all, I remember the sound of her laughter. Lauren laughed such a lot, perfect white teeth, sparkly eyes, the elegant, inelegant way she hoisted up her bustier, causing her tiara to wobble, making her giggle – she could never be serious for long. Then my pride, as Sam walked into shot, as always, her safety net, reaching to help her steady the fairy princess headwear. Just seconds of chaos, but I'll always treasure the photo on my phone, the tiara echoing the gossamer veil, with a whisper of freshwater pearls lopsided, the two of them looking into each other's eyes, laughing, their happiness caught in a web of sunshine.

But just three months later, Lauren was dead.

CHAPTER ONE

I'll never forget the night he called to tell me. It was exactly 2.17 a.m. I know this because, as I later told the police, I was woken by the shrill ring of my mobile and remember the dancing neon digits on the alarm clock by my bed. I just *knew* something had happened, and like most mothers, my first thought was my son, who might have been grown up and married but was still my baby. And why was he calling me in the middle of the night? His name flashing on my phone at an ungodly hour set my brain on high alert, while my physical self tried to catch up. Even as I held the phone to my ear, my head was too jumbled with alarm and fear to hear what he was saying at first.

'Mum, Mum?'

I remember opening my mouth to respond, but nothing came out.

'It's Lauren,' he said, and I heard the voice of the little boy he used to be.

And when he'd told me, I refused to believe it and had to ask him to repeat it.

'She's dead, Mum, Lauren's *dead*.'

Afterwards I kicked myself for making him say it twice, what kind of mother does that? But then I've kicked myself so many times since then, and I'm bruised all over. So many things I missed, so much was happening around me that I took at face value. I trusted everyone – when, really, I should have trusted no one.

That night, everything changed – a big, red line was drawn right through all our lives, and everything from then on was cut into two halves. There was *before* Lauren, and *after* Lauren.

For Sam, it seemed impossible to comprehend, not just because she was his love, his wife, his future, but because he'd never really known a life without Lauren in it. I remember walking Sam to nursery school on that first day, the leaves crisp like cornflakes, clouds swollen and dark with the threat of rain. I'd both welcomed and dreaded my only child's first day at nursery, the beginning of the long goodbye. I was sad and happy and nervous for both of us.

As a mum of one, I was only too aware that first days would also be lasts, each watershed moment more precious as it loomed on the horizon, then quickly disappeared. So I devoured the first times, ate them up like hot toasted teacakes on a winter afternoon. The memories of Sam's childhood are still Instagram-perfect curated collections of glossy photos in my head. And that first morning is especially clear, because I've looked back often, and thought about how much it shaped both our lives. I remember it like yesterday, me and Sam walking hand in hand, he in his new Paddington wellingtons, kicking leaves, hurling himself into the slightest puddle. It was a half-mile from home, which must have seemed a long walk for a little three-year-old, but he was so excited, driven by adrenalin, he didn't complain once.

When we got to the nursery, the clouds seemed to suddenly burst, and the heavens opened. We dashed inside, where it was warm and dry, and the daubed paintings on the bright nursery walls seemed to welcome us into the next chapter of our lives.

In all the chaos of abandoned outdoor clothes and wellies, we eventually found Sam's designated coat peg, which, to his delight, was a bright green frog, with SAM written above. I didn't see Lauren at first, but I heard her. She was commanding attention with Hammer Horror-style screaming and clinging to her mum's knees, as the poor woman desperately tried to extricate herself. She was clearly dressed for work, in a skirt suit, tight pencil skirt, her thick blonde hair cut in a sharp, mid-length bob. I remember looking down at my jeans and fleece, wishing I'd dressed up a little, even if my outfit *was* far more sticky-finger friendly.

I tried not to stare as the nursery nurse attempted to coax the little girl from her mother's legs with the promise of 'a story about a very hungry caterpillar', as the mum made for the door. Not surprisingly, the last thing the child wanted was to be presented with the concept of a big green hairy insect with an enormous appetite while dealing with the threat of her mother's departure.

I stood with Sam, both onlookers in this drama, and now I can't help but wonder, was this a portent for the future? Back then, we didn't know them as Lauren and her mum, Helen, and had no idea how much these people would impact our lives.

I remember feeling really bad for poor Helen in her suit and heels, desperately trying to make her escape as a screaming, mucus-dripping toddler clung like a limpet to her stockinged legs. This full-scale drama went on for several minutes, with nursery staff approaching Lauren cautiously, as though she were a wild beast, no one prepared to put their head in the lion's mouth, even the experts. But as this continued, I was suddenly aware of Sam's hand slipping from mine, breaking away from me, and doing the unthinkable – slowly walking towards the ear-piercing meltdown. I called him back, but in all the racket he either didn't hear me or chose not to, but he did stop and survey the situation, before putting his hands on his ears and yelling: 'Stop making that noise!'

To everyone's amazement, Lauren suddenly stopped screaming and turned to see the upstart that had dared to shout at her. We all stood in wide-eyed surprise.

'Sam, that's *rude*,' I murmured into the silence, fearing judgement from the other adults.

'She's being *too* noisy, Mummy,' he responded crossly, as Lauren now peered out from behind her mum's knees. I was fully expecting her to set off again any minute, but then Sam uncovered his ears and said, 'Will you play with me?'

After a moment's silence, she nodded slowly and released the stranglehold on her mother, who smiled gratefully at me, then Sam, and flew from the building.

I watched in amazement, as my son held out his hand to the little girl, and she allowed him to guide her to the home corner, where, I was later told by the nursery supervisor, they played all day together.

Over the years, Helen and I often told the kids about this first encounter, which neither of them really remembered. It became family folklore, as we exaggerated and recreated the scene to amuse them, and as dialogue was added, we presented them with a story they probably didn't really own. But Helen and I loved embellishing the memory as much as our kids enjoyed reliving it, even Tim, Lauren's dad, regaled guests of their first meeting in his wedding speech, and he hadn't even been there. We all marvelled at how life was so random, and in choosing a nursery school for our children, we'd also, inadvertently, set the course of their lives.

'I was going to send him to St George's down the road. I don't know what made me enrol him at Little Bee's,' I'd say, like there was some force of destiny guiding my hand as I'd clicked through day care options on the internet.

Their subsequent journey from nursery school led them, twenty-three years later, to the altar on that sunny spring day when they finally said, 'I do.'

As a single parent, I'd always appreciated the way Tim and Helen had embraced Sam and I, welcoming us into their family. Even after the wedding, when the kids had flown off to Paris for a romantic honeymoon, they were sensitive to the fact I was now alone, insisting I meet up with them for dinner, drinks, a walk in the park. 'I wonder what the kids are doing now?' Helen would say, referring to the young honeymooners, and Tim usually rolled his eyes. 'Can we not speculate?' he'd say, in his policeman's voice, and I'd catch his eye and giggle.

'I meant *sightseeing*, I wonder what they're *seeing* now...' Helen clarified, and Tim and I would look at each other again, with exaggerated expressions. 'Oh, you two!' she'd respond, in affectionate reprimand.

The dynamic between us was easy, natural, evolved over years, and I felt like we just *knew* each other. Tim and I were the sensible ones, and while Helen pushed us out of our comfort zone, I liked to think we held her back from doing anything too crazy. And our kids' relationship seemed to mirror this – Lauren was like her mum, always choosing the scariest rides at the funfair, whereas Sam would stand back, petrified and pale-faced, thinking only of potential danger.

Their wedding was a prime example of this yin and yang. As Tim and I stressed about everything, from catering to parking to accommodation, Helen secretly arranged a joke waiter to cause a scene. She certainly liked to disrupt things – even her daughter's wedding. And when the waiter began dropping plates and shouting during the meal, I thought I was going to be sick. I glanced over at Tim, who looked just about ready to punch him, I could see his clenched fists, and was about to go over when the waiter suddenly took a bow. After a few seconds of realisation, the guests started laughing and clapping, Tim's fists unclenched and we caught each other's eye in relief. Sam was the same, he looked like he was about to pass out at the top table, while Lauren laughed loudly, shouting, 'Bravo!'

Lauren loved being a bride and spent the day beaming, relaxed, taking everything in her stride. I wished Sam had been able to relax and enjoy their special day too, but my son could be difficult to understand sometimes, and sadly he seemed on edge throughout the wedding. I thought he was probably nervous, his relief when they finally took off for their honeymoon was palpable, as he waved from the car taking them to the airport.

I understood Sam – for him this wasn't just a lovely wedding with cake and flowers. This was a marriage, and along with all the wonderful things, marriage brought with it a lot of responsibility – and it weighed on him. Lauren often joked that Sam's glass was always half empty while hers was brimming, but I don't think he's a pessimist, he's a realist.

As always, though, Lauren responded differently, drinking champagne, laughing with friends and throwing her shoes off to dance barefoot. I remember Sam joining me at the table after everyone had eaten. 'Have you had a nice time, Mum?' he asked.

'It's been wonderful,' I said, truthfully. 'I've had the loveliest time. But what about you? Have you enjoyed it?'

He shrugged. 'Oh, you know me, I'd rather have got married outside with just a few mates and family – everyone sitting around on hay bales and drinking Devon cider,' he said with a smile. Then he turned to the dance floor. 'But Lauren's happy, just look at her,' and we both gazed over to where Lauren had hitched up her skirts and was doing the twist.

I laughed. 'I could see Helen doing that on her wedding day.'

'She's doing it now!' Sam said, pulling a mock-horrified expression and making us both laugh.

I hadn't realised one of the dancing group was Helen, but there she was dancing away, several bottles of wine down. 'Like mother like daughter,' I said, watching them both fondly.

'Yeah,' he laughed, 'you wouldn't think she was twenty-six, would you?'

'Twenty-six,' I said with a sigh. 'It's so hard to believe, isn't it, seems like yesterday when you two were at nursery,' I said, and put my hand on his.

'Sometimes I feel older,' he said, as we watched Helen, still dancing and grabbing Lauren's veil to put on her own head. 'I definitely feel older than Helen tonight,' he said, rolling his eyes in the direction of his new mother-in-law.

'Yes, Helen's always seemed like a teenager to me,' I said, affectionately.

'I hope we're as happy as Tim and Helen are,' he said. 'I told Tim I'd look after Lauren as well as he has.'

'You won't go far wrong following Tim's lead, love,' I said.

I loved that Sam was so protective and took his marriage seriously, despite being so young. I was sure those two would last forever, even though they were so very different, which is why I was so shocked when he told me just a few weeks into the marriage that he thought Lauren was bored by him.

'What do you mean?' I'd asked, trying to hide my alarm at this revelation.

'She gets pissed off with me if I don't feel like going out at night. But things are different now we have the mortgage and bills to pay. And I don't want to go out drinking, come in late and have to get up for work the next day.'

One would think, as a junior doctor, neither would Lauren, but she had more stamina than Sam, and could probably dance all night and still get up the following morning fresh as a daisy.

I mentioned to Helen that the kids seemed to be having a few issues adjusting to married life, but she said, 'Georgie, the first couple of years of *any* marriage are hell. It's all about expectations and different lifestyles merging together and making sense. They'll work it out, don't worry.'

Having never been married, I probably had a rather idealistic view of what it's like. But having been married to Tim for more than twenty years, I figured she knew what she was talking about. Perhaps the honeymoon period was more about getting used to each other rather than lying on a bed of rose petals every night?

After all, they had a lot going on in their lives already, both with physically and mentally taxing jobs. Sam was a conservationist, employed by Devon's Dartmoor National Park to oversee ecological surveys in the area. He'd always been quiet, reserved even, but passionate about wildlife, and for a child who at just three years old created his own beetle farm, this career was always on the cards. He worked so hard to get a 2:2 degree in Environmental Studies, while Lauren, who'd always been naturally bright, partied through her medicine degree and gained a first.

Sam adored Lauren and from a relatively young (too young?) age he'd wanted to settle down. In fact, he proposed twice, which was all a bit traumatic. Eventually, Lauren said yes, and they often joked about it – even at the wedding, he referred to her in his speech as, 'The one that almost got away.' But deep down, I think we all knew those two were meant to be, and one way or the other they'd wind up together.

But still, it didn't seem like smooth sailing in those early days. I remember a few weeks after they'd returned from honeymoon, showing Lauren photos of her crazy dancing at the wedding.

'OMG, Georgie, I was so pissed. Do you think that's bad, a bride drunk at her own wedding?'

'I think it's perfectly acceptable.' I scrolled through more photos on my phone, holding one up to her.

'Oh God! I just hope none of my patients ever see these,' she said with a laugh.

'I won't share them... For a price,' I joked. 'Besides, I think your patients would be impressed – being a good dancer doesn't make you a bad doctor.'

'No, but apparently it makes you a bad ecological officer if you dance or do anything social for that matter,' she said with a sigh, changing the mood completely.

My heart sank, so there *was* some friction between the newly-weds. 'Honestly, Georgie, I sometimes think Sam loves his job more than me. He works such long hours and I end up on my own most nights. I love the cottage when Sam's there, but on my own, it's a bit... creepy.'

'Oh, love, I'm sorry you feel like that,' I said, hoping that perhaps Lauren's comment to Sam about him being boring was more about her being left alone some nights. Before the wedding, they'd moved out of their rented flat and into a little cottage on the edge of Dartmoor. I hadn't visited the place yet but what she said about being alone there made me question the wisdom of them being so far away from civilisation. 'You've only been there a short time, once you've settled in, hopefully you'll feel differently,' I offered. 'You'll feel more at home and won't mind being on your own.'

'I know,' she sighed, 'and you're right, but we rarely have any time off together,' she looked at me, hesitated, then said, 'I've started to stay late at work, even when I'm on an early shift, because I don't want to go back there alone.'

'But you love the cottage?' I reminded her, feeling slightly defensive of Sam. He did work long hours, but I never realised he had to work so late, which was unfortunate, especially as they were only just married.

'I know, I didn't think it would bother me being out there, but it gets dark early, it's cold, and you hear things outside and get paranoid. A prisoner escaped from Dartmoor prison recently, you must have read about it?'

I nodded. The imposing 200-year-old Victorian prison, that had housed some of the country's most notorious killers, stood just a stone's throw from the cottage. 'Perhaps you should get some cameras installed – just for your peace of mind,' I said, trying to offer a solution and not dwell on the escaped prisoner story and scare her further.

'Yeah, perhaps. It might make me feel better. I'm probably just being silly, but I feel like...' She looked away.

'What?'

She turned to look at me. 'Like someone's out there, watching.'

CHAPTER TWO

Sam and Lauren had been married and in their cottage a few weeks when we all finally got to see it. They'd moved in just before the wedding, but it was very basic and they hadn't had time to make it a home. We were all keen to see it, but driving up through the moors, I could understand her feeling a bit isolated and a little scared on her own at night, but on a summer's day, it was idyllic. Tim drove, and I sat in the back of the car with Kate, their younger daughter, who, at eighteen, clearly had better things to do than spend the evening with 'old people' in her newly married sister's garden.

'I hate family get-togethers,' she'd complained, as she plonked herself on the back seat of the car.

'I know it's not exactly cool,' I'd said, 'but Lauren's making veggie curry, and you can watch me and your mum drink too much; that might be fun?' I added, with a wink.

I saw a smile flicker across her face, soon replaced with an eye-roll and a shrug. 'As hilarious as that would be, Georgie, it'll still be boring. No offence,' she'd added as an afterthought.

'None taken,' I'd said with a smile.

Once we'd set off and Tim and Helen chatted in the front, I did make a second attempt at conversation with Kate, but she seemed more interested in what her parents were saying and just gave me a sideways glance. I saw this as an indication to shut up, and the rest of the journey was endured in silence as I gazed out of the window.

Pulling up outside the cottage, I took in Sam and Lauren's new home. Built from local stone, it sat high on the exposed moorland peaks, all big blue skies meeting swirling purple heather over endless moorland. Just the house and the countryside; there was no one for miles.

As soon as we parked up, Sam rushed out to meet us. 'What do you think?' he called, standing on the doorstep, arms open wide.

'It's lovely darling,' I enthused, while climbing out of the car, gazing at the cottage. It could be pretty, with some tree clearing and work on the outside, which looked bruised and unloved and needed freshening up with a coat of white paint.

'It needs work out here, but inside it's been totally renovated,' Sam said proudly, helping with the cool boxes, ushering us into the cottage.

He was right; on the outside, it looked quite traditional, but inside it was very different.

'Ooh, you've got a trendy hallway,' Helen enthused as we took it all in. 'I know we've seen it online, but it doesn't do it justice, it's fab,' she said, as we all gazed at the surprising white spiral staircase twisting up from the black and white tiled floor. Kate scowled, and scuttled on past us into the living room, where she could crack on with vital matters on her phone.

'*Love* this,' I said, caressing the wrought-iron of the stair handrail. It was painted brilliant white, and looked like lace.

'Lauren and I fell for that as soon as we walked in,' Sam said. 'It swung it for us really, the game changer – it's great, isn't it?'

'Are these steps real marble?' Tim asked, bending down to touch them.

'Yeah, *solid* marble,' he said, proudly.

I made approving noises, but I guessed Tim was asking for safety reasons rather than aesthetic. Meanwhile, the mother in me was also wondering at the slipperiness of marble for little feet, should they one day have children, but I brushed it away and looked upwards at the circular stairs snaking up through the house. 'It's like looking up into infinity,' I said, suddenly feeling light-headed. I grabbed onto Helen's arm. 'Oh, I feel quite dizzy... I shouldn't have looked up like that,' I groaned with an embarrassed laugh.

'Are you okay?' she said, alarmed at my slight wobble.

I nodded, and being Helen, she had to test it for herself.

'Ooh, my God, I can see what you mean!' she exclaimed, looking up at the swirling infinity, while holding on to me in mock faint. 'Quite the high, eh, Georgie?' she joked.

Tim rolled his eyes and smiled indulgently at us. 'Will you two please behave,' he said before turning to Sam and asking in his dad voice, 'Is there a garage, I didn't see one?'

Sam's face dropped slightly. 'No, but there's room for three cars on the drive,' he offered.

Tim gave a doubtful look, before continuing his inspection of the hallway.

'You don't need a garage,' I murmured in support, and Helen agreed, and we both admired the wallpaper.

'It's quite a way out of town out here,' Tim said, holding open the door that led into the main room of the house, 'what about Lauren getting to work?'

'She's got a car,' Sam said, a hint of defensiveness in his voice. 'It isn't a problem.'

'Not for *you*, but it's quite a drive for Lauren – Plymouth's at least forty-five minutes away.'

I loved Tim, but he really was the overprotective father at times.

Sam's jaw twitched. Tim meant well, and obviously concerned for his daughter, but sometimes he didn't read the room. All Sam wanted that day was our approval, and in the absence of his own father, he wanted *Tim's* approval. Sam had always looked up to Tim, and over the years we'd both considered Tim to be something of a surrogate father.

'Lauren's happy to do the drive into Plymouth to the hospital, so...' Sam replied, edgy, still defensive.

Helen took a breath and gave me a knowing look. Here was Sam proudly showing us his lovely new home and all it needed was an ooh and ahh, and to tell them how happy we were for them. They'd already bought the house, signed for the mortgage and moved in, and it was up to them to decide if it worked, not Tim.

'I think it's lovely, so far, can't wait to see the rest,' Helen said, picking up on the tension coming from Sam.

'You've always liked it out here on the moors, haven't you, Mum,' Sam said, with a sideways glance at Tim.

The old silverback had better watch his step, I thought, as there were signs my son might challenge Tim, now he was married and king of his own castle.

'Yes, I love it out here, it's a place for all seasons,' I replied in an attempt to reassure Sam and show my support but sounding like a bloody tourist infomercial. I'd had many happy hours playing on the moors as a child, and later I'd brought Sam there as a child; I think it influenced his choice to pursue a life there that was outdoors and close to nature.

'It's great for wildlife, and feels so away from it all,' Sam was saying. 'I've worked on the moors for a while, but *living* here is something else.'

This was his dream – the location, the cottage itself was very Sam, who yearned for a simple, rustic life surrounded by the wilds of nature. I did ask myself if this was Lauren, and had to admit I wasn't sure; she'd always seemed sophisticated in her tastes. But what did I know? It was still early days, love changes people, marriage was as much about compromise as everything else.

We followed Sam into the living room, where Lauren greeted us with hugs and slight panic because one of the electricity points wasn't working in the kitchen. Tim immediately stepped in to help, and she took him through to show him, while calling over her shoulder, 'Sadie's on her way, she's already decided which room is hers,' and she laughed.

Lauren had met Sadie at secondary school, when they were both eleven. Sadie's parents had split up and, as she got older, she became pretty wild, skipped school and was eventually suspended. Sadie seemed to invite trouble, but in spite of her problems and her behaviour, Lauren always stood by her and Helen continued to welcome her into their home. Lauren and Sadie were like sisters, which I think made Kate feel left out sometimes, and I know she and Sadie didn't get on, but Kate didn't really try – with *anyone*.

Even now, as we looked around Lauren's brand-new lounge, Kate didn't make an effort and her mood hung like a grey plume of smoke over us. But Lauren wasn't bothered – she had her husband, her family and her best friend was on her way over. My daughter-in-law was so happy that day and any concerns I'd had about her unhappiness in this little cottage lost on the moors were gone.

'It's all high spec,' she said, walking back into the room, having given her father his instructions regarding the plug point in the kitchen. 'We just need some furniture now,' she said, while doing a little twirl in the middle of the room. I was reminded of the little girl at nursery school all those years before.

'Yeah, you do need furniture,' Helen agreed, with a laugh. 'Those sofas you fancied... the ones from Harvey Nichols? I could *so* see them in here,' she said, her eyes lit up, as she mentally placed the two sofas in the room.

'Oh my *God*, those cream ones, yes!' Lauren clapped her hands together excitedly. 'Facing each other, near the fire?'

'Exactly,' Helen nodded vigorously. 'And some beautiful throws?'

'Ooh yeah,' Lauren squealed.

Tim wandered back into the room slightly bemused at the excitement and glanced over at Sam who rolled his eyes. The two men were clearly unable to reach the same level of delirium as their wives over soft furnishings.

'Harvey Nicks, eh? That'll be a nice price.' Tim sighed.

'Oh shut up,' Helen chastised affectionately. 'It's her first home, everything has to be perfect.'

'*Perfect?* Remember *our* first home?' he said. 'We had your mother's second-hand furniture and a flea-ridden rug from a charity shop.' They both laughed at the memory, but even as he muttered about 'kids today' wanting everything, I knew he'd sign the cheque – nothing was too much for Lauren. It made me feel a little guilty that the Jacksons were buying expensive sofas. Fortunately, our friendship was such that I knew they wouldn't judge me or feel short-changed for not spending as much as they did on our children's home. I'd spent what I considered to be a fortune on four beautiful Emma Bridgewater mugs for their house-warming gift, but it was nothing like the cost of a sofa. And the kind of sofa that Lauren wanted would set me back a few months' salary in my office manager's job with a local children's charity. But I wasn't in the same league as Helen and Tim with their big careers and generous salaries. The Jacksons had never been short of money, but they certainly earned it, and Tim *lived* his role as Detective Chief Inspector.

I'd warned Sam before they married that Lauren wouldn't want any of his old stuff in the new cottage. 'Lauren's used to the best, and the cheap duvet covers and charity-shop stuff I bought for your student house won't be appreciated,' I'd said.

'We can't *afford* all new stuff,' he'd sighed, 'but she'll run to Mummy and Daddy and I guess they'll give her what she wants.' I'd heard a tinge of resentment, and wondered if this was because he wanted to be the one to buy these things for his wife, or he simply hated the materialism.

As a parent I could see that Tim and Helen just wanted the best for Lauren, and they had the money, so why not? They'd also helped with the deposit for the house; it was the only way Sam and Lauren could have afforded to buy a home. I'd asked Sam how much they'd given them, but he was deliberately vague.

'They don't want you to know,' he'd said. 'Helen doesn't want you to feel weird about it.'

'Do you feel weird about it?' I'd asked, knowing Sam's feelings were more important than mine regarding this.

He'd shrugged, which indicated to me that he did, and for that matter so did I.

I had no idea how much high-ranking police officers got paid or high-end estate agents, but judging by their lifestyle, Tim and Helen certainly did okay, and it wasn't just their own kids, I knew for a fact that they'd supported Sadie through university, and even now helped her sometimes with her rent. I was grateful that their generosity was being extended to my child, but at the same time felt guilty I couldn't contribute.

While Helen and Lauren continued to discuss where to put the sofas, I gravitated towards the double French doors, over-looking the garden and the moors beyond.

'Great views, Mum?' Sam said, wandering over to look out with me.

'I bet you're in heaven, aren't you, love?' I said, putting my arm around his waist. He was so much taller than me now, it was hard to imagine how I ever put my arm around his shoulders.

'Yeah, I love it but never thought I'd be lucky enough to live out here.'

'Is Lauren happy with it too?' I asked quietly, in my not very subtle way of reminding him this wasn't just about his happiness. Sam loved the national park, the wildlife, the history of this place of granite and dark clouds, but it wasn't everyone's cup of tea, and Lauren had already indicated she was lonely and a bit scared on her own. Sam could be quite single-minded about something if he wanted it badly enough, and I hoped he hadn't pushed Lauren into moving out here.

'She *loves* it,' he said dismissively and, without looking at me, turned to go into the kitchen, where Tim was fixing the electric point and Lauren was now wondering where best to put the coffee machine.

When she found 'the perfect spot', Tim had to break it to her there were no plug points there, but to avoid heartbreak, he was soon offering to put a new plug point in just as Sadie arrived.

I was still gazing through the French doors when Helen joined me.

'Gorgeous, isn't it?' she murmured.

'Beautiful,' I said with a sigh, happy that my son had a better start than I had.

'There's nothing for miles though, is there?' she noted, walking out onto the grass. 'I never imagined Lauren somewhere like this.'

'No, but they both seem to love it,' I replied.

'Miles and miles of granite,' she murmured, ignoring my attempt at optimism, and shivered, despite the warm day. 'On wintry days, those big, grey clouds come rolling in, swallowing you up.' She stared out at the landscape, which now seemed less appealing.

I wasn't sure how to respond to this sudden melancholy, something I'd rarely, if ever, seen from Helen.

Then she turned to me and smiled. 'I just hope they don't live to regret moving out here, with only each other for company.'

I left it a few seconds, then said, 'It's only forty-five minutes away from us.'

'Yeah, in good weather, but you know what it's like here. In winter, you can get snowed in for weeks.'

I wondered again how Sam had convinced Lauren to agree to living here, because as much as I loved the area for a day trip, or a bracing walk, Helen was right. Dartmoor had a wild, rugged beauty; in spring and summer it was dressed in swathes of purple-hued heather dotted with baby lambs and wild ponies. But in winter, it was a different place: thick, rising mists, extreme cold and in this bleak, beautiful emptiness lurked the foreboding grey-bricked, 200-year-old Dartmoor prison.

Having lived in Devon all my life, I knew that even in midsummer, you could walk outside in radiant sunshine and an hour later be surrounded by thunder clouds and torrential rain. Nothing was quite as it seemed, and looking back, I realise I should have seen the conflicting landscape concealing hidden, jagged flaws, the unpredictable climate, a perfect view bathed in sunshine, the threat of thunder just moments away. Life in all its beauty and darkness.

I looked beyond at the endless land, no one for miles, and I don't know why, but I felt the urge to turn around and glance behind me. Through the open door, I glimpsed the twisty white staircase, and suddenly felt very cold.

CHAPTER THREE

The day after our visit to the cottage I received a call from James Ronson, a former teacher of Sam's. He'd been a guest at the evening part of Sam and Lauren's wedding, and though I'd only met him a few times over the years at parents' evenings and school fetes, we chatted like old friends that evening at the wedding. 'I don't know anyone,' he'd said. 'I was invited in my formal capacity as former schoolteacher to the bride and groom,' he'd added, jokingly, which explained why he wasn't with his wife, a chatty blonde I remembered from some of the school events. Since leaving school, Lauren had kept in touch with James and had given talks to his sixth-formers about medicine as a career. Helen and Tim had been friends with James and his wife before they met me, and when the children were younger, would meet them for a drink. I remember Helen asking if I'd babysit for them, which I was happy to do, but it stung a little. My single status meant I wasn't always welcome when friends socialised with other couples, as I wasn't a member of that club. The friendship between the two couples seemed to fizzle out eventually, probably because the Ronsons didn't have children, and still wanted to enjoy a more sophisticated child-free social life. I wondered why James was alone at the wedding, but noticed he still had a wedding ring on, so had assumed that his wife wasn't able to attend. It didn't come up in conversation, and I didn't like to ask directly, so by the end of the night, I was none the wiser.

When, weeks later, my phone rang, I didn't for a moment expect it to be James, not least because I couldn't remember giving him my phone number.

'Hey, I hope you don't mind me calling, I got your number off Tim,' he'd started.

'Oh, it might have been nice if Tim had asked me if I minded him giving out my number to strange men,' I'd joked, while actually feeling a little pissed off at Tim.

'Oh, I begged him for it,' he'd said with a laugh. 'I know these days it's cool to "slip into" someone's DMs – I think that's what the kids call it?'

I'd laughed. 'Yeah, I mean a phone call is *so* old-fashioned.'

'Or *lame*, as my sixth-formers would say.'

There was a silence, and as he'd rung me, I didn't feel the need to fill it, so waited for him to speak.

'I had a good time at the wedding,' he'd suddenly said.

'Me too.' I could feel my heart beating. He was married, surely he wasn't going to ask me out?

'So, I was thinking, well – wondering, if you might like to meet for a coffee or a drink?'

'Aren't you married?' I'd asked, realising this sounded rather accusatory but it had to be addressed.

'I *was* married…' he'd replied.

'Oh, you aren't together anymore?' I recalled the ring on the third finger of his left hand.

'No, she died, two years ago,' he'd said, sadly.

'I'm so sorry,' I'd replied, a little embarrassed. I'd had no idea, but why should I? The fact he'd asked to meet made it quite clear that for him this was more than just finding someone to talk to at a wedding where you didn't know anyone. I did find him attractive, but I hadn't had a date for years and, in truth, it made me quite nervous talking to him on the phone like this, let alone a date.

'So, what do you think?' he'd asked. 'About meeting up, we could even do dinner if you'd like?'

So, with nothing in my diary for the foreseeable, I told myself it would be good for me to get out and took him up on his invitation.

We arranged to meet the following week, and just getting ready that evening shredded my nerves. I was so nervous I had to abandon the necklace I'd planned to wear because my anxious fingers couldn't fasten it. But when I arrived, he was sitting there waiting with a bottle of wine. 'I remembered from the wedding you drink Sauvignon Blanc,' he said, standing to greet me, and within minutes we were right back to where we'd been at Sam and Lauren's wedding, lots of easy-going laughter and intelligent conversation. We also discovered we had a lot in common, including, of course, our friends.

'So, do you get to see Helen and Tim much these days?' I asked.

Even in the semi-darkness, he looked slightly uncomfortable. 'It's difficult. We were friends when we were all much younger, and over the years we've got together, but until the wedding, I hadn't seen them since Becky's funeral.'

We sat in silence for a few moments, it was awful to think that someone in their forties, around my own age, had died. 'Sam invited me to the wedding,' James said, presumably in an attempt to fade the image of his wife's funeral from our minds.

'... it was very kind of him, people don't always want you at parties when you're single – especially weddings,' he added with a sad smile.

'Tell me about it.' I rolled my eyes and took a small sip of wine.

'Have you ever been married, Georgie?' he asked, rather suddenly.

'No. Sam's father wasn't interested in marriage,' I replied, shrugging it off but smiling at the same time. I didn't want his pity.

Years before, I'd fallen in love with brown-eyed, handsome Nathan and become pregnant with Sam very quickly, but he turned out to be an angry, abusive man and when I couldn't lift my son out of his cot because my back hurt from the previous night's beating, I knew I had to leave. I couldn't expose my two-year-old boy to that, so had packed a bag and ran to a women's refuge, and while there, life offered me a hand, as it sometimes does. A distant cousin died and I inherited enough money to put a small deposit down on a house, and eventually find work with the children's charity.

I felt it too soon to tell James about my life with Nathan – the only person I'd ever shared it with was Helen, and she understood why I found it hard to be with someone. But James seemed different; he was gentle and funny and kind, and when he dropped me off at the end of the evening and asked if he could see me again, I said yes.

Turned out we were both busy in the week and Lauren and Sam had invited us all over for a barbecue the following Saturday.

'Don't worry, I'll call you next week,' James said when I explained I was booked up at the weekend too. 'We can work something out then... but I do understand if you'd rather not and you're just being nice?'

'No, I am *genuinely* busy this week,' I stressed, concerned I might just be ending this before it started.

In retrospect, I can see it might not have been the best timing, but the next day, I called Sam and asked if he'd mind me bringing James to his barbecue.

'I know it's just close family, but everyone knows him, but if you think it's too much then—'

'Mum, I'm cool with it,' Sam said.

I'd never dated while he was growing up; I worried he'd already been exposed to someone he shouldn't with his father. The physical scars fade, but the emotional ones never do, and I still have nightmares about Nathan's fist landing on my cheek. I'd sometimes catch a flash of that remembered rage in my son's eyes, and though I'd brought him up to be kind and decent, a little part of me worried that Sam may have inherited traces of his father's anger. I just had to hope that nurture had overcome the undeniable power of nature.

'About time you got yourself a fella,' he teased, seemingly quite pleased about me seeing someone. Now he was married, perhaps he felt it should be my turn to find someone, probably because he didn't want to worry about me being alone.

So with Sam happy about my embryonic relationship, I felt it was time to tell Helen, but she and Tim had gone away to his brother's in Ireland, and I didn't like to phone her and interrupt their holiday just to tell her about James. Besides, I reckoned that Tim might already have told Helen he'd asked for my number, and knowing those two, it was possibly even a set-up. Their best female friend with one of their male friends – both single? It was begging to happen.

It was a bonus that James already knew everyone I was close to. He'd taught both Sam and Lauren and he'd been one of those teachers who always went the extra mile. He helped Sam to get a GCSE in maths, which he struggled with, and in her final year at school gave Lauren extra maths lessons in readiness for Oxbridge applications. To Tim and Helen's deep disappointment, Lauren never got into Oxford or Cambridge and chose to go to Manchester to do medicine. After a very difficult time at school, James had seen potential in Sadie, who was academically gifted, and along with other students, tutored her after school. She also chose to do medicine at Manchester like Lauren, but Helen still worried about the rather wayward Sadie's influence on her daughter. 'I'd hoped that Lauren could finally get away from her,' she'd said. 'It's a bit too *Single White Female* for me. Sadie follows Lauren wherever she goes, I can't believe she's followed her to uni.' Even now, the friendship had continued, Sadie didn't live too far from the cottage, so apparently was round there all the time. I wondered if perhaps Sadie being just a few miles down the road was one of the reasons Lauren had agreed to move there. I knew one thing, if Sam had a friend like Sadie, I'd have discouraged it from the beginning. From what I could gather, Sadie had no real home life, and was allowed to roam free, and without guidance she made bad choices. Helen said she bunked off school, had loads of boyfriends, and was sexually precocious from the age of about twelve. Still, in spite of all that, the Jacksons were kind enough to try to help, and from new school shoes to a university education, they'd basically funded her life. I'm not sure that even if I'd had the money I'd have been as kind and caring as they were.

Thankfully, Lauren and Sadie's friendship wasn't my problem, and now Sam wasn't a child anymore, I had my own life to think about and I was looking forward to seeing James again.

I felt quite a frisson putting on my make-up and getting dressed for the barbecue. I was excited to see the kids but also quite giggly at the prospect of turning up with a man on my arm after all the years of being single. I just knew Helen would be delighted, she was always trying to fix me up with Tim's colleagues, friends of her brother, random men on the street. I never took part in any of her real or imagined 'blind dates', telling her I was happy single and didn't need a man. And I was, but a good-looking guy who used to teach my son (therefore nothing like my cold, abusive ex) and someone my friends knew and liked was my kind of blind date.

I applied my lipstick, trying not to smile at the thought of Helen's face, when I walked in with James. In all the years I'd known her, I'd only ever had the odd date that never seemed to go any further, so it had always been 'just Georgie'. So for me to arrive that afternoon with a bottle of chilled Sauvignon and 'Mr Ronson', would bring squeals of delight from Helen. I smiled to myself imagining her dragging me off to the bottom of the garden demanding to know the details. She was so sophisticated, but could also be such a kid, and reminded me of the friends I'd had as a teenager, always ready for fun, a few drinks and a laugh. Helen was good for me, we all need to unleash our inner teenagers now and again, especially women in their forties who'd met someone that made them feel eighteen again. And that was how I felt.

I drove to the cottage with James – as this was my invite, I felt I should – plus it was way out on the moors and not easy to find.

As we pulled up outside, I could hear Lauren laughing in the garden. It still haunts me, her laughter.

'They're out the back,' I said to James, as we climbed out of the car, and I led him round the side of the house and through the gate into the back garden.

It was a lovely evening, in late May, birds still singing, the garden a beautiful, small sloping space, light dappling through the trees. Helen was stood by the French doors chatting to Sadie, Tim and Sam were doing their caveman thing with steaks on the barbie. As soon as Sam saw me, his face lit up, he looked older, more mature – perhaps it was just me, but I felt like being married had already altered his features.

I guided James past the prickly rose bush, and Sam and Tim immediately stepped out from behind the barbecue to greet him. Sam went off to get him a beer, while Tim looked from me to him. 'Didn't expect to see you here, James,' he said, smiling.

'Georgie kindly invited me,' James replied.

'Don't look surprised, you gave him my number,' I teased, expecting Tim to laugh, but he didn't. He just nodded slowly, looking from me to James, his face without expression. I was expecting this encounter to be fun, but there was an awkwardness between the men that made me long for Helen to intervene.

I turned around; she was still by the French doors with Sadie, they were talking, but I knew Helen only tolerated her for Lauren. She had seen me but hadn't come over to say hello, which was really odd. I gave her a little wave and a smile, but she seemed to be avoiding me, and looked away.

What the hell was going on here? Had I totally misjudged the response to me bringing James along? Had I got it wrong and she and Tim didn't *like* him? I couldn't work it out, so while the men stood in silence, I abandoned James and began to make my way over to Helen. Just at that moment, Lauren appeared, and Helen said something to her. I stopped heading towards them as I saw Lauren's face; she looked horrified, and Helen gently moved her inside and followed.

I was so confused, I didn't know which way to turn, but at that point, Sam reappeared with a bottle of beer for James and a glass of wine for me, so I turned and walked back to where James was stood. He was alone now; Tim had gone back to the barbecue. I smiled at him and thanked Sam for the drinks, feeling very vulnerable. Why were my friends behaving this way, and why did I feel like the Jacksons were forming a circle – and I wasn't in it?

Sam started talking to James about the cricket that day, so I took the opportunity to wander off and make my way into the house. I had to find out what the hell was going on with Helen and Lauren, but before I could get inside, Sadie emerged, smiling and holding up her glass. 'Can I get you another?' She must have seen I was holding a full glass – so was she just trying to keep me away from Helen?

'I'm fine thanks,' I said, holding up the glass.

We chatted for a little while about the wedding and the weather and found a few other tiny little corners of common ground. But all the time we were talking, I kept thinking, *Where's Helen and Lauren and why did they look so horrified? And is Sadie just chatting, or is she standing on guard?*

'Cute little garden, isn't it?' she was saying now.

I gazed around, I was probably overthinking things regarding Helen and Lauren, so I tried to push it from my mind. The garden wasn't what I would describe as cute. It really wasn't the bijou suburban garden with parasols, sofas and trendy firepit I would have expected for Lauren. No doubt that would come, but for now the garden furniture was rickety wicker and Sam had fashioned a rustic firepit from old breeze blocks. He didn't care how it looked; my son would sit for hours with his binoculars, gazing at the birds and wildlife, oblivious to what he was sitting on and whether it was fashionable for this year's garden. But it wasn't Lauren.

'It's an elevated woodland terrace,' I replied. 'That's what it said in the estate agent's blurb.'

Sadie looked at me. 'I guess.'

We stood in silence, nothing more to say, as she continued to stand in the doorway, blocking my entrance.

Then, to my relief, Helen popped her head out from behind Sadie. 'Sorry, Georgie, it's chaos – I'll be with you in a minute, just opening the champagne.' She was smiling broadly and waving a bottle in the air, the usual Helen energy had been restored, the megawatt smile, the reapplied lipstick, all was right with the world. Had I completely misinterpreted the look on her face when she saw me and James? And what about Lauren?

'Coming through, coming through,' Helen was calling now, and as she approached, Sadie seemed to decide it was okay to leave me. She wandered over to chat to Sam as soon as Helen appeared in the doorway, her voice raised in excitement – or was it nerves? It wasn't like Helen to be anxious; she was the coolest, calmest, most confident person I knew. She was now teetering onto the tiny patio with a large tray containing eight glasses and a misty bottle of champagne protruding from an ice bucket. Once she hit the slope of the garden, she staggered slightly and I rushed to help her, holding her arm with one hand and grabbing a couple of glasses.

'Damage limitation,' I said. 'If you hit the deck and the glasses break, at least there's one each for you and me.' We both laughed, as she negotiated the sloping ground in heels. We reached the rickety old garden table and safely deposited the tray. We were just a few feet away from where the men were now standing.

'What are we like, Georgie?' Helen said, laughing at the way we'd both almost collapsed due to the gradient of the garden. Then she looked up, as if she'd not seen him before. 'James,' she said, by way of welcome. It struck me as rather flat for Helen. And I started to feel slightly paranoid again. Perhaps she *was* pissed off because I'd brought him along? 'Did James come with *you*?' she suddenly said under her breath. The question was directed at me, but she was looking at the men drinking beer and talking meat.

I looked over at them, and in a voice that matched hers, said, 'Yes, I asked Sam if I could bring him.' I gave her a sideways glance, feeling uncomfortable as my suspicions were confirmed – Helen *was* pissed off with me.

She raised her head in a half nod. I didn't know where to take this, so just started talking, hoping she'd thaw.

'James and I... we got chatting, at the wedding and he... we went for dinner...' I offered, like it was an apology. Why did I feel the need to do this? I'd been so looking forward to telling her all about going out with James, I felt cheated, like I was defending myself against some kind of judgement I didn't understand.

'Oh, I see,' she said, lifting the champagne bottle from the bucket. I noticed she was chewing her lip, something Helen always did when she wasn't comfortable. I remembered her doing this when one of the mums at school said she'd seen Kate smoking weed. It's one of the few times I ever saw Helen speechless and unable to cope with something she didn't want to face – like now.

I had to get to the bottom of this. 'I thought you liked James, you and Tim,' I said, still under my breath. 'Didn't you used to go out with James and his wife?'

'Yeah,' she replied, then turned to look at me. '*She* was lovely...' And there it was, *whatever* it was, I hadn't been paranoid, Helen had a problem with me bringing James – and now it was hanging in the air.

'Are you annoyed that I brought him?' I murmured.

'No, oh no, no, no,' she said too many times, while reapplying that big, beaming smile.

'It's just... you seem, a bit pissed off?'

'Oh I'm sorry, George, just bloody exhausted from travelling... no, it's all good – all good,' she said, putting her free arm around me in a quick hug. Then she returned to the champagne. 'Come on, everyone, we have something to celebrate,' she said, 'the Jacksons and the Moores are finally family – to the Jackmoores!' She popped the cork and gave the bottle to Tim to pour, while she handed round the glasses, and I joined in smiling. But even as we raised our glasses to 'the happy couple', I was aware of her displeasure, an intangible thing I could see but couldn't fathom as it strung through the trees like fairy lights.

CHAPTER FOUR

Dusk and woodsmoke filled the air, the champagne bottle now empty, the barbecue cooling, napkins scattered on the table. Another celebration of our children's union, another celebration of us and, when I look back now and think about our friendship, it's evenings like this I remember. Our children were happy, everyone was well and life was good – or so we thought. I often wonder if I'd known then what I know now, could I have saved Lauren? But back then I had no idea that the gathering of old friends, the scent of jasmine clouding the dusk and tea lights flickering in jars were just dressing. If only I'd looked closer at that perfect summer scene and glimpsed what loitered in the shadows, watching and waiting.

As night came down like a blanket, the stars shivered, the drinks flowed, and Helen returned to her old self. The family dynamic seemed to have found itself again, as Tim played host and Helen giggled like a schoolgirl while the rest of the cast fell into their roles. Despite being sober, I started to enjoy myself. Sam and James were getting along, laughing too loudly, fuelled by beer and bonhomie. Kate, as usual, sat alone, gazing ahead, always around us, always quiet, but always listening too. She wore headphones, apparently listening to music, but was quick to comment if someone addressed her, or her name was mentioned. Sometimes

Kate made me feel quite uneasy. But that was just Kate – she was nothing like Lauren. Or Helen for that matter.

When Sam lit a small fire, everyone sat in a circle, chatting and drinking.

'That's something we need,' Lauren suddenly said, 'a decent firepit.'

'I made it,' Sam said, 'it *is* decent.' He snapped, clearly taking offence at her remark. Without looking at her, he took an angry swig from his beer bottle.

'It looks like shit though,' Lauren replied under her breath, but as I was sitting next to her, I heard it.

'Don't start, Lauren,' Sam replied wearily.

I looked around to see if anyone else was seeing this, but the others were caught up in their own conversations. I shifted uneasily in my chair and told myself this was nothing, all couples argue, but Sam wasn't letting this go. He never knew when to let go, always wound himself up and had to have the last word. I know it's hard to be objective about our children, but I never believed Sam had anger issues like his father; I put his 'passion' down to a strong sense of fairness. If he felt something was unjust, that someone wasn't being treated correctly, it made him angry. And now, I felt his hurt, and in my view, he was justified in his resentment of Lauren's criticism. I knew he'd worked hard to make that firepit, and was proud of what he'd done, so it must have hurt keenly for his wife to condemn it in that way.

'Why don't you get Mummy and Daddy to buy you a shiny new firepit,' he hissed.

Lauren shook her head, like she didn't want him to say anything else.

'I don't believe you,' he said, still quietly, but slurring slightly as the beer had taken over. 'You always run to them with your problems, and having the wrong firepit is obviously eating away at you.' Then he leaned in and said something in her ear that I didn't hear, but clearly made her uncomfortable, and she wrapped her arms around herself.

I took a sip of Coke to swallow my feelings. I was almost scared for them. This wasn't about a firepit, but about something far deeper. And the tension continued to shimmer over the fire, as Lauren gazed into it.

I didn't want to catch anyone's eye and get caught up in this, so turned to look into the flames. Through the smoke, I could see to the other side of the garden, where Sadie was talking to Tim, who nodded slowly as she talked; it looked to me like she was giving him instructions and he was just agreeing to them. I didn't know her very well, but I always felt that Sadie could be quite controlling, manipulative even, like she still hadn't got enough from them. I sometimes wondered if she really appreciated what they'd done for her. Did she realise the sacrifices they'd made to send her to university along with their own daughter? They didn't have to do that, they were good people, but Sadie was a survivor, and sometimes good people get taken advantage of by the Sadie's of the world.

I kept glancing over at Sam and Lauren. But they hadn't spoken since the flare-up a few minutes before, and I was glad when Helen joined me; I wanted to chat and take my mind off things. But she didn't seem to want to talk, so we just sat side by side watching the flames while Sam and James talked about football.

'You okay?' I asked Helen quietly.

'Yeah... it's just...'

'What?' I said, keen to know, assuming she was about to explain the weirdness earlier.

'Well, it's just... oh nothing.' She closed off, which wasn't like her.

'No, go on, what were you going to say?' I pressed.

'Oh... just... just that I can't see our grandchildren playing in *this* garden.' She turned to me, raised her eyebrows and sat back. That wasn't what she was going to say – why was she being like this?

'It's very dark out here, isn't it?' I sighed, unable to find the words I needed. If Helen wasn't prepared to talk to me about what was bothering her, I couldn't force it out, but perhaps I could try to gently tease it from her?

She nodded slowly, her eyes caught up in the fire. 'No street lamps to pollute the darkness, but that means you can see all the stars.'

I smiled, this was more like the Helen I knew, seeing the rainbow rather than the rain.

'I wonder if this time in five years we'll be grandmas,' I said, picking up on her earlier comment.

'Oh, I hope it's this time *next* year.'

'Yes, but *two* bedrooms,' I said under my breath so no one would hear. 'We want a grandchild each, don't we?'

She smiled and, reaching out, patted my hand. 'Let's hope it's in our stars. And let's hope Lauren allows me near her children.'

I started to laugh, but then realised she wasn't joking. 'What do you mean?'

'Oh... we're just not getting on at the moment.' She gave a shrug, didn't take her eyes from the fire. 'She doesn't approve of me, of my "life choices",' she made speech marks with her fingers.

'I don't understand. What does she mean by life choices?'

'Oh, something and nothing,' Helen said, dismissively.

'But you two get along so well, you always have. Why is she being like this?' I couldn't fathom it, they'd always been so close.

'Like what? A little bitch, you mean?'

I was shocked. I'd never heard Helen use a word like that about either of her children.

She seemed to register my reaction, so tried to temper it. 'Oh, it's just Lauren, she suddenly seems to think I'm a bad wife, a bad mother – like she's perfect. But God knows she's far from it. I mean, Christ, she's made some mistakes...' she started, then seemed to think better of it.

'What mistakes?' I pushed.

'It doesn't matter, ignore me, I shouldn't have said anything. I'm sure we'll be fine, once she sorts herself out.' She took a large sip from the plastic wine glass that was now almost empty, and I tried not to think too hard about what she'd just said. It was probably something and nothing, and as Helen said – we all make mistakes – even Lauren.

I wondered if the conflict with Sam and her mother had something to do with where Lauren was living. 'I know this isn't exactly what Lauren wanted, but I'm sure they'll be fine out here – Sam will look after her,' I offered.

'I know, love, I know.' She sighed. 'I mean our grandkids can romp along the moors and—'

'No romping, not alone!' I said in mock alarm. 'What if they went missing? Or got snatched by a serial killer who hunts the moors?' I joked.

Helen laughed – as a slightly more laid-back mother than me, she always found my unsubstantiated fears very amusing. 'Oh my God, Georgie, stop it! I've heard of helicopter mothers, but not helicopter *grand*mothers!' She gently slapped my hand and pulled her pashmina around her shoulders. 'As if we don't have enough to worry about.' She seemed to slip back into her sadness again.

'We've got *nothing* to worry about,' I said, being the positive one for once, 'everything is fine, isn't it?' I meant to reassure her, but it was a genuine question; the atmosphere was dark and broody, and I really wasn't sure if everything *was* fine.

She didn't answer me.

I wondered if perhaps we were all feeling a bit low after the wedding. Like any big event in life, there's always the comedown afterwards. For the previous two years, it had been wonderful to pore over venues, dresses, menus, and Helen and I had loved the whole process. I wondered now if, like me, she felt a bit directionless.

I glanced at her, and thought, *That's it – we've both landed with a bit of a bump*. Lauren's uncharacteristic disapproval of her adored mother was probably the same, we were all just coming down.

I remember thinking that we all needed a change, something different in our lives.

Little did I know, in just a few short months, things would be *very* different.

CHAPTER FIVE

Eventually when the wine and beer had been drunk, and it was too late and too chilly to stay, we all made a move to leave. I hadn't spent as much time with James as I'd have liked, but he seemed happy enough chatting to Sam and Tim.

'Oh, don't go yet,' Lauren pleaded, 'please stay a bit longer.' Then she paused for inspiration and said, 'Coffee? Would anyone like a coffee?' It was like she didn't want us to leave.

Helen said she'd love one and so did I. Having drunk mostly Diet Coke all night, I was sober, but a little sleepy, and coffee would give me the kick I needed to drive back.

As Lauren went inside, she brushed past Kate, who was coming out into the garden. They didn't even acknowledge each other.

'Where have *you* been?' Helen called to Kate.

'Just inside,' she said vaguely, 'midges have bitten me to f—' She stopped, clearly thinking twice about the final word in her sentence.

Helen glanced over at me. 'Once kids hit their teen years, they swear like sailors, don't they? Do you think it's hormonal?'

'I'm effed if I know,' I joked, and we both giggled.

'What's so funny?' Kate mumbled, as she wandered towards

us, barely taking her eyes from the screen of her phone. I didn't remember Sam being this obsessed with his phone, but then he was always out playing, or with his friends, and Kate seemed to be very insular.

'Nothing that would interest *you*, my darling, just two sad old mums trying to have fun.'

'Fun? I remember fun...' I murmured in response.

'I wish I did. It was so bloody long ago since I had any fun,' Helen said with a sigh. Then she turned to me. 'Oh, Georgie, where did it all go wrong? I was supposed to be in LA with a house in the hills and a gaggle of enthusiastic pool boys to descale my pool.'

'Descale your pool? Is that what they call it?' I said, laughing. She may have appeared to be joking, but Helen had always had such ambition, I knew she sometimes felt like she hadn't fulfilled her potential. She'd worked for Hayes and Cooper Estate Management since leaving university, but what had been a temporary job had seduced her into staying when she saw the huge commission to be earned. Then Lauren was born, and any plans for world domination had disappeared into the ether, but she worked hard and now made a good living selling some of the most expensive properties in Devon. 'You've got a lovely house, you don't need one in Hollywood, and I'm sure Tim would descale your pool with as much enthusiasm as a pool boy,' I added, jokingly. 'If you *had* a pool, that is.'

Kate was now standing over us, still on her phone, blocking out the fire, the warmth and the light.

'Sit down, darling?' Helen said to her, pulling forward another 'rustic' chair which had seen better days.

'Nah, I'm good,' Kate mumbled.

I always felt sorry for Helen at times like this; she'd been so used to dealing with bright, well-mannered Lauren, Kate had been a shock. She seemed to go out of her way to do the opposite of what was asked or expected of her. 'Bands have their difficult second album – I had my difficult second child,' Helen used to say. Sometimes in earshot of Kate.

I sympathised; with a boisterous, and rather stubborn son, I knew how frustrating and unnerving it could be to have gladiatorial stand-offs with your child. And we still had our moments. When the red mist came down, Sam could be a bit snappy with me, even now in his twenties – twenty-six to be precise. But on the whole, he was a good son.

'Kate, you're standing in front of the *fire*,' Helen warned, 'can you *move* please?'

'GOD!' she huffed and plonked herself hard on the seat next to Helen, who was clearly angry and about to have a go at her, so I tried to distract her.

'Well, Helen, I hope Sam gets a good lawn laid soon, or we will have to rethink our footwear next time we visit.' I gestured towards our feet, both clad in heels that were too high to venture into the garden.

After a few seconds, she responded to me. 'Yep until then, we're in trainers, George.'

'Kate's got the right idea,' I said, in an attempt to include her. She was wearing trainers so I thought it worth a go, but she didn't look up from her phone, just grunted.

'Kate, Georgie's talking to you,' Helen reprimanded.

Kate eventually dragged her eyes away from her phone screen and acknowledged me with a slight nod.

Helen was about to say something, but I shook my head and closed my eyes momentarily, I felt like I'd made things worse.

I looked around for James, who waved and gesticulated that he was going inside to use the bathroom. 'Are you okay?' I mouthed. He nodded and stuck his thumb up, and as he disappeared into the house, my eyes returned to where he'd been standing, with Sam and Tim.

'Look at those two,' I murmured, gesticulating my head over at the two of them, drinking beer, Tim talking intently, Sam nodding in agreement.

'If you didn't know, you'd think they were father and son,' Helen said with a smile.

'I wonder what they're talking about?'

'Oh, probably whatever Tim's obsessing about at work this week.' Helen sighed. 'Talk about bringing work home, he carries every case here,' she thumped her chest.

'Hit-and-run,' Kate muttered, responding to my earlier query. 'They're talking about the hit-and-run.'

'Oh... yes.' Helen was resting her head on the back of the chair and slowly turned to me. 'The case Tim's working on, it happened earlier this week, did you see it in the news?'

'Oh God, yes, an eighteen-year-old girl. They hoped she'd pull through, but she died, didn't she?'

'Yeah, yesterday.' She shook her head.

'Have they got the driver yet?'

Helen shrugged, shaking her head. 'Don't know, don't *think* they've caught him. It's all being kept very quiet; Tim's leading the case, so he can't really say too much.'

'It must be so hard for Tim sometimes, I mean, that girl was Kate's age,' I said, looking over at Tim. A six-foot-four chief inspector, he was one of the most conscientious men I knew. He really cared about what he did, and I could only imagine what this case was doing to him. 'It must hit home when you see something like that and think of your own kids,' I said with a sigh. 'He's always there for everyone Tim, and with work he has a lot to carry on his shoulders,' I added, feeling a little tearful. It had been an emotional evening with one thing and another.

I suddenly heard raised voices and Sam slammed his beer onto the ground, spilling it everywhere. Helen and I gasped, as he tramped past us into the house.

'What was that about?' Helen asked.

Tim shrugged. 'No idea, he just—'

'Oh, Sam,' I murmured under my breath, looking apologetically at Helen.

Helen put her arm around me and said, 'We are *officially*

family now, and families sometimes fall out, kids misbehave. Come on, it's nothing, I'm sure.'

'What are you saying about *"our kids"*,' Lauren said, returning with the coffee, handing Helen and I a steaming mug each, then sitting down cross-legged on the ground in front of us. It reminded me of when she was little, and I marvelled at the beautiful, accomplished young woman before me. How quickly they grow up.

'I was just saying that we're all family now.' Helen was stroking Lauren's hair and Lauren rested her head on her mum's knee. 'Sorry about before,' she murmured quietly to Lauren, 'I'm tired, work's busy – I just lost it, you know?'

Lauren nodded, but before she could answer, Kate dropped one of her little bombs.

'Sam just stormed off,' she trilled, barely able to conceal her delight at the drama. Sometimes I didn't like Kate very much.

'What?' Lauren lifted her head, looked from me to Helen and back again.

'Oh it's nothing, I'm sure,' Helen repeated the words she'd said to me with a sigh, gently pushing Lauren's head back down on her knee and continuing to stroke her hair.

'He was well pissed off,' Kate added, clearly thrilled with Lauren's reaction.

Lauren continued to look troubled. 'Has Sam said anything to you, Georgie?' Lauren asked, reaching out and resting her hand on my knee, where I covered it with mine.

'No, he just... He was talking to your dad, it wasn't you. And you know Sam, he sometimes gets a bit... overwhelmed, can't cope with his feelings,' I said, aware I might be excusing my son's anger. Did I need to worry? Did Sam have real issues or was he just having a bad day?

'He's probably still pissed off that you tried to get out of marrying him.' Kate's voice came as if from nowhere and I thought I must have misheard her.

'What?' I asked, putting a smile on my face, but preparing

myself for something I might not like. I looked from Kate to Lauren and Helen, who stopped stroking Lauren's hair.

The silence was deafening, until Lauren slowly lifted her head.

'I just... We just... I wasn't trying to get out of marrying him.' She shot a look of pure vitriol at Kate. 'I was having a wobble, that's all.'

Helen nodded vigorously. 'Yeah, it was nothing, and nothing for you to worry about. It's the bride's prerogative, isn't it, love? You needed to ask yourself the questions all women ask before we get married.'

I watched them both, desperately trying to escape something, to smooth something over that I mustn't see. And I suddenly got a prickly feeling, like I was being locked out again.

'Did Sam know?' I asked.

Helen and Lauren shook their heads in unison. 'No and I don't want him to,' Lauren said quickly. 'Don't say anything, Georgie.'

'Are you okay now?' I pressed, not willing to be fobbed off quite so easily.

'Absolutely. Honestly, it was *nothing*,' Helen stressed, coming to her daughter's rescue, but realising I wouldn't be fobbed off, she said, 'Look, a few weeks ago Lauren came over to see us and said she was worried about the future. Tim and I gave her one of our lectures about how she and Sam are amazing and perfect – but even amazing and perfect couples sometimes find marriage hard – bloody hard!' She rolled her eyes. 'And then you were fine, weren't you, love?' Helen went back to stroking Lauren's hair, but in the fire light I swear I saw something like fear in her daughter's eyes.

'Yeah... I talked to Mum and Dad,' Lauren said. 'They made me feel better and I went straight home to Sam,' Lauren said, which sounded rather rehearsed to me.

'I wish you'd mentioned it to me, Helen?' I said.

'Why?' she snapped, this was clearly touching nerves.

'Well, I know what he can be like. He's a bit single-minded, gets involved in work and doesn't see what's in front of him sometimes.'

She shrugged. 'It wasn't – and *isn't* – a big deal.'

I realised then, though, that apart from the flare-up earlier, the two of them hadn't been together all evening, I didn't want to press the point though.

'He loves this place so much, he'd probably been banging on about the bloody blue tits in the garden instead of telling Lauren how beautiful she is,' I said, smiling at Lauren, who looked up from her mother's lap and smiled fondly back. 'I could have had a word with him.'

'Georgie, this wasn't about *Sam,*' Helen snapped, 'it was about Lauren. And how would *having a word with him* help? You can't give advice on getting married, you're single!'

I felt a sharp sting. It wasn't like Helen to snap and what she said was cruel. No, I'd never been married, but I knew how hard relationships could be, and Helen was only too aware of that.

Then immediately she murmured, 'Sorry, I didn't mean that to sound... it's just that I know you worry and we didn't want to worry you with *nothing.*'

'I understand,' I said, truthfully. I was, and still am, a worrier. Sam may be twenty-six, but as a single parent I'd battled for him all his life; it was my default position to come out fighting. But what I *couldn't* understand was, if Lauren had doubts, why did she go to her parents and not to Sam?

'So, all good now,' Lauren said, drawing a line under it, sitting up, and moving slightly away from her mother, disengaging from the conversation and looking into the fire.

I wasn't convinced, but it was only when I shifted my chair slightly, I caught a glimpse of Lauren's face from the side. I was surprised and upset to see tears sliding down her face. Shocked, I looked at Helen to see if she'd realised her eldest daughter was crying, but she and Kate were also gazing into the flames, with the same sad expression as Lauren.

I've asked myself many times since, why I didn't say something, why I didn't ask them what was *really* going on? But all I can say is, they closed up and no one could push their way inside, even me. And just when I thought I couldn't feel any worse, I saw Sam emerge from the cottage through the French doors. Followed a few seconds later by Sadie.

CHAPTER SIX

Even now, I remember every single thing that was said the night Sam called to tell me. Each word is ringed in my memory, preserved in amber. I'll never be able to forget them, or the feelings they still evoke.

'Lauren's dead,' he'd cried down the phone.

It seems strange now, but I didn't ask how, or what had happened, I could barely comprehend what he was saying. Between us was a moment of thick, ugly silence, while I processed what he'd said. We would talk later; all I knew was that I had to go to him.

'Where are you?' I heard myself ask.

'Here, at home. I called Tim, but he's not answering his phone.'

'Is Lauren *there*?'

'Yes. I have to call Tim... I...' He sounded spaced-out, he must have been in shock.

'I'm on my way,' I said, before putting down the phone.

Like a zombie, I climbed into tracksuit bottoms and pulled a jumper over my head. It was late August, and as I walked out onto the drive, the cool of the night surprised me, waking me out of any remaining slumber.

I had barely woken and drove on autopilot, clutching the wheel like it was the only thing I could trust to hold on to. I stared ahead into the darkness, seeing nothing as my car climbed up through the moors, pitch black. Shots of gravel and grass and rock lit momentarily by my headlights. I kept thinking, *He must be mistaken, Lauren's not dead, she can't be, she's only twenty-six, and she's only just got married. Who dies three months after their wedding?* I shook my head in disbelief. Was I dreaming? Was this some horrific nightmare playing out my very worst fears – as nightmares do?

Suddenly, there was something in the road, a moorland sheep wandering into the lights of the car. I yelped and jumped on the brakes, my chest pumping.

An accident, he'd said. What *kind* of accident? Were they driving, did she fall in that steep garden? I'd been too stunned to ask and couldn't bear to do so, to make him tell me. He hadn't sounded like Sam, more like someone calling from another dimension. Terrified.

Arriving at the cottage, the air was lit up with flashing blue lights – an ambulance, a police car. I almost fell out of the car and, not even bothering to shut the door, ran into the cottage. The door was wide open; the tiny hallway full of people in uniform.

'I'm looking for my son, he lives here,' I said to a woman dressed in green – a paramedic, I assumed.

She looked towards the staircase, where Sam stood, a policewoman's hand on his shoulder, another officer was trying to get him to move, but he wouldn't. He was crying and reaching out for something at the bottom of the stairs, and when I looked down, I saw her.

It will always stay in my mind, like a dark tableau, Lauren's body twisted on the stark white stairs, her legs making a strange impossible shape, her arm wrenched somewhere up her back. It was grotesque, but what stays with me most is the blood, scarlet splashes, deep, dark pools, and Lauren, dressed in white pyjamas, soaked in red.

I had to look away. I had to go to my son, and when he saw me, he sobbed, and I cradled him in my arms and guided him away from the horror. My instinct was to save him, because until now, I hadn't believed it, but I could see that it was too late for Lauren.

We walked together into the living room, while the police and paramedics did what they had to do. I sat Sam down on a chair and went into the kitchen to get him a glass of water – like *that* would help. But these rituals comfort the giver as much as the receiver and just turning on the tap anchored me in some kind of reality. It was then I noticed a bright pink fur coat, hanging off the back of one of the chairs. I recognised it as Sadie's; she always wore it.

'Is that Sadie's coat, in the kitchen?' I asked Sam, as I handed him the glass of water.

He looked up at me, confused at first, then seemed to realise what I'd said. 'Yeah, I think so.' He was listless, lost.

'I didn't realise she was here,' I replied.

'She isn't, she must have left it, when she was last here.'

I didn't register this at the time but later wondered why Sadie had gone home and left her coat on the back of a chair in someone else's house. Then again, it was Sadie, and where she was concerned, nothing made sense.

I don't recall driving to the hospital, but I remember arriving and Sam and I being directed to a room, where Helen and Tim stood, holding each other up. Any hope I had of this being a mistake, a misunderstanding, some weird half-asleep dream, was shattered. I tried not to think of the twisted, blood-soaked limbs at the bottom of the stairs. I tried to hope there might be a chink of light, a possibility they could put Lauren back together again. But here, lit by fluorescence, in this impersonal place of plastic chairs and paper coffee cups, was the end of Lauren's story.

Through the heavy cloud of grief and tears, Sam shared – in sporadic, tearful bursts – that he'd come home late from work and found Lauren in the hallway. It seemed she'd probably been rushing down the stairs and slipped, banging her head on the stone floor. That stunning white spiral staircase we'd all admired, the beautiful game changer, the reason they'd bought the house, had taken Lauren.

'The blood... Mum, it was everywhere,' Sam kept saying.

'I know, love, I know.' He seemed to have forgotten I was there. His mind only able to focus on the red splashes on the walls, scarlet fingerprints on the white handrail where she'd perhaps tried to save herself.

Helen was inconsolable, a mess of tears and regret. 'Why? Why?' was all she could utter, between uncontrollable sobs. Every now and then, she'd let out a loud, guttural cry, like an animal in pain, and she'd pull herself away from whichever one of us was holding her up. I felt like she might make a run for it at any moment and tear through the hospital desperately searching for Lauren. She'd already been transported to the morgue, but as it was based at the hospital, we'd met up there, all hopelessly searching for answers.

Tim's cheeks were hollow, his colour was clay, as he kept asking to see 'the doctor in charge', like they might give him something to cling on to. But it was too late for any doctor, there was no hope, nothing to get hold of and we were all flailing around. It was particularly hard to see Tim, this strong oak of a man, so used to bearing other's troubles, now desperately bending with the weight of his own.

I didn't know what to do. I was comforting Sam because he was my son, but my best friends were suffering too, and I didn't have enough arms to hug everyone. She wasn't usually a welcome addition, but I was actually relieved when, after a few minutes, Sadie arrived. I glimpsed her through the glass windows as she ran past; she was running so fast she almost slammed into the door as she tried to open it. Her face was white, her eyes filled with questions, and closing the door behind her, she faced the room, seemingly wanting answers herself.

Apart from me, no one looked up, no one saw her. No one cared.

Eventually, she came and sat by me and Sam. 'Sammy, I'm so,

so sorry,' she was whispering as she gently pushed her arm through his and rested her head on his shoulder. Like Helen, I always felt Sam just put up with Sadie for Lauren's sake, and I was sure he didn't need this now. He still didn't seem to register that she was there; he just sat with tears running down his face, as pale and detached from everything as the rest of us. I wondered how she'd heard about Lauren and discovered that Tim had called her in tears and asked her to go to their house and sit with Kate. Being Sadie, she'd done what she wanted to do and turned up at the hospital first, which was of no help to anyone really, especially as Kate was at home all on her own.

'I thought you were going to be with Kate?' Tim said. He seemed understandably irritated that she was there and not with his younger daughter as he'd asked.

'I'm on my way to your house,' she said in the direction of Tim and Helen. 'I just asked the taxi to stop here first, he's waiting for me. I just wanted to see if I could do anything for you guys before I go to Kate?'

No one answered and eventually she pulled her arm from Sam, went over to Helen, hugged her and left.

'We didn't want Kate to come here,' Tim murmured to me, like he had to explain. 'It's too much for her.'

'Yes, you did the right thing,' I replied, not really sure what I was saying. Like the rest of them, I couldn't do anything but be inside my own head.

'My little girl,' Helen was crying, 'she had her life before her, what happened, what happened?' she said, looking at Sam, searching his face for an answer.

He shook his head. 'I don't *know* what happened. I just... found her.'

Helen continued to sob, then stopped for a moment, and glared back at Sam. 'And she was just *there*, was she, at the bottom of the stairs?'

'Now, love...' Tim started and tried to put his arm around her.

'NO!' Helen yelled in his face, shaking his arm off her. 'Why did you make her live out on the moors away from everyone, why did you take her away from us?' She was standing over Sam now, almost shouting in his face.

I wanted to pull her away, but how could I? She was in such a mess.

'Lauren was unhappy, and alone, but you wouldn't listen to her, would you? No, *you* wanted to live out there, you didn't care what *she* wanted. You were never there for her, always working... or were you doing something else? What were you up to on those late nights? Was there a reason you wanted Lauren alone and isolated? Why Sam? Why?' And she broke down again.

'She doesn't know what she's saying,' Tim cried, trying to hold her, contain her, stop the hurt. But it was clear his own was as much a burden, and the agony in his eyes revealed the horror and devastation of a parent losing a precious child.

Tim was right, I knew Helen didn't mean it, she was just lashing out in her pain. But still, I put a protective arm around Sam, to let him know I was there, and on his side, even if, in my heart I was asking the same questions as Helen.

Over the next couple of hours, a doctor and several nurses came to talk to us, they spoke of death certificates and coroners and things so foreign to me that I didn't even listen. They were all gentle passing on their information, but Lauren was dead, and anything the medical profession had to say to us now was worthless. Helen just kept talking over them, demanding to see Lauren, and when they wouldn't allow it, she railed against them, her sobs louder. 'I'm her mother, you can't stop me,' she yelled. But as we learned later, Lauren was in quite a mess; she'd landed face down on the stone floor and it took a while to make her presentable for loved ones.

While Tim and Sam spoke with the nurse, Helen came to sit with me, like a child seeking an adult for security. She leaned towards me and whispered in my ear, 'If they'd let me see her now, I could just hold her, talk to her, I might be able to waken her.' She pulled away, nodding, searching my face for confirmation. I didn't know what to say, and she sat there facing me, her head to one side, murmuring under breath. 'Am I going mad, Georgie?'

'No, you aren't,' I said quietly. 'It makes sense. We give our children life, so why shouldn't we be able to do that again?' Although I knew it was just the twisted logic of grief.

The nurse explained that Lauren would be 'ready' to see the following day. 'Until then, there's nothing you can do, perhaps you might spend this time at home and try to rest?' she suggested.

As she left the room, I felt the dynamic shift. It was like the adults had abandoned us; a group of people who'd never experienced this kind of grief, this horror, were now being left to ourselves.

'I can't leave her here,' Helen said, refusing to stand up, as Tim made vain attempts to ease her from her seat with firm arms and soothing tones. I remember thinking to myself, *At least she has Tim, he'll get them through this.* But looking at him desperately trying to coax her from her seat, then try again to physically move her, to no avail, I could see they needed help. Tim was also in tears again. He'd lost control, something I'd never seen before – he was as lost as Helen.

'Come on, love,' I tried, feeling like I now had to take charge. 'You and Tim can come back tomorrow and see her,' I said, gently.

'I *can't*, Georgie,' Tim suddenly said. 'I've seen so many... dead bodies in my time – but I can't see my own daughter's.'

'I'll come back with you, Helen,' Sam said, reaching out to her.

And I was reminded of the way he'd first reached out to her daughter in nursery school all those years before, when their journey began. Who would ever have believed it would end like this?

CHAPTER SEVEN

The days after Lauren's death crawled along. Nothing important was said, nothing happened, no one could think. Time was like a bridge leading us blindly from death to the next stage, and one day, hopefully, to the beginning of acceptance. But how could we *ever* accept what had happened?

Waiting for her daughter's body to be released was sending Helen down into a further spiral, and I'd go over there every day just to give Tim a break. He wanted to solve all her problems, but all she wanted was someone to listen to her, so I'd sit with her while he did stuff around the house or went for a walk.

'We need to put Lauren to rest,' she'd told me. 'I keep calling the police station, telling them to hurry up, but Tim says I shouldn't. I think he finds it *embarrassing*,' she added, curling her lip.

Understandably things between them weren't easy, and not helped by the limbo they were existing in. So when the coroner finally released the body, it was a relief to both of them, and as he knew people there, Tim got the news and called Sam straight away.

Sam nodded, didn't say very much, then put the phone down. 'That was Tim, Lauren's body's been released,' he said.

'Oh. How do you feel?' I asked, unsure how to react to this news.

He shrugged. 'I don't know. Numb?' he replied without looking at me and heading upstairs. He obviously needed to process this, so while he locked himself upstairs in his old bedroom, I went over to see if I could comfort Tim and Helen.

'You must be so relieved, you can have the funeral now,' I said gently to Tim, who opened the door. Kate was just coming down the stairs, apparently Helen was in bed; she spent a lot of time in bed these days, and who could blame her?

'Yeah, it's the beginning of some kind of closure, I suppose – but it's bittersweet, Georgie.'

'Of course, but the waiting is over, and that's been torture for you.'

'They needed to prepare a file for the coroner, had to try to establish a cause of death,' he continued, sounding like a robot. All the years of police information had been stored in his head for times like this, to explain to grieving families, broken-hearted children and spouses. I doubt he'd ever envisaged using this information to explain the delay of the release of his own daughter's body though. 'The usual, endless, pointless form-filling-in,' he added listlessly, walking into the kitchen.

I followed him through, and he filled the kettle to make a drink. Kate took her place on the same comfy chair she always sat in, her phone clutched to her, eyes locked on the screen.

'It just seems heartless to delay something like that for no good reason. I mean, how much paperwork is involved in establishing a horrible accident?' I said.

He turned off the tap, and put the kettle down on the counter. 'George, that's the point...' He looked at me, making proper eye contact for the first time since Lauren had died. 'It wasn't an accident.'

'Oh?'

'I told Sam when I called, didn't he say?'

'No... no he didn't, he was upset, he just went upstairs.' Sam would have dreaded telling me something like that, and I was glad in a way Tim had done it for him.

He was now spooning coffee into two mugs; he didn't need to ask how I liked it, he knew.

'So, it wasn't an accident,' I said, puzzled. 'Does that mean... that Lauren fell down the stairs *deliberately*?' I almost whispered. I suddenly saw Lauren's face the night of the barbecue when they'd talked about her doubts about getting married. *Was she so unhappy she'd killed herself?* I tried to shake the vision from my brain. 'Why would she do something like that?'

Tim was slowly shaking his head. 'You mean suicide?'

'I don't know, I... I mean, she's always been so happy and—' I backtracked, walking on eggshells. This was his child we were talking about; I had to be so careful.

He took a deep breath. 'I spoke to one of my colleagues earlier. From what I can gather, some of the forensic findings don't add up to it being an accident. Or suicide.'

'So, someone... *did* something to Lauren?' I found this hard to comprehend, and was unable to say the words *kill* or *murder* to my friend grieving for his child.

He nodded slowly, then turned away, back to the mugs, I knew he didn't want me to see the tears in his eyes. But it was too late.

'I don't understand, everyone *loved* Lauren, who could possibly... Why?' I pressed, convinced there was another explanation.

He didn't answer but continued to lean on the kitchen counter, with his back to me. He was stooped and diminished, the life and strength had been sucked from him.

'So that's why they've only just released her body, because they think someone... killed her?' I heard myself croak as the penny finally dropped.

'Yes.'

I was stunned, it didn't seem real. My subconscious just didn't want to believe that Lauren had been murdered.

'How has Helen taken it?' I asked.

'Angry, devastated. Before this, she was calling the coroner's office and the station day and night, demanding they release the body. And now, she's on the phone yelling at them to find the killer. She's desperate, says she won't rest until they find who did it.'

I felt so sorry for them both, this loving couple with a great life, a wonderful marriage and happy family had been reduced to this. 'It's understandable,' I said.

'Yeah... but I wish she'd stop phoning the station – they're my colleagues, my staff!'

'Oh dear,' I said, taking the mug of coffee he offered me. 'Have you spoken to her about it?'

'I've tried, but she just yells at me,' he said with a sigh. 'Reasonable isn't in Helen's vocabulary at the moment.'

I patted his arm, I felt for him, but at the same time, if I had been in Helen's shoes, 'reasonable' wouldn't have been in my vocabulary either. But people have different ways of processing trauma, of coping, I knew that from the way Sam had reacted to Lauren's death.

With police crawling all over the cottage, Sam couldn't go back there, so, in the initial aftermath of Lauren's death, had stayed with me. But this new development had distressed him and he couldn't rest; he wanted to be back home on Dartmoor, where he felt close to Lauren.

'Tim said that now they've established it wasn't an accident, the forensic team may need to spend longer at the cottage,' I explained. I knew this wasn't what Sam wanted to hear, but selfishly a part of me was relieved he couldn't go back there yet. I wanted to keep him close by, I could see he was struggling and didn't think it would be good for him to go back so soon.

'But I have stuff to do,' he said. 'I need to clean the blood off the stairs.'

This made me cringe. 'Oh, Sam. It won't be there now,' I said, knowing it would always be there, in his head. I was only at the cottage for a matter of minutes the night Lauren died, but what I saw will stay with me forever. I could only imagine the nightmares he still has. And now, knowing that someone was *responsible*, we could barely take it in.

'I left stuff on the stairs, went straight to the hospital,' he said, not making much sense.

'I'll talk to Tim, I'm sure there are people who'll clean up now the forensic team have left,' I said, trying not to think about my poor son scraping his new wife's blood and brain matter off the staircase.

'If it's left too long, the blood will stain,' he said, almost matter-of-factly. Then he paused, looked at me. 'I don't want Lauren's blood to stain everywhere.'

Sam fixed things, from broken fences, to the broken wings of birds on his beloved moorland. But this wasn't something he could fix, and his logical brain couldn't cope because Lauren dying was *not* logical. Everything had spiralled out of control in his life, he had no answers and no control over anything. One of the ways Sam could rein control back in was to return to a routine, go back to the cottage, deal with the physical mess, make his home clean and tidy again – as Lauren would have wanted.

So he didn't return to the cottage, and for the next couple of days he stayed in his room, sometimes wandering aimlessly through the house or garden. I was at my wits' end worrying about him, but he didn't seem to want to talk to me about Lauren.

'Were you and Lauren happy, in your marriage?' I asked him one evening. 'We all assumed it was the perfect union – was it?'

'Nothing and no one is perfect,' was all he'd say.

And when I gently tried to ask if he could remember anything about the night she died, if there was any sign of another person, he just shrugged. All I knew was that Sam came home from work around midnight, and found her.

'I walked in, calling her, thinking she'd be waiting up for me. I couldn't work it out,' he said. 'Then I saw the red... and it sounds stupid, but I thought someone had dropped a can of red paint on the bottom of the stairs. I worried what Lauren would say when she saw the mess... then I saw where it was coming from,' he shuddered.

After that I couldn't press him any further, so I left it, no point in making his pain worse by reliving it.

One day leaked into the next. We'd run out of conversation, just going over and over the same things – no one ever talks about the banality of grief, but that's what it became, waiting, and watching, day after day of nothing. Until the phone call.

I was upstairs when I heard Sam answering the landline and was coming downstairs as he put down the phone. His face was chalky, he looked like he was going to be sick.

'What is it?' I asked, trying to make my voice sound calm, while holding on to the handrail; this wasn't good news.

'That was the police,' he muttered.

'Oh, what did they want?'

He looked at me, his eyes dark, misty. 'To tell me they've taken tissue samples, and as far as the cottage is concerned, they've finished, I can go back there...'

'Good, good.' I nodded, my feelings mixed. I wanted him to have his space, and things had been tense with him around, but equally I didn't feel it would be good for his mental health to be holed up alone on the moors.

'Mum... the guy on the phone, he told me something else' – he paused, as if to take it in himself before telling me – 'he said Lauren was pregnant.'

I flopped onto the bottom stair. This wonderful, terrible news was something we'd waited a lifetime for. It was the dream Helen and I had longed for, and nurtured in our hearts and minds for such a long time. A baby. But now it just felt horrible. My eyes stung with tears.

'And you didn't know?' I asked.

Sam shook his head.

'I don't know what to say, love.' I was desperately trying not to let him see me cry, but it was obvious.

I was expecting him to burst into tears too, but the news seemed to have angered him more than anything.

'It was so *stupid*,' he spat. 'I used to tell her to calm down, slow down, but she never took any notice of me, *never*,' he added, raising his voice.

'It wasn't her *fault*, Sam,' I offered, feeling uncomfortable with the way he was blaming her. I understood that anger came with grief and loss – we blame the dead for leaving us, and now he was probably blaming her for taking their baby with her.

'If she'd just been more careful, thought before she did things, didn't take stupid risks.' He was pacing the hallway, muttering to himself. It was too painful to hear, I wanted to walk away and leave him to work through this, but I couldn't, I had to be there for him. Then he suddenly stopped pacing. 'She must have known, she *must* have known – they said she was almost three months, which means she conceived after we got married.' He was standing in the hallway, motionless, rigid with shock, and I was anchored to the bottom step, unable to lift myself even to support him. 'Why didn't she tell me?'

I couldn't answer him, all I could think about was how this huge loss had just grown bigger.

'Should I call Helen and Tim and tell them?' he asked, like a child, completely unsure of anything anymore.

'They'll find out at some point, Tim might find out from his colleagues,' I said, doubtful that any of them would volunteer this if it wasn't necessary. 'I'd leave it for now, it will be very hard for them to hear,' I said, knowing Sam would have to process this before telling Helen, who wouldn't be able to bear this news.

So we kept it to ourselves. It was so painful, we didn't talk about it again, but the following day Sam walked into the kitchen where I was making toast for breakfast, and suddenly said what I'd only dared think.

'I wonder if Lauren didn't tell me about the baby because it wasn't mine?'

CHAPTER EIGHT

Finally, a month after her death, the funeral could be planned and her family could begin their long goodbyes. The police apparently had all they needed to continue their investigation, and who knew what that may bring? But as Tim said, for us as a family, our priority for now was to lay Lauren to rest, and not allow the police or what they were doing to interfere with that.

Tim had asked to be informed of any new information, any evidence, and despite their initial reluctance, his team were now feeding him the information. I asked him about the clean-up; I didn't want Sam to go over there and be faced with the mess.

'I'll sort it,' he said.

'Do the police contract someone to...' I couldn't finish the sentence, it might have been Sam's wife's blood, but it was also his daughter's.

'No, people think that, but it's down to the householder to organise – I know a company though, it's fine... fine.' Understandably, he didn't want to go into details, and I was just grateful he was taking it out of my hands.

Even now, in all this, he was the one taking care of things, making life easier for the rest of us, and I wondered how much hurt he was hiding, to spare everyone else. I also wondered did he know Lauren was pregnant? But I couldn't bring myself to broach the subject, because if he didn't know, it wasn't for me to tell him, it was up to Sam to speak to Lauren's parents if and when he was ready.

Helen and Tim had insisted on paying for everything for the funeral. But they didn't take it over, they wanted us to be involved in the planning. As Tim said, 'She was like a daughter to you, Georgie – and we're all family.'

'It has to be a celebration of her life,' Helen said, trying desperately to find something positive in all this. So, typical Helen, in spite of her crippling grief, she organised a family supper, for the Jacksons, me and Sam and Sadie, so we could discuss the funeral together.

She tried to make the evening as sociable and as 'normal' as possible and greeted us at the door. Her hair had been brushed and she'd put foundation and lipstick on, something she hadn't done since Lauren had died. It made her look a little less pale and haunted, but it didn't hide the pain etched into her face.

'I've made my lasagne,' she said as we followed her through into the sitting room, where Tim got up from his chair and hugged Sam and I. He looked dreadful. As both a father and a detective, I knew that finding whoever had been responsible for Lauren's death was probably all he could think about. I wanted so much to talk to him about it, but I didn't want to distress Helen, who was struggling.

'I forgot how long it needed to cook, but looks like it's ready,' she added, as Sam and I sat down at the table, which had been set with Helen's expensive Mediterranean crockery. I felt a catch in my throat when I saw it. Inherited from Helen's mother, the crockery was Lauren's favourite; Helen had always promised her it would be hers one day.

'The table looks lovely, you shouldn't have gone to all this trouble,' I said.

'It's no trouble, it's called displacement activity.' She smiled wanly and took a glug of wine from her glass, passing the bottle down the table.

Kate then wandered in, and after a few minutes, Sadie turned up, noisy and dramatic, letting herself in through the back door and making a big fuss about the teatime traffic. Plonking herself on a chair, she announced that, 'It was the worst thing ever!' Which of course it wasn't. Something far worse had already happened. She threw off her leather jacket and, hanging it on the back of her chair, her eyes alighted on the serving dish Helen was putting on the table.

'Ooh, Helen, you've made your famous lasagne, Lauren's fave.' She looked around the table for a reaction, with a big, beaming smile. Then, finally, the penny dropped and she seemed to realise what she'd said and remember why we were meeting for dinner. She looked down at the table, wiped the smile from her face and stopped talking.

I'd always found Sadie a bit brash but Helen said she'd pretty much brought herself up, which I guess explained her lack of warmth or manners. But did it also explain her lack of empathy?

Sam and I just smiled politely, while Helen dished up rectangular wedges of layered pasta and oozing béchamel sauce. It looked and smelled delicious, but I found it hard to breathe, let alone eat. These suppers at the Jacksons' had always been noisy affairs, lots of teasing and talking over each other, sharing stories and jokes and demanding second helpings. But tonight we hardly spoke. What was there to say? We were all there to talk about the funeral of someone we loved, who'd died soon after her wedding.

I still believed in my heart that it was an accident. At that stage, I expected the police to call and say there'd been a mistake and Lauren had fallen after all. I couldn't comprehend the idea of anyone deliberately hurting her – and the fact she was pregnant made that even harder to contemplate, so I didn't. Instead, I took the same road as Helen and pretended to myself it wasn't murder. As for the pregnancy, I tried not to think about that either – it was too much. But it was hard to keep going, hard to pretend. Helen was trying to pretend with her Italian crockery and home-made family lasagne, but all it did was remind us of the empty chair. And as we made pointless comments about the texture of the bloody garlic bread, tension and sadness spiked the air, reminding us that nothing would ever be like it was.

Kate waved her hand when Helen went to put lasagne on her plate, but Helen pushed the serving spoon towards her.

'No, Mum, I don't *want* any,' she said. I hadn't seen much of Kate after Lauren's death, I hadn't seen much of anyone, but she seemed so diminished, with even lower energy and enthusiasm than before.

'Have some,' tried Tim. 'Your mum's cooked it specially.'

'I know she has. But it's not like she cooked it for *me*, is it?'

'She's cooked it for *everyone*, babe,' Sadie said, smiling at Kate and looking around the table like she was waiting for applause before taking a huge bite from her garlic bread.

'It was Lauren's favourite...' Helen started.

'Well, it isn't *mine*. And you can't bring her back by making lasagne!' she snapped.

I wasn't surprised at this, Kate never responded to being told what to do, she had to be encouraged. And whatever the truth about her dietary preferences, now wasn't the time to force-feed her lasagne.

'That's *enough*!' Tim said loudly, stopping everyone in their tracks and glaring at Kate. 'You will eat the meal your mum has made for you.'

'I won't!'

'You will,' he spat, both of them now staring the other down.

It was distressing to witness, I could never have imagined Tim losing his temper like that. But Kate had always been a difficult child, and in my view had become even more testing. Since Lauren's death, her resentment towards Helen and Tim seemed to have grown so much it shaped everything she did.

Me, Sam and even Sadie kept our heads down, eating slowly, tasting nothing.

'Just *try*, Kate,' Helen said. 'I've spent all afternoon—' she pressed.

'MUM, I'm not eating it – I'm *fucking* vegetarian!' She slammed her fist on her plate, which caused Helen to rear back with her spoonful of lasagne, catching Kate on the arm.

'Ouch, that's hot,' she hissed, glaring at her mother as Helen put the spoon back in the dish and sat down.

'Sorry, I didn't mean to...' she murmured. I thought Helen was going to burst into tears.

Kate stared ahead, eyes glassy, her chin dimpled like she might cry too. Then she slowly and carefully took a salad leaf and placed it on her plate, spreading and flattening it vigorously with the palm of her hand. Then, as we all tried to pretend we weren't watching, she reached over and took a small piece of bread and put that next to the salad leaf, flattening the bread with a thump of the heel of her hand. Thump, thump, thump. It filled the silence like a heartbeat. No one said a word.

As Kate continued to frown at her plate, I felt like the veil had been lifted, this was their home now: Helen in pieces, Tim trying to keep everything together while Kate demanded attention. Tonight, desperation simmered beneath their attempts to try to make everything the same as before. Helen had told me the doctor had given them both something to take that would help calm them, but she was obviously adding her own prescription of wine.

What Kate said about not being able to bring Lauren back by making lasagne was cruel, but I understood how she felt. I didn't want to eat something that Lauren loved in the vain hope we could somehow metaphorically reincarnate her. But Helen and Tim each had their own ways of dealing with things too, and it might have been kinder if Kate had, for now, gone along with them instead of being critical and confronting them over everything they said and did.

We all continued to eat in silence until Helen said in a trembling voice, 'Eat up, everyone, there's plenty, so don't be shy, help yourselves.'

Tim's jaw was clenched, this all felt so fragile, like the whole thing might tear apart any moment. The evening clearly hadn't been his idea and his still full plate betrayed him. Apart from Sadie, who'd almost emptied her plate and wolfed half the garlic bread, the only other person whose appetite wasn't affected by the sadness of the occasion was Sam.

'Great lasagne, Helen,' he said, continuing to shovel pasta on his fork.

I hated myself for even thinking it given what he was going through, but I wished he wouldn't eat with such gusto. It felt somehow disrespectful of him.

'*You've* still got your appetite then?' Helen remarked. I detected a slight slur and a hint of disapproval in her voice. She'd abandoned her food and was now sitting back in her chair with another glass of wine while watching Sam tuck in. I could feel my face burning, she was clearly thinking the same as me, that it wasn't appropriate for him to be behaving like this, as though nothing had happened. She wanted everything to be normal, and yet at the same time needed us all to acknowledge that it wasn't, and Sam wasn't playing by those rules.

'He's had no appetite,' I offered apologetically.

'Well, he's certainly got an appetite now,' she murmured, sarcasm oozing from her voice.

Sam carried on eating; he was never one for putting on an act or playing games. He wasn't oblivious to the complexity of Helen's feelings, he was choosing not to take them on. He'd already learned that his wife had been murdered and she was pregnant, it was a lot to take on – he had enough conflict of his own to deal with.

'It's good to see him eating,' I said, hearing my voice fade into the awkwardness. I nibbled on a piece of garlic bread. Hurt and shame and anger welled up in my chest. It was too raw, too soon for all this bonhomie, all sitting round the dinner table smiling and pretending felt false, a cruel parody of what we'd had before. Were we being naïve and foolish to think we could have that again?

Kate looked up from her plate of flattened bread, her eyes moving around the table, watching, waiting. Sadie checked her phone, while Sam continued to eat like his life depended on it.

Helen sipped on her drink, observing silently from behind the wine glass, her food untouched. No one spoke, and when Tim dropped his fork into a half-eaten plate of now congealed pasta, I jumped, like I'd been shattered into a million pieces. Even he wasn't keeping up the pretence and Tim always liked to pretend things were better than they really were.

Once we'd eaten, everyone helped clear the table in silence. Helen and I made coffee; she'd asked Sam to lay the wedding photos out and Kate to bring down the stack of family albums from upstairs.

'I thought we could choose the ones for the order of service card together?' Helen said, as she carried a tray of cups through, and I followed with a pot of coffee.

'Do you remember this, Helen?' Sadie asked, holding up a photo of her and Lauren.

Helen put down the tray, and gently took the photo from her hand like it was a precious jewel, studying it for ages.

I looked over her shoulder, the girls must have been about twelve, both blonde, wearing matching T-shirts, laughing into the camera.

She turned to Tim, and he took the photo, and they both gazed lovingly at their little girl. It was heartbreaking to watch, and I had to take a sip of coffee to swallow my own tears.

'Here's one of me and Lauren,' Kate offered, slightly more animated than usual. 'We loved that holiday,' she said with a sigh. 'Can we use *this* one for the service card?'

She forced the photo into Helen's slightly reluctant hand – it was Kate and Lauren when they were very small, sitting on the beach, eating ice cream and smiling in the sunshine.

'It's a lovely photo, darling,' Helen said, 'but Lauren's eyes are closed on this one, I'm not sure it's—'

Kate turned scarlet. 'It's fine. Go with Sadie and Lauren then, after all she's more like your daughter than I am!'

'Oh, love, I didn't mean... We can use a photo with you and Lauren, just not that one,' Helen tried to placate her.

'Come on now, this isn't about any of us,' Tim said, 'it's about Lauren.' I thought he might break down, but he held on. 'Let's look at *all* the photos before we decide on anything.'

So, for a little while, we climbed back into the past, before Lauren's death, and allowed ourselves to wallow there, on the beaches, making sandcastles, in swimming pools, birthday parties. We marvelled at how young we once were, and how the trees in our gardens had grown, but it only made us silently question why they had continued to live and thrive, when Lauren had been cut down. And so we continued to torture ourselves with what had been, and what might have been, from bald, smiling baby, to white-haired little girl holding a puppy, big sister to baby Kate, a birthday disco with Sadie and the skinny, beautiful teen. A life with such promise, such ambition and happiness smashed at the bottom of a staircase.

'Oh God, remember this, when you cut our hair the same.' Sadie covered her face in embarrassment and we all laughed mirth-lessly at the photo of two little friends with matching basin cuts. Helen laughed. A bit too loudly. I wondered how many glasses of wine she'd had. My next thought was, *Drink up*, because it can't have been much fun being a sober Helen around that time.

Then Helen found a photo of Lauren, Sam and Sadie, and just broke down. Tim immediately rushed to her side, his arms around her, rocking her like a baby. Even Sam looked like he might cry at the sight of Helen in tears, but Kate sat stony-faced as Sadie poured Helen another glass of wine. Eventually Helen rallied, emerging from Tim's arms, pushing him aside to reach for her glass, and after a few glugs she was able to carry on.

'Lauren loved that dress.' She sighed, picking up a photo of Lauren and Sam at the prom.

'She wanted the red one with the split up the side, but you wouldn't buy it for her.' Sadie giggled.

Helen turned to her, looking hurt. 'I wasn't even aware there *was* a red one,' she said defensively. 'I wouldn't have *made* her wear the blue one, she told me she loved it.' It was nothing, but everything. Helen was finding out things about her daughter she didn't know, and things about herself too. I remembered how Lauren hated the blue dress, and how Helen had made her wear it, but it felt unkind to remind her of that now. But Sadie had no filter, and usually said what was on her mind, she never wrapped anything up for anyone. Being sensitive to others' feelings wasn't something she excelled at and she just shrugged and raised her eyebrows as if to say, 'I know what really happened.'

Helen went pink with anger, and the two women stared at each other. I could have cried for Helen; as parents, we all make mistakes, some of us spend our lives making up for them, but Helen couldn't do that, so it was easier to recall her own version of the past. Perhaps Sadie was unaware of this – or perhaps she didn't care?

In an attempt to ease the tension, I quickly shuffled through the photos and found one of Lauren in her school uniform with Sadie, arms around each other, cheeky faces.

'Look at these two,' I said, holding the photo up to everyone.

'Thick as thieves,' Tim said with a smile, taking the photo and offering it to Helen, who seemed to have gone off into her own little world. We all looked at each other, the silence was awkward, and I was beginning to wonder if this tortuous night would ever end.

Sam clearly felt the same, and rubbing his hands together said, 'Okay, are we going to choose the music for Lauren's service now?'

Everyone nodded and murmured in agreement.

'Helen?' Tim said, and she looked up at him, bewildered. 'The music for Lauren, that's why everyone's here, love...'

She seemed to suddenly remember this and nodded uncertainly.

As Lauren wasn't religious, we all felt it would be more appropriate to play her favourite songs. 'Music from her life, we need music that meant something to Lauren,' Helen said, her words slurred as they landed.

'I still think we should have hymns,' Tim was muttering.

'Oh no, no, we need something that was relevant to her, she loved Lana Del Rey,' Helen continued. 'She loved the lyrics, that kind of music is far more Lauren.'

'Her favourite song of all time, and one I think she should come into the church with is James Taylor's "You've Got a Friend",' Sam offered.

'No *way*, she hated old hippie stuff,' Sadie said. 'She loved Ed Sheeran, Liam Gallagher—'

'She wasn't *fifty*!' Kate spat. 'Did any of you know her at *all?*' She went on to offer some suggestions, which, to me, sounded like a stream of consciousness. I didn't know about Lauren's taste in music, but Kate was right about one thing, it was beginning to look like no one had a clue what Lauren's favourite music was. Each person close to her seemed to have a different opinion and saw her from a completely different perspective. It made me wonder how well any of us really know the people we love.

CHAPTER NINE

The funeral was in September – my favourite month, a time of new beginnings, harvest festivals, back to school, leaves crunching like cornflakes underfoot, and tea and toast by the fire. But for us that September was very different.

What made this funeral so much worse was it had so many echoes of the wedding that had taken place just four months before. We were returning with Lauren to the same church where she'd walked in the sunshine, dazzling in white lace, with a bouquet of blush pink roses. Only this time she arrived in a white coffin, covered in the same blush pink roses she'd carried as a bride. I tried so hard not to think about her inside that box, along with the baby that died with her.

'I'm sure everyone here is asking why?' the vicar said in his sermon. He was right, it was all any of us could think as he tried to suggest this untimely death was all part of God's plan. I wasn't buying it, I couldn't reconcile any plan with such a cruel event.

Helen and Tim were like zombies and Kate was a mess – I'd never seen her so emotional. The monosyllabic teen who rarely made eye contact and played the spectre at the feast at most family events, even her sister's wedding, was sobbing loudly. Inconsolable, she clung to her mother, who in turn clung to Tim, who was trying so hard to be strong for them both, when inside he must have been crumbling. Lauren was close to both parents but had always been a daddy's girl. They had such a strong father-daughter bond, and when she was younger, they'd often be found kicking a ball around the garden or watching a test match on TV. Lauren always said her dad felt left out as the only boy, and I think, subconsciously, she tried to compensate for that by joining him in his hobbies.

'Those two are always whispering,' Helen used to say with a giggle, and watching Tim at the funeral, I couldn't help but think not only had he lost a daughter, he'd lost a friend too.

Later, we all went to a nearby hotel, where we ate beige food and people said obvious things. 'Such a shock,' Helen's auntie Penelope said. 'I'm ninety-four, it should have been me.' The rest made tearful small talk and tried not to mention the wedding – for many it was the last time they'd met.

'I can't bear it,' Helen murmured to me under her breath, as yet another distant relative staggered towards her, weighed down with grief and awkwardness. I felt so helpless. I couldn't fix the brides-maid's dress or find the missing notes for Tim's speech (in his pock-et), as I had at the wedding, we just had to get through it.

Tim was equally lost, just standing in the middle of the func-tion room holding a glass of something, like he was floating out to sea, completely directionless. I went to stand by him, and together we silently grieved for Lauren, the daughter I never had, the daughter he adored, standing in a sea of black, while mourners swam around us. After the funeral, Sam and I went back to Tim and Helen's. Sadie and Sam made coffee, while I cut up a home-made carrot cake – Helen's favourite. I wanted to soften the jagged edges of her grief and hoped – ridiculously – that the cake could make everything taste less bitter – literally. But none of this could be soothed or softened or sweetened. And as hard as we tried, by looking through old photos, and sharing memories, nothing really helped, because it always led back to the same conclusion – Lauren was dead. It was like reading a story over and over, hoping this time the ending would be different, but it was always the same.

We all sat in the living room with our drinks; Helen was in a daze, Tim had opened the whisky, and Sam seemed lost in his own world. He still hadn't returned to the cottage; I think he was conflicted, he wanted to be there, but at the same time couldn't face it. He was planning to move back there after the funeral though, and as much as I'd miss him being around, he'd spent a lot of time out walking, or alone in his room.

'How are you, love?' I asked him, knowing it was a stupid question, but wanting to acknowledge his pain along with everyone else's.

He lifted his head. 'I'm okay. In a way, I'm glad it's over,' he said with a sigh.

'Yes, I understand. It's hard to grieve properly until after the funeral,' I added, pointlessly, and we all sipped our drinks in unison and toyed with the cake on our plates in the silence that followed.

Then into that silence, Sam suddenly said, 'I grieved enough before the funeral, today was a watershed. Lauren wouldn't want us to grieve for too long.'

I felt this was a little too soon to be talking about ending his grief, especially in front of Lauren's parents, whose grieving would continue all their lives. The way he spoke, Sam made it seem like it was possible to just turn off all his feelings.

'She would have hated all that.' He gestured towards the coffee table, where photographs of Lauren lay scattered, her life spread before us. He looked angry and, of all the emotions I expected from my son that day, anger wasn't one of them. But the news of her pregnancy had seemed to stir it up in him, like he'd given her something precious to look after and she'd dropped it. Or was it because he still couldn't understand why she hadn't told him? I didn't know, and he didn't want to talk to me about it.

'I know Lauren wouldn't want you to be sad,' I started, trying desperately to edit what he'd said, 'but you are allowed to take some time to mourn her loss, love, she was your wife.' I reached out and rested my hand on top of his, and he looked at me.

'I didn't mean, I just meant...'

'I know, love, and I'm sure you'll do what you need to do,' I said. 'But don't make the mistake of thinking you can throw yourself back into work, and your old life, because you'll burn yourself out. What you think you're ready for and what you really are ready for are two different things.'

'Your mum's right, Sam, we all want to get back to our lives, but it's only because we think we'll be able to escape,' Tim said. 'We think by going back to the things we used to do, we can get our old life back with Lauren in it,' he added, gazing down into his almost empty cup.

'Yeah, I guess,' he replied, 'but we can't escape, can we?' Sam's eyes were pure fire, and I worried he might say something he shouldn't. I held my breath just praying he didn't mention the pregnancy. Even if Tim knew about it, that didn't mean he'd told Helen, and it may not be something they'd want Kate or Sadie to hear.

Sam picked up a photo from the coffee table and held it in two fingers, then tossed it back onto the pile like it was rubbish. I winced, as it sat, abandoned on top of all the photos of Lauren. Helen seemed to have had every single digital photo printed, a desperate attempt to have something of her little girl to hold. Sam stared ahead, his jaw flexing, his eyes filling with tears. I could see he was hurting, which is why what he said next surprised me.

'I must get back into running,' he said. 'I'm getting really unfit.'

I heard a titter behind me, Helen got up to fetch another glass of red wine. 'Go, Sam,' she said, sarcastically, and plonked herself down onto a chair, spilling some of the wine on her white silk shirt – it looked like blood. She continued to stare at Sam. 'You're not going to let the grass grow under your feet, are you?' she said bitterly.

You could cut the atmosphere with a knife, and I had to say something in my son's defence.

'Helen, I think you're misinterpreting what Sam said, he didn't mean it in a disrespectful way to Lauren,' I said.

'Don't bother, Georgie, he doesn't deserve your support,' she slurred, emptying her glass and looking around for the bottle.

My stomach churned, this wasn't the time for confrontation. Nor was it the time for Sam to talk about his plans to go running because he was out of shape! In fairness, I understood Helen's resentment, hearing this just hours after her daughter's funeral. How could he even *think* about that right now?

In an effort to clear the air and to show Helen and Tim that Sam wasn't 'moving on' obscenely early, I said, 'Helen, I should just explain, I think Sam wants to run because he used to run with Lauren, don't you, Sam?'

I looked at him for confirmation, but to my horror, he shook his head. 'No. I've been running on my own a lot since we moved to Dartmoor. Lauren was never very good at running over hills; the altitude gave her nosebleeds.'

I flinched at the mention of Lauren's blood and took a sideways glance at Helen, who raised her eyebrows as if to say, 'Nothing surprises me anymore.'

'You may not have *run* together lately,' I conceded, 'but you and Lauren *loved* walking, you went walking a lot.' I heard my voice fading on each word and realised how desperate I must sound. I was begging him with my eyes to come up with a lovely memory to soften the tone of what he'd said, erase the nosebleed comment, and show Helen that he was hurting too. I knew he was, and this was just his way of coping, but it still sounded insensitive, uncaring even.

'Look, all I'm saying is I need to get my life back, Mum,' he said softly and touched my hand, 'and running would be a start.'

I understood; he was just being honest, positive even, deleting all the stock phrases, the 'time will heal' and 'she's in a good place now', that we'd overdosed on at the funeral. He was just being real, saying what he felt. I just wished he hadn't chosen to say this in front of Lauren's parents. But before I could do any damage limitation, Sadie jumped in.

'I'll go running with you, Sam, and there's some great trekking near your place – we could do that?'

'Great,' Sam said. 'Let's start tomorrow.' Sadie's response had been bad enough – almost childlike in her enthusiasm, but Sam sounded even worse – so flippant, so carefree.

Sadie now clapped her hands together, and looked around expectantly, presumably thinking everyone would be high-fiving at the prospect of Sadie and Sam running together. She was making herself and Sam look really bad, would she ever grow up and learn to keep her feelings to herself? I felt a shimmer of disapproval in the air, and this time it wasn't just Helen.

Mortified, my cheeks were hot with fury and embarrassment at my son's total lack of sensitivity. I kind of expected it from Sadie, nothing surprised me there, but not Sam, my caring, sensitive child, who used to bring me gifts of daisies from the garden crushed in his hot little hand. I just wanted to get up and leave. I had this urge to drag Sam out with me before he said anything else, and slap Sadie hard across the face on the way. Hadn't she taken enough from this family already? Surely she didn't think she could now take Lauren's place with Sam? But watching her watching him from across the table, it crossed my mind that that was exactly what Sadie thought she could do.

CHAPTER TEN

'I think I'll get off now,' Sam said. He had apparently agreed to take Sadie home. 'Do you want to come, Mum?'

I shook my head. 'Thanks, but I feel like a walk.' I didn't particularly relish the idea of a journey into Dartmoor with Sadie. I didn't see why Sam should have to drive all that way either. 'Can't Sadie get a taxi?' I asked, pointedly. 'I mean, today *was*—'

'I'm fine to drive,' he said, putting his arm around me.

'He said he wants to,' Sadie added defensively. She was either brazen or completely unaware of the inappropriateness of expecting him to drive a round trip of an hour and a half on the day of his wife's funeral.

Tim hugged both Sam and Sadie, and Helen made a half-hearted attempt. 'Don't be a stranger, Sadie,' she said, her head wobbly, her eyes red. She'd never been keen on Sadie, and I'd wondered why she'd continued to include her in everything. I guess seeing Sadie was just a way of holding on to a part of Lauren's life. Kate just sat in the corner, making no attempt to get up and say goodbye. On the way out, Sam offered her a high-five and she almost smiled and high-fived him back.

'Is Sadie okay?' Tim asked Helen when they'd gone.

Helen shrugged. 'As okay as any of us, I suppose. It was her best friend, they did everything together.' Helen sighed and stood up, leaving her empty glass on the coffee table and wandering into the kitchen. I heard the fridge door open and close, then she came back in with a bottle of white, already opening the screw top. The zip of her black skirt was open at the side, she had no shoes on, and her hair was a mess, and it made my heart hurt to see her like this.

'Oh, love,' I said, standing up, putting both my arms around her. And she sobbed, and sobbed, her whole body shook with pain and loss. I wanted to tell her it would all be okay, but we both knew I'd be lying.

She suddenly pulled away. 'I'm fine, fine,' she said, pushing me with the bottle she was still clutching. 'Does anyone else want one?' she asked, as she sat down.

Kate mumbled something, and Tim said no, so Helen went to pour some in my glass, but I put my hand over it. She rolled her eyes, plonked herself on the sofa next to me and started to pour herself a large one.

'You sure you want that?' Tim said under his breath, he nodded towards the glass of wine Helen was already downing defiantly.

'How would you know what I do or don't want?' she hissed, picking up the bottle and sloshing in yet more wine.

I was surprised at the apparent bitterness between them, I'd never seen this before.

I felt my throat constrict as Helen emptied another glass. 'I'm going to bed,' she suddenly said and, still clutching her glass, picked up the bottle and stood up. Without acknowledging anyone, she staggered out of the room, brushing past Tim as she went.

Kate disappeared too and it was just me and Tim, which was a relief really.

'How are you?' I asked. It seemed like everyone else's feelings had been considered except Tim's, even Helen seemed to have abandoned him emotionally. I figured things like that happened when a couple lost a child, but I wanted Tim to know I was there for him, just as I was for Helen. He needed support as much as anyone.

'I'm... I'm okay.' He paused. 'No, I'm not, but what else can you say when someone asks you that?'

'Yeah, sorry,' I replied, feeling stupid, thinking I could help at all. Tim obviously needed space and me being there was just an irritant.

'No, I didn't mean...' Tim sat down, put his head back on the chair.

'I'll get off,' I said.

'No, no, don't, Georgie. Just stay a little longer?' he asked.

'Of course. Can I get you a drink... cup of tea?' I added quickly, not wanting to sit in silence. I was in danger of coming up with clichés or putting my foot in it again.

'Tea would be nice,' he said and almost smiled.

I got up and went into the kitchen and he followed me.

'I'll always be grateful to Sam,' he said, as I took two mugs from the cupboard, this kitchen as familiar to me as my own.

I glanced at him as I put teabags in the cups and saw tears in his eyes. I was touched that in all his grief he'd found the strength to convey that to me.

'I just feel like Helen's all over the place, and I... well, I feel close to Sam.'

I wanted him to have the opportunity to talk, so made the tea slowly, and just listened.

'He gave Lauren the chance to lead a good life, be proud of herself – he made her a better person,' he continued, hands in pockets, leaning against the kitchen island.

I guess it was just a phrase, but I wasn't sure quite what he meant by Sam making Lauren a better person and giving her the chance to lead a good life. She'd always led a good life – hadn't she?

Tim was now looking down, hands in pockets. I felt I should say something.

'Sam might have been responsible for her happiness, Tim, but you and Helen showed her how to lead a good life, you made her the best person she could be. Don't forget that.'

And then he said something that surprised me: 'Ah, me and Helen... we've made our mistakes, George.'

'You *haven't* made mistakes,' I insisted. 'I think you're blaming yourself because what happened to Lauren was something you had no control over, you couldn't save her. You're always saving people, you've saved me before now,' I said with a smile as I handed him a steaming mug. 'Remember when Sam fell off the trampoline in the garden?'

He nodded, as he took the mug from me.

I'll never forget the high-pitched scream coming from outside, a strange animal sound that my mother's ear was attuned to. I still remember the way my finger ends tingled as my body carried me out of the back door, my mind desperately needing, but *not* wanting, to know what was happening. I can still see Sam now, in my mind's eye, standing there unable to move for the pain, a pain that went through me as much as it did him.

'He just couldn't stop screaming. I called Helen and within minutes you arrived and I was comforted by your presence, straight away. You're brilliant in a crisis – well, you don't need me to tell you that, it's your job to be brilliant in a crisis,' I added. His skill was probably partly his personality and partly his police training, but that day I witnessed it first-hand. 'I need you to be very brave and stop making that noise,' he'd said firmly but kindly to Sam, who immediately stopped screaming, comforted by the father figure in his life. Within minutes, Sam and I were in the back of his car and Tim was driving us to the hospital, where he waited with us, distracting my six-year-old while a nurse injected him with a painkiller. After a scan, I was told he'd have to have an operation. 'I was traumatised,' I continued, 'but you sat and waited with me outside the operating theatre in the middle of the night. I don't know what I'd have done without you.'

He smiled. 'Ah, you know how I feel about Sam, and I want you both to know, that won't change. I'll always be there for him, whatever happens.'

And I knew he meant it. But I also knew Lauren's death hadn't just hit him, it had felled him. He'd lost so much weight in the past month and was a shadow of the man he'd once been. It was in his demeanour too, he walked like an old man, talked more quietly, like he didn't deserve his allotted space on the earth, like he wasn't worthy. We were all worried about Helen, but being with him now, I felt Tim was the one we should be keeping an eye on.

I suggested we sit down in the sitting room with our mugs of tea.

'It's a bad business, Georgie,' he murmured, following me through. 'I don't know where all this is gonna take us.'

My stomach plunged, as I sat down on their beautiful grey sofa. 'Do you know anything, have they... I mean the *police* said—?' I couldn't finish the sentence.

He shook his head slowly and paused, like he was garnering all his courage, then he said, 'I'll do what I can, but I just hope we're not all dragged into this. I just hope they find out who did it, what happened.' He held his mug in both hands, gazing down into the steam from his tea like it was a crystal ball and he might just find an answer in there.

'Are they *absolutely* sure it wasn't an accident?' I asked, still finding it hard to comprehend. In my naivety, I'd assumed that because no one had mentioned this again it had gone away, that the police had returned to their original theory about it being an accident. Stupid I know, but sometimes the reality is too much, and like children we think if we wish hard enough what we want to be true, will come true.

'Apparently they found some evidence,' he muttered.

'What?'

'I don't know yet, I'm not on the case, and everyone is keeping their cards close to their chests.'

'I wonder what they could possibly have found that's made them think it's—'

'Murder?' he asked, his voice hoarse with tears. He looked at me, red-rimmed eyes, hollow cheeks. I wanted to be sick.

'The injuries aren't conducive to accidental death. Apparently there were signs of a struggle.' He started to cry.

I put my hand on his shoulder, a vain attempt at comfort, another pointless gesture as Tim sobbed into his hands. I was trying to think back to that night, my mind was going up and down that whirling white staircase, but all I saw was blood and Sam's tears.

As Tim's sobs eased, I asked, 'Do they have any idea what might have happened, do they have any suspects?' I didn't want to mention Dartmoor prison and the possibility that a prisoner might have escaped, but I'm sure Tim had considered it.

'The problem is it's so remote out there, someone could have been on the moors that night before Sam got home, but there'd be no witnesses, and there are no CCTV cameras.'

'I wonder if we'll ever know what really happened?' I said with a sigh.

'Helen's a mess,' he said and started crying again, a quiet, throbbing cry that seemed to go right through him and through me too. Eventually he emerged, and looked up at me. 'Sorry, Georgie.'

'God, Tim, don't ever apologise.'

'It just, the idea that someone *killed* her – it changes everything, you know?'

'Yes, yes,' I said, now rubbing his back, wishing there was something I could do for him. He'd done so much for me and Sam over the years, yet I felt so impotent.

'I keep thinking about her, the last thing she saw, the pain as she landed – you should have seen her face, Georgie, it was smashed,' and as he said the word, the pain and horror showed on his face. 'You wouldn't know it was *her*,' he said through sobs. 'Her face was such a mess and her limbs were so twisted...'

'Oh, Tim,' was all I could muster. I'd seen her that night too of course, but I'd had to look away, I really thought that by the time she was in the morgue and Tim got to see her, they'd have cleaned the body, covered her injuries somehow, but clearly not. I don't know how Tim and Helen were able to view the damaged body of their child. At the time, Tim was reluctant, but Helen was desperate to see her daughter and must have persuaded him to go with her. I don't think I could do that as a parent, but given the choice of seeing your child badly injured or never seeing them again, who knew what you would choose to do? I wondered if it had been something Helen had to do, but perhaps wasn't so good for Tim. The horror on his face as he remembered told me he gained no comfort from seeing Lauren after death.

'Sorry, I'm sorry,' he said. 'I don't want Helen to hear me crying like a bloody baby. She'll only worry – she doesn't need any more worry.' He glanced upwards, in the direction of the bedroom.

'Neither do you, and you need to cry, to let it out,' I said. 'Do you think Lauren was happy?' I heard myself ask.

Tim lifted his head and looked at me. 'Yeah, yeah I *think* so. Don't you?'

'I *did*, I do – but I wonder if something happened that might provide an answer.'

'I don't...'

'I mean – Helen said Lauren had told you both she had cold feet, just before the wedding, have you any idea what it was, or *who* it was, that gave her cold feet?' This had plagued me ever since that night Lauren and Helen had tried to convince me it was nothing. And I couldn't shake the feeling that Lauren perhaps hadn't been as happy as she made out.

He stroked his cheek. 'I... I don't remember,' he said, but this surprised me, surely he'd remember his daughter getting cold feet just before her wedding? Had he really forgotten, or did he not want to tell me?

'Yeah,' he paused, changing the subject and returning to what we'd previously talked about, 'I thought this was going to be open and shut – a tragic accident. God, the alternative is just so hard to bear.

'You know, I really dreaded today. Her funeral was like this big cloud coming towards me and I thought if I can get through it, and get Helen through it, we can finally start to grieve. But knowing the police think it was murder leaves it open, a big, gaping wound of questions with no answers.'

'What do you think happened?' I asked.

'I don't know,' he said with a sigh. 'Perhaps Sam might know something?' He looked at me like I might have the answers, and I felt a weight in my chest. 'I don't think... He hasn't talked about it. He just *found* her...' I added, feeling uncomfortable. After all, Tim was a detective, he was trained to question, not believe.

'Have any of your colleagues found any new evidence?' I asked.

He shook his head. 'No. I reckon they're being cagey because they're looking at someone I know.'

Nausea swept through me, if it was someone Tim knew, it was likely someone I knew too.

'But I'm telling you now,' he continued, 'if I find out who did this, even if it was my own brother, I would kill him with my bare hands.'

I didn't doubt it; if Tim Jackson ever found out who'd killed his daughter, he would be capable of murder himself.

CHAPTER ELEVEN

I arrived home from Helen and Tim's around eleven and Sam came downstairs looking groggy; he was still wearing the shirt and the trousers he'd worn to the funeral.

'I'll make us some hot chocolate,' I said.

'I'm tired, Mum, I just want to—'

'I know, Sam, but I think we need to *talk*,' I said gently, and he seemed to realise by my tone that this was serious.

Ten minutes later, we were sitting in the kitchen with mugs of hot chocolate – the mother in me hoped the drink would soothe him, that it might dig deep into his childhood and give him some kind of succour, especially as what I was going to say wouldn't be easy for him, but I needed to get through to him, get him to open up.

'I just wanted to talk to you about this thing with the police. Tim said they aren't telling him anything, but I wondered if there was anything *you* could tell the police?'

'What do you mean?' he said defensively; so much for my gentle approach.

'Lauren was your wife and we've found out she was pregnant.' I reached out and put my hand on his, trying to soften the blow that was about to come. 'You said yourself that there was a chance it might not be yours?'

'I didn't *say* that, I just don't understand why she didn't tell me.'

I kept my voice gentle. 'Exactly, and it made me wonder if perhaps there were other things she didn't tell you. Did she ever behave suspiciously, did you ever think something was odd?'

This made him so uncomfortable, he almost stood up. I was his mother, and I knew there was something he wasn't telling me.

'Whatever it is, you can share it with me, Sam,' I suggested.

'There isn't anything. I just don't want to talk about this...' he said, sounding like the truculent teen he used to be.

But I knew that it was something we needed to talk about, so I pressed on. 'Apparently the police have evidence, but Tim doesn't know what it is,' I said, sipping my drink. 'How do you feel?' I asked.

'How do you *think* I feel? Pissed off, upset, angry.'

I found his anger unsettling and wasn't sure where to take the conversation next. I was aware that any minute he would finish his drink, go back upstairs and that would be it. Sam and I had always been able to talk, but since Lauren died, he seemed defensive and irritated, and I was finding it hard to communicate with him. I understood it was incredibly difficult for him, especially as this was about his marriage, but I had this instinctive feeling that there was something Sam wasn't telling me. And that something might just give the police what they needed to catch whoever had done this. So I took a deep breath, and went in. 'I hate to say this, but did Lauren perhaps have an admirer?'

'A stalker you mean?'

'Yeah, well, someone who liked her in that way?' I was trying to be as discreet as possible, not spell it out and hurt him any more than I had to.

'Nah, she'd have told me,' he said defiantly.

'She might *not* have,' I started gently, 'if she thought it might upset you, or you'd be jealous?' I said, trying to lighten this with a faint smile.

'Mum, for God's sake, just drop it,' he snapped.

I could feel my chin trembling at his outburst and he put his hand over mine.

'Mum, I didn't mean to snap, I'm just shocked. When I found her... she... well, she was already gone and it freaks me out to think that someone else might have been there, that someone deliberately hurt her... and the baby.'

'I know, I know. I do understand.'

We sipped our hot chocolate in silence, then he suddenly said, 'I don't know how I'd have got through this last month without you, Mum, you've been brilliant.'

'Why do I feel a but coming on?' I said, squeezing his hand.

'I'm thinking of going back to the cottage at the weekend.'

'Oh. For good?'

'Yeah, I can't leave it any longer. I have to check everything's okay and with no neighbours for miles, it's not like anyone can keep an eye on it for me. If the local hoodlums find out it's empty, they'll be having parties there.'

'Does Dartmoor *have* hoodlums?' I asked, smiling at the prospect. 'It's not exactly the hood, is it?'

'You'd be surprised,' he joked. He was now standing next to me, a tall, slim man, with the world on his shoulders. I desperately hoped that one day his future would open up for him again.

'Okay, I can drive out with you, help take some of your stuff?' I suggested.

'I'll be fine, I haven't got much to take. Oh God, I just thought...'

'What?' I said, assuming his head, like mine, was full of potential murder suspects. 'What, Sam?' I repeated, as he took out his phone to check something.

'Shit, I totally forgot,' he said again.

I was now on tenterhooks, holding my breath, waiting for what he had to say. Had he thought of someone who may have wanted to harm Lauren?

'It's the sofas for the cottage, they're being delivered tomorrow, but I have a meeting with my boss about going back to work. Mum, can I ask a huge favour, would you mind going to the cottage tomorrow and waiting in for the delivery?'

It wasn't exactly the breakthrough news I'd been expecting. In fact, it seemed surreal to be thinking about sofas at all, but Sam had a lot going on in his head. The very thought of driving out there and being in that place, the place where Lauren died, gave me chills. I didn't really want to be there on my own. 'Is it worth trying to cancel them, Sam, I mean I know Lauren wanted them, but—'

'I've probably left it too late. And anyway, Helen ordered them, she's got all the paperwork, she'd need to do it. I could call her tomorrow?' he offered.

'No, no. Leave it,' I said, remembering the state Helen was in. The last thing she needed was a phone call at dawn about her daughter's sofa delivery. 'I'll go out there in the morning.'

'Sorry, Mum, I wouldn't ask, but...' Then he thought of something. 'Sadie could go?'

'Isn't she working?' I asked.

'No, she's between jobs,' he said absently, appearing to now text her. 'She's only down the road and she's got keys so can let herself in. She'll be glad of something to do,' he said, putting his phone down.

'No, text her back, tell her I'll do it.'

'But you don't really *want* to drive out there, it's a hike for you, and Sadie's cool—'

'No,' I said, holding my hand up in a stop sign.

'Why not?'

I didn't *know* why, I just *knew* I wasn't happy about her being there, call it instinct.

'To be honest, Sam, I'm not sure I trust her,' I answered truthfully. 'She might forget to lock up afterwards, or take one of her shady boyfriends over there.' And the thought of her poking around, inveigling her way into the scene of the crime made me uneasy.

He started laughing. 'You're terrible, Sadie doesn't have a boyfriend, let alone a shady one.'

Helen had a different story to tell regarding Sadie's love life, but Sam clearly didn't want to hear that.

'*And* she smokes,' I added.

'That doesn't matter,' he said, which surprised me; he abhorred smoking, and Lauren said he wouldn't let Sadie smoke in the garden when she was over at the cottage. 'Sadie's great, and she'll be happy to stay at the cottage all day.'

'Yes, rifling through your stuff,' I snapped, recalling the missing money from mine and Helen's purses when she was younger.

Sam looked at me with such shock on his face. 'Mum, you can't say things like that.'

'I just did.'

He took a deep breath. 'Sadie gets blamed for everything that goes wrong, but she's—'

'*Manipulative?*' I hated myself for saying this, but I had to get it off my chest.

'She is *not* manipulative,' he said, scrolling through his phone.

'You're vulnerable at the moment, and I get the feeling she's got you wrapped around her little finger.'

'Mum, that's not fair, she hasn't. And I'm not stupid!'

'Helen and Tim aren't stupid, but look what happened there – she managed to get university fees, help with rent for her flat, Helen once even hinted they'd paid for her driving lessons.'

'You don't know anything about that,' he sighed.

'Well tell me then.'

'There's nothing to tell,' he said, going back to his phone. 'But you can't blame Sadie because—'

'I *know* she had a difficult upbringing.' I rolled my eyes at the age-old excuse. 'And I can empathise, but having a difficult childhood doesn't mean a person can be forgiven for being cold, for taking people's money and ignoring other's feelings.'

'There are good reasons,' he replied, sounding vague.

'Yes, I'm sure there are, but I won't stand around and watch her use you like she's used Tim and Helen. So please text her back and say it's fine, you don't need her to go to the cottage. *I'll* go in the morning, and stay there all day if necessary,' I said, getting down from my stool and washing the mugs, signifying the end of the conversation. 'Now go to bed, or you'll never get up in the morning,' I said, just like I used to when he was younger.

'Okay, okay. Thanks, Ma,' he said, smiling and not taking my diatribe about Sadie seriously, if anything he seemed amused by it. I was glad, I didn't want Sam and I to fall out over her, she wasn't worth it. 'Love you.' He kissed my cheek, which softened me slightly, and went off to bed.

After he'd gone, I still felt extremely prickly about Sadie and his defence of her. He didn't seem to want to hear a bad word against her, but I hoped he'd taken *some* of what I'd said on board. Sadie seemed to get a hold over people, and I'd never really understood her connection with the Jacksons. She was Lauren's friend, but Tim and Helen seemed to treat her like their third daughter, even if Helen did find her irritating. Over the years they'd bailed Sadie out of trouble many times, but the worst was when the girls went out in Lauren's new car and Sadie insisted on driving it.

They were seventeen, Lauren had only just passed her test, and Sadie hadn't even had a driving lesson. She'd had too much to drink and ploughed into another car. Poor Lauren was distraught and called her dad at 2 a.m. from the local police station, sobbing down the phone. Both Tim and Helen rushed out to rescue them, and the cheek of it, Sadie tried to say *Lauren* was driving. Back then, both girls were blonde and the same build, so the driver of the other car couldn't tell who'd been driving, and Sadie took advantage of this. Tim put his job as Detective Chief Inspector on the line to try to help Sadie, who eventually admitted it was her. They threw the book at Sadie and she got a five-year driving ban, Helen said it served her right. 'She could have killed someone, she could have killed *Lauren* – she's reckless, and dangerous.' But Sadie was devastated, and moaned about it for ages, she was never prepared to take responsibility for her actions.

Looking at it from my perspective, it seemed to me that Sadie had controlled Lauren, perhaps even bullied her into doing what she wanted. But Tim and Helen couldn't see this, and being far kinder human beings than me, they had continued to help her out with spending money when she needed it.

'We can't stand by and let her ruin her life, we can afford to give her the support her own family can't,' Tim had said. And not only did they continue to welcome her into their lives, they'd even paid her university fees. I thought about how James had also helped her, mentoring her so she could get the A levels she needed for the same university as Lauren.

I hadn't been able to see James for a while, it felt inappropriate to be embarking on a romantic relationship after Lauren died. Obviously he was at the funeral, and we'd kept in touch over text and the odd phone call. But I'd been caring for Sam, and swept up into the Jacksons' grief, and anything outside of that felt like I was letting them all down. One evening he called to ask if I'd like to just go over to his and have a takeaway with him, but even that would have felt like a betrayal to Sam and the Jacksons torturing themselves at home. I told him I'd love to see him again once everyone was settled, and my son and my friends didn't need me quite so much. James' own experience of grief meant he understood, and rather touchingly, he'd said, 'You don't have to explain, just know I'm here when you're ready.'

I thought about our very short but sweet romance, and felt a warm rush as I washed and dried the hot chocolate mugs. But staring out of the window at the dark garden, I was reminded of the cottage on the moors with no street lights and how the next day I had to return to the place my daughter-in-law had been murdered. But rather that than letting Sadie in.

CHAPTER TWELVE

The following morning, I set off to the cottage at 6.30 whilst it was still dark. There was an early-morning eeriness about the empty roads, which wasn't helped by the fact my car was old with a small engine and struggling with the climb. It would take at least an hour to get to the cottage, and only once I was climbing the moors did it begin to get light. It was late September, and the trees were laced with morning frost and, ghostlike, they watched from the side of the road. As I climbed higher, the road gave way to rough tracks and I suddenly felt very alone. I turned the volume up on the radio and tried not to think about how vulnerable I was to the elements. But what the hell would I do if my car broke down? The phone signal was really weak out here. I couldn't even comfort myself by thinking I'd arrive soon, because I really didn't want to *get* there. The last time I'd been at the cottage was the night of Lauren's death.

When I finally arrived, I was surprised all over again at the sheer remoteness of this little cottage tucked behind the trees. The thick veil of silence was a reminder of how isolated it was, no one for miles, just me, and a very weak phone signal. As Tim said, there was no CCTV anywhere, and no neighbours. I shuddered as I thought that out here *no one* would hear you scream.

The untended front garden and the darkness inside the cottage made me feel so sad. Sam and Lauren should have been here now. Lauren getting ready for work or sleeping off a night shift, lights on, the kettle whistling on the stove, the smell of toast. But opening the front door, the taste of bleach and metal permeated the hall, and I realised, to my horror, the metallic smell must have been Lauren's blood. Tim had obviously organised the cleaners to come in and cover up the smell of death with disinfectant and elbow grease. I was suddenly reminded of a book I'd read where the detective remarked that brain matter hardens to a cement-like consistency. I shivered and tried not to think about it, but the tang of her blood still in the air told me Lauren wasn't giving up that easily. I remembered her laughter, the swish of the pearl-dotted veil, her perfect teeth, the picture of new-wife happiness in the spring sunshine. But was she? Was Lauren happy? Did she have secrets, and if so what were they? And who else knew Lauren's secrets?

Pushing these unbidden thoughts from my mind, I reluctantly walked into the living room, feeling the need to glance behind me as I went. *Just in case.* But, of course, there was no one there. It was freezing inside the house, the battered old sofa donated by a friend sat in the middle of the room, a silent witness to Lauren's death, to her life. There were ashes in the fire grate and I imagined them both, sitting by the fire, Lauren's legs across Sam, a bottle of beer each, Netflix on the TV. Then, all of a sudden, I recalled those legs twisted at an impossible angle at the foot of the stairs. I took a deep breath, and tried hard to focus on something else, and searched for the boiler to turn on the heating. I wanted to warm up the pipes after the place had been empty so long, and I was bloody freezing.

I finally found the boiler and switched it on. As I walked away, it rattled into life, making me start. Then I saw the chair where I'd seen Sadie's bright pink fur coat on the night of Lauren's death. It was gone now. Had the police moved it, or taken it as evidence? If so, evidence for what? With this in mind, I had this rather irrational need to check the house over. I told myself this was to make sure there weren't any leaks or breakages, after the visits from police and forensics, but really it was my unease that someone was here, or had been here, and as much as I didn't want to, I had to check the cottage was empty. So I went back into the hall and walked up the staircase, purposely striding, trying not to think about her lying in a twisted mess at the bottom. But as fast as I wanted to get up those stairs, I knew I had to respect them, and carefully approached each slippery marble step, a potential killer on the beautiful white twisting monster that had already taken Lauren. Once at the top, I looked down into the eternal circle, and wondered for the millionth time what had happened there that night, and who had been with her.

I moved away and checked the bedrooms, the bathroom, even the en suite. The first bedroom I wandered into was the smallest one, and the one Helen and I hoped might one day be a nursery. Tears sprang to my eyes as I gazed around, imagining where the cot would have stood, the little mobile hanging just above, soft bed linen, furry toys. It had been so much closer than we'd realised with Lauren being pregnant, and unable to think about it anymore, I left and closed the door. I had to give myself a moment and pause before going into Sam and Lauren's room, and after a few seconds to gather my strength, I walked in.

I was confused to see the bedclothes turned over, like someone had just got out of bed – surely the crime scene cleaners wouldn't have left it like that? I walked towards the bed, planning to take off the sheets and wash them for when Sam came back at the weekend, but as I did, I saw something that almost made my heart stop. The wedding picture on Lauren's bedside table, the beautiful photo of her and Sam on the happiest day of their life, had been turned face down. And when I went to pick it up, the glass of the frame had been smashed.

The hairs on the back of my neck stood on end. What the hell?

I knew Sam hadn't been here since they'd finished, so either this room had been untouched since the night Lauren died or *someone* had been staying here since the cleaners left. Was the smashed wedding picture frame from the night Lauren died? Did

Sam and Lauren have a row? My stomach dipped at the prospect, what did it mean?

I checked the wardrobe, not sure what I was looking for. The pink fur coat was nowhere to be seen, but Lauren's clothes were still there, and I reached out to touch them, moving them gently along the rail, a whiff of her perfume was on the air. If I believed in ghosts, in that moment she was with me.

Suddenly something fell from the wardrobe, I jumped back slightly, my whole body rigid with fear. I looked down to see what it was, dreading a rat or a mouse – but some clothing had fallen out of the wardrobe. It looked like Lauren's wedding dress, but it hadn't fallen off a hanger; the dress had been stuffed into the bottom of the wardrobe.

I carefully picked it up, soft, ivory silk as beautiful as it had been on the day, save for a few creases from being jammed into the wardrobe. But what intrigued me was that the dress wasn't in a protective plastic cover, and I know for a fact, just days before Lauren died, it had been hanging from the wardrobe in the cover.

'I want it to stay as lovely as it was on the day,' she'd said to me and, as she was working, asked if I'd mind collecting it from the dry cleaners. When I'd collected it, the dress had been covered, so why take it out of the plastic and shove it to the back of the wardrobe in a heap? That just wasn't Lauren, she liked everything neat and in its place – and anyway, who would do *that* to a wedding dress? Even if she'd tried it on, she'd have put it back, carefully. I lay it on the bed, then searched for the protective cover, which had also been shoved to the back of the wardrobe. I pulled it out and was about to put it on the dress, when I noticed a stark, red stain on the ivory silk. My stomach lurched. Blood? I looked more closely, touching it with my fingertips. It was hard to tell what it was, but it definitely hadn't come back from the cleaners like that. I remember dropping it off for her at Helen's and we checked every inch of it, remarking how fresh and perfect it looked.

'It could be yours one day, Kate,' Helen had remarked.

'I'm too fat, I'd never get into it,' Kate had muttered, rolling her eyes.

'Oh but, darling, you'd diet for your wedding. Every girl goes on a diet for her big day, even Lauren cut down a few weeks before, and she didn't *need* to,' Helen had said. I'd winced silently at this, but fortunately Kate was too busy looking at the dress with Lauren to take any notice of what her mother was saying. But in the last month, I noticed Kate becoming thinner, her hair blacker, eyes more sooty, and the words emblazoned across her dark T-shirts, increasingly vile.

'Even the strawberry mousse stain's gone,' Lauren had said of the dress, and I wondered now if that's what the red was on the bodice, but no, this was darker – it was lipstick, or blood.

I touched the dress now as it lay on the bed. My fingers followed the fine freshwater pearls threaded through the bodice, all the way to the shimmery fish tail. I smiled, remembering how happy Lauren had been, her laughter, light and musical, the first dance, the last dance, and everything in between.

I carefully put the wedding dress back in its cover and returned it to the wardrobe. I'd ask Sam about it later, but I doubted he'd know anything about his wife's wedding dress after the wedding.

I left the room, feeling like I had more questions now than I had before, and heading back onto the landing, I was met with the spectacle again. The staircase looming large, a white, glacial killer unfurling upwards. But who was its accomplice?

CHAPTER THIRTEEN

It was strange sitting in the house without either Lauren or Sam, and I was finding it hard to relax and lose myself in the book I'd brought with me, so I turned on the TV. I wasn't really watching it, and every time I heard a noise, I turned the volume down, but after a while I got used to the creaks and the cranking from the boiler. So when I heard a different noise, one that sounded like it was coming from outside, my heart started pumping.

I looked through the front window and couldn't see anything, so it wasn't the sofa delivery. Then I walked over to the French windows, where beyond the garden went on for infinity, miles and miles of moorland, and I was reminded once more of how alone I was in the cottage. I moved back to the chair I'd been sitting on, telling myself I was simply hearing things, but as I turned the TV volume up again, I *definitely* heard something. Tapping on glass?

My back was now to the French windows, and I slowly turned around. I couldn't see anything, it must have been the wind blowing through the tree branches, but even so, a chill ran down my spine. I went back to the book, then the TV, but I couldn't settle, so I called Sam, who was obviously busy with work, because his phone was engaged.

A woman on TV was talking about how HRT had changed her life and I wondered momentarily if it might change mine? But before I could delve deeper, daytime TV had swiftly moved on. 'Now, what are you buying for your pet this Christmas?' the presenter asked earnestly, like she wanted to know the meaning of life. Turned out there was quite some soul-searching going on among dog owners. Oh how I wished that was all I'd had to worry about.

I stood up again and walked to the window, it was raining heavily now, and the skies had darkened. I remembered Lauren telling me she was scared in the house alone, and I felt guilty for not taking her more seriously, talking to Sam about leaving her here all hours of the night. Was she scared that night? Was it someone she knew? Or was it a random thing, a burglar maybe? Perhaps she'd run from the living room and in a desperate attempt to escape ran upstairs and tripped? Would we ever know?

I tried not to think about it, tried to take my mind off what might have happened, but it kept dragging me there. I owed it to Lauren to know what happened, and to Sam too. And I couldn't take my mind away from the fact that the intruder might come back. He could turn up when Sam was here alone and do the same to him? Then I remembered the attic – what if he didn't need to come back, what if he'd never left? And suddenly everything went silent. The TV stopped, the lamps went out and the boiler stopped cranking.

I held my breath; what was going on? Had someone cut the power? Suddenly a knock. I gasped, as the knock became harder, more desperate. I thought I was going to be sick. Fear ran through me like a knife. I heard something I couldn't identify. It had started to rain, was that the noise? Or was *someone* outside, and was that *someone* now banging so hard on the French window because they wanted to get in? Is this what happened to Lauren? Did they come in through there and chase her into the hall, and she couldn't get out through the front door because she'd locked it when she came home. Locked herself in. Just like I had.

I still had my back to the window, unable to move for fear whoever was outside might see me. My whole body stiffened as a voice called to me, 'Georgie, let me IN!' It sounded like Lauren, young and girlish but desperate, pleading and banging on the door. I couldn't bring myself to turn my head around to see. I looked at my phone, no signal. I took a deep breath and hoped if I ignored it, the person might go away.

'GEORGIE,' whoever it was, was now screaming my name. Was this real, or was I going mad?

I managed to turn slightly, and slowly got up from the chair. Walking towards the window, I saw the shape of someone. They were wearing a hood, so I couldn't see their face, and the rain on the glass was blurring everything. Then I heard something that chilled me to the bone. Lauren's laughter. I was going mad, or perhaps I was having a nightmare I couldn't wake up from? I tried to push myself forward, wake up and make my legs walk to the windows. And as I did, the rain seemed to slow down and I could finally make out the face in the window. Sadie. My stomach lurched, I was almost relieved to see her, at least I think I was.

I rushed to my bag to get the keys, ran to the window and opened the doors. She almost fell in, the icy wind followed her, along with splashes of cold rain as I quickly closed the door, making sure to lock it behind me.

'What are you doing here?' I asked, rushing into the downstairs toilet and grabbing a towel, her hair was wet through.

'I've been banging on the windows for ages, didn't you *hear* me?' she said, almost snatching the towel from my hands. 'Christ's sake,' she spat.

Why did she always have to be so bloody confrontational?

'I didn't know it was you,' I said, defensively. 'Anyway, I thought you had keys?'

'I have.' She dangled them in the air in an almost taunting gesture. 'But you've left *your* keys in the front door, so I couldn't unlock it from the outside, and I don't have a key to the French doors,' she added, clearly furious.

'I was just being safe,' I snapped back. 'You could have been *anyone*, an intruder or—'

She stopped towelling her hair and looked at me. 'An intruder? I was calling your *name* – how would an intruder know your name, for f—?'

'I don't know,' I said; she was making me feel so stupid. 'And you were laughing, like some madwoman,' I added. I could make her feel stupid too.

'Yes, I was laughing at *you*! I was talking to Sam, he's still on the phone. I was telling him I couldn't get in because *you* were watching a bloody dog dressed up in a sleigh on the telly. You couldn't take your eyes off it,' she said. '*That's* what I was laughing at, I was telling him how mad it was, me in the bloody wind and rain and you just completely ignoring me!'

'You were just laughing, you *weren't* on the phone,' I said, matching her rather challenging tone – Sadie always brought out the worst in me. I understood that she'd had to fight for everything, but she'd find life so much easier if she were a little more pleasant. But Helen told me Sadie's mother always spoke to her in an aggressive way, so I guess that's how she learned to communicate.

'Yeah, yeah, she's here. No, she's fine, she thought I was an intruder. Yeah, I know, hilarious. Laters,' she said. I was confused until I saw the Bluetooth thing in her ear and realised she *was* talking to Sam on the phone. Though she'd just put the phone down without asking if I wanted to speak to him or him to me. Typical.

'So, Sadie, *why* are you here?' I asked again, not exactly pleased to see her but relieved she wasn't an intruder, or a sign I'd lost the plot.

She threw the towel on a chair, crumpled. 'Sam texted me last night. He asked me to wait here for a sofa to be delivered or something?' She wasn't even looking at me, just gazing into her phone. I never really understood why Lauren was friends with her, they were so different.

'Yes, I was with him when he texted you, but I said I'd come over. He should have texted you and let you know I came instead, sorry,' I said, hoping if I treated her with some kindness and respect, it might come back.

She didn't look up.

'So we seem to have had a power cut,' I announced, abandoning kindness and respect for facts.

'Oh, we're always getting them here.' She shrugged, again without taking her eyes from the phone.

'*We?*' I asked, questioningly. I didn't like the way she seemed so at home here. Already she'd taken over the chair I'd been sitting on, one leg over the arm like she lived there.

'Yeah, *we!*' She looked puzzled. 'Remember, I live just down the road, I get power cuts too.'

'Oh. Right.'

God she was so aggressive and was now leafing through my bloody book. She had no manners, no respect for anyone or anything. I'd tried so many times but really couldn't warm to her.

Then, suddenly, miraculously, the lamps came on, flooding the room with light, and the TV began to buzz in standby mode, the cottage now resuscitated back to life.

It seemed the power was back on and I, relieved, decided to go and check other electricals and test the kettle. I walked into the tiny kitchen which had an old-fashioned hatch and called through to ask Sadie if she'd like a cup of tea. I admit, I wasn't just being kind with this gesture; I was keen to know how long she intended to stay, and her response might give me an indication of this. In spite of not really being comfortable here on my own, I didn't want to spend any more time in her company than I had to. But she didn't answer, so I repeated the question. 'Tea, Sadie?'

'Coffee,' she replied, without even a please.

My stomach dropped and I breathed deeply before turning on the kettle. I told myself to be more like the Jacksons, and I owed it to the memory of their daughter to be nice to Lauren's best friend. Then I suddenly remembered something, and walked back into the sitting room where she was still half-sprawled with her phone.

'Sadie, you left your coat behind, it was on that chair.' I didn't say 'on the night Lauren died'. I thought that might be a little too pointed. I gestured to the chair, and she followed my hand with her eyes, then made a puzzled face.

'Coat? Which one?'

'The bright pink furry one.' You couldn't miss it if you tried.

'Oh *that* one. I gave it to Lauren ages ago.'

'Oh, it's just that Sam thought it was yours,' I said, trying to find out in my clumsy way if she'd been at the cottage (and perhaps been the one who'd played brides with Lauren's dress).

'Sam hasn't got a clue.' She rolled her eyes.

'It seems to have disappeared – or have you got it?'

'No, God, why are you getting so wound up about a coat?'

'Because it was here the night Lauren died and now it isn't,' I snapped.

'Oh, take a chill pill, it's probably in the wardrobe, or something...'

'I can't understand it – it's quite the mystery,' I said, putting on a puzzled expression for her benefit.

She glanced up at me, gave me a filthy look and went back to her phone, which was rude and irritating. Perhaps now wasn't the time to take a chill pill, perhaps it was the time to ask her annoying questions I wanted the answers to. If she didn't like it, she might go? So I walked further into the room, and perched on the arm of one of the old easy chairs that were going to be skipped when the sofas arrived.

'Sadie,' I started, 'did you ever try Lauren's wedding dress on here?'

She scowled without looking up. 'No, why would I?'

'Oh I don't know. It's just that I found Lauren's dress in the back of the wardrobe. It had a red stain on it.'

She went pale. 'A red stain?'

I nodded.

'What makes you think I know anything about it?' she said, immediately regaining her composure. 'And don't get any ideas – I didn't play weddings with it. I'm not exactly a wannabe bride,' she huffed.

But I wondered if that's exactly what she was – a wannabe bride, a wannabe Lauren too.

'I'm not *saying* it was you,' I lied. 'I just thought you might... feel close to her, trying on her clothes?' I suggested, desperately trying not to make it sound like an accusation, but wanting to gauge her response.

At this, she finally looked up, this time in anger. 'God. Georgie, you make me sound like a weirdo. Do you really think I'd get off trying on her *clothes?*' For a moment I didn't know if she was going to say something else, but then suddenly she went from anger to amusement, and started to giggle.

It occurred to me that she too was suffering from grief and might be feeling slightly unhinged.

'What?' I asked.

'Well, I'm not a bloody stalker. Jesus, Georgie, what do you think I am?' She'd stopped giggling now, and I saw a shadow of sadness, or something similar, move across her face.

'I just meant, as you spent a lot of time here, you might be missing her and...'

'Trying on her clothes? Yeah *right*,' she added sarcastically.

But instead of going straight back to her phone, she stared ahead, then suddenly said, 'Actually, what you just said was bonkers, but we used to share clothes, me and Lauren. Sometimes she'd pretend to be me and I'd pretend to be her.'

I was surprised at this little chink of information; Sadie rarely shared anything, with anyone.

'I remember you both dyeing your hair the same colour,' I replied, with a smile.

'Yeah, we did.' Her eyes glazed over like she was remembering. 'I first met Lauren when we were eleven and in the same class at our new school. I thought she was the most hilarious person I'd ever met – she was mad, just *mad*. And I was so excited when she invited me to her house for tea, I'd never been to anyone's house for tea before. Her mum called my mum to ask if I could go after school and my mum was like "What the fuck?" because she didn't care whose house I went to after school.' She gave a hollow laugh. 'But that day we walked to her house, to me it was like a mansion, and I thought she was really posh. They had napkins on the table, I didn't even know what they were!' She giggled at the memory, and glanced over at me, like she'd forgotten I was there.

I couldn't remember Sadie ever saying this much to me, she clearly wanted to talk, and I doubt anyone ever listened. She must have been missing Lauren, so I stayed perched on the arm of the chair.

'I fell in love with Lauren's parents the moment I met them,' she was saying. 'They weren't anything like my mum, or my step-dad, or any other man she'd brought home and told me to call "Dad". They spoke quietly, they didn't shout – they were gentle and didn't smack Lauren over the head when she spilt some juice on the carpet. They were like parents in a film on the telly, I didn't think they existed in real life, but her mum asked us about school, and her dad teased us and made us laugh. And I was just like "Oh. My. God. I want to *live* with these people, I want to be part of this amazing Disney family."'

I had to smile at this, recognising a bit of myself and how starstruck I'd been when I first met Helen and Tim, but I'd been a fully grown woman, not an eleven-year-old schoolgirl.

'Anyway, after tea we went to play in the garden,' she continued, 'and Lauren threw this ball and it smashed a neighbour's window.' She lifted the back of her hand to her mouth, reliving the moment, it was obviously still very clear in her mind. 'We were both horrified and when the neighbour came out and started shouting, Lauren said, "I'm sorry my friend did it, but my dad will pay for the damage." The woman told me off, and I was mortified, but then it got worse because we went inside the house and she told her dad the same thing, "Sadie did it." I was so embarrassed and upset and Tim looked at me with such disappointment, I burst into tears.'

'Oh, Sadie, that's really sad,' I said, wondering why she was telling me this, but at the same time feeling a tug at my heart-strings. 'Why didn't you tell Tim that it wasn't you?'

She shrugged. 'I dunno. I was their guest, I felt sort of *honoured* to be there, you know? I was in their lovely house having tea with napkins and cream jugs, and everyone was so... *nice*. At home, me and Mum had chips out of the bag, or beans from a tin, or nothing, and we never talked, she just yelled. It really was a different world, and I didn't want to annoy Lauren, or upset her parents. I thought if I made a fuss and said Lauren wasn't telling the truth, they wouldn't *like* me, and I'd never be able to go there again.'

This was a glimpse of the real Sadie, where she came from, who she was. I was beginning to understand why she clung to the Jacksons, but was surprised at what she'd said about Lauren blaming her.

'I'm sure Tim wasn't disappointed with you, probably just pissed off he had to pay for the window,' I said.

'Yeah, but it made me determined to be good, and never give them any reason to stop inviting me,' she said with a smile. 'And when Lauren stole some make-up from Boots, and the store detective stopped us at the door, she'd pushed it in my pocket and said, "I'll give you all my pocket money for a month if you say you did it."'

'I can't imagine Lauren doing anything like that?' I said, not sure I believed her.

'Oh she did all sorts of crazy stuff – wrote rude words on the girls' toilet walls at school, skipped classes. And she'd often drag me in on it, but she always paid me, and when she offered me all that money to say I'd shoplifted, I know it sounds bad, but I took it and took the shit from the store detective. He threatened to tell my mum, but I didn't care because she didn't care, and I had a whole month of Lauren's pocket money, it was like winning the bloody lottery.'

'Wow, I guess teenage girls are even more complicated than teenage boys,' I said.

'She always made me laugh though,' she murmured, a caveat sweetener to what she'd just told me. Was that to assuage her guilt for lying about her friend? Or had Sadie simply remembered it differently? Because I was sure Helen told me that it was Sadie who had the issues with shoplifting. As hard as I tried, I could never imagine Lauren doing something like that. She could have anything she wanted from Tim and Helen; she didn't *need* to steal. But Sadie did.

Lauren wasn't around to defend herself now, and Sadie could say what she liked. She could rewrite the narrative of their friendship, swap their lives around, *become* Lauren, and kill off the old Sadie. Just thinking about that made me shudder, because if that *was* the case, Sadie could now hand all her misdemeanours over to Lauren. From the shoplifting to the crude graffiti in the school toilets – it could all be Lauren's now, and she wasn't here to deny it. I wondered what else Sadie had done in her young and difficult life that might have found its way to Lauren's door?

She stopped talking and went back to her phone, so with my head full of tangled thoughts, I went back into the kitchen to continue making the drinks.

'There's really no need for you to stay and wait for the sofas,' I called, putting coffee into a mug for her and a teabag for me. Being organised, I'd brought milk from home and biscuits and a sandwich. I'd been planning to diet, but it was the kind of day only chocolate biscuits could cure. 'No need for you to stick around here all day,' I repeated, walking in with two mugs and putting them down on the coffee table.

'I've got nowhere else to go,' she said, as I headed back into the kitchen and picked up the packet of chocolate digestives, taking them through on a plate.

'Up to you,' I said, mirroring her indifference as I walked into the room and offered her the plate. But after being so chatty only seconds before, she just shook her head at the proffered biscuits. It was on the tip of my tongue to say, 'No thank you,' but having just had a tiny glimpse of her childhood, I realised that it wouldn't even occur to Sadie to say thank you.

I sat down, silently chastising myself for not being a bit more sympathetic, and at least taking on the fact that she'd had a tough upbringing.

'Is the coffee okay, enough milk?' I asked, trying to open up communication again.

She barely nodded, and didn't even acknowledge me.

I considered her earlier suggestion of taking a chill pill, and decided to take her advice, so settled down with my copy of *Good Housekeeping*, which was about as 'chill' as I got these days. I flicked through the magazine, realising that to someone young and carefree like Sadie, I was probably just an uptight old bag. Perhaps I was? I'd felt like an old bag for quite a while, which was a shame because I was forty-five, younger than Nicole Kidman, and no one would ever describe *her* as an old bag. I didn't used to feel like an old bag with Helen, we were the same age and used to laugh about our wrinkles and stiff joints. And as much as she hated getting older, she could always find something funny to say, and we'd soon be laughing. God how I missed that. The becoming old. Now there was nothing to laugh about, I wondered if poor Helen would ever be able to smile again. I was also permanently low, worrying about Sam, and the Jacksons, and constantly trying to make everyone feel better. But while I was looking after everyone else, I felt like I was going downhill, and spending that time with Sadie made me feel very much like an uptight old lady. I wondered if perhaps I needed to start the journey back to my own life? I thought about James, his smile, the way he made me feel attractive, younger, and not like an old bag at all. Now the funeral was over and Sam was planning to come back to the cottage, I could see a chink of light, a kind of future – and James fit into that future. But for now, I was stuck here with 'charming' Sadie, waiting for sofas; my life, like everyone else's, still on hold.

We sipped our drinks in silence – the morning show had now finished and the news was on the TV. I was watching passively, still thinking about James, when I suddenly saw a photo of a bride on the TV screen. I sat forward, to make sure I was seeing this correctly – it was Lauren, on her wedding day, smiling.

'What the hell?' I grabbed the remote and turned the volume right up. 'Sadie, look!'

She slowly dragged her eyes from her phone, but by the time she saw the screen, the photo was gone.

'What?' she said, irritated.

'It's on the news – about Lauren.'

She sat up now and watched avidly, gesturing with her hand to turn up the volume even louder, and despite the situation, I still wanted to remind her of her bloody manners. But I did as I was told and turned it up to hear the newsreader say, '... the young newly-wed whose body was discovered in her home on Dartmoor last month.' The camera was panning on the cottage, it looked so familiar yet strange seeing it on the TV, but before I had chance to take it in, a detective was making a statement: 'This is now a murder investigation,' he said. Sadie and I looked at each other wide-eyed. 'The murder took place on a remote section of the moors, but it's an area popular with hikers and tourists and someone may have seen something. We would ask for the public's help in identifying anyone or anything they may have seen that might have appeared suspicious or unusual in the area around this time.'

'Christ,' Sadie gasped. Her face was deathly white; she looked like she'd been punched.

'Are you okay?' I asked; she looked like she was about to faint.

She shook her head, her arms were now wrapped around her body, and she huddled on the chair. All the nonchalance and bravado had fizzed away, and here, in front of me, was a scared little girl. She clearly hadn't been told that the 'accident' was now considered by the police to be murder and was being investigated as such. 'It's just... it's scary, isn't it?'

'Yeah, very.'

'I mean, if someone killed her – *why*? What do the police know?'

I shrugged. 'Do *you* know anything?' I asked gently, leaning forward in my seat.

'Nothing, nothing,' she repeated. But the way she said this, and the fear on her face, told me Sadie knew *something*.

CHAPTER FOURTEEN

Sadie left soon after we'd seen the news on the TV. Her cold and indifferent demeanour had been replaced with a more flustered, worried look, and she certainly didn't want to hang around the cottage with me any longer. I called Sam to see how he was, but he didn't answer, he was probably still in the meeting with his boss.

The sofas arrived at 2 p.m., and when I let the men in, they asked me where I'd like them to be put, so I pointed to the places I'd heard Helen and Lauren discussing on that first visit to the cottage. Today would have been exciting for them both; they loved shopping for new things. After Helen's enthusiastic suggestion about the Harvey Nichols' sofas on our first visit, I thought it was decided, but no, they did what Sam called 'deep sofa research' – they just loved the process. The two of them had spent days, no, weeks, going through swatches in different shades and fabrics. I'd often turned up at Helen's to find them with a pile of little squares, the computer on and a bottle of wine between them. But today was the culmination of all that planning, and neither of them were here.

The sofa arrival would be treated with great importance in the Jackson household. Lauren would have taken a day off from the hospital, and no doubt there would have been a 'sofa celebration' lined up for later on. Helen would've produced nibbles and chilled white, and friends would have been invited to view the sofas like installations at an art gallery. But without Helen and Lauren sprinkling their sparkle, this was just sad and empty. I missed the fun. I missed Helen getting very drunk and being hilarious, while Kate rolled her eyes and Tim tried to get her to bed. Just thinking about it all and how it would have been made me want to cry, and once the delivery men had gone, I did.

Then I called Helen, I wanted to see if she was okay after the news on TV. I didn't know if it was insensitive or not to tell her I was here and the sofas had just been delivered. But depending on how she was, I might mention it. These days, I had to second-guess my best friend's feelings, and sometimes I got it wrong, because she wasn't the carefree, happy woman I'd known. Only the previous week I'd suggested the two of us go out to dinner, and she just looked at me in horror and said, 'Georgie, my daughter died,' like I didn't know.

I called her now and waited. But no answer. So I tried the landline. It rang out quite a few times, and I was about to put the phone down when Tim picked up.

'Hi, Tim.'

'Hey, Georgie,' he said, his voice raw.

'I'm sorry, I just wanted to speak to Helen,' I said, aware I'd just apologised; I did that a lot these days with Tim and Helen. Only a couple of nights before I'd got no answer at their door so left a cooked pasta dish on the doorstep, which only seemed appropriate if I accompanied it with a text that began with 'sorry'.

'Helen's taking a nap,' he said, and I knew what that meant – she didn't want to speak to anyone. Even me.

'Good, good, glad she's getting some rest,' I said, going along with the lie. 'I'm at the cottage.'

'What? Why?' He seemed alarmed.

'I... I've been waiting in for the new sofas.'

'I don't think that's wise, Georgie. The police won't want anyone in there now this is a murder investigation. They might need to do more forensics.'

'Oh yes... of course,' I said, feeling like I was being told off. 'But the murder investigation was only announced once I was there... it was on the TV, so...' I started.

'Sorry, Georgie, I have to go. I'll tell Helen you called,' he added. I was shocked at the abruptness in his voice, he'd never been like that with me before and it stung.

'Tim,' I said, finding it hard to let him put the phone down on me like that. 'Do you think, now the media are involved, people will phone in... someone might have seen something?'

'I don't know,' he said doubtfully, and I realised it had been insensitive of me to call. Presumably that's why Helen didn't want to talk, she was upset and so was Tim. I could have kicked myself. Then it occurred to me – as I'd called on the landline, they might have thought it was the police with news? How stupid of me! Why on earth would Helen want to know about the delivery of bloody sofas at her dead daughter's cottage when her daughter's death had just been declared to be a murder?

'Okay, I'll get off, Tim, and leave you. But let me know if I can do anything,' I said, before adding, 'and if you hear anything?'

'Georgie,' he paused, 'the road might get a little bumpy, but just remember, we're family,' he added, 'we will stick together, and get through this, okay?'

'Yes, yes, of course we will. The Jackmoores,' I said, relieved to hear echoes of the old Tim, who wouldn't be defeated. 'And let's hope to God they get the right man and charge him quickly before he can hurt anyone else,' I added.

'You know where I am if you need me,' he replied, which seemed an odd response to my comment. 'It's just very difficult, you know?' he added, before finally putting down the phone.

I understood, Tim was like Atlas holding everything and everyone on his shoulders. No one seemed to be taking care of him though, and I made a mental note to ask James to check in on him.

I called Sam, but again no answer, so I left a message to say the sofas had arrived and I was leaving now, I didn't want to hang around any longer, this place was bad news. So I grabbed my keys and bag, checked everything had been turned off and headed out for the car. I opened the cottage door to be hit by the autumn evening chill. It was still raining hard, with some hail, and the wind was getting up, I could hear it sweeping across the moors. I couldn't wait to get in my car and pull away from that dark little cottage that smelled of death.

I set off driving through the rain, my car smashing into puddles on what was little more than a dirt track as I negotiated my way off the moors. After my conversation with Tim, my thoughts wandered to the many times over the years when the Jacksons had been there for me. They always knew just what to do and never made me feel guilty asking for help. 'You're family,' they'd say, and just thinking about this brought tears as I drove along.

I'd sometimes wondered what such a free-spirited, impulsive woman like Helen had seen in Tim, who was attractive but in a fatherly way. He was only five years older than her, but as she always said, 'Tim's so much wiser, he just knows everything.'

And he did, and even now it's hard to describe how safe he made you feel, but he was like this great big wooden door that kept all the badness out. After he'd stayed with me and Sam at the hospital after Sam's trampoline accident, I'd envied her. I'd never had that support, a man who stepped in and commanded respect, asked the right questions, and got the right answers. I remember a nurse commenting that, 'Your hubby's lovely,' and I didn't contradict her, because it felt nice. And, I confess, after that night, I sometimes imagined what it would be like to be married to someone like Tim and was horrified to realise I had a tiny crush on him for a while. I'd been so touched by his caring, and it was such a relief to share my worries about Sam with someone else, another adult who cared about Sam too. Luckily, the longer I got to know them, the more incestuous the very idea began to feel, and eventually, my feelings for him naturally reverted back to friendship.

I smiled at the memory as my phone started ringing. On Tim's 'police safety' advice, I always kept it on the passenger seat when I was driving. So I glanced down at it, to see Sam's name flashing on the screen.

I was minutes away from home, so didn't answer; he'd know I was driving and he'd leave me a text or message if necessary. But then my phone rang again, and then again, and eventually, when I got somewhere near civilisation, I pulled the car over. Sam had left me a message, but when I opened the voicemail, my heart almost stopped.

'Mum. Mum, the police are here.' He sounded shocked, tearful. 'They think I killed Lauren.'

CHAPTER FIFTEEN

I couldn't get home quick enough and pulled up outside the house just as Sam was being put into a police car. It's a scene I never thought I'd witness, my son, who loves animals, works with nature, was being arrested for murder. And this wasn't some random road accident, an unavoidable death that he'd witnessed, or couldn't save someone from. This was the actual murder of his wife! I couldn't get my breath as I abandoned the car, running towards him. Our eyes met, he looked devastated. But before I had chance to say anything, the officer put his hand on Sam's head and guided him onto the back seat.

'Sam, Sam,' I called, running to the car. The police officer nodded, giving me permission to say goodbye. There was another officer sitting on the back seat next to him, like he was some fugitive who might escape any minute.

Sam was crying. 'Mum, I didn't do it, I didn't.'

'I know, love, don't worry, I'm going to sort it out,' I said blindly, not sure what the hell I was going to do.

'Will you call Tim?'

'Yes, yes, right now,' I said, knowing that was the only thing to do.

Two other police officers climbed into the front of the car, and the engine started, so I stepped away, my heart breaking as the window was wound up, and the car began to pull away.

'I'll call Tim,' I mouthed, and Sam's face lifted slightly at this. I watched as he was driven off, making an attempt to smile, like I was seeing him off for a day at work, trying not to let him see I was crying too. He didn't look at me, just kept his head forward.

I took a deep breath and slowly headed into the house. I needed to talk to Tim, he'd know what to do. He'd probably known Sam would be arrested when I'd called him earlier, that would explain his odd responses, his reluctance to be drawn into a conversation. He told me he knew nothing, but I was sure he was able to find out what was going on. So I called him, something I'd always done in the past when faced with an emergency, but no answer. I'd call back later, straighten everything out, it wasn't like Sam was guilty. Then I called the station and asked if Sam had arrived and the woman I spoke to confirmed that he had.

'So, what happens now? This has never happened before, I don't know anyone who's ever been arrested,' I said, tearfully.

'Yes, I understand, Mrs...'

'*Ms* Moore, I'm single,' I said, thinking *for Christ's sake why do I always feel I have to explain my marital status?*

'Well, Ms Moore, it's hard to say really. They could keep your son in for twenty-four hours for questioning, but your son will have given your number as next of kin, so just wait to be contacted,' she said, clearly about to hang up.

'Wait... wait. While I'm waiting... What do I *do?*' I said, aware I sounded completely helpless.

She gave a sigh, she probably dealt with parents like me all the time. 'Just wait, I'm afraid.'

'Well, they'll soon know he's innocent, they only have to talk to him to find that out, so is it likely he'll be home *before* the twenty-four hours. That means he could be released in the middle of the night, couldn't he?'

'He *could* be released any time, in theory,' she said doubtfully, 'but I wouldn't wait up. I'd go to bed if I were you, love, and if he *is* released, he'll be allowed to phone you. If not, give us a call in the morning, someone might be able to tell you what's happening by then.'

I thanked her, took a deep breath and slowly headed into the sitting room, where I plugged my mobile into the charger. Never had I ever considered something like this, but how stupid was I not to realise that's what Tim was trying to warn me about, he must have known that Sam would be in the frame. But he obviously didn't expect him to be arrested tonight; he'd be horrified. I quickly dialled his number, again, but still no answer. I considered driving over there, but it felt too intrusive. Even in the light of what had just happened with Sam, their plight would always be worse than mine.

I paced around the sitting room, then realised that this was in fact an emergency, and I'd be quite justified to call my friend, detective or not, to discuss with him the fact that my son had just been arrested for the murder of his daughter.

So this time I called the Jacksons' landline and was surprised when Helen picked up. 'Yes?' she snapped, obviously not realising it was me.

'Helen, I'm so sorry, did I wake you?'

'No, Georgie... I—' But before she could say anything Tim came on the line.

'Georgie,' he said, sounding like the mention of my name was about to be followed by, 'what are we going to do with you?'

'Sam's been arrested,' I blurted.

'Yeah, I just found out. Can't believe it.'

'I know, I can't either. I mean, it's ridiculous.'

'Absolutely,' he murmured, something Tim always said when he was at a loss for words.

'What can we do, Tim?' He didn't immediately respond, so I ploughed on, this was no time for politeness, for waiting to hear his theories, I was desperate. 'I understand that they might think that he... Sam *did* something, but we know he didn't.'

'Absolutely,' he repeated, and I felt like I was losing my

foothold. Tim wasn't raging, he wasn't furious with the police for arresting an innocent man, he was trying to placate *me*.

I had to be forthright. 'Tim, would you mind coming to the police station with me and explaining?' I hated to ask, but I had no idea of police procedure, and Tim *was* the police. He was also my friend, and he'd have Sam out of there in no time.

'Thing is...' His tone made me feel uneasy, Tim often started bad news with 'thing is... I can only do so much. I told you before, this isn't my case.' He sounded tired, irritated.

'Oh, I just thought—' I was taken aback, and was in such a state, I sat down on the nearest easy chair seeking some kind of grounding. It was velvet, and I began rubbing the arms with my fingertips in a futile attempt at self-comfort. This wasn't like only a few hours before, he'd told me he was there for us. He'd *always* been there for us and now Sam and I needed him more than ever.

'It's *my daughter's* case, Georgie...' he said, helplessly, and then I realised, he was conflicted. He might even be wondering if Sam was in some way involved in his daughter's murder.

'Of course, I understand.' I had never felt so utterly alone. I wanted to put down the phone, but he just kept listing the reasons why he couldn't help me.

'You see, any potential suspects could be my family members. This isn't a US cop show where the sheriff Dad sets out to avenge his daughter's... death,' the word faded on his lips.

'No, I understand.' I now felt embarrassed for even asking. I'd just assumed Tim would step in, but this wasn't like the time he used his position to make Helen's ticket for driving over the limit disappear (something they were both uncomfortable about, and if Kate hadn't mentioned it no one would have been any the wiser). This was something quite different and, as he said, it involved his daughter.

'Do you have any advice for me?' I asked in desperation.

Silence again while he thought of a gentle way to say this. 'It depends on what they think happened, what forensic reports say, what they found, and where they found it.' He took a long breath, and I heard Helen muttering in the background. 'No, it's fine,' he was saying to her. I guessed she was offering to take the phone from him, he was going through enough and she could probably see that, and I felt bad that my best friends were now protecting each other from my phone calls. 'Trouble is, if they find who did it, they can't risk a miscarriage of justice,' he continued. I could hear the conflict in his voice, he wanted to help Sam, but he couldn't. 'If I try to get involved with Sam's arrest now, and someone else becomes a suspect, then I could be accused of planting evidence. If someone else did this, we want a watertight case, and me being around doesn't help that.'

I found this vaguely comforting, that he felt someone else might be a suspect. Did he know this; was he trying to tell me something? Or was I reading too much into a sentence he uttered just to be kind, to give me false hope?

'You know Sam, he isn't violent. He adored Lauren, they were perfect together, you *know* that, Tim,' I said, aware of the pleading in my voice.

'Absolutely. And trust me, love, I'm there for you, and if I can, I will get in there and make it go away. But they have to follow procedure, and as you're probably aware, the first people, or person, they'll be considering is—'

'I know, I know, the husband,' I breathed.

'Obviously he's innocent and if things get difficult, I'll vouch for the lad, you know I will,' he whispered. I wondered if a police liaison officer was within earshot, I hoped that was why he was whispering, because the alternative was that he didn't want Helen to hear him making this promise. Which meant she didn't want Tim to help Sam.

'Will you? Will you tell them – your colleagues?'

'Of course, of *course*,' but I heard helplessness in his voice. I'd never heard helplessness in Tim's voice before.

'The officer on the phone said they could keep him in twenty-four hours.'

'Yes, that's right. Although if they apply for an extension, it could be longer. But at this stage it's just supposition, on everyone's part. They don't *know* he did it and we don't know what they've got and why they've arrested him. We can talk all day but we won't know anything until he's been questioned. You just have to be brave, Georgie.'

I started to cry, big heaving sobs.

'Look,' he said, '*officially* I can't do anything, and if the police question Sam, or you, I can't be there even as a friend, as you know I would under different circumstances.'

I nodded through my tears. 'I understand,' I said, 'but if you can't help me officially, can you tell me how to help him if I need advice?'

'Absolutely,' he said, that word again. That meaningless word that meant he was lost for something to say.

'Thanks, Tim.' I was tearing at the tissue paper in my hands, making damp strips of white.

'As soon as they talk to him, they'll know he had nothing to do with it,' he reassured me.

'And then they'll start looking elsewhere?' I asked hopefully.

'Absolutely. They just need to eliminate him as a suspect, and once they've interviewed him, then they'll know he's innocent and he'll be home.'

I hoped Sam didn't, in his confusion and upset, say anything that might make him *look* guilty.

'One thing you have to remember, Georgie, is that I think very highly of him,' Tim was saying, but I felt like this was just a palliative, he was trying to soothe me. Because, of course, he had to be wondering now if my son had killed his daughter.

I thanked him, asked him to give my love to Helen, and tell her I'd see her soon. Then I put down the phone. The silence in the house was deafening, thoughts were whirling round my head, the cottage, late at night, Lauren falling, the white staircase. Blood. Sam discovering her there, on the floor, trying to bring her back to life. It's all I could see.

I didn't go to bed that night, just napped on the sofa, and at 6 a.m. I called the station. They said they had no information regarding Sam Moore but would call me as soon as they knew anything. This took it straight out of my hands and the 'don't call us we'll call you' message made me feel so impotent.

I waited, and waited, and at 9.30, when I was just considering calling again, even though I'd virtually been told not to, the call came through. It was Sam, he was in tears, and I could barely hear what he was saying, but the gist of it was that he was being kept in for another twelve hours.

'Mum, I didn't do it. I *didn't* hurt Lauren, I *wouldn't*,' he spluttered. 'Things hadn't been great between us, but—'

'What do you mean?' I pounced.

'Nothing. It had nothing to do with what happened.'

'You can tell me anything, Sam,' I offered, trying to shake away the tentacles of doubt slowly twisting around my brain.

'I know, but I can't talk here anyway.'

I took a deep breath. 'Okay,' I said, unwilling for him to say anything over the phone that might wrongly incriminate him. 'Just keep telling the truth, don't let anyone put you under pressure – I'm going to get you out.'

'What did Tim say?' he asked. I heard a faint vein of hope in his voice.

'He's working on it, love, he's furious, he's going to speak to someone. But until then, just hang on and I'm here. Is there anything you need?'

'No, Mum, I've got to go, my solicitor is telling me they're ready to carry on with the interview. I'll try to keep in touch.'

And with that, he was gone.

CHAPTER SIXTEEN

Later that day, the police arrived. Two smiley female officers, standing on the doorstep. In a strange way, I was pleased to see them, I thought they might have news of Sam.

'Have you brought him home?' I asked, looking beyond them out onto the street. 'Is he with you?'

They both looked sympathetically at me. 'No, sorry, love, we're not involved in that side of things. I'm PC Shelley Rawlins and this is my colleague, PC Karen Johnson, we'd just like to ask you a few questions if we may?'

They both smiled expectantly. I hadn't anticipated this, and I certainly didn't want it, but I invited them in; it wasn't as if I had much choice. And surely, I could make them see Sam was innocent. Once inside, I led them to the sitting room and offered them coffee. PC Rawlins was blonde, whilst PC Johnson had red hair. They were so young, probably around the same age as Sam. PC Rawlins had eyeliner on just like Lauren used to wear, and my heart broke a little.

I took a tray of coffee and biscuits into the sitting room, where I was surprised to find them admiring my bookshelves. A bookcase, in my view, is a peek into someone's life, and given the circumstances, this felt slightly uncomfortable. Were they looking for clues? I knew it was probably me feeling protective of my privacy in light of what was happening.

'I love a good old romcom,' Rawlins said with a smile. 'I deal in death and destruction all day, so a bit of Bridget Jones is all I need with my cup of cocoa.'

Johnson smiled in agreement, as I put the tray down on the coffee table. 'I like a bit of erotica,' she confided, and they both giggled conspiratorially.

I invited them to sit down and passed around the plate of biscuits as we discussed our favourite authors. It was like a bizarre, uniformed book club. If I hadn't been so distraught and nervous, I'd have found it quite amusing. PC Johnson talking about Mr Grey from *Fifty Shades*, while PC Rawlins giggled, giving her a knowing look.

'So, Ms Moore,' Rawlins said, suddenly remembering where she was and why she was there, 'we're here to get some background, ask you a few questions, about Sam?' There was an upward inflection, like she was wondering if I knew who Sam was. 'Is that okay?' she asked, like I had a choice.

'Yes, fine, anything that will help get him home,' I said.

'So, Sam and your daughter-in-law, Lauren Moore,' she began. She had dimples just like Lauren. 'We just want to get a picture of them, is that okay?'

'Yes.' I sipped my coffee, knowing I had little choice but to say yes. I'd never encountered the police like this before, and as nice as they both seemed, I felt I'd been ambushed. My throat was bone dry with nerves. I couldn't face a cookie.

'So...' Rawlins leaned so far forward, her knees were nearly touching mine, her radio almost fell from her breast pocket. She began to ask all the questions one would expect, like how long the kids had known each other, when did I last see Lauren. And since he's been home, how did Sam seem to me.

'He's seemed, sad... of course,' I answered, not knowing quite where to go with this.

'Has he said anything, about the night Mrs Moore died, talked about what happened?'

'I know that he discovered her, and he can't get the horror from his mind. I know his life has changed, his future is—' I looked helplessly from one to the other.

Rawlins nodded and made a note in her pad, her knees still too close to mine. I was beginning to feel slightly claustrophobic.

'Do you know when Sam will be able to leave the station?' I asked, desperate for this to be over. I caught a glance between them, and it made me feel very uneasy.

'As far as I know, he's still being questioned,' Johnson said. 'So, to your knowledge, was everything okay between Sam and Lauren?' They seemed keen to get the interview back on track, to ask even more questions, but I wasn't sure I had anything to tell them.

I nodded.

'The marriage didn't have any problems?' she pressed gently.

'No. Well not as far as I know.' I thought about Lauren having cold feet and wondered if that was relevant, but I was scared to say anything that might lead to them further suspecting Sam. 'They'd only been married for three months. I can't imagine anyone being *unhappy* in that honeymoon period,' I added.

'You'd be surprised.' Rawlins whistled under her breath.

'No, they were *very* happy,' I said firmly, wanting to erase any doubts about Sam and Lauren's relationship. 'It just doesn't make any sense.' I sighed, reaching for a tissue.

'You mean her death?' Johnson asked, suddenly perking up.

I nodded, trying to get the words out. 'She fell down the stairs after a long shift at work. She's a junior doctor, she was *exhausted*. She wasn't killed, she just fell!' I said, exasperated. 'Her parents are inconsolable. I think it was easier for all of us when we thought it was an accident, and I still believe it was.'

'Well, it's early days yet. Let's see what comes from the investigation,' Johnson said brightly.

'Sam's devastated, being questioned will destroy him, as if he needed anything else on top of this.'

'The interview with your son is pretty routine at this stage.'

'He was *arrested*!' I cried.

'Yes, but he hasn't been charged yet. And no news is good news.' She smiled at me as if this would make everything better.

'I... Tim, Lauren's father, he says Sam is innocent. He's a detective—' I started, irrationally making the point that if a detective, and father of the victim, thought Sam's innocent, then he must be.

'Yes, you mean DCI Jackson?'

I nodded. 'Yes, he knows Sam didn't do it... I mean he didn't.'

I saw a look pass between them that made my blood run cold. Convincing these two that the police had got the wrong man was going to be quite a battle, and I wasn't sure I had all the facts with which to fight that battle. There were things even I was finding difficult to understand about Lauren and Sam and their marriage.

'Tim says once they've interviewed Sam, they'll discharge him. He's known Sam since he was three years old, he'll vouch for him,' I continued blindly on.

'Yeah, try not to worry too much,' Rawlins said, her head to one side in mock concern.

'Lovely cottage, that your son has out there on Dartmoor,' Johnson said, changing gear and taking a sip of coffee. 'I love it out there, so remote.'

'Scary at night though, especially where your son and his wife lived, eh, Ms Moore?' Rawlins countered. So they were playing that game, were they? Pointing out how easy it would be to kill someone, a rather clumsy attempt to make me slip up and accidentally incriminate my son. I wasn't stupid, and I had nothing to hide either, so answered her question with confidence.

'Yes, it *can* be, but Sam loves it out there. Lauren did too,' I added quickly.

'Oh? *Did* she?' Johnson looked questioningly at me. 'It's just that Lauren's mother said it didn't make sense that Lauren had moved out there.' She made a big play about checking her notes. Then read from them, like a script: '"Not her at all," was what she said.'

'Helen said *that*?' I asked, surprised. Yes, we'd both remarked that it wasn't the kind of area we'd expected Lauren to live, but for Helen to say this now, to the police, had different connotations. Couldn't she see that to indicate that Lauren wouldn't *choose* to live there, might make it look like Sam had *forced* her? By saying this, she'd made it sound like he had an ulterior motive. That he wanted her in an isolated cottage far from anywhere – so he could kill her. I took a deep breath. 'No one *forced* Lauren to live there,' I said. 'Yes, it was a drive, and yes Lauren loved the city, but I was under the impression, as was Helen, that she loved the cottage, she seemed happy there. She was planning all kinds for the interior—'

'It's a *spiral* staircase, isn't it?' Rawlins asked, like I hadn't just spoken.

'Yes, it's beautiful, quirky,' I said, before anyone could accuse Sam of having it installed as a murder weapon. 'They loved the staircase, it's one of the reasons they chose the cottage.'

'So *Sam* loved the staircase?'

'Yes, and so did *Lauren*,' I repeated.

'Yes, according to Mrs Jackson, Lauren's mum,' she added, like I didn't know, 'Sam said the staircase played a big part in *his* decision to buy the cottage.'

'I don't... well, yes, I suppose.' I couldn't deny that, but they were making every innocent fact look like some kind of murderous hidden motive.

'I have it in my notes—' She looked down, then back at me. 'Yes, according to Lauren's mum, Sam said that...' she looked back at her notes, '"the spiral staircase was a game changer."'

I shrugged. 'I think he *may* have said that.'

'So you agree that your son was keen to purchase the property *because* of the stairs?'

'No,' I cried. 'I mean, yes, he *loved* the staircase, we all did, but there were other things he loved too, like the garden. I'm sure the garden was also a *game changer* – he loves wildlife, and there are so many birds, and he works there, he loves the moors, says it's so peaceful,' I added, aware I was beginning to ramble, desperately grabbing at things for ballast as I fell.

'Away from it all?' Johnson murmured.

'*Very* isolated. He liked that, did he?' Rawlins added. She was smiling and nodding, willing me to say yes. Despite being a PC, it seemed to me that she was playing a detective in a crime drama; I was sure it was not her job to trick me.

'You said you came here just for background,' I said. 'And the only background I can give you is the truth. My son loved the cottage, he loved the staircase, and he loved *Lauren!*' I added, raising my voice on her name. 'And nothing anyone can say will change that. They were a wonderful couple, and she was the loveliest girl. They'd known each other from being tiny, and nothing, *nothing* would ever—'

'Yes, yes, we understand,' Johnson said gently. 'We're just wanting to know a little more about them, about day-to-day things. Like why they decided to live there, what made them suddenly sell their flat in town and move out there?'

'Because they were getting married and wanted somewhere bigger, I guess. Perhaps they wanted children one day like many newly-weds?' I was trying to keep the exasperation out of my voice, wondering why they were twisting perfectly normal things into something more.

Rawlins jumped on that. 'Did *they* tell you that?'

'No, but—'

'It's just that there aren't any schools out that far, it's a journey into town and quite a schlepp for Lauren to get to the hospital. A long school run and a lot of driving for a doctor working long shifts,' she commented.

'Yes, it was. But it was *their* choice, what they *both* wanted,' I said, trying not to sound angry at the obvious game-playing. 'Sam can work mostly from home, and Lauren probably wanted some peace after a day in a busy hospital.'

'When Sam called you, on the night,' Rawlins continued, before I could finish, 'did he sound... upset?'

'Of course, he was in a terrible state,' I answered firmly. 'He'd just found his wife dead at the bottom of the stairs.'

She nodded. 'And you say Lauren was tired, after her shift?'

'I assumed she was and I thought that was why she'd fallen, I still think that might be the case, because I can't think *anyone* would—'

'Have you ever known your son to take any medication – drugs, Ms Moore?' Rawlins said, not allowing me to finish.

I took a breath. 'No, no I haven't. He's very healthy, he hikes, he's never smoked, and the only thing he drinks is organic cider. No, he wouldn't put anything poisonous in his body.'

They both sat looking at me, like I was going to add a caveat like, 'Only on a Sunday when he treats himself to a bag of heroin and chases the dragon.'

'Is there anything you can tell us about Sadie Marsden?' Johnson started, the segue from drugs to Sadie was not lost on me. I wasn't sure how much I should say, but let's put it this way, Lauren had sometimes referred to Sadie as 'the chem queen'.

'I don't really know her. She was a friend of Lauren's,' I said, truthfully.

'And a friend of your son's too?'

'Yes, through Lauren,' I added, making the implication clear – she was a friend of a friend and not a direct associate of my son.

'And do you know if Sadie was at the cottage on the night Lauren died?'

I thought about Sadie's pink fur coat sitting on the back of the chair that night. She'd told me she'd given it to Lauren, but I hadn't seen it anywhere in the house on my last visit, but was it relevant? I wasn't sure, so decided not to mention it. 'I don't know. I think Lauren was alone, and Sam came home later. Why do you ask? Has someone *said* she was at the cottage?'

'No, we just need to establish where *everyone* was on that night. And it seems that Sadie spent a lot of time at the cottage, she stayed over a lot, didn't she?'

'Yes, she and Lauren were very close, had been since they were about eleven, they were like sisters really.'

'And Sam?'

'What?' I wasn't sure what they were asking.

'Was he close to Sadie?'

'No, not close, not... just friends, only friends. She likes football and hiking and stuff and Lauren didn't. Sometimes they'd go...' I was about to say that Sadie and Sam went to football together, but something told me I shouldn't. Something told me that the further Sam was from Sadie during this investigation, the better. And I had to ask myself again, why Sadie was suddenly at the heart of this, why was she always at the heart of everything?

CHAPTER SEVENTEEN

The police officers eventually left after about an hour, though it felt like they'd been there much longer. As they got up to leave, PC Johnson was looking down at my hands, and as she lifted her eyes, they met mine. I realised after they'd gone, that I was still clutching a tissue that I'd ripped into tiny shreds.

I felt uneasy about Helen's apparent sabotage of Sam to the police, I couldn't believe she'd tried to drop him in it, and wanted to talk to her. I was keen to work out where her head was in all this, and if I needed to worry about what else she might say. So I called her, the phone rang out for ages, but eventually she picked up.

'Georgie?'

'Hi, how are you?'

'Not good. Just feel so empty.'

'I'm sorry. Look, I haven't seen you for a while, I wondered if I could come over?'

'Yeah, that would be nice.'

'The police have just left,' I said, waiting for her response.

'Oh?'

'They said they'd spoken to you?'

'Yeah, they came over first thing.' I got the feeling she hadn't intended to share this with me. 'Sorry about Sam being arrested...' She seemed spaced out.

I didn't acknowledge this, she can't have been so sorry; it sounded like what she'd said had been enough to get him convicted. 'They asked me if Sam and Lauren were unhappy; did they ask you questions about their marriage too?'

'Yeah,' she replied, this was followed by silence – she clearly didn't want to elaborate. I'd never known her like this, Helen and I shared everything, we knew each other's lives inside out, and this was hard. As upset as I was about the distance in the conversation, I was equally concerned that Helen might have mentioned to the police Lauren's 'second thoughts' about getting married. I also worried that Helen may have elaborated with her theories about their marriage and talked too much without thinking how it might look.

'Shall I come over now?' I asked, thinking that perhaps speaking face to face might be easier.

'Yeah,' she sighed.

'Okay, I'm on my way,' I said, clicking off the phone, grabbing my jacket and handbag and running out to the car.

It was no surprise Helen sounded a bit weird. Her daughter's funeral was only days ago, how could I possibly expect her to have a normal conversation with me? But then again, talking was what we'd always done in a crisis; me and Helen, we'd joined forces. We'd supported each other since our twenties, with little kids. We'd done all the worrying and wondering in late-night chats over bottles of wine. We'd shared childcare, holidays, doctors' and dentists' appointments, swimming lessons and later driving lessons. We'd also shared our grown-up concern for our lives, apart from the children. Although now poor Helen faced the real meaning of being apart from her child. She'd lost her daughter and I worried about her fragility.

Everything had changed, but I was convinced that Helen, Tim and I would ride this terrible storm together, like we had the lesser ones in our lives.

The sun will shine again, I thought as I started the car.

I wasn't sure I believed it though.

It was less than a mile to Tim and Helen's; they lived on an adjoining estate of much bigger houses than my two-bedroomed semi. I could easily have walked there, but it was cold and rainy and I also had a twinkle of hope that Sam might call to ask if I'd fetch him when he was released. Surely there'd be news soon?

I was just pulling off the drive when my phone rang, so I stopped and scrabbled frantically in my bag to pick up in case it was Sam. But it was Helen.

'Hi, did you want me to pick you something up on the way to yours?' I asked, knowing she wouldn't have shopped for anything.

'No, no. Thanks, Georgie, I don't need anything, but I just... Look, I'm exhausted, I'm going to bed, so let's do a rain check.'

'Oh, are you sure?' I was disappointed, I wanted to talk and find out where her head was. I worried she might be thinking Sam was guilty, and I wanted to put her right. 'Shall I call round later instead?' I asked.

There was an awkward silence.

'To be honest, Georgie, I'm just not really up to seeing anyone at the moment,' she said with a sigh.

'I understand,' I lied. I wasn't *anyone*, I was her friend. 'Look, just call me when you feel like you want some company,' I offered. But I couldn't help it, I said, 'I'm really worried, Helen.'

There was another lengthy silence, and eventually I heard her take a breath. 'I know. I'm sure it'll all work out.'

'I hate all this...' I said, and I started crying quietly. It was mostly for Sam, but a little part of me felt like a teen who'd been rejected by her best friend at the worst possible time. I thought the Jacksons were our friends, I thought they'd always be there for us, but I could feel the ranks closing. So much for 'we are family'.

Helen didn't answer, just abandoned me in the silence as the rain pattered on the car roof.

'What did you say to the police about Sam?' I asked. Now I'd been robbed of my visit, I had to ask the question over the phone. Sam was a victim in this too, not only had he lost his wife, but he was now a suspect, being accused of something he didn't do and I needed to look after him.

Again, the horrible, deafening silence, accompanied by an endless tip tap, tip tap as the rain came harder and harder.

'I'm sorry. I just don't want to talk about this now,' I heard her say. And before I could respond, the phone went dead.

I sat there, in the car, the engine still running, rain lashing down on the windscreen, trying to work out what to do next. Then my phone rang again, and this time it was Sam calling from the station, I was so relieved.

'Are you ready to come home? I'll come and collect you—' I started.

'Mum, mum, listen to me.'

'Yes?'

There was a pause, then, 'They're charging me with Lauren's murder.'

CHAPTER EIGHTEEN

I tried to be strong for Sam, but it wasn't easy. He was a few hours behind too, still under the impression that Tim would somehow save him. As I had been.

'Is Tim coming to the station?' he asked. 'I told them that he knows me and he knows I'd never harm Lauren.'

I couldn't lie to make my son feel better; I had to be brutally honest.

'Tim can't get involved.'

I heard a groan coming from the other end of the phone.

'But... *but* he *will*... he says the police will be looking at other suspects, and you just need to keep telling them the truth, that you're innocent,' I encouraged.

'Other suspects, like who?'

'I don't know. Is there anyone *you* can think of, anyone at all?'

'No, no, if there was anyone I could think of, I would have said,' he was starting to sound exasperated, and I knew I was pushing a little hard, but I had to make him focus.

'I know, love, but just try to *think*. Did Lauren have any colleagues who might have been jealous? Might someone have followed her back to your place from the hospital that night?'

He sighed. 'I can't think of anyone at all. And I can't think of anyone who would want to hurt her.'

I knew how hard this must be. Everyone loved Lauren; the patients often gave her chocolates and flowers because she was so sweet to them, especially children. I thought about the baby she was carrying and wanted to hug Sam, whose heart had been broken twice.

'I promise you, Sam, I *will* find who did this.' I'd been about to say, 'Don't change your story,' but aware the calls were probably not private from a police station when you've been charged with murder, I didn't. Later, I wondered why I even thought to say it, because I knew Sam was telling the truth, so why would he change it?

'Yeah, yeah,' he sounded despondent, like he didn't have faith in me. 'I go to the magistrates' court first thing and if I don't get bail, that's it, I'm locked up until it goes to court.'

'We can get through this, love. Me and you have battled through all our lives, this is just one more challenge. You know your tiger mother,' I said, trying not to let my voice break, 'and woe betide anyone who thinks they can get away with this. I will find them, and when I do, they will sleep with the fishes,' I joked.

He didn't laugh.

'I know, Mum, and thanks, but we need Tim,' was all he said and put down the phone.

He was right, and I only wished we had Tim, but it was clear that wasn't an option. Helen's knee-jerk reaction to Sam being arrested wasn't helping either, and she would be furious if she thought Tim was trying to help. My real fear in all this was that once he'd been charged, the police could make it fit. Would they even bother to look for other suspects? We couldn't come up with any idea of who might have done this, so how on earth would they have a clue where to start. Even more worryingly, would the lack of an alternative theory mean there was only one theory? That Sam did it?

. . .

It was now 8 p.m., and I couldn't face a long night ahead, so I called James. He sounded pleased to hear from me, and when I'd told him the basics, he offered to come over.

'I bet you haven't eaten,' he said. He was right.

'Just a dozen chocolate digestives this morning,' I replied, 'but I can't face food anyway.'

'I'll bring something, do you like curry, Chinese?'

That's how little we knew about each other, we didn't even know what we liked to eat. But it was nice though to have someone to turn to now, someone who was there for me – and the fact he didn't know me all that well didn't matter.

'Nothing, thanks,' I said. 'I just couldn't face it.'

Half an hour later, he appeared on the doorstep with a Tesco bag. He asked me to point him to the kitchen, which I did, realising he'd never even been to my house before.

'I'm going to force-feed you,' he announced, as I followed him into the kitchen.

'Oh, really?' I said, doubtfully.

He was producing tins of soup, bread rolls, a bunch of bananas and a large tub of strawberry ice cream from his shopping bag.

'Aren't these the kinds of foods you give to sick people?' I asked, then remembered his wife had died from cancer. He probably gave them to her, and I felt a moment of such tenderness towards him I wanted to wrap my arms around him.

'Yes, I suppose they are,' he said, folding the plastic carrier bag, the food now laid out on the counter. 'I appreciate you aren't *sick* as such. But you're stressed, and as I always say to my students before exams, what you eat now you'll be glad of later. These things,' he wafted his hand across the tins and the bread like a magician, 'will give you the strength you need to face whatever's on its way.'

'Thanks, but I think it'll take a bit more than tinned soup to face what I've got to face,' I said with a sigh.

'So what you're saying is that you feel it may be necessary to go straight for the A Class? The ice cream?'

And I smiled. It was probably the first time I'd genuinely smiled in weeks. 'Yeah, leave it in the tub, I'll inject it straight into my veins.'

'A spoon *might* be easier?' He opened a drawer and then another, as I watched him search for the one with cutlery. 'Okay, here we go, I want you to take this, and let's go and sit down and talk.' He handed me the huge tub of ice cream, meant for at least four people, with the spoon sticking out of the top. I took it from him and we went and sat in the sitting room, where I took a few, soothing strawberry spoonfuls and told him all about Sam and the police, and Tim and Helen.

He was surprisingly in tune for someone who'd only recently come into my life. 'You mustn't be hurt about Tim and Helen not being there for you. As you said yourself, they're dealing with their own struggles at the moment, and they are going to have to come to terms with a lot of things.'

'No, I know, but surely they don't think he did it any more than I do.'

'I know how much Tim thinks of Sam and he'll be as upset as you about what's happened today.'

I sighed. 'I know this sounds horribly selfish, but I just hope he can summon up the strength to make a call to the station, say something on Sam's behalf.'

James took a deep breath. 'It's hard for him, given his position. He lost his daughter but if he gets too involved, he could lose his job and the police is Tim's life, it's everything, you know that.'

'I know, but I'd put my hopes in Tim, so has Sam. I feel so helpless, this isn't something I've ever had to deal with, I'm so out of my comfort zone, but this is my son and I have to do whatever I possibly can to prove his innocence.'

He gave me a considered look. 'You're a good mum, Georgie. I always thought that. You'd come to parents' evenings and know exactly what Sam was doing. You knew his friends, his dreams, his strengths and weaknesses – you always impressed me.'

This lifted me, especially given Sam's current predicament.

And as a single mother there was no one to reassure me, to say I was doing the right thing, I hadn't realised, but I needed that. 'Thanks, and you always knew a lot about the kids, treated them as equals, gave them respect. I know Sam and Lauren, even Sadie, thought the world of you.'

'Ah Sadie, Sadie Marsden. She had it tough,' he said with a sigh.

'So I gather. Helen never really went into details, but I know she'd had a terrible home life.'

'God, yeah, she used to come into school sometimes half-awake because she hadn't slept for the noise of her mother fighting – or otherwise – with her latest boyfriend. I remember the PE teacher, Miss Morris, commenting to me that she'd seen bruises on her in the shower.'

I felt a rush of sympathy for Sadie, I'd always found her difficult and Helen had hinted at a 'difficult' childhood, but I didn't realise it involved violence. 'I had no idea it was that bad.'

He nodded. 'Yeah. She and her mother had a very volatile relationship.'

'I saw her the other day at the cottage when I was waiting for sofas to be delivered. Lauren would have been so excited. I just keep thinking about the night she died, all alone – except for whoever—'

'It doesn't bear thinking about, does it? Do you know if they have any other suspects, any other theories about what happened?'

'No. They're keeping Tim out of the loop, but now Sam's been arrested I don't suppose he'll tell me much.' I sighed. 'It's so distressing, James. I know he isn't guilty but—'

'But what?' he asked.

'Oh it's nothing, just something Sam said.'

'You can tell me.'

James was impartial, he was fair, and he wasn't involved, so I guessed it was okay to tell him stuff. In fact, now I felt Helen and Tim didn't want to discuss things with me, I *needed* to talk to someone. I was driving myself mad.

'It's just that Sam said things hadn't been great between him and Lauren, and I wondered if perhaps she was seeing someone?'

He sat back, looking shocked. 'No, no, not Lauren.'

'I don't know. I would have said the same a few months ago, but the more things I hear, the more I wonder what was real and what wasn't.'

'What do you mean?'

'Well, *why* weren't things great between Sam and Lauren? They'd only been married a few months, that time should be the happiest of their lives.'

'I suppose there could be a number of reasons, it might have just been teething problems, some people find it hard to accept they're going to be with someone forever, it can take a while to adjust.'

'Mmm, I suppose so.' But after my visit to the cottage, I wasn't convinced. 'I haven't told anyone this – because I don't know what to make of it, but I found Lauren's wedding dress shoved at the back of the wardrobe, it was crumpled and stained and I know it had been dry-cleaned after the wedding. It doesn't make sense.'

'Perhaps Lauren just tried it on and didn't put it back?' he suggested reasonably.

'I don't think so, she wouldn't have put it back in that way, all crumpled.' I shook my head slowly. 'And it looked like their bed had been slept in, and their wedding photo had been smashed and placed face down.'

'Perhaps they hadn't made their bed? Or the police had moved stuff, pushed things into the wardrobe, broken something as they searched?'

What he said made perfect sense, but I still wasn't convinced. 'I don't know, it just doesn't add up for me. And then there's Sadie – she seemed to spend a lot of time at the cottage. I don't think a third wheel is a good idea for any newly married couple, and she has a key.'

'You said she was at the cottage the other day?'

'Yeah, she was.' I told him about the mix-up. 'She was so rude, I sometimes want to say to her, that if she was nicer, more polite, showed respect, then people might show her some back. She's such hard work.'

'Ah yes, but you're dealing with a damaged child. She doesn't know about respect or manners – she knows about survival, about getting the slap in first before she gets slapped. It's a different world for someone like Sadie.'

'I'm sure you're right.'

He smiled. 'Don't get me wrong, she'd try the patience of a bloody saint, and there were times in school when I had to send her out of the classroom, even yelled at her on a few occasions. But then she'd come and see me after class, when the others had gone home and I was working late, and she was different. Vulnerable, somehow *nicer*.'

'I think I may have seen her more vulnerable side when I told her that Lauren's death was now a murder investigation. She seemed to lose her bravado – not for long though,' I added with a wry smile.

'Yes, there is a softer side to Sadie.' He rolled his eyes and laughed. 'But then she had this, this... well, I think you'd call it sexual precociousness. It started when she was about fourteen or fifteen, I don't remember exactly. A few times I gave her a lift home, it was late and dark, and I worried about her. It's not like her mother would know where she was and if something had happened to her on the way home from school. But I remember one night when she got in the car, she started to touch my leg. I was horrified and told her it was inappropriate, and she must never do anything like that with anyone other than a boyfriend. And do you know what she said?'

I shook my head.

'She said, "Mum's boyfriend likes it when I do that, he makes me do other stuff as well."'

I shook my head, horrified. 'Oh God. That's messed up. No wonder Tim and Helen took her under their wing,' I said. This began to explain why they hadn't given up on Sadie, especially when her own mother had. 'I've never really understood why Lauren was so friendly with her though. They were chalk and cheese.'

'Who knows what brings two people together?' he acknowledged. 'As a teacher, you often see these friendships blossom between the unlikeliest kids. I see it a lot, a power dynamic usually.' He raised his eyebrows.

'I can imagine,' I said, thinking how Sadie probably had quite a hold over Lauren, and being like her parents, she just invited her in.

'I'd thought that by tutoring her I could help her, but she started to hang around outside the classroom at home time asking for a lift, and I realised how inappropriate that might look. Sadie's relationship with the truth can be a little hit and miss, and I worried she might make trouble. I told Becky and she said, "Steer clear of that one."' He smiled. 'She was more intuitive than me, she understood people, you know? I'd just wanted to help a young girl achieve her dreams, but Becky could see I was putting myself in a dangerous position.'

I nodded. Despite the struggles James had been through, he still seemed to want to help others, and he obviously had a good, honest relationship with his late wife.

'At the wedding I saw a different girl,' he said. 'She's grown up and I think she's come through the worst, I really do. I know she can be slightly abrasive, but her heart's in the right place.'

I wasn't sure how best to broach what I wanted to say, so put down the tub of ice cream that was now starting to melt, and said, 'Do you think Sadie knows anything about Lauren's death?'

James looked at me with surprise, but not complete shock. 'Why do you think that?'

'I don't know, I just have a feeling she's hiding something.'

He shifted in his seat. 'I doubt that, but who really knows what a person could do, until they are tested?'

CHAPTER NINETEEN

The following day, Sam called me. He'd been taken to the magistrates' court that morning and told me he'd been charged with murder and there was no bail. It was going straight to Crown Court and he would be taken to Dartmoor prison, where he'd have to wait for a court date. I'd had a vain hope that things might have turned out differently, but tried to be positive with him, only to burst into tears as soon as I put down the phone. Then, I wiped my eyes, told myself this was sheer self-indulgence and not helping anyone and called the prison to find out when I could visit. I was told that a remand prisoner was allowed three one-hour visits a week, so immediately booked a visit for the next day.

After the longest twenty-four hours of my life, having barely slept since his arrest, this was only compounded by the fact he would now be in prison. And Dartmoor prison is an imposing place, high on the moors, its bleak, granite walls dominate that part of the area, above the small village of Princetown. It's just a few minutes' drive from the cottage, escaped prisoners being one of the worries Lauren had about living there. Who would ever have thought that one day Sam would be an inmate?

Driving there was the saddest, most depressing journey. Dark, heavy clouds hung over the sprawling grey building in a landscape of rocks. There was nothing for miles, save a few wild ponies wandering the heather. I could see why Arthur Conan Doyle and Agatha Christie were inspired to write books about crime and murder in this rather bleak part of Devon.

'I could have come to the court,' I said to Sam, once I'd gone through the humiliating security checks and been ushered into a visiting area. I felt like someone else, surely this wasn't me coming to visit my son in this godforsaken place?

'I didn't want you there, Mum. It would have been too upsetting,' he said, sounding near to tears. 'I didn't really want you here – but I'm glad you came.'

I looked around at the other prisoners and visitors.

'Funny, they all look so normal,' I said. 'That sounds stupid, but I'd never really thought about it.'

'I know. I used to drive past here often and imagine all these caged beasts.' He smiled a sad smile at the memory, the irony too. 'But everyone has their story.'

I looked at my son and wondered what his story was. He wasn't a murderer, of that I was sure, but had there been struggles, problems I didn't know about?

'Has Tim said anything?' he asked.

'Not yet. It's not easy – he's dealing with all the fallout from this and he's also looking after Helen and Kate. They're all having to come to terms with the fact it wasn't an accident, and that's hard.'

He didn't answer. Sam seemed to think that Tim would solve even this huge problem because that's what he'd always done. But he wasn't there for us now, and we had to get through this without him.

'The thing we have to look at, Sam, is if *you* didn't do it, who *did*? Can you remember anything unusual that happened before Lauren died? *Anything* at all?'

'No, I told you and everyone else. How many times do I have to say it, she called me from work, I was working late, I came home and—' he said, irritated. Rocking back so his chair was on two legs, he gazed around as if looking for an escape.

But I wasn't giving up, even if he was. 'Sam, *think* – was there anything *before* then, a few weeks or days before?'

'Nothing,' he said, allowing his chair to bounce forward, back on four legs, like a bored, frustrated kid in a classroom.

'Nothing?' I repeated.

'Just the usual.' He didn't look at me, seemed unable to concentrate, to focus.

'Tell me *the usual*,' I said, frustrated now.

'Just working, sleeping, eating.'

'Anything else?'

'I'd been running every day, and Lauren had been doing crazy shifts, so she went to the gym. The day before, she'd started work late, and I think she went for a walk with Sadie. They went up across the moors. She said it was cold up there considering it was August... but she'd enjoyed the walk, said she was starting to understand why I liked it there.'

'Okay, good, and she said that the day before she died?' I was trying to think like a solicitor and banking that it might come in useful if, in court, anyone tried to say Lauren didn't like living out there. 'Just keep thinking, rack your brains, Sam, because at the moment there's no one else in the frame, and we know it wasn't you. So someone somewhere knows *something*.'

He looked up at me.

'What?'

'I don't think this is relevant, but... there was...' he started, then shrugged.

'Go on, tell me anyway,' I pressed.

'Well, it probably isn't anything, but about two weeks before the wedding, Lauren came home very late,' he paused. 'She'd been with Sadie, and when she wasn't home by eleven, I called her just to check she was okay. But her phone was off. I tried a few times and when she still wasn't home and I was a bit worried, I called Sadie to see if Lauren was still with her. But according to Sadie, she'd left her about 10 p.m.'

'And what time was it when you called Sadie?'

'About midnight?'

I took a deep breath. 'Did you tell the police about this?'

'No, because I didn't... I still *don't* think it's relevant.'

'Sam, at this stage *anything* could be relevant, and it's down to you to remember. It could be the difference between you being locked up for years or home next week!' I blurted. I didn't want to scare or depress him, but he *did* need to wake up.

'I hate to say this, but the *only* other person who could prove you didn't do it was Lauren.'

We sat in silence at that thought, and he leaned forwards, putting his head in his hands. An hour wasn't long to talk and I felt like the clock was ticking, every moment was precious and I was determined to leave there with something.

'So what happened when Lauren finally came home, did she tell you where she'd been?' I asked.

After a few seconds, he lifted his head, his eyes were red, and my heart lurched, but I didn't say anything, just waited for his answer.

'She seemed, I dunno, upset, and it looked like she'd been crying. But when I asked her, she just said she was stressed and exhausted from work and planning the wedding.'

'Did you ask where she'd been when you were trying to call her, after she left Sadie?' I felt like one of those pushy detectives on TV, but this was too important to let go. We were fighting to keep Sam out of prison, saving him from a murder conviction, but I had this horrible feeling that he was already defeated. He'd been to hell and back losing Lauren, and then to be arrested, and thrown in here. Even Tim couldn't help us, so it was up to me to find out exactly what happened, *who* did this – and get Sam home.

'Yeah, I asked her and she said she'd just sat in her car and had some quiet time.'

'So you're telling me she left Sadie, then sat in her car in the dark for *two* hours?'

'That's what she said.' He shrugged.

'Around that time did she give you the impression at all that she was having second thoughts about getting married?' I asked.

'No, she was excited, said she couldn't wait.' He looked amazed I'd even suggest this. Then his face looked doubtful.

'What?'

'Well, out there it can get really cold, and that night was freezing. I remember because we found a dead pony the next day, died of hypothermia.'

'Was there a blanket in the car?'

'No, not in Lauren's, and she had this thin little dress on. I said to her, "You must be freezing!"'

'Did you ask why she'd been crying?' This was like getting blood from a stone. I understood that Sam found conversations about Lauren painful after her death, he seemed unable, or unwilling, to really open up, but I needed him to talk to me.

'Yeah, and she just said the same, that it was tiredness, the wedding, work...'

Whatever happened that night, was it connected to Lauren having second thoughts about the marriage? Perhaps *that* was the night she'd gone to her parents? She could have left Sadie at 10 p.m. and gone straight to her mum and dad's? But it was late for a forty-five-minute drive and she'd have to have driven back too, in the two hours since she left Sadie. It didn't add up.

I hated myself for even thinking it, but I kept returning to my theory that Lauren's wedding doubts might have been because she was seeing someone else? But *who*?

'Mum, I have to go,' Sam was saying.

A faint bell was ringing and the other prisoners were stirring, grabbing hands with their visitors, wiping tears from the faces of their wives and girlfriends.

'Okay, keep thinking, Sam,' I urged. 'I can do three visits a week, so I'll put in for a visiting order on Wednesday, okay?' I said, standing up to leave.

'Er, actually, Sadie's coming then,' he said.

I bristled, I know I shouldn't have but I couldn't help it.

'Is something going on with you two?' I asked.

'Look, apart from you, she's the only one who seems to believe me. You're both on the same side, Mum.'

I scowled slightly. I knew James said she'd changed from the wild teenager, but I wasn't convinced. As far as I was concerned, she had TROUBLE tattooed across her forehead. I really couldn't see how she would help the situation. But if it was what Sam wanted, I wasn't going to argue.

'Okay, so shall I come on Friday? That will be your third visit of the week – you aren't allowed any more,' I pointed out, frustrated because I felt that seeing Sam was the only way I could try to sort this. Talking through everything that happened was vital, but meanwhile, good old Sadie was happy to kill an hour and waste everyone's precious time.

'Yeah, yeah, that'd be great, Mum, see you Friday then?'

'Yes, I'll be here. And meanwhile, think, think, think. And tell your solicitor everything – he might see some significance in Lauren's missing two hours.'

'Mum, for Christ's sake, this isn't *Murder She Wrote*,' he rolled his eyes.

'No, it isn't, it's more serious than that. So if you think of something, call me – if you're allowed to. I don't want to be visiting you here in ten years' time!' I didn't want to be harsh, but I needed to be sure he realised how important this was, to him, and to me.

I fastened my jacket, wrapped my scarf around me, knowing I'd probably have to unwrap it for the prison guards before I was allowed to leave. This really was a different world. I could never get used to this.

'Mum,' Sam said, as I walked away, 'will you talk to Tim, ask him to come and see me?'

I nodded uncertainly but didn't answer him. 'Just stay strong, this will all be over soon, I promise,' I said instead. But as I drove away from the prison, I knew I had no right to promise my son anything at this stage. But I knew too that I would do anything to prove his innocence. And there was only one place I could think to go – Tim and Helen's.

Thinking of Sam's last words, I decided to go and ask for Tim's help, or at least see if he could give me any information or advice. Tim was the only person who could help me defend my son, because he knew him – and knew as much as I did that Sam would never kill anyone, and certainly not Lauren, the girl he'd loved for most of his young life.

CHAPTER TWENTY

I drove straight to Tim and Helen's after seeing Sam, and where usually I would let myself in through the back door, which Helen left on the latch, I knocked on the front door instead. For the first time ever, I felt that I might not be wanted and I didn't know how I'd find them. It wasn't long before Tim opened the door, and ushered me in.

'You don't need to knock, Georgie,' he said kindly. I was so relieved at this welcome, I hadn't been quite sure what to expect, especially with Helen being so erratic.

I'd half-hoped to find a blooming Helen in full make-up waiting to hug me as I followed Tim through into the sitting room. But of course, that wasn't to be, she was sitting in an easy chair, staring ahead. She looked terrible. Her hair was limp, her face pale, and her eyes ringed red, dark shadows beneath them. I walked over and gave her a hug, which she barely reciprocated.

'Cup of tea?' Tim asked, clearly still trying to keep everything as normal as possible.

I nodded and thanked him.

'How are you?' I asked, sitting down on the sofa next to Helen.

She didn't respond, seemed unaware of my presence.

I gently took her hand and held it until Tim wandered back into the room, his face a study in pain.

'She's having a bad day, aren't you, my love?'

Her eyes slowly rose to meet his. For a moment, they just looked at each other. I wasn't sure whether they were communicating, or she was simply resting her eyes on something familiar, something she loved.

It was so hard to see my friends like this. I was there for them and I hoped they knew that. But I was also concerned about Sam, and it was filling my mind, so when Tim set the mugs of tea down, I started the conversation.

'You know Sam's been charged?'

Tim's face dropped. 'Yes, I heard. I'm so sorry.'

'I don't know what to do, I don't know what evidence they have, or why they're suddenly *accusing* him?'

'Yes, well that will all come out in court. Have they told Sam what they've found?'

'He says not, but I think he's trying to protect me.'

'Aye, that's Sam, isn't it?' he said with a sigh. 'Always looking after his mum.'

'Well, he's the man of the house, always has been, he's one of life's carers is Sam,' I said, and as I said it, I heard a snort come from Helen.

'*Carers?* One of life's *carers?*' she spat.

I was taken aback. 'I think so, he's *very* caring, and gentle and—'

'Can you hear yourself?' she asked, viciously.

I was confused. 'I don't... What do you mean?'

'*Caring? Gentle?* For Christ's sake, Georgie, wake up! *Your* son is facing charges for murdering his wife, *my* daughter!'

I had to swallow hard to stop myself from crying. 'Helen, you *know* he didn't do it.'

'Do I? Do *you?* How well do you *really* know your son?' she hissed, hate spilling from her lips.

I didn't know what to say, the shock took my breath away. Helen was my best friend, she'd never ever said anything derogatory about me or Sam, and this was sharp and painful.

I looked from her to Tim, who sighed and shook his head.

'That's enough, Helen,' he muttered under his breath.

'No, let her say what she really means,' I urged, and looking at Helen, asked, 'Do you think Sam's *guilty*?'

She raised her eyebrows. 'I now know it wasn't an accident, and that your son was the only other person there that night... he *apparently* found her.'

'Come on, love,' Tim was saying to her. 'It's not fair on Georgie, she's suffering too in all this.' He glanced over at me. 'We don't believe Sam's guilty.'

'Don't *we*?' Helen snapped. 'I've seen the way *she* gazes at him.'

'What are you talking about?'

'Sadie, who else?' she giggled maniacally, and didn't pick up her mug of tea, but reached for a half-empty wine glass on the coffee table.

I couldn't believe Helen was saying this. 'Sam wasn't interested in Sadie, he loved Lauren.'

'*Loved*, loved. In the past tense, he got bored,' she spat.

'That's just not true, Helen. How can you *say* that?'

'How? Let's see,' she pretended to be thinking and I couldn't get over how cruel she was being, 'Lauren wasn't cold and those two were already going running together... She always wanted what Lauren had.'

'It wasn't like that,' I said, desperately trying to believe what I was saying, trying not to let her words pierce my faith, my trust in Sam. 'They're friends, they are both grieving for Lauren and supporting each other.'

'*Supporting?* Is that what you call it?' She threw her head back. 'It doesn't take a detective to work out what was going on there. Lauren became an inconvenience.'

'That's just not true, Helen, you're imagining it, you're grieving.'

She sniffed. 'You sound just like him.' She pointed at Tim, sitting on the sofa, his head down. 'What about the witness who saw Sam's car outside Sadie's flat the night Lauren died? Did I *imagine* that?'

This took my breath away. 'I don't know anything about a witness. Sam was at work, he came home late, he didn't go to Sadie's,' I said, unsure of what was happening here. Had Sam lied to me? Had he lied to Lauren? And, even more worryingly, had he lied to the police?

'Not so sure now, are you?' Helen growled, before taking another sip from her glass.

'Helen, for Christ's sake,' Tim groaned. 'Enough!'

She got up then and walked over to where he was sitting, and as he looked up, she slapped him hard across the face. The crack of the slap made me gasp, but he just sat there, taking it.

Then she staggered from the room, leaving Tim in embarrassed, hurt silence. After a while, he said, 'Forgive Helen, she's had a bad day and needed a couple of drinks.'

'I understand,' I said. Although, in truth, I was trying to get my head round everything that had happened here. 'I just don't know why she'd *think* that Sam would... And the witness, I didn't even know about that.' I felt betrayed, both Helen and Tim knew about it, so Sam must have, but he didn't tell me.

He looked uncomfortable. 'Oh, she's got it into her head that Sam and... and Sadie...' His voice drifted away, he couldn't even finish the sentence. Couldn't look at me.

All my fears came rushing in, and as scared as I was for Sam, I was scared for me too, these people had been my life, they'd always been there for me and I valued them. I'd lost both my parents years before, my sister moved to Australia in her teens, and for more than twenty years, I'd had the Jacksons, they were my family. Tim was like my brother and Helen, my sister. A day didn't go by when Helen and I would either see or call each other, and there was never a weekend when I wasn't included in their plans. Holidays were the same – 'Where shall we go this year, George?' Helen would ask, before she'd even discussed it with Tim, who said he felt like he had two wives and would sometimes jokingly refer to me as 'wife number two'!

And it wasn't just about me. For me and Sam to have a ready-made extended family was wonderful, it had made being a single parent easier, and given a child with no father or siblings a family. Tim would take Sam to football, play cricket with him in the garden and watch sport with him on TV. Even now they talked about sport in a kind of shorthand I couldn't understand. I knew I could never have provided that for Sam, and I was eternally grateful for Tim's male input. 'He's the son I never had,' he used to say, in much the same way I felt Lauren was the daughter I never had.

But here we were, in my friends' home, where I'd always been so welcome and Helen had just told me she thought Sam had killed Lauren and Tim was trying desperately to think of something to say to repair the damage. But this was a huge rip across the fabric of our friendship and it made me realise that perhaps our friendship hadn't been the miracle I'd always believed it to be. Despite our strong bond, when it came down to it, our relationship was as parents and therefore an ecosystem based around the children. And if there came a point where any of us had to choose between our kids and our friends, it was a no-brainer, we'd always choose our kids. We'd been through tumultuous times before, like when our children were teenagers and other love interests had drifted through their landscape. But we understood it for what it was, 'being a teenager', and our friendship was so strong, it barely felt the strain. Until now.

'I'm shocked though, about the witness. Perhaps Sam had called in to see Sadie? They were, and are, friends, it doesn't mean anything,' I said to myself as much as Tim. 'You don't believe it, do you, Tim?' I asked. 'You don't think Sam and Sadie...?'

He lifted his arms to cradle the back of his head and leaned back in the chair. 'I think Sadie's a girl who gets what she wants. Sam's a great lad, good-looking, a good catch... and who's to say they didn't get close, and weren't attracted to each other?'

'No way.' I could hear the horror in my own voice but at the same time wondered if to someone like Sadie, who'd never had anything, a husband in a cosy little cottage on Dartmoor could be quite the prize. I remembered the way she turned up at the cottage, making herself at home. Then I had a thought. 'Has Sadie been questioned by the police like the rest of us?'

Tim nodded. 'Today apparently.'

I shook my head. 'If she opens her mouth and starts saying stupid things to the police, Sam's had it.'

'She won't, she wouldn't.'

'Tim, she'll probably have bragged to them about how wonderful he is, how they go to football together. She could make it look like something was going on even if it isn't.'

'It doesn't really matter what she says. If she and Sam weren't... aren't together, then whatever she says won't make any difference.'

I tried to calm myself. 'Yeah, I guess you're right.' He then sat forward in his chair, and looked directly at me. 'Our kids don't always tell us everything, Georgie.'

'What do you mean?' I said anxiously.

'Well, don't take this the wrong way, but are you sure Sam's telling you the truth?'

CHAPTER TWENTY-ONE

I drove back home from Helen and Tim's feeling really low. Tim's comment about our kids not telling us everything really bothered me, but when I'd pressed him, he wouldn't elaborate. It made me wonder if Sam had said things to Tim that he didn't feel he could tell me, because Tim was definitely hinting at something.

The look on Helen's face when she talked about Sam was pure hatred. And that hate was also aimed at me; she hated me for trying to support my child, because she believed Sam was guilty. And now even Tim seemed to be questioning Sam's innocence, and that was the biggest blow.

I drove the familiar roads back home from theirs, as I had so many times, only this time I felt lost and alone. I couldn't imagine my life without Helen's friendship, but seriously doubted we'd ever come back from this.

I recalled how Helen and I used to sit in their big, sunny kitchen, two steaming mugs of coffee. 'Shopping spree!' she'd announce, opening up her laptop and laying it all before us. Beautiful cushions, a profanely priced chair, a dress that cost a month's salary. 'Let's play rich bitches,' she'd say, giggling, and we'd fill our online basket until we'd spent thousands of pounds and then she'd get the wine out and close the laptop. 'All the fun, without spending a penny,' she'd say, 'and now the wine will help us to forget those fabulous cushions.' The kids were usually playing close by and most of the time they were pretty self-sufficient, but Kate, being younger, was the odd one out, and the older ones found her annoying. Helen and I were constantly asking Sam and Lauren to include her in their games, but poor Kate was too young to understand how 'uncool' she was. Meanwhile, Helen and I were probably too *old* to understand how 'uncool' we were.

I smiled at this as I turned the corner onto Wellington Lane, moving away from the big double-fronted Georgian homes like the Jacksons', to my semi. It was only a few minutes between the two but might as well have been in different continents.

Their house was on the way home from school for me and Sam, and Helen always invited us in, or if I was picking the children up, I'd go back there and have a coffee with her. Tim worked long hours, and she was usually on her own, and as we loved spending time together, a coffee would turn into wine, and then Helen would cook or we'd order takeaway. She always offered to pay. Tim too, but I was proud and insisted on paying my way.

School holidays were the same, Helen planned all kinds of things with the kids, but it could be quite expensive. Days at theme parks, galleries, stately homes, day trips to Cornwall, or to London to the Natural History Museum or a child-friendly show. It was all great fun, and Tim always said, 'Thanks for babysitting, I can only relax when Helen has a grown-up with her.' I knew what he meant, Helen could be a bit flaky sometimes. She forgot the family passports when we all went to Italy and Tim had to jump in a taxi on a forty-mile round trip to collect them. It was so stressful waiting for him at the airport as they called our names to board the flight. Like Superman, he arrived with passports and just moments to spare, and we all had a very large gin on that journey. I remember looking across at Tim asleep, his daughters sleeping on his shoulders, either side of him on the flight. Helen and I sat together with Sam, and we both looked across and smiled at the tableau of the three Jacksons asleep.

'Look at them,' she'd said, '*his girls*... I don't know what we'd do without him. He's our rescuer.' She'd beamed with such love.

'Yep,' I replied, 'they say there's no such thing as the perfect husband, but I reckon he must come close.'

'Yeah. Sometimes I just have to be reminded,' she'd said, and looked at me, 'because I'm *not* the perfect wife.'

I'd tried to reassure her, 'You're a fabulous wife...' but she was more concerned about grabbing the stewardess 'for a cheeky glass of wine'. We'd enjoyed that holiday, like we had all the others, the beach, the kids, the endless sunshine. I never wanted those holidays to end. Back then, I couldn't imagine anything ever coming between us.

Little did we know then the dark shadow that would one day cross our lives and our children's lives, and how easily it would break us apart. Like delicate fabric, we seemed to have ripped at the first tug.

Having arrived home, I was putting my key in the lock when my mobile rang. It was Tim; I quickly answered it. I was hoping he was ringing to say that Helen felt awful, of course she didn't think Sam had hurt Lauren, and could I go back and have supper with them?

'Georgie, I feel like I've let you and Sam down,' he started.

I didn't say anything. If he thought my son was guilty, then yes, he was letting him down.

'Thing is, Helen's all over the place, she doesn't know what she's saying.'

'You don't have to apologise again for her, Tim. I'm sure if the shoe was on the other foot, I'd feel so devastated I wouldn't know who to trust.'

'Absolutely. Look, I want to help, but as I've said—'

'It's fine, Tim, honestly,' I lied. 'I just feel like I'm the only one who believes he's innocent. Even the police have given up on him. If this was different and you were in charge, I know you'd be searching for who really did it.'

'Georgie, I'm sure they haven't given up on him. Police work takes time, it's a process...' He seemed to hesitate, then said, 'Look, one thing you *could* do...'

'Yes?' I jumped on it.

'You could call the station. Ask to speak to DCI Weston, she's a mate, tell her I said to call and ask if she can give you any information. She might not be able to say much, but it might put your mind at rest, if she talks you through the process.'

'Okay, thanks for that, Tim,' I said, gratefully.

We said our goodbyes and I put down the phone. I knew he was only offering me a palliative, and even his friends in the police could only tell me so much. Sam being on remand now was a whole new ball game, not only was it going to be emotionally traumatic, but financially too. I'd checked online and neither me or Sam were eligible for Legal Aid, so I'd probably have to remortgage the house, I would need to take on more work too, but that wouldn't be easy. The charity I worked for had let me work from home under the circumstances, and I was grateful, I had an understanding boss, who, after Lauren's death, had approved compassionate leave. But I wasn't on full pay and it was eating into my savings. Right now, I didn't care about any of that, I just wanted Sam home and free.

Tim had suggested I ring the station to find out more about the process, but rather than ask for information, I had some to impart, so I dialled the station and was eventually put through to DCI Weston.

'Good afternoon – or should I say evening?' she said.

I looked at my watch, it was already 5 p.m.

'Hi, I'm Georgie, a friend of Tim's – Tim Jackson. He suggested I call you about the murder investigation... Lauren Moore's murder,' I added awkwardly. I wasn't used to using words like murder outside books and films, it all still felt so surreal.

'Hi there, Georgie, how's Tim, I haven't spoken to him for a couple of days?' She sounded friendly, to my great relief.

'He's... he's good.'

'So how can I help you?'

'Well, I believe I may have some information that might help in the Lauren Jackson investigation?'

'Okay,' she said, sounding rather cautious.

'I'm... Yes, I might have something of interest,' I added and began to explain about the night Lauren seemed to be missing for two hours, but before I could get very far, DCI Weston stopped me.

'Oh, hang on, you're Mrs Moore? You're the defendant's *mother*?'

'Yes,' I almost whispered, like if I said it quietly she wouldn't judge.

'Okay. Carry on, Mrs Moore,' she said.

So I did, without correcting her about my marital status, because I had the feeling that the minute she knew I was 'the mother' I was on a timer. So, I just rattled on until I got to the end, waiting for her to show some signs of being intrigued by the two missing hours.

But instead she said, 'And?'

I was a bit nonplussed. 'Well, she disappeared for *two* hours. No one knows where she was.'

'But she didn't actually disappear, did she? As you said, she told your son she was sitting in her car, thinking. We've all done it. I spend ages in my car working out stuff. With three young kids, trust me, it's the most peaceful spot I know.'

This wasn't going to be easy, but I needed the police to listen. 'Yes, but she doesn't have kids, and Sam was waiting at home worried about her... My son will go to court later this year and probably be convicted of murder – and *no one is listening to me*.'

'I think you're probably overwrought, Mrs Moore, and I don't blame you—'

I was not in the mood for being patronised or placated. 'He's a graduate, he works with nature, for God's sake, he wouldn't harm anything or anyone.'

'I understand how you feel,' she said. 'But, as one mother

speaking to another, I have to remind you that sometimes our children live quite different lives than we *think* they do.'

Why wouldn't anyone listen? 'I know my son's life, DCI Weston, and I know he's blameless. But I feel like the police have just charged him for convenience.'

'Convenience?' Suddenly her tone changed at the implied criticism, and if she ever had been, she certainly wasn't on my side now.

'Yes, "the husband did it". And yes, his DNA is everywhere, because he lives there. And yes, he was the one who found her, BECAUSE he LIVES there!' I probably shouldn't have lost it, but I'd had high hopes this call might be a chance to save Sam, but there it was again, a big, fat brick wall.

'Okay, okay. Firstly, I'd like to reassure you that nothing, *nothing* is done here at this station for *convenience*.'

'I'm sorry, I didn't mean...'

'You mentioned the DNA?' she said, talking over me, like she just didn't have the time for this silly woman. 'We are fully aware that Sam Moore's DNA will be all over the cottage, but that isn't *why* he's been charged. There were signs of a struggle and, as we explained to your son when he was arrested, the blood spatter and the fact that your son was the only one there...'

'*Blood* spatter?' I blurted, before she could finish.

'Yes, it indicates that the victim was pushed. If she'd fallen, the body would have been in a different position, the spatter would have made a different pattern. And there were also signs of a struggle, paint from the upper staircase under the victim's nails and *someone* had tried to scrape it off post-mortem.'

I gasped. I could now see how incriminating this was for Sam and why the police had just assumed it was him and charged him, but there must be another alternative. 'But what about other DNA?' I asked, refusing to be fobbed off. 'My son didn't do it – so either Lauren fell, and your forensic people have got this wrong. Or someone *else* pushed her, in which case—'

'DNA isn't the one-stop shop everyone imagines, and I don't

mean to be rude, but since *CSI*, everyone is an armchair forensic and it isn't that simple. We might find there is *other* DNA, but it isn't looking likely from the samples. And once again, I would like to reassure you of the competency of employees at this station, our forensic team have not "got this wrong",' she snapped officiously.

'I still feel like you're forcing this,' I said, in a small voice, up against Goliath but still battling in my own way.

'And the jumper?' she queried.

'What jumper?'

'Your son didn't tell you about that?'

It wasn't what she said, it was the way she said it. All hope died in that sentence.

'What about a jumper?' I repeated, desperate to know, while at the same time not wanting to. I had this urge to throw my phone across the room and run away.

'We searched the cottage just after the death. We were very thorough and took some of Sam's clothes. One of the items we removed is a jumper.'

I almost couldn't bear to hear any more.

'It's a big Aran-style jumper?'

'Yes, yes I know it. I bought it for him a couple of years ago, it's hand-knitted – why is it significant?' I asked, holding on to the kitchen counter, waiting for her answer.

'The forensics have confirmed...' A swish of paper, she was reading from her notes.

'Forensics confirmed what?'

'That it has Lauren Moore's blood on it.'

CHAPTER TWENTY-TWO

I'd naively thought I could offer my own theories and evidence and set the police off on a manhunt to find the real killer. How stupid I must have seemed to the DCI. Why hadn't Sam told me about the jumper, and the blood spatter too? Then there was the witness Helen mentioned who'd seen his car at Sadie's? I'd have to wait until Friday to find out why he'd kept all this to himself, and I guessed his answer would be, 'I didn't want to worry you,' but it had now been made so much worse. After the conversation with DCI Weston, my heart was still strong, but my head kept taunting me, inviting me to go down another path. *But what if...?*

I thought again about what I'd just told the detective, and though it was the last thing I wanted to do, I knew I had to try asking Helen again about the night Lauren went over there with concerns about getting married, because I just knew it would lead me somewhere. Whether I wanted to go where it led me was another matter, because what DCI Weston said about not knowing our kids' lives was playing on a loop in my head.

I was scared to know why Lauren was having second thoughts, but I had to know. And if Helen could confirm it was the same night Sam told me about, when Lauren said she sat in her car, then her two missing hours were accounted for. If it was a different evening, then where had Lauren been that night? Was it what she told Sam, the usual pre-wedding nerves along with the extreme tiredness caused by long hours as a junior doctor? Or were the missing hours, and the concern about getting married, because she'd met someone else?

I was only too aware that I had to be careful how I broached this with Helen. I obviously didn't want to hurt her by suggesting her daughter might have been having an affair, and after our last encounter I needed to approach this with her cautiously. I had to subtly plant the seed, so she could see the evidence for herself. It wouldn't be easy, but I had to try.

So I took a deep breath and called Helen's mobile. It rang for a while, but eventually she picked up.

'Hi, sweetie,' I started softly.

'Hi. Look, I'm sorry, Georgie, about what I said.'

'It's fine, I understand,' I said, relieved at this unexpected apology.

'Tim loves Sam like a son, it would break his heart all over again if it turns out to be him,' she said, hitting me in the face with my son's perceived guilt. Helen was still wrapped so tightly in her grief, she was just talking as if to herself.

'Helen, it *won't* turn out to be Sam, so don't worry about that,' I said, trying to sound calm.

'Oh, Georgie,' she said with a big sigh like she was exhausted, 'you're not doing this again, are you?'

'Doing *what?*'

'Deluding yourself. "Sam's perfect, Sam would never do anything."' Her voice turned sarcastic again.

'I never said that. But if I am deluding myself about my child, perhaps I'm not the only one? For example, why, two weeks before the wedding, did Lauren get home late, in tears? And when Sam asked where she'd been, she said she'd been sitting in her car in the cold for two hours, thinking?'

'Perhaps she *was* thinking?' She sounded confused.

'It was midnight. It was cold. She was wearing a thin dress.'

Helen didn't say anything – or couldn't?

'Can you remember the date she came to see you about having second thoughts about getting married?' I pressed.

'Second thoughts? What the hell are you going on about, Georgie?'

She'd had a drink earlier, and from her demeanour I guessed she'd had more in the interim. I wouldn't be able to get any sense out of her now, but I gave it another try.

'You told me at the barbecue Lauren had doubts about marrying Sam. She went to see you one night before the wedding, talked to you and Tim.'

'Oh *that*, no. I don't know. Tim sorted it.'

She was completely pissed. It was impossible to get any sense out of her when she was like this. On the other hand, I thought ruthlessly, if Lauren had confided in her mum, the red wine might cause Helen to let something out. So I continued to talk. 'Okay, well, I just wondered what Lauren might have been doing the night she said she sat in the car. Did she meet someone?'

'She was with Sadie that night. Wasn't she?'

'No, she'd left Sadie by then, but she didn't go straight home – did she come to you?'

'God knows, I can't remember what happened yesterday, let alone before...' she suddenly stopped mid-sentence. 'Oh God, I wish she was here now, Georgie.'

'I know, love.' I sighed. Perhaps I was barking up the wrong tree? Perhaps all the police forces in all the country couldn't solve this one. So what made me think I could just waltz in and ask Helen a few questions and put two and two together? I'd fooled myself on so many counts, and Helen wasn't exactly a reliable witness – to anything!

'It was all Sadie's fault,' she suddenly blurted.

'Helen, what are you talking about? What was Sadie's fault?' I felt a cold wave wash over me.

'She wasn't a true friend,' she slurred. There was some shuffling and muted voices.

'What makes you say that?' She'd said stuff like this before, but

I felt that through her alcoholic haze she was trying to tell me something.

'Hello? Hello?' Another voice picked up the phone.

'Is that Kate?' I asked.

'Yeah, oh hi, Georgie, Mum's just... she's just gone to the bathroom.'

Had I just missed some vital information, or was Helen so pissed she was just repeating what she'd said a million times before. I reckoned she was merely expressing her disapproval of Sadie, which was meaningless in the context of Lauren's murder.

'Hope Mum's okay, oh how are you?' I said to Kate. It sounded like an afterthought; it was. Poor Kate was always an afterthought.

'Yeah. It's just... Everything's a bit shit at the moment.'

'I know, love.'

'I heard about Sam. I'm sorry. Mum thinks he did it, but I keep telling her he didn't,' she said, and I had the feeling she wanted to talk, which was highly unusual for Kate, and must have taken a lot, so I reciprocated.

'Thanks for your faith, Kate. I know he didn't. But until I can find out who *did*, the police are going to continue the case and Sam could end up staying in prison.'

'Oh God, Georgie, that would be awful.'

'Yeah, well...' I never really felt like I had much to say to Kate and was just about to say goodbye, when she said:

'Sadie was jealous, you know.'

I was surprised and intrigued by this. 'What was she jealous of?'

'Lauren and Sam. She fancied Sam,' she said, like it was the most obvious thing in the world and she was amazed I didn't know. Of course I'd had my suspicions, but Kate's blatant confirmation piqued my interest.

'Did Sadie *say* she fancied Sam?'

'Didn't have to. It was common knowledge, she'd always had the hots for him, used to write his name all over her exercise books at school. "Shady Sadie" we used to call her.'

I had so many questions for this eighteen-year-old who suddenly seemed to have been privy to stuff no one else seemed to be aware of. Even Sam as far as I knew.

'Did Lauren know about this?' I pressed.

'Yeah, she was the one who christened her "Shady Sadie". Lauren showed me the exercise books in her school bag when Sadie stayed over – which was all the bloody time!'

'Yes, she stayed over a lot, didn't she?' If what Kate had just told me was true, and she hadn't misinterpreted Lauren's feelings towards Sadie – it didn't sound like the perfect friendship. 'Sadie was close to Lauren, they were best friends,' I said, playing devil's advocate.

'Yeah, I guess, but they were always falling out. Lauren hated her staying over all the time, said she wanted to see other friends, but Sadie wouldn't let her.'

I'd always suspected that there was an unhealthy dynamic between the two girls, and I knew Sadie could be difficult, but never suspected she stopped Lauren from having other friends.

'Did Lauren tell your mum and dad she didn't want Sadie to stay over?' I asked. Helen and Tim were probably being kind to Sadie and had no idea how their daughter really felt.

'All the time. She'd cry when Sadie was coming over, begged them not to let her come in, but Mum and Dad said she was being mean. I guess she was.'

'Well, perhaps not if Sadie was being mean to her?' I suggested. 'Perhaps Lauren just didn't want her there because she was upsetting her?'

'I dunno…' Kate was about to say something, when I heard Tim's voice calling her. 'I need some help with your mother,' he was saying, obviously unaware that Kate was on the phone.

'Oh, I'd better go. Give Sam my love, won't you?'

'Yes, of course, take care, darling,' I said, putting down the phone, with a whole new scenario whizzing around my head. What I took away from the conversation with Kate was that, first of all, I didn't know she could be so chatty – I don't think she'd spoken so many words to me in one conversation ever. But more important was *what* she said, and it sounded like Lauren had felt trapped, bullied by Sadie even? And on top of that, Sadie fancied her husband.

Either way, it looked like Sam and I were still on our own in all this. Perhaps in truth we'd always been on our own, because when it comes to family, everyone sticks together. So, in the absence of a trained police officer, or wily detective, it looked like Sam still had only one person on his team, with the time and the faith to find out what really happened. His mother.

CHAPTER TWENTY-THREE

Her name had been mentioned too many times for me to ignore it and I had a lot of questions, so I grabbed my phone and called Sadie. She'd given me her number before the wedding, when we'd had to collect the flowers together.

She answered straight away.

'Sadie, it's me Georgie.'

'Yeah, I can see that,' she replied with her usual sarcasm.

I took a deep breath. 'Sadie, I was wondering if we could talk. Would it be okay with you if I call by?' She didn't have a car, she'd never passed her driving test, in spite of Tim and Helen paying for her lessons, so the only way I could see her is if I drove out there.

'Busy...'

'Sorry, what did you say?'

'I'm busy, can you come tomorrow?'

I knew if I left it until the following day she'd probably cancel, say she had to go somewhere, I really had to press her on this. 'I'm up that way to check on the cottage,' I lied.

Silence.

'And it's important we talk,' I continued, then added, 'Important for Sam.'

'Sam?' Now she seemed interested.

'I don't want to talk over the phone,' I said. I had to go there, I *had* to see her face when I asked her about that night, about her feelings for Sam, her friendship with Lauren. 'Please, Sadie?'

'Okay... come over later then.'

'I can be there in about forty minutes.'

'No, later. Come at seven.'

I checked the time, it was 5.30, I doubted she was busy until seven, I reckoned she was just keeping me waiting, and making it difficult for me, she clearly wasn't keen on talking.

I clicked off the phone before she changed her mind and gave it half an hour, then, unable to rest, I picked up my handbag and car keys and headed out to the car. I might not succeed in this, but I was going to damn well give it a go. There would be a battle ahead, but I was used to fighting by now. And as I started the car, and pulled away, I knew that saving Sam was going to be the hardest fight of my life.

I eventually arrived in Sadie's village, which was about a mile or so from the cottage. She lived in a flat over a fish and chip shop and she was always complaining of smelling like grease. I'd have thought she'd have been grateful for anything, without Helen and Tim helping with her rent, she wouldn't have been able to afford anything.

I was about twenty minutes early, but as I'd been told by Sadie to arrive at seven, I decided to wait in the car, planning to park in the space that belonged to the flat. But when I reached it, someone was already parked there. As I looked more closely at the car, I froze. It was James' car. But it was a long way from where James lived. We texted or spoke most days now, and when I'd spoken to him earlier, he'd told me he had loads of marking to do that night. So, what was he doing here, parked outside Sadie's flat? And why was he even visiting her? It didn't make sense. My throat constricted, what was going on?

But in my heart I knew, or at least had a good idea of why

James was there, at the flat of a young woman who he'd described as once being sexually precocious.

I reversed the car and parked under a tree so I could observe. But when it got to almost seven, I decided to just knock on Sadie's door and deal with whatever awaited me. Perhaps I could then see for myself what was going on, why James was there. If Sadie let me in.

So, taking the keys out the ignition, I picked up my handbag from the passenger seat and started to leave the car, but as I did, I noticed the front door of the house opening, so stayed where I was. Through the car window, I could see a figure in the doorway, and by the light coming from the hall, I could see Sadie standing on the doorstep. Her arms were wrapped around herself in the cold and, as the figure walked away, she lifted her arm to wave.

From the lights of the fish and chip shop, I saw his face – I think I'd hoped I was wrong, that someone had perhaps borrowed his car, but it *was* James. As he left, he turned and called something to Sadie and she nodded, then he climbed into his car, started the engine and slowly pulled away. I stayed still and watched, giving it a few seconds for him to pass me, stunned and confused by what I'd just seen.

I took a few moments to compose myself, before getting out of the car and walking across the street to Sadie's door. I decided not to ask Sadie about James, I'd keep that information to myself until I knew exactly what was going on, but I was pretty shaken.

Approaching the door, I rang Sadie's bell. She answered quite quickly, opening the door slowly, like she didn't want to know who was on the other side.

'Hey, it's me,' I said, over-brightly, trying to sound positive, desperately hoping she'd mirror it. She didn't.

'Oh yeah, hi, Georgie,' she mumbled, like she'd forgotten I was coming over. She opened the door wider, her eyes searching beyond me, scanning the road.

'Are you looking for someone?' I asked, turning to look behind.

She shook her head. 'Come in. Shut the door behind you, make sure it locks.'

I did as she asked, following on down the hall and upstairs to her flat. As I reached the door she'd gone through, not waiting to welcome me in, I felt like an intruder. I stepped into the tiny, cramped flat, which was more of a bedsit with a kitchenette attached. The odour of chip fat had followed us upstairs and was now fusing with the smell of damp and cooked cabbage. I tried not to take deep breaths, the taste of grease filled my mouth and, taking it all in, I felt immediately sorry for Sadie, no wonder her default setting was miserable. A single bed was pushed up against a wall, a throw and two flat cushions were strewn onto it give the impression of seating. I thought of the profanely priced, perfect cream sofas Lauren had chosen, and I was struck by the stark difference between the lives of these two best friends.

It was a bleak space, the kind of room that someone else might try to brighten with fresh flowers, a bookcase, a nice lamp, but apart from the strewn cushions, Sadie had made no attempt to lift it. This dank little corner of the world lacked any permanence, it was no one's home, just somewhere to exist and sleep. I couldn't help but compare it to the gorgeous little cottage Sam and Lauren had lived in, and even though now it felt rather cold and unloved, it had once been cosy and full of life. I wondered how Sadie felt going from this to their home? Now I'd seen where she lived, I wasn't surprised Sadie was at the cottage so much. I wondered fleetingly if Sadie had coveted the cottage as much as Kate said she'd coveted Sam.

'So, you wanted to see me?' she said, dragging me back into the dank little room. She was standing by a table against the window, there were two chairs, and an open laptop. She was about to sit down at one of the chairs, then changed her mind. Then, leaning over the table, she hastily picked up two coffee mugs, I hadn't seen them because they'd been behind the open laptop. Presumably she and James had had coffee together? But as she clutched them to her and moved quickly towards the kitchenette, I saw them more clearly and recognised them. I felt my hackles rise. I'd bought Sam and Lauren a set of four Emma

Bridgewater mugs *exactly* like this for their housewarming gift. I'd been delighted to find a present that would suit them both; it wasn't always easy as they had such different tastes. They were beautiful, depicting birds, rabbits, flowers – pictures of nature for Sam, and a stylish crockery brand for Lauren. The mugs had looked right in the kitchen of the little cottage, but as Sadie put them down by the sink in that dimly lit half-kitchen they seemed completely out of place.

My first thoughts were that Sadie had keys to the cottage and had helped herself to Sam and Lauren's stuff. But as I stood in the middle of the room staring at her back, I tried to be kind, give her the benefit of the doubt. Had Sadie simply copied Lauren, liked the mugs and bought them for herself? After all, Helen always said Sadie copied Lauren, from her clothes to her hair to her university choice; had she simply bought the same mugs?

I doubted it, because four of these mugs cost around £80, and Sadie didn't *have* £80 for mugs. She didn't even have £80 for her *rent* and had to get Tim and Helen to chip in! Also, it was clear she hadn't wanted me to see the mugs, but unfortunately for her, there was nowhere to hide in a one-roomed flat. I watched her now, still standing with her back to me in the kitchenette. She hadn't moved since she'd put the mugs down; she was leaning against the sink. Was she thinking? Was she wondering if I'd realised? Was she working out how to explain this? I couldn't help it, I had to say something.

'They're just like Lauren and Sam's mugs, aren't they?' I heard the words burst out of me into the silence.

She didn't respond, just continued to stand with her back to me, not moving. In the dim hush, I began to feel rather uncomfortable. What was she doing? She was just standing there so still and silent, it was unnerving.

I stood a few more seconds in the stillness waiting for a response, but getting nothing. And it was then I finally saw Sadie and understood what she was, who she was. She lived on the periphery of other people's lives, most of her time spent in the dark, alone, living off the kindness of other people. Sadie was a parasite seeking second-hand happiness, finding a door ajar and creeping in. She'd used Lauren to get to the Jacksons, to live off them, to be part of the family, to belong. But it didn't matter how hard she tried, what university she went to, or what mugs she drank from, because the tragedy of Sadie was that she could never truly belong. And she would never be Lauren.

We continued to stand in the dimly lit space, just feet away from each other but oceans apart. Eventually she turned around, slowly.

'They aren't Sam and Lauren's, they're *mine*,' she said, slowly, clearly, almost without emotion. 'Everyone seems to think Lauren had good taste, but she copied me.'

I could feel the heat rising in my cheeks, how dare she? Imagine saying something like that about your best friend – after her death? 'Well, not in this case,' I said, trying not to sound as sharp as I felt, 'because I bought those mugs for her.'

'Why are you here, Georgie?' she asked then.

I'd almost forgotten why – seeing James and now the mugs had completely thrown me, but I had to focus. I walked backwards, away from her, instinctively not willing to turn my back on her. I didn't trust Sadie, never had, and now wished I'd met her somewhere public. She was unpredictable, and now, as she walked further into the lamplit room, there was something like madness in her eyes, but I needed to do this for Sam.

'Sadie, I want to ask you something, and I need you to be honest with me.'

She just stared in my direction dead-eyed. I wondered if she'd even heard me but decided to continue.

'Did Sam come here on the night Lauren died?'

'I don't remember,' she said too quickly and immediately started twisting the necklace she was wearing. She was twisting it so tightly, it was making a red welt on her neck, but she didn't seem to notice.

'Have the police already asked you? Because they have CCTV and could find out.'

She sighed. 'I told the police so might as well tell you. He was here for about twenty minutes.'

My heart started thumping, there was so much I didn't know, and so much I didn't want to know. 'Why?'

'Chat.'

'Just *chat*?'

'Yeah, what else?' she asked defensively.

I felt uneasy imagining Sam here in this grungy flat with Sadie whilst Lauren was alone in the cottage. 'I just wondered if you two were… in any way—'

'Sleeping with each other?' she said in a mocking tone, and I wondered if she was enjoying this.

'Well, yeah, I suppose so?'

'Nah. He's not my type,' she replied matter-of-factly.

'Oh? I thought—' I was glad, but remembered Kate's words about Sadie being into Sam, so continued, 'I heard you liked Sam, a lot?'

She shrugged. 'That was a long time ago… but Lauren got him, didn't she?'

'So nothing was going on, with you and Sam?'

'I like older men,' Sadie announced, defiantly.

I immediately thought of James and felt sick. But I had to pull myself together.

'I… I also wanted to ask you about something that happened about two weeks before the wedding,' I said, watching her intently.

'Go on, Miss Marple.' She had a look of defiance now, like she was waiting for me to ask her a difficult question.

'Sam told me that Lauren got home late,' I continued. 'She seemed upset. She'd been out with you?'

Sadie shrugged; she wasn't going to make this easy.

'Well, I wondered if *you* remembered anything from that evening? I mean, do you have any idea why she'd be upset? Do you know why she was late after leaving you?'

'Nothing to do with me. That was between her and Sam,' she

said, now folding her arms.

I put my hand on the back of the chair that was by the desk, I needed some support.

'You're right,' I said, placating. 'Of course it's between the two of them, but I'm not asking because I'm nosy or I want to know what Lauren was up to when she wasn't with my son. This is about Sam, about what happens to him, and as cold as it sounds, Lauren is dead.'

She didn't flinch, just stood facing me, arms still folded.

'I know he didn't do it, Sadie, and I can't let him go to prison for something he didn't do, so if you know something, anything...'

She tightened her mouth and shook her head.

'All I want is to try to find out who killed Lauren,' I said gently. 'Perhaps someone was following her... or she might have been seeing someone, I *need* to know. It isn't about judging her, it's about putting the pieces together and saving Sam from prison – someone knows something, Sadie.'

'I don't want to see Sam rot in prison either, but I think you should butt out, because if you go around asking too many questions, you're going to make things worse.'

This was the most she'd ever said to me, but it only served to unsettle me even more. 'What do you mean?'

Keeping her arms folded across her chest, she began to shake her head slowly, as if addressing a little child. 'There's so much you don't know, and trust me – you don't want to.'

'I do. I have to know. Tell me. TELL ME!' I yelled, frustrated.

Then, still staring at me, she started to giggle, almost under her breath. Then it got louder and louder until she was laughing maniacally, and I was so freaked out, I ran for the door. She didn't try to stop me, she just kept laughing and continued as I hurled myself down the stairs and out into the cold night. And as I ran towards my car, I heard her voice behind me, shouting out of the now open window, 'That's it, run away. As soon as it gets hard, you people can't handle it, can you? People like you *need* people like me to clear up your shit!'

CHAPTER TWENTY-FOUR

I jumped in my car and locked the door. Sadie definitely knew more than she'd been letting on.

I set off for home, but something was bugging me, and after about ten minutes' drive, I turned around and headed back towards the moors and the cottage.

Perhaps I was overreacting, but something turned my car around on that lonely, dark November night. It was fear for my son, for what would happen to him, and the desperate need to know the truth. This seemed like the craziest thing, to head out onto the moors now; it was around 8 p.m. and already pitch black, and as the car climbed up into the moors, a hailstorm started. This wasn't just about two mugs, it was about so much more, but I couldn't quite put my finger on why this felt so big. I tried to work it through in my head as I drove along. I knew Sadie was lying – they were Lauren's mugs, but even if Sadie *had* taken them, did it matter? Lauren was dead and Sam was locked up, that's all that mattered. And if it gave Sadie pleasure to use two of her best friends' mugs to drink her coffee from, then who was I to take that from her?

But if she could take those mugs from the cottage kitchen after Lauren's death, what did that say about her feelings for Lauren, and for the family who'd done so much for her? And why take only two when they were a set of four? Now I really was just going mad. I was totally overthinking this – wasn't I? I wished I had someone to talk to about this, but it sounded so stupid even Tim would refuse to entertain it.

I almost turned the car round again to go straight home, but something pushed me on – I *had* to know if she'd taken them.

I pulled up outside the cottage, my stomach a pit of dread just seeing it lurking in the dark, the place Lauren lived and died. Keeping the car doors locked for a few moments, I sat and contemplated what I was doing. I had to check those mugs were there now, because if Sadie *had* taken them, I reckoned she was sly enough to come back in the morning and put them back. If they were there, it would prove she was telling the truth, and if they weren't, if the set of four had been split, it meant Sadie had lied to me and had no compunction but to take her dead friend's possessions from her home. I felt that was indicative of something, and it made me question what else Sadie would do, and what happened the night Lauren had been with her and returned home upset. Had Sadie upset her in some way? Was this a prelude to her death, or just a random incident? I didn't know, but I just knew if I didn't check those mugs I wouldn't have slept that night.

I was reluctant to go into the dark little cottage alone. I fleetingly considered calling James. But then I remembered him leaving Sadie's just as I'd arrived and my stomach lurched recalling the two chairs at the table and the two mugs. She hadn't asked me if I wanted a coffee – she hadn't even invited me to sit down in her flat – so clearly James was a more welcome guest than me.

I took a deep breath, enough procrastinating, I had to grasp the nettle, go inside and find out if the mugs were there, and if she'd taken anything else.

Since I'd visited only a few days ago, there'd been some high winds, and tree branches scattered the path to the door, so I turned my phone torch on and took tentative steps towards the front door. I let myself in and, turning on the hall light, was met with the stark white staircase, the treacherously polished marble steps. I shuddered and bent down to pick up some post from the floor. Some of it was addressed to Lauren and it was still a jolt to realise she wasn't here anymore. I put the post on the hall table. In the corner of my eye, I could see the staircase rising up through the floor. I turned away; it was like watching a car crash, my eyes drawn to the horrible beauty of the swirling stairs, the infinity of the circle. Putting lights on everywhere as I went, I made for the kitchen.

I went straight to the cupboards where I knew Lauren kept the mugs. I'd seen all four mugs when I'd been at the cottage for the sofa delivery. I went straight to the cupboard, hoping I was wrong, but knowing when I opened it what I'd see. And I was right. There were just two mugs from the set of four sitting on the shelf, evidence if it was ever needed that Sadie lied and she stole. I made sure to check all the other cupboards thoroughly, just in case they were hiding somewhere, but as I'd suspected, they were nowhere to be seen.

Walking into the sitting room, I turned on a lamp and scanned every surface, to check if anything else had been taken. I touched a sofa arm with the tips of my fingers and leaned on the two new, fat, comfy sofas sat in the room, waiting to be loved. It was then I had this creepy feeling, like I wasn't alone, and turned around quickly, my eyes searching the room into the dark corners untouched by lamplight. The cottage was hundreds of years old, and I tried not to think of the lives that had been lived here, the people who'd died, the ghosts that still remained. I suddenly had an urge to get out, so turned off the lamp and moved into the hall, where the light was still on. I tried not to think about it, but all I could see was blood sprayed on white walls, Lauren on the floor; Tim's voice cramming in my head with all the spilled blood, *You should have seen her face, Georgie, it was smashed* and I imagined her lying there, at the bottom of the staircase. Her face a mess, her limbs twisted...

I felt my head spinning, whirling around, just like the stairs, going round and round into infinity. Red on white, splashes and sprays and scarlet. *The game changer*.

Triggered, I remembered Lauren's wedding dress, the red

stain, like lipstick, or blood, on white silk. I wondered again if it had been Sadie who'd tried it on? That stained wedding gown was as much evidence as the mugs – even more, it would have her DNA all over it. I could take it to the police station that night and hand it over to DCI Weston.

I took each step carefully and, as soon as I got to the top, went straight to Sam and Lauren's room, knowing I'd put the dress away neatly after I'd found it crumpled and stained. But when I opened the wardrobe door and leaned in to reach for the dress, it wasn't there, so I searched along the rail, but I couldn't put my hands on it. In the unlikely event the dress had come loose from the hanger and fallen, I then got down on my knees and searched lower down in the wardrobe. 'Damn,' I said to myself, wondering if, after our conversation about it, Sadie had thought it made her look guilty and removed it. Was it now hanging in her wardrobe, damp and smelling of chip fat? Had she moved it because it was evidence? And if so, evidence of what?

I was about to close the wardrobe door when I suddenly saw the plastic cover peeping out of the far end of the wardrobe. *Not where I'd hung it.* Goosebumps prickled my arms as I reached nervously for the covering, *knowing* this was significant, knowing *someone* had moved it. I lifted the plastic carrier out of the wardrobe and carried it to the bed with the intention of inspecting the stain again so I'd know exactly where it was before taking it to the police station. As I lay the dress down on the duvet and unzipped the plastic, I heard a loud sigh. It sounded so clear, so sad, it shook me, and, my head fizzing with fear, I stopped for a moment and took a step back. Standing very still in the silence, knowing it was the sound of air escaping plastic, the irrational side of my brain seriously wondered if Lauren was trying to tell me something. I took a deep breath, told myself not to be so stupid, and pulled the dress from its plastic womb, laying it on the bed. I turned on the ceiling light so I could see the stain properly. But to my confusion and dismay, it looked whiter and cleaner than ever. And as hard as I looked, I couldn't see any stain. Yards and yards of unblemished snowy silk. I was in no doubt, there had been a stain, I hadn't imagined this. But still, I momentarily questioned myself as doubt crept in. I wasn't going mad, was I? No I wasn't, the stain had been there, just above the waist, a scarlet splash on white silk. *Someone* had cleaned it. And for me there was only one person that could be.

The stain *had* been there, but how could I prove it now? I wished I'd taken a photo before, but it never occurred to me to do that, why would I?

A groan echoed through the old timber, telling me to leave, so I quickly zipped the dress back up and returned it to the wardrobe. Then, as I tried to shake off the feeling that I wasn't alone, I turned out all the lights and headed downstairs, taking each treacherous step carefully and slowly. In my haste to run, each step was agony, but in the dimness of the old cottage, with its secrets and sighs, I wasn't taking any chances on unfaithful, slippery marble. As soon as my foot left the last step, I was unlocking the door with nervous hands and jangling keys. Seconds later I was outside, the wind was whistling, there was no one for miles, but still it felt safer than being inside that place.

Not for the first time, I climbed into the car relieved to be leaving the cottage, but my head was going round in circles at what I'd discovered and how Sadie had to be involved. She'd lived a difficult life, and it was bound to have had an effect. She was closed in, secretive, I shuddered to think what had been going on in her head all those years? The irony was that if she'd have ever let me in, Sadie might have realised that we had more in common than she realised. I'd had a tough time too, with Sam's father, a slightly older man, who manipulated and diminished me.

I'd found out years before that Sam's father had died, which was a relief, because I'd often worried he might come and find us. If I'm honest, his death had been convenient for me because I never wanted Sam to know the truth, he didn't need to. He had a couple of treasured photos of him with his dad as a baby, so he thought of his father with sadness rather than with fear. The only person I'd trusted enough to tell the truth to was Helen. I'd shared my experience, the terrible wounds and the devastation to my self-esteem. Helen knew why I'd never gone speed dating or on Tinder like the other single mums at the school gate, and if anyone suggested it to me in her company, she'd quickly change the subject. Like Tim, Helen had been a rescuer, and while Tim specialised in the practical side of things, Helen did emotional rescue. Cold tears ran down my cheeks now as I realised I would have gone straight to their home, told them everything, and they'd have listened. I missed them both so much.

The irony was that the children who'd brought us together were now the reason we were being torn apart and I drove back from Dartmoor, remembering Sam and Lauren's first proper date. They were sixteen and went to McDonald's and, as Sam had volunteered nothing on his return, I'd texted Helen to see if she knew if it had been a success, which of course it had. She always had more intel being the mother of a girl.

I smiled at the memory and told myself even if Helen found it difficult, Tim would rally, and one day, when all this was over and Sam's innocence was proven, we would be friends again. The family get-togethers at their big table, the late suppers, the Christmases, they all went through my head on a reel of film. So many memories, so much happiness. No one was ever left out with the Jacksons.

I was reminded again of the way they'd also welcomed Sadie and treated her like a daughter, but where was she when they needed her? She never seemed to be at the Jacksons' now. She'd been happy to spend time at the cottage when Lauren was there, but she wasn't prepared to jump on a bus or in a taxi and go and visit Helen and Tim. After all they'd done for her too. She'd been given so much by them and how did she repay them? By staying away, 'appropriating' Lauren's coffee mugs and staining her wedding dress. Often it's the little things that tell you a lot about the person, and however hard I tried to find justification for her behaviour, I kept coming back to Sadie in my mind's eye, wandering around their bedroom after Lauren died. Sadie dressed in her dead friend's wedding gown, pretending to be a bride, no doubt envisaging a life with Lauren's new husband. I recalled Helen saying Sadie was a bit, 'Single White Female,' and I could see it now. If she ensnared Sam, the cottage, and the Jacksons, Sadie could finally be who she wanted to be – Lauren.

I was no detective, but from where I was, it looked like Sadie had every reason to want Lauren dead.

CHAPTER TWENTY-FIVE

'Are you okay, Georgie?' James asked, as we sat together drinking coffee the following day. 'I feel like I haven't seen you for ages,' he said softly, slipping his arm around my shoulder. I wasn't comfortable with even this level of intimacy, knowing he'd been to see Sadie the previous evening. I hadn't planned to see him, I was convinced something was going on with Sadie, and until I knew what, I had no intention of continuing our burgeoning relationship.

'Yeah. Did you get your marking done last night?' I asked, to see if he was going to lie.

'Eventually,' he replied, 'it was about midnight before I finished the last one. I'm exhausted, hopefully this will wake me up.' He took a sip of coffee, and rested it on his knee.

'Midnight? Wow, that was late, did you have lots to do?'

'Yeah, new term and all that. It takes time to get to know the kids, where they are coming from.'

I smiled, my heart sinking, he wasn't going to tell me.

'Oh,' he lifted his arm from around me, leaned forward and put his mug on the coffee table, 'and I went over to see Sadie Marsden.'

'Sadie?' Relief swept through me, if he was telling me he'd been there, then he had nothing to hide. *Right?*

'She's applying for university again,' he said, nodding.

'Really?' I was surprised. 'What does she want to do?'

'Medicine *again*,' he gave a grimace.

This news was out of the blue. Sadie had started Medicine at Manchester University with Lauren but dropped out in the second year. Lauren seemed to miss Sadie after she left and Tim and Helen worried she might leave too, perhaps Sadie was pursuing her dream of medicine after all? Or was the dream still to be Lauren, especially as there was now a vacancy for that role?

'Did she call you over to help with the application?' I asked, pleased there was an innocent explanation but still a little uncertain if Sadie was just using James in some way.

'Yes, I gave her some advice, just helped with her letter to the uni. She has the grades of course, but whether they'd take her a second time, I don't know.' He shrugged.

'I seem to remember Helen saying Sadie dropped out because she suffered from anxiety?' I said, wondering if the Jacksons would be stepping in to foot the bill for her university course this time around too.

'I don't know why she dropped out,' he said, almost too quickly. But something in his eyes told me he knew more than he was letting on. Perhaps James was in Sadie's thrall too and was in danger of getting caught up in her tangled web?

'If you vouch for her, or support her application, you have to be sure there are no issues, don't you?' I said – it was my subtle way of warning him. I didn't want to ruin Sadie's hopes and dreams but at the same time was concerned for James' academic reputation if he supported her. After the previous evening, it was clear to me there were plenty of issues.

'No. I only advise, I'm a sounding board as she doesn't have anyone else.'

'I think she's probably very lonely, especially now Lauren's not here. From what I gather she spent a lot of time at the cottage, didn't she?' I probed, wondering if he knew any more than I did about her visits to the cottage before or after Lauren's death.

'Yeah. A lost kid always looking for sanctuary somewhere, that's Sadie,' he said with a sigh.

'Mmm.' More like *Shady Sadie*, I thought, remembering Kate's comment about it being her nickname at school.

'You know Lauren's death has had a profound effect on her,' he suddenly said, leaning back, resting his hand on my knee. Now reassured he wasn't having any inappropriate rendezvous with Sadie, I was comfortable with this and put my hand over his. He looked at me and something in his eyes made my heart jump, in a good way.

I turned to face him. Before anything else happened between us, I just wanted to get everything out into the open. 'Actually, I saw Sadie last night too,' I said.

'Oh, I didn't know?' he seemed genuinely surprised.

'No, well it was after your visit – she didn't tell me you'd been there.'

'She probably doesn't realise we know each other?' he offered.

'She does. I took you to the family barbecue at the cottage. Remember?'

'Oh, yeah, of course,' he said. 'She just called me yesterday, out of the blue. You mentioned about issues earlier, and I do think she's struggling. She's all over the place. I mean, just the stuff she said about Lauren—'

'What?' I asked, almost jumping down his throat.

'She's angry about her death. *Really* angry.'

'Is she? I wonder if she's more angry about Lauren being dead – or Sam being in prison?' I asked, bluntly.

He hesitated. 'That's a strange question. I don't know, is she angry about Sam being in prison?'

'I think she might be.'

We sat there for a few moments, and then I leaned forward, my elbows on my knees, 'James... I want to talk to you about something.'

'Are you going to propose?' he joked.

I rolled my eyes. 'No.'

'Oh you wound me.' He put both hands on his chest in a jokey way, but I didn't laugh, I wanted him to take what I was about to say seriously. 'Look, I have this theory about Lauren's death and it's going round and round in my head. It just won't go and...' I hesitated.

'Okay, what is your theory?'

'Well,' I started, 'my biggest fear, and I don't even want to say this, is was Sadie in love with Sam?' I told him about the stolen mugs, the wedding dress, the smashed wedding photo.

He looked incredulous.

'And this all ties in, because according to Kate, Sadie always had a thing for Sam.'

'Did she?' He nodded slowly, taking it in, contemplating my theory. So far so good.

'And, okay, this might be a stretch – but I wonder if something happened between Lauren and Sadie, an argument or whatever. Did Sadie lose her temper, did they have a fight, a physical fight and did Sadie perhaps push Lauren down the stairs...?'

He looked at me under his eyebrows, a doubtful scowl if ever I saw one, but I ploughed on.

'Did Sadie hope that if Lauren wasn't there, she might end up with Sam?'

'It's feasible,' he said, then paused as if considering this. 'But, if she *did*, it backfired spectacularly.'

'Yes, but she probably didn't expect him to be *arrested*? I mean, if Lauren died and it was made to look like an accident, then no one would be to blame, she could move into the cottage, "console" Sam and—'

'I don't know, I...'

'It all fits though, James, surely you can see that? Or do you think I'm mad?'

'You're utterly mad,' he said, smiling. He reached across and kissed my forehead.

'So you think it's bonkers, that Sadie had nothing to do with it?'

'I don't know,' he hesitated. 'Of course anything's possible, but as far as anyone knows, no one else was there that night and no one else had *been* there.'

I looked at him. 'So you're saying it's Sam?' I asked defensively.

'No. No I don't... I think it was probably an intruder—'

'But you just said no one else was there?' I said, feeling hurt.

'I know Sam didn't do it,' he emphasised, 'but equally, I don't think Sadie did it either.'

'But who else *is* there?' I asked.

He sat back on the sofa, slightly away from me. 'Look, I just... I'm not very good at this. I take people as I see them, and I see Sadie as a troubled child, I see Sam as a potential miscarriage of justice, and I see Lauren as the tragic victim of... something random, a break-in that went wrong.'

'But if it was a break-in, the locks would be broken, whoever did it was someone Lauren knew, she invited them in, James!' I said, exasperated.

'I'm sorry, Georgie, I don't want to spend the evening sitting here wondering who it might have been.'

'Believe it or not, James, it isn't how I would choose to spend my evening either,' I said angrily. 'But I have no choice because my son is in prison, and if I don't sit here thinking about it, he might be in there for life.'

His expression softened, and he reached out and gently touched my face. 'I'm sorry, that wasn't fair of me. Of course you have to consider everything, and you're doing it for Sam. But the police are working on this too, and you're driving yourself mad.'

'I know, I know,' I said, calming down slightly. 'You have a point, I'm just used to doing everything, and I don't trust other people to fight for Sam like I would – and I include the police in that.'

'Well you have to, you have to trust me too, Georgie, and you're not alone, I know *Sam* didn't do it.'

'But *someone* did. According to the police there was a struggle at the top of the stairs. There was paint from the staircase under Lauren's nails, which *someone* had tried to scrape off. And... and the blood spatter at the bottom of the stairs shows she landed in a way she wouldn't have if she'd just fallen.'

James put both his hands up to cover his face.

'Are you okay?' I asked. He seemed quite distressed.

He nodded and lifted his hands away from his face; he looked very pale. 'Yeah, I just, hearing those details – I just... find all this a bit much. I'm a maths teacher, we deal in reality. Numbers add up or subtract and you know what you're getting. But blood spatters? Human mess? I'm not so good with that, I can't control it, the outcome isn't predictable.'

I couldn't bring myself to tell him about Sam's blood-covered jumper. Perhaps I *was* adjusting the facts to fit the picture I wanted to see after all?

'I understand how you feel, James. But I just feel so alone in this and it scares the hell out of me.' I felt my eyes welling with tears, I was exhausted from thinking, from trying to work out what to do next.

He put both arms around me, hugging me, his face in my neck. 'I can see why you feel like this and I know Sam, he's a great lad, I can't imagine...' He pulled away gently, and looked at me. 'Why don't we go out for dinner, you're driving yourself mad with your crazy theories.'

'Okay,' I said, nodding. It would be good to get away from my own head, the fear that filled my sleep, and taunted my waking hours. My son's incarceration, his wife's death, and the absolute torture my friends were living through was almost too much. But someone knew *something*, and my thoughts kept returning to Sadie – the one person, the *only* person, who loved Lauren's life so much, she had every reason to end it.

CHAPTER TWENTY-SIX

I woke the next morning with James in bed next to me and it felt right. It wasn't the first time we'd spent the night together, but as we'd started our relationship just before Lauren's death, and Sam's arrest, it hadn't been the easiest start. It can't have been much fun for him to be thrown into a relationship with all that going on, but he was still here, and I hoped in the future when all this was sorted I could make it up to him.

'I think I'll go and visit Helen and Tim,' I said, over toast and coffee once we were up.

'Would you like me to come with you?'

'No thanks, I think I should probably go alone. It's very delicate at the moment.' I took a sip of coffee. 'I'm finding it rather difficult. Tim's been as helpful and supportive as possible, given his position, and said he doesn't believe Sam's guilty. But Helen told the police that Sam wanted the house *because* of the staircase and that he virtually *forced* Lauren to live somewhere isolated – like he had an ulterior motive all the time. It's as if she *wants* him to be guilty, and… it just hurts,' I added sadly.

James was sitting at the kitchen table opposite me, scrolling through his phone, and he looked up. 'Helen's not an easy person to understand,' he said.

'No, I thought I knew her, but I really don't,' I said with a sad smile. 'I know she's going through hell, but you'd think that would make her want to reach out to friends, but she's just being distant, and I don't think the alcohol helps.'

'It never does.'

I continued, 'And I have this survivor's guilt when I'm around her – my child lived, hers died. You know? I want to help her, but because it was Lauren and not Sam, I feel like she hates me and blames him.' My vision blurred with tears.

James immediately got up from his chair, walked round the table and put both arms around me. 'Helen's all mixed up and *you* mustn't feel guilty,' he said, getting down on his knees, wiping my tears with the heel of his hand.

'I know, I know, but me and Helen, we're so close, I can't help but see things through her eyes, and she really thinks he did it. She thinks I'm defending him, but it's more than that.'

'What?'

I sighed. 'It's as though Helen *wants* Sam to be convicted, whether he's guilty or not.'

'I don't understand,' he said, standing up and moving away from me.

'I don't either, but it seems to me that Helen will only be happy when Sam's locked away. I remember not long after Lauren died, she kept calling the police, demanding to know what was happening, offering "information". God knows what she told them. And I can't help but wonder why she's being like this.'

'She's just upset and lashing out. It's easier if there's someone to blame.'

'Perhaps,' I conceded. 'But I don't think Helen would... I mean, I can't see a situation where...' I was thinking, thinking. Helen and Lauren had had a difficult time during Lauren's teen years, which wasn't helped by Sadie leading her into all kinds of trouble. But as far as I knew, things between them had improved, especially during the lead-up to the wedding. 'You don't think Helen would cover for Sadie, do you?' I blurted out.

James sighed. 'Look we talked about Sadie, and I think you're barking up the wrong tree. You're right to consider every situation, but you can't treat everyone as a suspect. I'm worried you're going to start imagining stuff about *me* next. I was Sadie's teacher *and* Lauren's after all,' he said, sounding irritated.

'I'm sorry,' I said. But I wasn't. I knew James wasn't involved, of course, but I *still* felt strongly that Sadie was. I also felt that James had been taken in by her 'innocent best friend' act.

'I've said it before,' he continued, 'it could have been a stranger, an intruder.'

'Yeah, it could have been a random thing, teenage lads trying the door or window, getting in, scaring Lauren...'

'Exactly, and she fell in such a way that it looked like she was pushed.'

'Hence the blood spatter,' I said. But in my heart I just knew this was all too simple, and if it was just a burglary gone wrong, surely the police would have someone by now?

I thought of the scene that greeted me on the night Lauren died. And however much James tried to convince me, the image of her twisted body, the pool of blood – and the secrets she seemed to hold, made me believe it was more than just an accident.

CHAPTER TWENTY-SEVEN

After a second coffee, James left, as it was Wednesday, he was in school, so once he'd left, I decided I'd pop round to see the Jacksons. I was particularly keen to make my peace with Helen, I was unhappy being at loggerheads, it felt like a constant toothache, this was a time we should be supporting each other, not falling out. So that afternoon, I called at the little French bakery and bought a dozen macarons in different flavours, making sure there were several lemon ones because they were Helen's favourite. Then I walked round to their house.

I rang the bell for quite a while, and eventually Helen came to the door. She looked dreadful.

I stood holding up the bag of macarons. 'I have come bearing gifts,' I said with a smile. 'Fancy a girlie afternoon?'

She didn't even try to hide the fact this horrified her but she ushered me in, with a stiff smile on her face.

'I'll make the coffee, you sit down,' I said.

'No, I can still make bloody coffee,' she snapped.

'Sorry,' I said, as she pushed passed me into the kitchen and turned on the coffee machine. 'That's nice, is it new?' I asked, desperately trying to find something neutral to talk about.

She looked at the coffee machine and took a step back like she hadn't seen it before. 'Yeah, Tim bought it. He thinks if we have a new coffee machine we'll forget about our dead daughter.'

The rawness of her words cut through me. 'I'm here for you, Helen,' was all I could say.

But she wasn't listening, she was trying to force pods of coffee into the contraption and was pushing so hard, they weren't fitting and water seemed to be going everywhere. I didn't feel I could help, but in the end she just stood there, sobbing, as boiling water dribbled out of the machine.

'I... I didn't want coffee anyway,' I heard myself say.

She turned to look at me and, through her tears, she almost smiled. 'Good job,' she replied, a glimmer of her old self fighting to come to the surface. Reaching across the kitchen counter, she grabbed a bottle of gin from her 'collection', as she called it. 'Come on, join me in some mother's ruin,' she said, taking two glasses from the cupboard.

I didn't want to drink. Apart from the fact it was the middle of the afternoon, I wanted to stay clear-headed. But to keep her happy, I let her pour me some.

'Do we not do tonic anymore in this bar?' I asked when she poured a more than generous measure.

'Oh you bloody wimp, the gin works faster on its own. I prefer it to wine these days,' she said, as if to herself, as she wandered over to the fridge. It seemed the sun had already slipped over the yardarm for Helen. 'There you go.' She sloshed some fizzy tonic into my glass and I followed her through to the living room, where she plonked herself down heavily in an easy chair. She was wearing tracksuit bottoms and a thick sweatshirt, which looked stained. Her skin was pale yellow; it didn't look like Helen.

'I've been wanting to catch up,' I said.

'Catch up on what? Nothing happens here, everything's the same, just him nagging me to get dressed, have a bath.' She looked round before leaning in to me. 'I told him to fuck off this morning,' she hissed, then took a large gulp.

I'd seen Helen drunk before, but that was at family parties, Christmas, her birthday, but not to this extent, and alone, on a Wednesday afternoon. And she'd always been happy when tipsy, always singing and dancing, socialising. But this was different. This wasn't a chilled glass of white on the patio, or a couple of 'cheeky G & Ts'. Like it used to be for Helen. This was dark, and desperate, a woman hopelessly seeking respite from despair. This was what grief had done.

I just kept talking, asking how she was, and how she felt, trying to get her to open up.

'I feel like absolute shit,' she slurred, pouring herself another glass from the bottle.

'I can't begin to imagine how you feel,' I started.

And she looked at me, weighing me up and down. 'No, you can't. Losing a child is like belonging to a club, and only other members of that club know how it feels – you don't belong to that club, Georgie.'

'No, but I'm still your friend, please don't shut me out, Helen.'

She threw her hands up in the air. 'Do you just think we can go back to being how we used to be?'

'I... I hope so. We go back years—'

'Your son is currently in custody for killing *my* daughter!' She looked at me incredulously. 'And you turn up with a bag of *cake* expecting me to forget that?'

'I promise you it wasn't him, what could Sam possibly gain by hurting her?' I asked, unable to use the word 'killing'.

'Well, for a start he'd get half the cottage and his freedom to go his own sweet way,' she held her glass to her lips and before sipping added, 'and she had life insurance—'

'So does Sam. They have a mortgage they *had* to—'

'Whatever,' she said, taking a large swig of gin.

I shook my head. 'Sam wouldn't even *think* like that. You've known him since he was three years old, Helen, you know him as well as *we* know each other...'

She rolled her eyes. 'So just because we're friends, we know each other's kids? We don't even know *everything* about each other!'

'Of course we do,' I said gently and leaned forward. 'I know you always wanted to be a ballerina when you grew up, but you got too tall, and I know you hate the way your sister still picks on you. Your mother used to force-feed you cabbage and you still hate it. Tim's the love of your life and rescued you from your mad family, *and* the cabbage.' I smiled, offering this as a gesture, an opportunity to laugh, or at least smile in recognition. But she didn't even look at me. I continued regardless, because memories bind us, and the history we share with each friend, each loved one, is unique. 'I know Kate had a lisp when she was little, and after speech therapy it disappeared. I know Lauren inherited your eyebrows, and you both think they're terrible, but I think they're beautiful and... and you and Tim are the strongest couple I know.' I touched her arm. 'And if ever I had a relationship, I hope it's half what yours is with Tim.'

'Oh, Georgie,' she wailed, and her eyes filled with tears.

Had I just made things worse by talking about the past? I wanted to cry, but managed to hold on. 'I just wanted to remind you how precious our friendship is. It means a lot to me.'

She turned to me and, looking into my eyes, unsmiling, said, 'Georgie, we *are* friends, but I'm not who you think I am. No one knows me, no one knows my life, how I feel. And right now, I don't care about my life, it's nothing – I've got nothing to live for.'

Losing a child must make you feel like that, but I tried to remind her of what she *did* have. 'You've been through the worst thing ever, but you still have a future. Lauren wouldn't *want* you to give up and you have another child who needs you, a wonderful husband who loves you—'

She gave a mirthless laugh. 'You really don't have a clue, do you?' she said, and the hate in her eyes stung me.

I found it hard to open my mouth to respond.

'Tim doesn't love me,' she spat. 'And I don't love him, our

marriage has been like a dying dog, for years. But no one has the guts to PUT IT DOWN!' she yelled.

I tried to respond to this calmly, and gently, although this confession had rocked me. Even though she was clearly drunk, she seemed to mean what she said. 'Oh, love, it might feel like it at the moment because of what's happened, but you two—'

'What?' she snapped.

'You two are... strong,' was all I could say.

She shook her head. 'Strong? Ha. We hate each other. We barely speak except to ask where the paracetamol is or work out what we're having for dinner.'

'Isn't that what all marriages are like after a long time?' I offered, hoping this might be just the grief and the gin talking. 'They morph and change and—'

'It's SHIT, Georgie, and it's been like that for years, long before Lauren.'

'But...' I started, unable or unwilling to believe the couple I knew were so unhappy; surely this wasn't true? Surely I'd have known?

'We haven't had sex for years... YEARS,' she spat.

'But I've seen you together, you've always seemed close.' I'd always thought there'd been a frisson between them, even joked to them about getting a room sometimes.

She snorted. 'What? A peck on the cheek, me putting my arm through his because I was too pissed to walk?' She slowly shook her head. 'That's not love, it's what my therapist calls co-dependency. And I find the only solution is to drink myself into a place where I don't feel anything anymore.'

I was finding this hard to process. I'd thought Tim and Helen were the perfect couple, had the perfect marriage. 'You never said, just kept all this inside. You could have talked to me.'

'Why would I talk to *you*?' she asked, and genuinely waited for an answer.

'Because I thought we were friends and I assumed—'

'You think you have all the answers, don't you? Georgie, you don't even know your own son!'

Her words wounded me, and I flailed around for a response. 'I do... I...'

'Your *son* couldn't wait to get my daughter out on the moors.' Helen was stabbing her finger at me in the air now. 'Why? Why did he want to live out there, when she obviously didn't?'

'She did. She liked it, Sam said that she was growing to love it...'

'Sam *said*,' she curled her lip. 'And you believe him?'

'Yes I do. Sam and I have always had an honest relationship—'

'Er, no you haven't.'

I looked at her, puzzled.

'You've never told Sam his dad was a violent woman beater and you only ended it when he'd given you two black eyes and a broken arm.'

'He doesn't need to know about that,' I said, hurt that she'd use this now.

'Oh – I see, there are different kinds of truth in your world, are there? Some we talk about and some we don't *need to know* about?'

I had no idea she could be so vicious. It was probably still the drink talking but it really stung. 'I told you about my ex in confidence.'

'Yeah well, it's all up for grabs now, the police have to know everything so we can get justice for Lauren. Don't think because we're friends, I held back.'

'But what you told the police wasn't true, Helen. There's so much more going on here—'

'Tell me about it.' She rolled her eyes.

I knew I had to get through to her. 'Did you know that Sadie has some of Lauren's mugs? And someone's been wearing her wedding dress?'

'Look, I'm no fan of Sadie, but you can't say she did it and just hope that she takes Sam's place. You keep coming up with all these crackpot ideas to save him, but don't think a wedding dress and a few mugs will take the police off the scent. They *know* it was him. I mean, who the hell else could it be? Your son has issues.'

'What are you talking about?'

'All I'm saying is the fruit doesn't fall far from the tree, Georgie.'

'Sam isn't violent. You know that's why I got out when I did, so Sam wouldn't become his father.'

'Looks like your plan backfired. You should have told him everything and put him in therapy. You hid stuff from him, and looks like he hid stuff from you. He didn't tell you *everything* after all, *did* he?' she said coldly, turning to look at me.

'I understand why you're upset, but this isn't about Sam's father, it isn't about Sam.'

She shrugged. 'Well, you're wrong, it has everything to do with Sam. Anger and violence is genetic.'

'Don't be so stupid,' I spat. Yes, Sam could get angry, he had a bit of a temper, but it didn't mean he killed his wife.

I was determined not to let her see the doubt flicker in my eyes, because, there was, growing inside me, a seed of doubt. It was a tiny seed, but nonetheless it was there, and I couldn't let it grow, I had to stamp it down.

Helen poured herself another straight gin, like she'd just beaten me in a battle. Perhaps she had?

I saw the blood-spattered walls, the red-stained wedding dress, and wedding photo smashed in its frame. Was there a fight? Had Sam somehow lost his temper? Then I remembered his jumper with Lauren's blood on it and wanted to cry.

I tried to remember the little boy who'd reached out to Lauren on that first day in nursery school. *That* was Sam, he wasn't someone who murdered his new wife in temper. He was a kind, caring, protective man, who'd once been a loving little boy who made Mother's Day cards with folded paper and misspelt, vividly-crayoned messages of love. I wasn't going to sit here with Helen, getting swallowed up in her grief-stricken theories, while drinking away the pain. Gin wasn't a cure for sadness and it certainly wasn't going to help me get my son out of prison.

'I know Sam,' I heard myself say, 'he wouldn't hurt her. I think you know that too, Helen, deep down.'

She looked up from her glass. 'Oh, Georgie. You see the good in everyone, even when there isn't any.' She was trying to sit back in her chair with a full glass, some spilling onto the floor as she did. The old Helen would be rushing to the kitchen for a cloth, but not this one.

'Sorry, I'm really sorry that you're unhappy—' I started.

'You just can't see what's right in front of you, can you? There's so much you don't know.'

'Tell me then?' I looked at her, swaying in her seat, trickles of gin now splashed on her already stained sweatshirt, her hair matted.

'I CAN'T!' she yelled, stabbing her finger at her head.

'What are you hiding?' I asked.

'Shut up. SHUT UP!!!' she screeched and put both hands over her ears.

She kept them there, and didn't stir, just sat, staring ahead in a hopeless stupor. This was getting us nowhere and I couldn't stay there a minute longer.

I picked up my handbag and, with my head down, walked to the door. She didn't try to stop me and I was relieved because this was *my* fight now and it wouldn't be fettered by our friendship.

I reached the hall, and turned before I left, wondering if I'd ever go back there, glancing through into the kitchen, the big table where we'd sat together on so many loud and happy occasions. All quiet now. I glimpsed the sitting room next door, where Helen nursed her glass, staring ahead, and I wondered what darkness the Jacksons shared, what secrets they'd kept, that I'd never even imagined.

I turned to leave and jumped slightly. At the top of the stairs were two feet, not moving. Kate. My heart sank as I wondered what she'd heard. The disembodied feet didn't stir as I left quietly, closing the door behind me.

CHAPTER TWENTY-EIGHT

After seeing Helen, I felt wretched. I hated to see her like that, but I also hated what she'd said. When my phone rang, I jumped, still on edge. It was a recorded message from the prison, asking if I'd accept the call.

'Sam, is everything okay?' I asked anxiously.

'Yeah, yeah – well, as okay as it could be in here.'

'I wasn't expecting you to call.'

'I wondered if you had any news?'

I felt terrible; I wished I had great news for him, but there was nothing. 'No, love. Helen's slowly going off her rocker and—'

'Oh yeah, Sadie said she's drinking a lot.'

The mention of Sadie rattled me. 'Did she?' I hesitated, but couldn't help myself. 'Did you know Sadie's got two of yours and Lauren's mugs, the ones I bought you both for your housewarming?' I said suddenly.

'Has she? Well I can't use them in here, can I?' He said this with such nonchalance I wondered if he knew, maybe he'd even told her she could have them?

'Did Lauren try her wedding dress on?' I pressed now. I was making far more of the bloody mugs than I needed to, but surely the same couldn't be said of Lauren's wedding dress?

'You mean did she try it on before the wedding?' he asked, confused.

'No, I mean *after* the wedding. I found it at the back of Lauren's wardrobe with a stain on. But then it had been put back and cleaned.'

'Oh. Good.'

I shook my head, thrown by his indifference. 'Not "good", Sam. Weird is the word you're looking for.'

'Okay weird,' he said in a funny voice, completely missing my point and taking the mickey out of his mother, who he'd presumably thought had lost it.

But I continued, 'The day I waited for the sofas, the bed... *your* bed had been slept in.'

Silence.

'Sadie?' was all I said.

I heard him take a breath. 'She stayed over a few times, kept an eye on the place.'

I bet she did, I thought. 'I don't think the police would be too happy about *that*, she could have been tampering with evidence,' I said.

'It was *after* forensics had been in. Remember, we had permission to go back there, Mum. She wasn't doing anything illegal.'

'Perhaps not, but Tim was pissed off at me going in there for the sofas, and that was after you'd had permission to go back. It's a murder investigation and it doesn't look good, Sam. And then there's this witness who saw your car outside her flat the day Lauren—'

He sighed. 'I called in to see Sadie, that's all.'

I wasn't sure I believed him, and thought again about the way Sam and Sadie seemed so comfortable in each other's company. How she chatted on the phone with him when she turned up at the cottage, like they were besties... or more? And she had keys for the cottage, I wouldn't be surprised if that's why the bed was unmade, she wasn't just staying over to keep an eye on the place – she was probably already living there. Was that why Sam was so keen to move back to the cottage? There was me worried about him being alone with the memories, but perhaps that wasn't the plan? Perhaps the plan was to make *new* memories?

'To someone on the outside it could look like you and Sadie were having an affair or something.' I couldn't help it, I just launched in. If something was going on, they were both being very stupid if they thought they were hiding it.

He sighed. 'Mum, there's nothing going on. Sadie's just looking out for me.'

'Was she looking out for your marriage?' I suddenly heard myself say.

Another silence and then he cleared his throat and whispered, 'Look, there's stuff... stuff I can't tell you – but believe me when I say that Sadie can be trusted.'

My mouth went dry. 'What stuff?'

'I can't *tell* you,' he hissed.

'I... you can't just say that and not *tell* me, Sam? I'm worried.'

'I'm not telling you for your own good. I want to respect Lauren's memory and, if I can, but if I have to use the information to stay out of prison, I will. Please, Mum, don't ask me again. I can't talk in here, our calls are recorded.'

Every part of me wanted to ask Sam what he meant, what wasn't he telling me, why was he speaking about Lauren's memory and what information did he have, but I needed to have faith in my son, now more than ever.

'Look, I've got to go. Thanks for being there, Mum.'

'We're all behind you, love, just remember that. It's not going to be easy, but stay strong, and I promise you it will all work out,' I said, but it was a lie. I was less certain about this than ever, I couldn't promise Sam anything.

'And you'll talk to Tim, ask for his help?'

'I can try,' I said. If it helped him get through this time on remand thinking he had Tim fighting behind the scenes, then I wasn't going to disillusion him.

Eventually I put down the phone, and all the tears I'd held

back while talking to Sam came flooding out. A few minutes later, my phone went again.

'Hey, Georgie, are you okay?' It sounded like Lauren, and it gave me a start, until I realised it was Kate.

'I'm good thanks, Kate. How are you? I called to see your mum earlier.' I didn't want to embarrass her and say I'd seen her on the stairs.

'Yeah, I must have been in my room,' she said. 'Dad's home now.'

'Is your mum okay?' I asked. I felt like we were talking in code. Kate was almost nineteen, she knew the score with Helen's drinking, I think that's why she kept out of the way.

'Mmm, I think she's okay, *you* know.'

'Yeah, she just needs time. But what about you? How are *you* coping?' I wanted her to know I cared, that *someone* cared, about how she was feeling. Her mum was swallowed up in grief and gin, and her dad was dealing with his loss while trying to save the rest of the world.

'I'm okay,' she said with a sigh, but I knew she wasn't.

'Everyone's just trying to cope. People are saying stuff they don't mean because they're so upset. But it will get better, I promise.' If Kate *had* heard anything Helen said about her unhappy marriage, or family secrets, I didn't want Kate to dwell on things and get them out of proportion.

'Yeah. I know.' There was a moment's silence and then she said, 'I just wondered if I could call over to see you?'

This was unexpected, as Kate had always been a bit of an awkward girl, but our last telephone conversation had been a revelation. She'd told me so much, and I'd never known her quite so engaged, perhaps she needed someone other than her parents to talk to. And if I could be there for her, I would.

'Of course, love. Come over whenever you like, you know you're always welcome!'

'Now? Could I come over now?'

I had hoped to do some work, but this was more important.

'Yes, yes, come over now, I'll get the kettle on.'

Twenty minutes later, we were sitting in my kitchen eating chocolate brownies and drinking coffee. We'd never really had a one-to-one like this, I was usually talking to Helen or Tim or Lauren, and Kate was on the outskirts.

'What are you doing about university?' I asked. Kate had deferred a year and was due to start in October, but it was already September.

'Next year now. After Lauren, I couldn't leave Mum and Dad, so I've put it off and Newcastle have agreed to defer my place until next year. But I'm just wondering if I should stay nearer home, stay in Devon, go to Exeter instead?'

'You *could*,' I said, 'but it might be good for you to get away?'

She nodded. 'I guess so.'

I reached out and touched her arm. 'You need to do whatever feels right, Kate, but don't stay out of duty. I know your parents are struggling, but you need to think about *you* in all this too – you're grieving and coping with such a lot of turmoil. I think going off to Newcastle for three years might be just what you need.'

'Yeah, sometimes I think it's exactly what I need. I just worry about them, Mum and Dad.'

'That's understandable. But don't stay indefinitely. You've paused your life – but don't stop it.'

'No, no I won't. I'm sure they'll work it out, I just can't stand the rows.'

'After what happened to Lauren, they are probably just lashing out at each other,' I said gently. 'They don't mean it – it's just grief.'

'No, it's not, they've always rowed.'

'Oh, I'm sure that's not true.'

'They hate each other,' she snapped, the surly Kate emerging finally.

'They're just going through a difficult patch,' I tried.

'Is that what you call it? And what do you call Mum's affair, it went on for years. Was that a difficult patch?' she scoffed.

I was stunned. 'No, not your mum?'

She nodded.

'When did... it happen?' I asked, unable to use the word affair.

'Oh years ago. Lauren told me about it, and I believe her.'

'Well, she was your sister, I'm sure you did, but things aren't always what they seem, and—'

'No, this was real, Lauren said she'd seen love letters from years ago. But she found out on her tenth birthday – I was only about two then, so obviously it was years later she told me,' she added as an aside.

I almost smiled at this, poor Kate, always watching from the sidelines, reporting on other people's lives, other's experiences.

'Lauren remembered Mum going into the back garden to use her phone during the party. When it was time for the birthday cake, everyone was looking for Mum and Lauren found her outside, and she was telling some guy on the phone how she wished she was with him, how she still loved him, yada yada.'

'Oh, that must have been very difficult for Lauren to hear.' I was struggling with this and didn't want to say too much, it was a ten-year-old girl's interpretation of these events recounted to her little sister years later. How true could it be? But it tied in with Helen's rant about her marriage, and how unhappy she was.

'Lauren said she felt really weird about it and went back into the house. You were there and Dad was putting music on, and you asked if she knew where Mum was. She said no, because she thought she might cry, but they had to sing happy birthday because some of her friends were leaving. So you found the candles and lit the cake and you got everyone to sing while my bitch of a mother carried on talking to her lover.'

Shocked at the vitriol, I took a breath, I wanted to defend Helen, but it seemed easier just to let Kate talk.

'Lauren said Mum was furious when she came in, she hated that you'd all done the birthday candles without her.'

I suddenly remembered it then, Helen walking into the party

from outside. She was really put out about something. At the time I couldn't work out why she was so upset. Now it made sense, but still I tried to make Kate see it from her mum's side.

'Well she *had* made the cake, I think she just wanted to be there when we sang happy birthday to Lauren,' I offered.

Kate looked at me like I was mad. 'That wasn't why. It was because she wanted to take photos of the cake so she could show it to her boyfriend, Lauren said she realised after that that Mum was always sending pictures to him. Anyway, when everyone had gone, Lauren kept saying, "Mum, why weren't you there to help me blow out my candles?" And Mum was pissed and Dad tried to get involved and Mum gave Dad a smack right across the face. Dad was so upset, Lauren was screaming, apparently I was crying, and she was pushing Dad, telling him she wished she'd married someone else. I just feel for Dad. He's such a good person and she speaks to him like shit, always having a go at him, blaming him for everything that goes wrong in her sad life.'

I couldn't believe this had all happened after we'd left the birthday party. And being horrible to Tim didn't sound like the Helen I knew at all. I wondered if perhaps Kate was adding her own drama, as teens sometimes do, but if it was bad enough to upset Kate like this, then that was a worry. I found it hard to believe that Helen had this other life, yet after what she'd said about her unhappy marriage, a picture was forming – but I wasn't sure I wanted to see it.

I made more coffee and suggested we finish off the brownies. 'I think we need all the sugar we can get at the moment,' I said, bringing two fresh mugs to the table. 'I made the brownies for Sam,' I said with a sigh, taking a bite of the fudgy chocolate cake. 'I was hoping against hope he'd get bail and be home, but...' I wasn't sure how much Tim had told Kate or Helen, so I didn't elaborate.

'I heard they'd found a jumper with Lauren's blood?' she said. 'I heard Mum and Dad talking about it.'

So, Kate listening at doors was working for her then?

'Yes, but it doesn't mean anything. There are other things that point to other people,' I said vaguely.

She looked at me like she was about to say something, then turned quite pink. Her face was glowing, and despite being something of an enigma, I'd known Kate since she was born, and there was something she wanted to tell me.

'What is it?' I asked.

'Nothing.'

'Kate, do you know something?'

Along with Tim, Kate had seemed to be on my side where Sam's innocence was concerned, but she'd clammed up now.

'He didn't do it, Kate,' I said.

Suddenly her head shot up and she snapped, 'I bloody know he didn't and I've got a good idea who did.'

I had to catch my breath. 'Who, Kate? Please tell me.'

For a moment, she seemed to have second thoughts. I held my breath, waiting, not wanting to push too hard.

'Sadie,' she hissed.

I had to be careful what I said. As much as I wanted to share my theories with Kate, I didn't want her repeating anything I'd said, not until I was absolutely sure.

She continued, 'I told you. She has the hots for Sam, she was jealous of Lauren. I wouldn't trust her one millimetre.'

I deflated slightly. So that was it? The same story about Sadie being in love with Sam wouldn't get him off a murder charge, even if it was true – in fact it might even make things worse. Kate didn't like Sadie and that was probably all there was to her accusation. For a moment, I really thought she might have had something to share, but it was just grief, jealousy even.

'Mmm, I know Sadie's not an easy girl to like, but Sam says they're just good friends—'

'Georgie – she was crying at Lauren's *wedding*.'

I almost smiled at this. 'I think we *all* were, love. She was probably crying happy tears?' I suggested, though in truth I doubted Sadie could do 'happy' anything, but it was hardly damning evidence.

But Kate was shaking her head. 'Nah, she was jealous. I heard her telling one of the bridesmaids it wouldn't last, and then later she was crying and leaning on Sam.'

'*Leaning* on him, you mean at the reception?' I asked, thinking perhaps Kate had seen them dancing and was trying to make more of it.

'No. After the wedding, the photographer was asking for the groom, and no one could find him, so Lauren asked me to look for him. She was such a bridezilla,' she rolled her eyes.

'So did you find him?' I pressed.

'Yeah, I found him all right.' She pursed her lips, and I was reminded of Helen when she gossiped about someone.

I was beginning to feel a little unsettled, did I really want to hear this? Was it just going to make Sam look worse? I took a breath. 'And when you found him, what was he *doing*?'

'They were hiding round the back of the church, they didn't see me at first, so they kept talking. Sadie was crying and kept saying, "I can't bear this, I can't go through with it – I don't know why I even agreed to it."'

'What was Sam saying?'

'He kept telling her it would all be okay.' She paused. 'And he just kept stroking her hair.'

CHAPTER TWENTY-NINE

The picture Kate painted of Sam behind the church, stroking Sadie's hair on his wedding day, was an image I couldn't erase. I told myself it was probably innocent, but something about it made my skin prickle – the idea of them being caught up in what seemed quite an intimate conversation, while Lauren, married only minutes, searched for her groom. It felt so wrong, and even when Kate and I moved on to other subjects, I kept going over it.

It would all be okay, Sam had apparently said to Sadie. *What* would be okay? And why was he stroking his bride's best friend's hair?

I was aware that Kate didn't like Sadie and may have an axe to grind, so tried to take some of what she'd said with a pinch of salt, but I needed to speak to Sam so I could ask him outright about this, and only then would my mind be calmed. I was sure there must be an innocent explanation, but for the life of me, I couldn't think what that might be.

Kate seemed desperate to talk, about everything and nothing. I guessed it must have been lonely in that house with her parents, so I just listened. But from time to time, my mind wandered off, and I'd go back to the constant ache gnawing away at me – my son's predicament. I thought about the way Sadie looked at Lauren on her wedding day. At the time, I'd thought it was an admiring, proud, sideways look at her best friend in her bridal veil, but now I wondered, was it *Sam* she'd been looking at with admiring eyes?

I cast my mind back to the day and recalled a brief conversation with Sadie outside the church in her blush pink bridesmaid dress. 'I hate weddings,' she'd announced, cigarette in hand, blowing smoke up into the fresh air, 'I'm always the bloody bridesmaid.'

I'd thought it was just a throwaway comment but maybe it was something more?

When Kate paused in telling me about some girl in her sixth form that she hated, I stepped in. 'I always felt that Sadie had some kind of hold over Lauren,' I murmured, aware I was saying far more than I should to her younger sister, but I wondered if Kate could shed any light.

'I never really understood why Lauren put up with her,' she said. 'I mean they were always falling out. Lauren was always hating on her, and I asked her why she stayed friends with her because if I had a friend like Sadie I'd dump her straight away.'

'And did Lauren say why she stayed friends?' I asked.

She said she'd promised Mum and Dad she'd be nice to her, Kate shrugged. 'I wouldn't be friends with someone I didn't like just because Mum and Dad told me to.'

'No,' I muttered. 'I wouldn't have thought Lauren would either.' She was as headstrong and stubborn as her little sister, she just did it with more charm.

'After Lauren got married, even Mum started bitching about Sadie being round there. She was always hanging out at the cottage. I heard Mum on the phone saying, "It's not healthy, Lauren – your husband calling your best friend 'wife number two' isn't funny."'

'It was a joke though, right?' I asked.

'Yeah, I guess. But Lauren had told Mum Sam was getting up in her grill about working late and Lauren was saying, "He's got Sadie for company." Mum didn't like that.'

'I can see why your mum thought this might be a bit inappropriate,' I offered.

'Yes, totally. I wouldn't let my best friend hang out with my husband while I was at work, especially if he was as cute as Sam,' she flushed slightly. 'Lauren worked too hard and too long...' She gave me a sidelong look, and my antennae picked something up.

'What?'

'Nothing.'

'If there's anything, *anything* you can remember, Kate, it could make all the difference. And it would mean the world to Sam,' I said.

'It was just something that happened a couple of days before she died,' she started. 'I didn't think it was important, but...'

'Tell me.'

'Well, I'd borrowed Mum's car and went round there to see her. I knocked on the door, but she didn't answer, so I went round the back and slid in through the French windows, they never locked them.'

'Oh. Really?' I made a mental note.

'Yeah. Anyway, Lauren was on the phone when I got inside, she hadn't even noticed me come in. She was saying, "Yes, of course I'm ashamed, and I'll do what I need to do. You can't just call me up and start telling me what to do. I don't *love* you, you're nothing to me... I hate you." Then she said something like, "You've ruined my life..." I can't remember the conversation exactly.' But it sounded pretty word-perfect to me, it seemed to me that all of the practice Kate seemed to have of listening to other people's conversations at the top of stairs and behind closed doors had paid off. 'She had him on speaker, so I could hear him quite clearly, and he said, "Let's stop this now, it's already gone too far."'

I could barely take this in. Is *that* why Lauren had second thoughts about the wedding, because she'd been seeing someone else? Was it the aftermath of the break-up that Kate heard? And where did Sadie fit into all this, because, as I was beginning to discover, she was never too far away from trouble?

I sighed, deeply. This wasn't good, and though it might provide another suspect in the man Lauren was seeing, if any of *this* was said in court, it would be the end of Sam. To anyone other than me, it gave Sam a very good reason to be angry and hurt and everyone would be thinking, what if they'd argued at the top of the stairs... *and Sam pushed her?*

'Lauren didn't even know I was there!' Kate continued. 'And after she'd turned her phone off, she stood there staring ahead, all creepy-like, so I tapped her on the shoulder and she screamed SO loud.' She laughed at the memory. Kate was very young for her age, too young to really grasp what might have been going on in Lauren's head and heart at that moment.

As worrying as all this information was, if handled sensitively, it had a potential silver lining for Sam. If Lauren *was* seeing someone, then *he* might well be 'someone of interest' to the police?

'So, when Lauren came off the phone, did you ask her who she'd been talking to?'

'Yeah, course I did, but she lied; she said it was Sadie, but I'd heard a man's voice, so when she left her phone on the side to go to the bathroom, I checked out her recent calls.'

'You could get into her phone?' I was taken aback by Kate's seeming lack of boundaries with her sister.

'Yeah, course.' She scowled, like I was crazy to even question this. 'I knew her passcode, it was always something lame. Anyway, on her recent calls there was a number with no name, but I didn't see it all before she came back.'

'Have you told the police any of this?'

'No, I don't want to drop some innocent guy in it and break Mum and Dad's... or Sam's heart. I mean, looks like she'd had a fling, he was ending it and she was saying, "Yeah, okay, I'm married now so let's not."'

'*Still* it might be significant to the police?' I offered, wondering now if Sam had known about this? I thought about what he'd said in our phone call, that he'd wanted to respect Lauren's memory but if he had to use information to stay out of prison, he would. Was this 'information' what he couldn't tell me?

Kate shrugged. 'Everyone saw Lauren as this golden girl who never did anything wrong, but she was no angel.' She scowled again. 'When we were younger, she was always getting me into trouble. She stole a load of Mum's wine and gin from the kitchen and her and Sadie went off in her car onto the moors to drink it, and when Mum saw it was missing, Lauren told her I'd smashed the bottles when she was out, and she'd had to clear them up!' The injustice at this was still clear on her face, and as difficult as it was to reconcile this image of Lauren as a deceitful, cunning girl with the one that I'd known, I was beginning to wonder if I'd ever known any of the Jacksons. Even Kate, who I'd always seen as surly and monosyllabic seemed like a different person chatting away openly. 'Then, another time, Mum and Dad went out for the night and Sadie and Lauren had these boys over and they drank loads. Then, when I was asleep, they put the empty bottles in my wardrobe. Mum found them a few days later and went mad. I didn't even know they were there. I told them it was Lauren, but she denied it all and Mum and Dad believed her. They always believed Lauren over me.' She glowered at the memory.

As a younger sibling myself, I understood how she felt. But I did feel that perhaps she played the 'poor little sister' trope too well. She often played the victim, and even when they were younger, Kate would always make a huge fuss, crying at the slightest thing. And she hated to be left out, which she usually was.

'I'm sure she did some mean things to her baby sister, and it's no excuse, but that's what siblings do.'

'I guess, but sometimes I thought she was worse than Sadie.' She frowned and I remembered the cross little girl standing by the paddling pool, because Lauren and Sadie wouldn't let her in. I'd envied Helen and Tim their second child, wished I had the opportunity to go once more round the baby block, but Kate and Lauren didn't get along. She was intelligent, free-spirited and pretty like her big sister. But she lacked Lauren's charm and humour and she seemed permanently angry at someone or something. 'She stirs the pot that one,' Helen had once said, laughing about her youngest daughter's talent for causing trouble. I guessed perhaps she'd coloured things she'd seen and heard more vividly, for the attention she so desperately craved.

It was about 7 p.m. by the time we'd finished talking, and I walked her home. I didn't want her heading back in the dark and I also needed the cold night air to clear my head. I didn't go inside the house with her, as I would usually have done. Instead, we said goodbye at the gate and I cleared off quickly. I didn't want another encounter with Helen.

CHAPTER THIRTY

Once home, I called James to tell him I was worried and he immediately offered to come round. When I opened the door, he had with him a big bunch of flowers and a bottle of wine.

'Thought you might need cheering up,' he said, 'you sounded upset on the phone.'

'I've never been more happy to see you,' I said, hugging him in the doorway. 'James, I didn't think things could get any worse, but I've had a horrible day.'

He put down the wine and flowers and, holding my face in both his hands, looked at me, his eyes taking me in, and I felt a real connection.

'So tell me all about your horrible day,' James said, putting his arm around me and guiding me to the sofa.

'Where do I start? Helen is convinced Sam is guilty, Kate told me she'd overheard Lauren talking to some guy, sounds like she was cheating on Sam, which might be good or bad news, but the way things are going—'

'Georgie, Georgie,' he said softly, taking his arm from around my shoulder, 'I understand, this is all very upsetting, but you're torturing yourself. You can't take on *everything*. You have to trust in the police, they know what they're doing. I bet you haven't eaten all day, have you?' James was saying now, presumably trying to avoid a difficult conversation.

'No,' I said, realising I'd only eaten chocolate brownies when Kate came round earlier.

'Okay, well, why don't I go and get us a curry? You decide what you'd like, I'll phone the order through and I'll pick it up, there's a takeaway just a few minutes away, isn't there?'

'Yes, thanks, that would be nice,' I said, knowing this would make me feel slightly better. It wouldn't resolve any problems, but a chicken tikka masala with pilau rice would certainly make me feel more ready to tackle them.

James made the phone order, and as he did, I glanced over at him and thought how considerate and kind he was. I really appreciated the fact he was arranging dinner, because being single it was rare for someone to think of my welfare. No one ever said, 'Have you eaten?' or 'How was your day?' And this simple gesture had helped to erase some of the darkness, it gave me hope and the twists and turns in my head loosened. Little did I know, this was only a temporary reprieve, because just around the corner, something far darker was waiting.

'You're still worrying, aren't you?' James said, as he put down the phone from the takeaway.

'Yes,' I said with a smile, 'he's my baby, I won't be me again until he's home.'

'I understand, I don't have children myself, but I can imagine how all-encompassing they are to a parent.'

'Yes, it's true. I've given my life for Sam, from being a screaming ball of mucus, to a stroppy, selfish teenager who could barely acknowledge me. And now, I'd give my life for him. There's no one else in the world who I'd do that for, I just love him unconditionally.'

'I know it's not the same, but I've felt a degree of that sometimes for my students – I've worried about them, tried to guide them, and no, I wouldn't give my life for them – but it's a *kind* of love.'

I softened at this. Our relationship was becoming about me and my feelings because of everything that happened, and I needed to acknowledge his feelings more. 'Of course, of course you would care, I can see that.'

He shrugged. 'It's been a heavy day for you, let's lighten the mood, open that wine, and I'll go and get the curry.' He kissed me, and then stood up, putting his jacket on.

'Yes, hurry up back with that curry,' I urged with a smile as he set off down the hall. I felt the draught as he opened the front door, and I was suddenly plunged back into silence and the relentless cycle of Sam and Sadie, and Lauren and her mystery caller still going around my head.

James had only been gone a few minutes when a text pinged, making me jump.

It was from Tim, asking if I'd give him a call. I hadn't heard from him for a few days so was pleased he was in touch. He might have news, so I immediately called him back, but it was engaged. I tried again, and again. Then I waited, perhaps he was trying to get through to me? I had a lot to tell him, but mostly I wanted to discuss the phone call Kate overheard. I know she didn't want her parents upset, but we were beyond that, and while I waited for Tim, I decided to text Kate. There was something I'd been thinking about.

> *Hey Kate. So good to chat this afternoon, hope you're OK, love. Just wanted to ask, you said you saw some of the digits of the phone number from Lauren's call. It's a long shot, I know, but can you remember them?*

I sent it and tried Tim again, still engaged. I knew asking Kate for the number was a bit naughty, especially as I was going to tell Tim, and I did feel bad, but if I could get the numbers to Tim, he might be able to trace it.

I called Tim again, and this time he answered.

'Tim, hi, got your message to call you?'

'They've found new evidence, Georgie,' he said without

preamble.

I put my head back onto the sofa. 'What?' I heard myself whisper.

'Well, it's too soon to say, but me and some of the team were at the cottage earlier this week – I basically invited myself along – and some of the stuff we sent to the lab has come back with unknown fingerprints.'

I caught my breath. 'What?' I clutched the phone like my life depended on it. 'What does unknown mean, Tim?'

There was a slight pause and then: 'It means... they aren't Sam's.'

A wave of relief crashed over me, dare I hope?

'So an intruder?'

'Mmm, not exactly. But it's good news for Sam because it means someone else had been at the cottage, we just need to match up the prints.'

'Oh God. Does this mean Sam's going to be released, can he come home?' In that moment, it was all I cared about.

'Hopefully, but we just haven't worked out the details yet, and Sam isn't home and dry. We still need to establish why there's blood on his jumper, and once we do that we can arrest the bastard who did this. I just wanted to let you know.'

'Oh, Tim, I'm so grateful. Thank you.' I paused. 'Can you find out who else was there from the fingerprints, even if it was a random stranger?'

There was silence for a few seconds, I heard him take a breath, and what he said next gave me chills: 'I can't say too much at the moment. But it wasn't random, and it wasn't a stranger.'

CHAPTER THIRTY-ONE

I clutched the phone long after Tim had hung up. I was both elated and horrified. Sam could be free, but at the same time, it sounded like whoever killed Lauren had meant for this to happen. 'It wasn't random, and it wasn't a stranger,' Tim had said, which opened up so many horrible possibilities I didn't even want to think about. I fleetingly wondered if I might know the non-stranger, but what mattered was that Tim *had* believed me after all, and he'd believed in Sam. And as a result of Tim's faith he'd searched for the real culprit, he hadn't let us down and now my son would be free. We owed him such a lot, and my only regret was that his wife, my best friend, hadn't shared his faith.

I couldn't wait to tell James, I felt so happy I couldn't hide it – he'd know as soon as he walked in the house, that everything had changed.

I virtually skipped into the kitchen to get the plates and crockery ready for James' return.

'I got extra poppadoms,' he was saying, ten minutes later, as he walked into the kitchen where I was waiting. He stopped. 'Has something happened?'

I nodded vigorously. 'Tim called, I shouldn't really say anything yet – but they've found fingerprints at the cottage – and they're not Sam's. I think it could be the man Lauren was seeing.'

'Well, let's keep our fingers crossed.' He started taking the lids off the food.

I felt a little deflated, I hadn't expected him to be as delighted as I was, but still, I was surprised at James' rather lacklustre response. He was now dishing up bloody tikka masala and talking about how busy it was in the takeaway. But nothing was going to dampen my sparkle of hope, so I opened the wine and set the cutlery out on the kitchen table. Then I popped back into the sitting room for my phone, in case Tim rang again.

'Would you like a chapatti?' James was saying as I walked back into the kitchen.

'Yeah, that would be nice,' I replied, just as my phone pinged – a text. Desperately hoping it was Tim, I glanced down to see Kate's name. She was responding to my earlier text about the phone number she'd seen on Lauren's phone, which, I'd rather forgotten about. I wasn't sure how much use it was now the police knew who it was, but still.

Hey Georgie, thanks for the brownies they were sick! The number was 07256051. I put it in my phone, but nothing came up, so it's no one I know. Not sure how much use it is with the last 3 digits missing. LOL x

I sat down at the table, tore at a piece of chapatti and started eating the curry. I was starving, and it was delicious, but then I started to think about the number. If the police had fingerprints or DNA from someone, and they needed further proof, three-quarters of a phone number might just be what got Sam out of prison.

'Did you hear a word I said?' James suddenly said.

I looked up, almost surprised to see him there. 'I'm so sorry, James, I was just thinking.'

He smiled sympathetically and briefly abandoned his curry to cover my hand with his. 'It's okay. I was saying, would you like me to stay over tonight?'

'Yeah, I'd like that.' I smiled. As he started talking again, I went back to Kate's message. She had said the phone number wasn't anyone's she knew, but it might be worth checking it against the directory on *my* phone. I'd almost ignored James throughout this meal, but I was desperate to check the number. Not wanting to offend him, I slid the phone in my jeans pocket and said I was just popping to the bathroom.

Once inside, I locked the door and started to put the number into my phone contacts list. The first two digits were apparently common, several of my friends' numbers started with those, but as I put more in, the names disappeared.

I was left with just one.

Even without the last three digits, it was clear I knew this person. I wanted to be sick.

The number belonged to James.

CHAPTER THIRTY-TWO

My whole body tingled with fear. I couldn't believe what I was seeing on my phone. Was it *James* that Lauren had been talking to when Kate overheard? Was it *James* ending their relationship when Lauren was married? I couldn't believe it. *No, it's not fair on her, and I have to think about Sam, it's not fair on him either...* I'd just started to see James before Lauren died, and when she said that it wasn't fair on her or him, were they talking about me and Sam?

But that couldn't be true. I found it so hard to believe, my head was hurting as I tried desperately to put a different spin on it. James had been her teacher, and the only time she was in touch with him had been about her career talks at the school. Was that what they'd been talking about? I reminded myself that this whole conversation was Kate's retelling, Kate's interpretation, but still, the words seemed like that shorthand intimacy one uses with a friend or a lover. How could the stuff about it not being fair and '*We should never have let it happen*' be applied in any way to school career talks? No, the phone conversation Kate heard *couldn't* be misconstrued. It seemed none of us had seen it, but apparently this relationship had been staring us all in the face.

I thought back to less than an hour ago, when James had sat on my sofa, his arm around me, saying he'd felt *a kind of love* for his students. I shuddered.

Just *when* had this started? Was it when James was Lauren's teacher and she was his teenage pupil?

I sat there on the toilet lid, clutching my phone. *What should I do?*

So many things were going through my head, I had to hold on to the sink to steady myself. Was James the one who had pushed Lauren down the stairs that night? If it wasn't him, then in the many, many conversations we'd had about Lauren's murder – why had he not mentioned calling her, just days before her death, and having a heart-to-heart? If it was innocent, he'd have told me about it, but, of course, it wasn't – how could it be? Even his visit to Sadie's which he'd passed off as helping her with a university application seemed a bit suspect now.

I walked slowly back into the kitchen, and the world had changed. I turned on the tap for water, filled a glass and stood with my back to him. Eventually, I found the courage to turn around. He was tearing at a chapatti, blissfully unaware that we were now in a very different place. I glared down at him and he looked up at me with such softness in his eyes, that, for a moment, I doubted he was capable of anything bad. His smile was so open, so *genuine*. But I was the one who'd also believed Helen and Tim had the perfect marriage, that Sam and Lauren were blissfully happy. My judgement was clearly rubbish.

'Yours will be cold if you don't eat it,' he said, nodding towards the plate of congealed curry I'd left a few lifetimes ago. The very thought of it made me feel sick now, as I sat down gingerly on the edge of my chair.

I had to get rid of him. 'I... I was thinking, I need to get up early tomorrow, probably best you don't stay tonight.'

He stopped eating, looked at me, slightly puzzled, his head to one side.

'So much work to do. I've been putting it off...'

He seemed disappointed, but nodded and went back to his

curry. 'Okay, if you'd rather I didn't,' he said, now dipping his chapatti in tikka masala and taking a large bite. 'You're okay, aren't you?' he asked.

I nodded. 'It's just been a tough week.'

He smiled. 'Tell me about it.' He stopped eating a moment and paused. 'You know, I'm often conflicted about my role as a teacher. My subjects are so young, so *innocent*,' his eyes seemed to light up at this, 'and I tell them what to think, how to *feel*. As teachers we have this huge responsibility shaping young minds.' He gave a little laugh, and wiped his hands on a napkin. 'Scary, isn't it?' he said, looking up from his plate.

I nodded, it *was* scary. I couldn't bring myself to look at him, and had to keep my hands on the table, because they were starting to shake. My mind was sifting through what I'd just discovered, had James shaped Lauren's young mind and started something with her when she was still at school? Or was this something that began when she went back, as a junior doctor, to give career talks to his class?

'Such a responsibility,' he was saying, 'but I *love* those kids.' He nodded and went back to his curry.

I swallowed hard, unable now to eat anything. I pushed my plate away.

'You not finishing that?' he asked, amazed.

I shook my head. 'I don't feel great to be honest.'

'I'm sorry, is there anything I can get you?'

I shook my head. *No, just go!* I thought. Had this man sitting here at my table, who I'd been sleeping with, been sleeping with my daughter-in-law? But, worse than that, had he killed her?

'You're very pale,' he said, abandoning what was left on his plate and reaching over, his palm coming towards my face. I flinched. 'Whoa, Georgie.' He looked at me questioningly, then laughed. 'I was just going to check your temperature?'

'Oh no, no, I'm okay, just tired.'

'Let me make you a nice cup of tea,' he offered, and I nodded, glad I'd only taken a couple of sips of wine, aware that any moment, I may need to run or drive.

My plan was to keep everything as normal as possible, not alert him to anything. All I had to do was drink the bloody tea, get him out of the house, lock all the doors, and call Tim.

James began to fill the kettle, talking now about next summer and how we could perhaps go to a Greek island. 'Imagine – just you and me, away from everything and everyone, somewhere warm. I wish we were there now,' he said with a sigh, as he opened the cupboard looking for teabags.

I wished *he* was there too. I couldn't just sit there, I wanted to scream and run, but got up and carried my plate to the sink, wondering if I could make a run for it. Just then, my phone started buzzing. I was so jumpy, I dropped the plate, and watched helplessly as it crashed to the floor, throwing white splinters everywhere.

'Shit,' I said, pulling out my phone and seeing Tim's name.

'You've got no slippers on, you'll cut your feet to ribbons,' James was saying as I picked up. 'Go into the living room, I'll clear it up.'

'Thanks,' I said, and then answered, 'Hi there,' brightly into the phone, for James' benefit.

I walked into the sitting room and pushed the door slightly with my foot to close it. James was running water and singing to himself, so hopefully couldn't hear me.

'Tim, Tim—' I started.

'Georgie, it's all systems go, Sam's good – the real perpetrator is about to be arrested.'

'Who is it?' I hissed down the phone.

'I can't say, love.'

'Would I know him?'

'Yeah, yeah, you do,' he said, in a quiet voice, presumably he was with colleagues.

'Oh God, Tim, you have to tell me,' I said. 'I've been through so much, I have to know.' My heart was thumping so loudly, I thought James might be able to hear it in the kitchen.

'Well, I shouldn't really, you'll know soon enough.' He paused. 'It's James Ronson.'

Even though I'd half expected this, it was still a body blow. I almost threw up on the carpet. 'Oh God, he's here now!'

'What, at your *house*?'

'Yess!' I hissed.

'Shit. I didn't realise you and he were still—'

'Yeah, we are... *were*.' I was so frightened I could barely speak. The man who'd murdered Lauren was in my home and we were alone.

'Hang on. We're on our way to his house, but I'm redirecting.' I heard Tim talk urgently into his radio, then he came back to me. 'Georgie, are you still there?'

'Yes?'

'We're on our way,' he yelled, 'stay on the line if you can, try not to engage with him – trust me, Georgie, you can't negotiate with someone like Ronson. He's *extremely* dangerous.'

My whole body stiffened, I had visions of myself at the bottom of my *own* stairs.

'I think I know why he did it,' I whispered. 'I'm sorry, Tim, but I think he might have been sleeping with Lauren.' I thought about the pregnancy but couldn't bring myself to say anything.

'Christ! No.' Tim sounded like he might cry. I almost wished I hadn't blurted this out, but the police had to know as soon as possible

'He isn't the man we all thought he was, Tim, he—' I stopped talking, suddenly aware that everything had gone quiet. No running water, and James had stopped singing. I felt a movement and knew he was now standing behind me. I turned round slowly, and he was standing there, glaring at me.

'What's going on, Georgie?'

Still gripping my phone, I took it away from my ear, Tim was talking, but I couldn't hear what he was saying. Pins and needles were shooting through me. I was terrified.

'Georgie, what were you saying about me?' His face looked different, *he* looked different – bigger, fiercer. 'I don't understand, I thought you liked me,' he was saying, as he moved closer.

I backed away, clasping my phone with one hand, holding the other one out to keep him back, but it was little defence if he lunged at me.

'Georgie, it's *me*,' he was trying to say this gently, but the fear and anger bubbling in his voice betrayed him.

I nodded. 'I know it is, I know it's you – and I don't want you to come a step nearer.'

He stopped immediately, his face now a study in confusion.

'Tim's on the phone,' I said, 'and the police are on their way.'

He gasped. 'Oh, Georgie, what have you done...?'

'I know about your affair with Lauren and the police have found your DNA at the cottage. You've been found out, James. All the sneaking around playing the kind teacher—'

He tried to look shocked. 'I don't know what you're talking about.'

'Yes, you do. I know you called Lauren just before she died to break it off. Even she admitted she was ashamed, and said you'd ruined her life.'

'That isn't how it sounds...' he started, so I waited for an explanation, but he couldn't give me one.

'Then there was your intimate little evening coffee stop at Sadie's, were you hoping she could take over where Lauren left—'

'What?' Now he feigned surprise.

But I kept going. 'Why did you kill Lauren? Had she become difficult when you wanted to end things, was she threatening to tell on you? Was she just too old for you, James, I guess you like them young – and still in school!'

'How could you say such vile things? I really liked you, Georgie, I thought we had something...'

I was about to say more, but just at that moment, the police came crashing through the front door, with Tim leading the way. He and three other officers grabbed him and read him his rights. As the others took him away, Tim stayed behind to comfort me.

'I can't tell you how grateful I am for what you did,' I said, clinging on to him as he hugged me close.

'As they say in the films, I was just doing my job,' he said with a faint laugh. 'I'd have got there sooner if they'd let me, but rules are rules, and the powers that be were a bit...' he waggled his hands, 'a bit iffy about me getting involved.'

'But if you hadn't... no one would have done anything, they'd have let Sam rot in that prison. You were the only one who believed in him. Everyone else seemed so convinced it was Sam.'

'Yeah, but that was too easy, too *lazy*, to pin it on the husband. So, I had to talk to my mate, Tony, who was leading the case, and he let me in on it. I worked on it by proxy if you like,' he said with a smile. 'I pointed him in the right direction.'

'I'm so shocked to realise how little I knew James,' I mumbled.

'Yeah, he's a mate of mine too and I never in a million years thought it possible. But I also knew Sam wasn't capable. I told Tony that Sam didn't do it. Told him I'd put my life on it. I knew all I needed was to go back to the cottage, take a forensic with me, and do another sweep. I was convinced we'd find *something*.'

I'd be forever grateful to Tim, but now I just wanted to know one thing: 'When will Sam be free?'

Tim looked at his watch. 'I have it on good authority that he's down the station now, filling in forms and being released. Come on, Georgie, I've come in my cop car, I'll drive you there in style,' he said with a big, beaming smile.

While I grabbed my coat, Tim arranged for an officer to stay at the house and keep guard until I got back, as the front door had been smashed open when the police arrived.

'Sorry about that,' he said, gesturing at the smashed glass with his thumb as I followed him out to the waiting police car.

'That's nothing,' I said with a smile, 'who cares about smashed glass when you saved my life, and got Sam out of prison. It's a small price to pay,' I added, buckling myself in the police car. 'Apart from the night Sam was born, this is the happiest night of my life.'

Tim smiled. 'Ahh, Georgie, I'm as happy as you are. You know he's like a son to me. I'd never have let it get as far as court.' He started the car. 'Let's go get our boy.'

CHAPTER THIRTY-THREE

'I still can't believe it,' Sam said, when we finally arrived home the next day, 'not James, not Mr Ronson.'

'I know, it's hard to take in,' I said, my happiness at Sam's return slightly tainted by the discovery about James. I'd been asked to go down to the station that morning to give a statement; I told them everything I knew about James. It gave me no pleasure to be proven right over Sam, because just hearing myself answering their questions about James made me realise how stupid I'd been not to see the red flags. I still had questions for Sam too and needed to clear my head of all the rubble I'd accumulated these past few weeks.

'Sam, you know when we spoke on the phone, and you said there were things you knew, things you didn't want to tell me. What were they?'

He took a breath. 'Oh nothing important. It was about Lauren, but I don't really want to talk at the moment.'

I was desperate to know, but couldn't press him, he'd been through enough, losing his wife and then being accused of killing her and spending too long in prison. 'Okay, but if you want to talk, I'm here,' I said. I assumed it was about Lauren's affair with James, he must have found out she'd been seeing someone but at the time didn't know who. And, quite understandably, he was now feeling very raw and didn't want to dwell on it, which was how Sam dealt with pain. He kept it all inside, and wasn't a great talker.

'I... thanks, Mum – for everything,' he suddenly said.

'It's my job,' I said. 'But, to be honest, in the end, Tim was the one who pulled off a miracle.'

'Yeah, I knew all along that Tim wouldn't let me down.'

'You were right. The original investigation just wanted to pin it on the most obvious suspect, but he wasn't going to allow them to do that. He ordered a second forensic examination and basically it was his faith in you that urged him on.'

'Yeah, I owe him big time. But you were pushing too, harassing the police.' He laughed.

I smiled. 'I'm just glad you're home, love. And now Tim and I can say "we told you so" to Helen and everyone else who thought you'd done it.'

'Sadie believed in me too,' he said, which I admit made my heart sink slightly.

'Yes, yes, she did,' I conceded, reluctantly. She might have been off the hook for Lauren's murder, but I still found her difficult to like as a person simply by the way she behaved, scrounging off the Jacksons and not being the friend she should have been to Lauren. And I still hadn't forgiven her for the theft of the mugs and for staining Lauren's wedding dress then being so sneaky about getting it cleaned. I just hoped she'd give Sam some space now to move on, but just a few hours later she was on the doorstep holding a *Welcome Home* balloon! I couldn't bring myself to look at the bloody cake she produced with *You're Free!* plastered across in thick blue icing.

'James hasn't been charged yet,' I reminded her, 'so it's a bit soon to be celebrating.'

'I'm glad he's locked up, the creep.' She addressed Sam, ignoring me.

I couldn't help but show my disapproval. As far as I was concerned, her rather buoyant cheerleading wasn't just out of character, but also unfitting. Lauren had been murdered by her old teacher, who had also possibly had an inappropriate relationship with her. In my book, this was hardly a cause for celebration, and I couldn't bring myself to join in, so didn't hang around in her company. And while she made herself very comfy on the sofa with Sam, I went upstairs and watched TV in my bedroom. I couldn't concentrate on anything on screen though as I could hear her laughter downstairs, it made me feel really uncomfortable.

'Just don't get too close, Sam,' I said, after she'd gone.

'What do you mean?' he asked, all innocence.

'You know *exactly* what I mean. I reckon Sadie's got a soft spot for you and I'm sure she'd love to take it further, so don't lead her on. Besides, you're only just out of the woods, let's have a drama-free time for now, eh?'

'You're the one who's being dramatic; no one cares who I hang around with,' he shot back.

'Well, for a start, the Jacksons do, not to mention the police. If they can't actually pin this on James and charge him, they might come back to you.' I wasn't sure this was the case, but until James was firmly behind bars, I couldn't relax.

The only good thing to come out of Sadie's friendship with Sam and Lauren was that she was able to address and eliminate the one solid piece of evidence that the police seemed unable to get over. Lauren's blood on Sam's jumper. Sadie had, in all the horror, apparently forgotten, but she and Lauren had been for a walk together across the moors the day before she died, and Lauren had worn Sam's jumper. They'd gone quite high up and Lauren had a nosebleed, which had stained the jumper. Fortunately, Sadie had taken a selfie of her and Lauren on the day. They were walking through the mist, and even in the photo the red stain was clear to see. Plus, the picture was already on Instagram, so no one could doubt the timeline.

By the second day after his release, Sam was chomping at the bit to get to the cottage.

'I'm going to have a drive out there,' he said over dinner. 'I need to check that everything's okay, I'll go tomorrow.'

'But I thought you'd asked Sadie to go over and check, she's only down the road from there?'

'She did, but I just want to see it myself, you know?'

'Would you like me to come along *too*?' I didn't ever want to go back there, but if Sam wanted some support I'd go with him.

'No,' he said, almost too quickly. 'I just want to go there on my own, and—'

'Get back to who you were, the Sam you used to be?' I offered.

He smiled. 'Yeah, something like that.'

'Okay, love, whatever makes you happy,' I said.

He put his arm around me. Since his time in prison I think he'd come to appreciate what he had, even though he'd lost a huge part of his life when Lauren died. 'What about *you*, Mum? What would make you happy?'

'I am happy, because you're home. I wish Lauren was here too, but after what we've been through, I'll take this.'

He stopped eating, put his fork on the side of his plate. 'I haven't really liked to ask you, but how do you feel – about the James thing?'

I sighed. 'I feel stupid for being so taken in by him but also a bit fearful thinking how it could have ended? Other than that, I'm hurt, humiliated, angry, betrayed – call me superficial, but I'm also *embarrassed*!'

'Sorry, Mum, I feel like I should have known,' Sam said apologetically.

'God, you weren't to know, I didn't have a clue. I've been rather naïve, taking people at face value, believing what they put out there, never questioning...'

'Oh?' Sam looked up, curiously.

'Oh, just Helen, it seems the Jacksons don't have the perfect marriage after all,' I said. 'Did Lauren ever say anything about her parents?'

He shook his head.

'Oh, well I'm sure it will all work out one way or another,' I said vaguely. It wasn't fair of me to reveal that Helen had an affair. It was also a bit near the knuckle – both she and Lauren had been seeing other people during their marriage, and she'd had the cheek to say to me, *the fruit doesn't fall far from the tree*.

'Did Helen ever say anything about James... and Lauren?' Sam was saying, dragging me back from the awful confrontation with Helen.

'No, but...' I looked at him, 'are you okay talking about this?'

'Yes, I want to know, I need to understand what was going on with Lauren.'

'Well, I'm not sure if this is anything, but I remembered that barbecue at your cottage. It was the first time I'd taken James anywhere, and I hadn't had chance to tell Helen I was seeing him. I thought it would be a nice surprise, he was their friend and they liked him, and I was their friend too and...' I paused, remembering the scene. 'But it was really odd, because instead of being pleased to see him, Helen was really off.'

'In what way?'

'It's hard to explain, but she didn't greet me until I'd been there ages, and she was whispering to Lauren, and they both looked really horrified to see him. The atmosphere was quite tense.'

'I had no idea.' Sam shook his head. 'Just the thought of him touching her...'

'I can't help but feel angry towards Helen, she obviously knew something and for some reason kept it between her and Lauren.'

He looked down at the table, nodding slowly. 'Perhaps she was keeping it from Tim. Jesus, he'd have had James for breakfast if he thought for one minute...'

'Yeah, that might be it.' I started to clear the plates away.

'So you think the police have got the right man?' he asked.

'Yes, I do think James killed Lauren, and though we don't know officially why, it looks like there was something between them, and I think he was worried she'd talk.' I stood up, holding the plates and looked at him. 'What do you think? Do you think James did it?'

He didn't answer me, just nodded, and shifted uncomfortably in his seat, pushing the table mat away, as I walked past him with the plates. I can't explain it, but as I glanced back at him, I knew Sam knew something, and I shuddered to think what he might be hiding.

CHAPTER THIRTY-FOUR

The next day, Sam was leaving to go to the cottage when I got a call from Tim. 'Hey, Georgie, I've been meaning to call.'

'What's happening with James?' I asked without preamble.

'I'm off now, but from what I heard, they've applied for an extension, so will be keeping him in for questioning for another thirty-six hours. They'll get him, I just wish I could interview him, I'd pin the bastard down.'

'Thanks, Tim, for everything. Lauren would be proud—' I started.

'I know, I know, but I'm not calling to talk about that,' he said, as usual not wanting to take the credit. 'I'm calling because I thought... well, *Helen* and I thought it was time the Jacksons and the Moores got together. We've been through a lot and we'd like to draw a line through it. Lauren would have wanted us all to stay friends, support each other.'

'You're so right,' I said, a flush of happiness curling in my chest. 'We'd love to see you guys.'

'Okay, us too. So how about tonight – about 7.30?'

I was delighted. This was obviously something orchestrated by Helen, but she'd asked Tim to do the inviting as she was probably feeling bad about not supporting Sam and this was her way of saying sorry. I appreciated that, and knowing Helen, she'd now be cooking and creating a fabulous spread. Without Lauren, it would never be the same as it was, but we could still all be friends.

'Tim and Helen have invited us round tonight,' I said to Sam, who was about to leave to go to the cottage.

'Do we have to?' he asked, standing in the hallway like he couldn't wait to leave.

'Well, I think we should, Tim's been amazing, if it wasn't for him—'

'Yeah, yeah, I know.'

I was surprised by his lack of interest. I put it down to tiredness, but there was something else. 'I think they've invited us because Helen feels guilty that she doubted you. It's her way of saying sorry, and we're still family,' I said.

'It just feels a bit uncomfortable, after *everything*.' He started unlocking the front door.

'It won't once we get there, it'll be lovely to get together,' I said, hoping to God he wasn't going to back out. It wouldn't be the same as it used to be, but it would be the start of the healing process between the two families, and Sam had to be there.

Sam clearly didn't feel the same. 'Okay, I can't promise, but I'll see what time we get back from the cottage.'

'*We?*'

'Yeah, I'll pick Sadie up on my way back from the cottage. I take it she's invited too?'

'Tim didn't say, but I suppose so,' I said, trying not to let my feelings show. I got the impression from Tim this was about the two families bonding again, and I felt it might be easier without any spectators. It was a delicate situation, Sadie could be unpredictable at the best of times, and was bound to say something tactless. She didn't read the room, and if she started flirting with Sam, it could ruin the fragile olive branch that Helen was holding out to us. I'd assumed as Sadie lived miles out and with no Lauren to ferry her around anymore, she wouldn't even consider attending, even if she *had* been invited. But it seemed Sam was her taxi now.

'Just try and be there,' I said to Sam.

He rolled his eyes and let himself out, leaving me to do some much-needed admin work for the charity, while trying not to ponder the many ways Sadie could ruin the evening.

At about 5.30, I noticed the time and decided to get changed. I picked up my phone from the desk and, wandering upstairs, checked for messages, as I always had it on silent when I was working. Someone had tried to call twice, and now there was a voice-mail. I clicked on it and heard James' voice. I turned cold at the sound.

'Georgie, I tried to call, but I guess you aren't answering. It isn't easy to get a call booked here in the remand centre, but you'll know that from when Sam was here. I just wanted to clarify a few things that I'm finding pretty impossible to live with, they just keep rolling around my head.' He gave a little laugh. 'I understand how you felt now, always looking for answers, always playing the detective. The police don't seem to want to hear me, they have some evidence, they have DNA, and of course your witness statement about how I said I love my students. It's since been taken out of context and used to prove that I've spent my whole career as a predator strolling the corridors of secondary schools in search of my young prey.' Another little laugh. 'Of course, it isn't true.'

There was a long silence now. I wondered if he had given up on his message, but then I heard him breathe, he was obviously finding this hard.

'I don't know who killed Lauren, but it wasn't me. I had no reason. If I'm found guilty of murder, I'll go to prison for something I didn't do, and it also makes me fair game for all kinds of sick, twisted accusations regarding the kids I spent my life trying to help.' He hesitated, 'I can't stress enough, nothing happened between me and Lauren, *nothing!*' Then he paused, before adding, 'I'm sorry it ended like this, Georgie – I thought you and me had a future, I really liked you.'

I stood holding my phone as he clicked off, thinking about everything he'd said.

My mind was going backwards and forwards. Perhaps James

wasn't involved in anything inappropriate with his students? Perhaps his relationship with Lauren began after she'd left school, and she was old enough to make her own choices? He'd sounded so plausible, so sad, so genuine, that I almost believed that he was innocent of the murder too. Then I thought about the evidence against James. The phone call between him and Lauren and the new forensic evidence were damning, and I told myself to stop being so bloody naïve, because he did it. I just hoped they'd charge him soon and put us all out of our misery.

CHAPTER THIRTY-FIVE

I was strangely nervous about going over to the Jacksons' that evening. It wasn't helped by Sam; it was half past six and he still wasn't home, with or without Sadie. I held on to the vain hope that Sadie might not be able to come along, that she might have other arrangements. But Sadie never had 'other arrangements', she didn't have any other friends and I reckoned she'd jump at the chance for free food and drinks as usual.

Couldn't Sam see how this would look, turning up with Sadie? Helen was finally prepared to accept that Sam was innocent, but faced with the prospect that Sam was moving on with Lauren's best friend might set off her doubts about his innocence again.

When he wasn't home by seven, and I hadn't heard from him, I decided to go alone. I didn't want to make things worse by being late, so walked the few minutes to Tim and Helen's, telling myself it was going to be like every other evening I'd enjoyed there.

Kate opened the door to me, which was unusual. She was scowling, which wasn't.

'Are you okay, darling?' I asked, hugging her, knowing she probably wasn't okay. The lovely brownies and bonding moment we'd had only days earlier seemed to have gone in a puff of smoke.

'No, I'm not okay,' she snapped. '*She's* here!'

'Who?' I said, taking off the warm parka I'd thrown over my dress.

'*Sadie!*' she hissed.

Just hearing her name set me on edge these days, but I tried not to react.

'Mum's furious,' she continued to hiss at me as I walked down the hall, 'and she's all over Sam.'

I felt a frisson of irritation, and sure enough, as I walked into the room, I was greeted with the sight of Sam and Sadie sitting together chatting on the sofa. Helen was sitting on a chair in the corner, she looked miles away.

'Hi, Mum.' Sam extricated himself from Sadie and wandered over to me.

'I've been waiting for you at home, Sam.'

'Sorry.' He was vaguely apologetic, but seemed agitated, probably something to do with Sadie. 'I called, but you were engaged. I left a message,' he added.

He must have called when I was listening to James' message.

'Is everything okay?' I asked.

'Yeah, why?'

'I mean, at the cottage? That's where you've been all day, isn't it?'

'Oh... yeah, yeah. It's fine.'

He was definitely slightly off, like he wasn't really concentrating, but I didn't have chance to continue the conversation because Helen suddenly seemed to notice me. 'Where the hell have you been, my old mucker?' she slurred.

'I see you're on your throne?' I joked. She was sitting on a pink velvet chair she'd bought a few years before, it cost a fortune, but she loved it, said it was called 'a cocktail chair'. 'When sitting on it you *have* to drink,' she'd joked, and it certainly looked like she'd been fulfilling that requirement.

'Tim, get Georgie a drink,' she yelled at the kitchen, and Tim appeared, walked into the room and hugged me.

'So glad you could come, Georgie, really appreciate it,' he said.

Tim looked tired, I'd hoped that finding Lauren's killer would have given him a lift, but he looked worse than ever.

'You okay?' I asked.

He shrugged. 'Just exhausted, you know?'

'Yeah, yeah, give it a rest, Tim,' Helen shouted over him, 'we don't want to hear it, just get her a drink.'

I felt so sorry for him, he'd done so much and tonight should have been about him, about him finding his daughter's killer and saving Sam. But it looked like Helen had other plans, and wasn't going to let him have that. Tim caught my eye and left the room, immediately returning with a bottle of champagne. 'Only the best for Georgie,' he said, grabbing a flute and pouring a glass. 'Same over there?' he said in Sam and Sadie's direction.

'No thanks,' Sam replied.

I sat down awkwardly, holding the flute. 'I'm not the only one drinking champagne, am I?'

'You're the only one celebrating, if that's what you mean,' Helen said, and laughed at her own private joke.

I sipped guiltily at the champagne.

Within minutes, Helen had decamped from her cocktail chair and was now almost snuggling me on the sofa. She often sat close, especially when she'd had a drink, but what was different tonight was that Sadie seemed to be in Lauren's place – literally, she was sitting so close to Sam, whispering in his ear like a lover – just as I'd feared. Kate was huddled in a corner scrolling on her phone, no doubt taking everything in, and Tim was now apparently preparing 'a feast'.

'I've been in the kitchen in my apron all day, haven't I, Kate?' he said, and she looked up and smiled. It touched me, to see Kate throwing him a lifeline, even in her bad mood, she could see he needed some support; hell, he *deserved* it. Poor Tim, desperately trying to bring us all together, juggling hard to keep it all in the air, pretending everything was fine, while his wife just sat there, refusing to even look at him.

I was beginning to wonder how much of this evening was her

idea – she wasn't engaging at all – except with her glass. Helen was a good cook, and in the past enjoyed being in the kitchen, we all joked about how she was a domestic goddess, but not any more. Tim's cooking was hit and miss, to say the least, but my heart went out to him for trying.

So while Tim did his worst in the kitchen, Kate listened to something on her earphones, and Sadie and Sam continued to whisper to each other. From the corner of my eye, I saw Helen looking over at them disapprovingly and I felt like I had to stick up for Sam. Whatever might be going on with Sadie, he was innocent, someone else had killed Lauren, not my son.

'It's all worked out, hasn't it, the police have the right man now?' I said quietly, I didn't want Sam to hear me talking about it.

'What do you mean?' She looked at me, puzzled.

'Well, it was James.'

She rolled her eyes. 'Oh *that*! Yeah, poor James.'

'Poor S*am*,' I said. 'He could have ended up in prison, serving time for a crime James had committed.'

'He hasn't been charged,' she replied coldly.

'No, but he soon will be. Tim says they have the evidence—'

'Oh Tim says that, does he?' she spat.

I realised I wasn't going to get any sense out of her in the state she was in so abandoned the conversation, and we both sat in silence for a while. I felt so deflated, I'd desperately wanted this to be a new start for us, to try to begin moving forward, but Helen seemed determined not to.

'Lovely, lovely James,' she eventually said with a sigh and began humming to herself. I found this quite alarming and looked around to see if anyone else had noticed, but Sam was busy talking to Sadie and Kate was still apparently absorbed in her phone.

Helen suddenly stopped singing and sat up, her movements jerky. She was so drunk she could barely focus as she took another gulp of gin.

'Are you okay, Helen?'

'YES! Jesus, you sound like Tim. Why am I always surrounded

by sodding Tims!' she slurred, her head wobbly, like it might topple right off. 'Yeah, Georgie – I'm bloody wonderful. I'm far better now I've had a couple of drinks, I LOVE oblivion!' she said loudly, causing the others to finally look up and Tim to pop his head around the door.

He looked frantic, and I attempted to give him a reassuring smile, which seemed to have the required effect, and he gave me a discreet thumbs up and disappeared back to his buffet. In the past few weeks he'd aged so much and I wondered just what he'd had to endure in this house with his wife.

'I drink because it makes everything bearable, and for a little while I can forget life's crushing disappointments,' Helen was saying now, 'where we thought we'd be, and where we *are*, our expectations slammed against the rocks.' On the word slammed, she banged her glass on the coffee table. The contents splashed out, and she laughed like a child.

Sam, Sadie and Kate were now all watching, nonplussed.

'I know things seem insurmountable now, but give it time and —' I started, knowing I was wasting my breath. Perhaps I just kept on using comforting words to soothe myself, because it certainly wasn't improving Helen's mood.

She lifted her shaky hand, almost lunging at me. 'Don't you *dare* tell me time heals, because I've been married for twenty-six years, and *nothing* has healed!'

I closed my eyes; it was hard to see my friend in such pain, Lauren's death had infected everything for her, even the past, her marriage.

'I never knew you were so unhappy,' I said into the silence.

She turned to look at me on that still wobbly head. 'I've always been unhappy – except for four years – four blissful years in my marriage.'

'So you had that once, you can have it again,' I said, desperately clutching at straws.

'You stupid cow,' she hissed in my direction. 'I never had four blissful years with *him*. Old Tim, with his starched shirts and his uniform and his regulation bedtime, he never left the bloody station! No, you silly cow.'

I saw Kate lift her head. She'd already told me about the affair, but I didn't want her or Tim, or even Sam and Sadie to hear something that couldn't be taken back.

I glanced through the window, it would soon be dark, but there was still about half an hour of dusk left, so I suggested to Helen we take a walk round the garden. I knew it was the drink talking, so wasn't offended by Helen, but it wasn't fair to inflict this on the kids.

She didn't resist, and once outside, I led her to the garden bench and I sat there shivering slightly in the early autumn chill. But Helen didn't seem to feel the cold, it was like all her senses had died with Lauren.

She put her head down, and I saw tears on her chin, landing on the pale pink top she was wearing.

'You and Tim, you've been through more than most couples go through in a lifetime. Stop beating yourself up – people have affairs, but you can move on from it,' I said softly.

She shook her head. 'I can't. I can't move on from any of it. My heart is weighed down with guilt about Lauren...'

'Helen, don't do this to yourself. Of course you feel guilty, but who wouldn't. How does anyone ever get over seeing their child – like that? You two have been through something terrible, but you have each other,' I said. 'You're mourning for your child, so why not do that together, share your feelings, because you must both feel the same and can help each other.'

She put her head in her hands. 'I can't, it's like a horror film, when I think about her, all I can see is the blood... her lying there...'

I recalled the image that Tim shared with me of Lauren in the morgue; *her face was such a mess, I didn't recognise her, and her limbs were so twisted....*

'I can't imagine how it feels seeing your child after she passed,' I said gently. 'But Tim says he can't get it out of his head either, and feels just the same, so perhaps if you talked about it, to each other...?' I offered blindly.

'It isn't that,' she said. 'In fact, we didn't see her after she'd died.' She paused. 'Tim said from the beginning he couldn't face it, he wanted to remember her how she was. In the end, I felt the same. No, thank God, neither of us could go through with it. So we asked Pete, a colleague of Tim's, to identify the body, he'd known Lauren since she was little. It felt right, you know?'

I could see this was making Helen more agitated and was about to suggest we go back inside, when she suddenly said, 'Why did Sam come here tonight?'

'Because you invited him, didn't you?'

'Not me. I didn't want *anyone* here, but Tim's trying desperately to bring everyone together.'

I was stung by this. 'James is with the police now, there's DNA evidence that damns him, he is the one who killed Lauren, so why do you still refuse to believe that Sam's innocent?'

'Because James isn't guilty,' she replied confidently.

'But the police are saying differently?'

'The police are idiots,' she said, wafting her hand dismissively. 'I'm telling you, Georgie, it *wasn't* James.'

'How can you say he didn't do it? There's evidence—'

'Look, trust me... I *know* it wasn't James!' She was staring at me, then she took a breath, and leaned in, about to say something, when she apparently thought better of it. 'I just know, that's all. James would *not* have hurt Lauren. *Never!*' She shook her head vigorously.

'He's been arrested for the murder. Tim says the police also think he was having inappropriate relationships with his underage students.'

She scoffed at this. 'Tim thinks he knows James, *you* think you know James, you *think* you know me. But you don't know any of us. We're just in your head, Georgie, you create this image of how you *want* people to be,' she murmured, sounding more sober now. 'But you can't squash everyone into your little pigeonholes, because we don't fit, we're not who you think we are, none of us,' she hissed.

'So why don't you tell me?' I asked, calmly.

She looked at me. 'I told Lauren and she was never the same. She hated me for what I'd done.'

'Are you talking about the affair you had? Is that what she found out?'

She nodded. 'I had to tell her, she knew something, she'd found letters, she'd seen us together... I loved him, I wanted to be with him, but it was all too complicated.'

'I see.'

'No, you don't, that's what I'm saying – you *think* you do, Georgie. But me and Tim, we had to get married, I was pregnant with Lauren and... Tim isn't Lauren's father.'

I felt like I'd been punched in the stomach. 'Did he know?'

'He hasn't got a clue, but I stupidly told Lauren and sent her into some sort of spiral. What I hadn't realised was that she wanted Tim to be her dad, I thought she'd want to know the truth, but she said she could never accept James as her dad.'

'James?' For a moment I didn't understand what this had to do with him. 'James is Lauren's father?' I said in disbelief.

She nodded. 'And *that's* why I know he didn't do it.'

CHAPTER THIRTY-SIX

I was trying desperately to process what Helen had just told me. I'd put Helen and her family on a pedestal for so long, seduced by their big family suppers, board games at Christmas and crazy camping holidays. They were everything I'd wanted for me and Sam. A ready-made family of cut-out dolls in their lovely home, all perfectly proportioned with flawless skin and an outfit for every occasion. I'd envied the way Helen and Tim held hands in front of everyone, how they'd throw a party at the drop of a hat. On the surface, their home was always so happy, like a glossy TV commercial for stock cubes or family holidays. I wanted what they had, and thought merely by being there, that some of it might rub off on me. But now I knew, those parties were just a respite from the regrets, the secrets, the misery of their real lives.

We were still outside, it was getting cooler, and though Helen's body now shivered, her mind seemed unaware of the cold. She was animated, as she detailed how, before she even knew Tim, she and James were friends, and she'd always carried a torch for him. 'He was married, I was engaged,' she said, gazing out onto the garden that Tim tamed into a perfectly manicured plot. 'We'd known each other as friends, and suddenly this mad, crazy passion hit us – I saw him as my last lover. I was getting married to sensible old Tim, who I loved in my own way, but wanted that big, windswept thing we all want – and James was it.'

I just listened while she told me how over the years, James had stayed in touch, keen to know everything about his daughter's life.

'I'd update him with everything she did, but he had to watch her from afar,' she said, sadly. 'I sent him photos of when she took her first steps, called him when she spoke her first words, then when everyone started using mobile phones it was easier, I could send him the photos to his phone. Becky never knew,' she said, turning to me. 'I sent him photos of her birthday parties, and he kept them all, he particularly loved the ones of her blowing out her candles.' She smiled at this, and I remembered what Kate had told me about Lauren's tenth birthday party and Helen going mad because she'd missed the candles being blown out. It made sense now.

'So for all these years, you and James kept this a secret?' I asked. I watched her, still a beautiful woman in her late forties, still capable of turning heads. She'd brought her glass with her, and sipped on her gin like it was purely social. But Helen's drinking was real, and why she was usually carried out early from her own lovely parties. Now I knew why she sought her own personal oblivion in the wine bottle.

'Yeah, it was just between me and James, until I told Lauren. I told her just before she got married, I'd never intended to, I just blurted it out, and I don't know, it felt right. But from that moment, things weren't the same, and Lauren was distant from me, I guess that's why I wanted it to be Sam, because I didn't want it to be that she'd taken her own life. That would have been my fault...' She started to cry.

I put my arm around her, and eventually, she emerged from her tears and carried on talking.

'I really wanted James at the wedding. He'd missed all her milestones, her birthdays, everything, and I felt he should be there, but when I suggested it, she said no. She said it was bad enough finding out he was her father, she didn't want him there on her special day, and I respected that. But then Sam – who doesn't know about James – bumped into him, and invited him, no invitation, just a "why don't you pop in?" so he did.'

I shifted slightly on the garden bench, I'd spent all evening with James at the wedding, and later he'd asked me out, but Helen didn't seem to register my relationship with James. I realised now I was just a side note in their love story, there was so much else going on. This was all too much to take in, I couldn't speak. Meanwhile, Helen seemed sober and seemed more alive than I'd seen her in weeks. Her eyes were sparkling, she was like a different woman when she talked about James.

'We made the decision never to tell anyone because it would have broken Becky, his wife's heart, she'd suffered ill health for years and it would probably kill her,' she was saying.

'I had no idea, no idea at all,' I said, feeling terrible and weird and, given the history, I had to wonder what the hell James was doing going out with me, Helen's best friend. 'If I had, I obviously wouldn't have gone out with James,' I said, awkwardly.

'Oh, it was over by then...' she said dismissively, but the fact she was finding it hard to acknowledge my very minor role in all this told me differently.

'I remember you seemed a bit put out when I took him to the barbecue at the cottage?' I said.

'Put out? No, no, it was all so difficult because I'd only recently told Lauren, and you'd brought him, which was a shock to both of us. She didn't want him there, she refused to even talk about him. It caused some rows between us, and it hurts to think that her last few months were spent hating me.'

'I doubt that, she was obviously just shocked, and I'm sure she'd have come round to things eventually,' I said, not sure at all if that was the case, Lauren could be very determined.

'Her feelings were understandable, to Lauren Tim was her dad, and always would be.'

I had so many questions, but before I could even start, the back doors opened, and I heard Tim's gentle voice.

'There you are. I wondered where you girls had got to. The kids said you'd gone out for a walk. I didn't realise you were in the garden,' he said as he walked towards us across the lawn. 'Aren't you cold, it's getting chilly out here? Come on inside.' I saw the steam on his breath as he held his hand out to Helen.

After what seemed like an eternity, she reluctantly took it and staggered to her feet. She seemed lost again, the enthusiasm, and engagement of just a few seconds ago had dissipated into the night air like breath.

I stood up, and never wanting to leave me out, Tim then offered me his other hand, and the three of us walked together, back to the house.

Looking at us, three middle-aged people walking through the garden at dusk, this could have been any evening, at any time in the past twenty-odd years. We'd trod this path so many times, the three of us in the garden, going inside for supper, but this was so different from the last time I was in their garden. It had been warmer the previous year, and Helen had cooked, we'd sat under the pergola, smothered in vine leaves and honeysuckle and ate from huge tureens of pasta and sauce. Tim and Helen had seemed happy, we laughed a lot, even Kate – and Lauren was there. The sun shone down on us then, but now it was dark, the garden was dying, furniture stowed away, the pergola now entwined with dead stems and black leaves. Death had been here, and you could taste it.

CHAPTER THIRTY-SEVEN

Once inside the house, Helen wandered into the living room, while I went into the kitchen to help Tim with the cutlery and plates. I found it hard to make conversation with him, I was still in shock at what Helen had told me outside, and the implications it now had. Given that James knew Lauren was his biological daughter, it was hard to imagine they were having an affair. It was also hard to imagine James killing his own child, but perhaps it was because she couldn't accept him as her biological father? Did it hurt him so much he lashed out at her? Who knew? My mind was scrambled with everything that was going on. I glanced over at Tim, who clearly had no idea about any of this, he was flailing about in his own grief, trying desperately to help his family heal, and he was being deceived by his wife and a man he thought of as a friend. He didn't deserve any of this, but it had landed at his door, and without questioning it, he was clearing up the mess like he always did. I just wanted to put my arms around him. It broke my heart to watch him in the kitchen, trying to do his very best to make a meal for the family he loved, while grieving for the child he adored, with no idea she wasn't even his.

Eventually he opened the oven and took out a lot of beige pastries, some burned around the edges, some waxy and uncooked. He went to lift one of the baking trays from the oven and, catching his hand on the white-hot heat of the tray, whimpered, almost dropping everything on the kitchen floor. I quickly grabbed a tea towel to help him and tried to deal with what was happening – forget the human mess and deal with the kitchen mess – and be in the present for Tim.

'I got frozen pizza too. Should I cook that?' he asked me help-lessly, and my heart hurt for him as he fumbled in the freezer.

'Tim, this is *fine*,' I said, putting the slightly burnt sausage rolls, samosas and little meat pies on a large platter, knowing this was all pointless, as no one had an appetite anyway.

Once we'd put the pastries onto serving plates, he grabbed two and headed off into the dining room; 'Grub's up!' he called, in an attempt to be jovial, to return to the past, when he and Helen were a team. But now, in the light of what had happened, and what I knew, it sounded hollow and desperate, like a cry for help.

Kate, Sam and Sadie all responded quickly and came through into the dining room, Kate plonking herself on a chair and giving daggers to Sadie, and Sam apparently oblivious to the bad feeling Sadie had created. I tried not to meet Kate's eyes; she was glaring at me, obviously seeking an ally, but she needed calming down not buoying up, so I did as Tim was doing and smiled, while passing round plates like everything was fine. The last thing we needed now was a confrontation between Kate and Sadie.

Meanwhile, poor Tim was now handing round napkins like his life depended on it and anxiously calling for Helen to join us. Even Kate must have picked up on his desperation and went back into the living room, where after a few angry mumblings seemed to convince Helen to come through.

'What's all this?' she asked, on entering the room, glass in hand. She stood at the table, waiting for a response, and, fuelled by alcohol, was definitely up for a fight. No one looked up, the tension was palpable, as the rest of us nibbled on the burnt offerings in front of us and tried to ignore the bubbling hate seemingly directed at all of us, but especially Tim.

He was the only one to acknowledge her, as she stood hands on her hips by the table. 'Sit down, love, you need to eat something,' he said.

'Yeah, but not *this*.' She put down her glass, and, reaching over to Tim's plate, picked up a frazzled sausage roll between finger and thumb. She looked at the black around the edges and, holding it up in the air, she laughed at it. The sounds she was making bordered on hysteria, on hurt and hate and screaming, as she threw her head back. Eventually she stopped, and from a height, she dropped the pastry back onto his plate. In the silence it made a thudding sound on the china, and her lips curled into a cruel shape as she looked around the table for her next victim.

'Sit *down*, Mum,' Kate urged, under her breath.

'Why, so we can all play happy families?' she hissed back at her daughter.

Kate looked mortified.

'Helen...' I murmured, reluctant to get involved, but knowing I should, if only to spare Kate.

'Don't *Helen* me,' she snapped. 'You think you're so perfect don't you, sitting there at my table, judging me because I've had a little drink...'

'Helen, I'm not judging you, I thought tonight was about us getting together, being kind to each other...'

She moved along the table towards me, already victorious; she'd found her next victim. I'd offered myself up as a sacrifice, and as she came closer, really wished I hadn't. '*Kindness?*' she hissed into the embarrassed silence.

'Ugh, you make me want to puke.' She put her hand to her mouth in a vomiting gesture, which seemed, in her state, to make her unsteady on her feet. 'Who do you think you are, Georgie...' she started, and I straightened up, ready to retaliate, but before I could say anything, Kate slammed her plate onto the table.

'STOP!' she yelled. 'Just stop it, Mum. Dad's tried so hard tonight, and Georgie's only trying to help. Why do you always have to spoil everything?'

'Coming from you Miss Congeniality, that's rich,' she hissed, then laughed again, too loudly.

Kate threw down her napkin, stood up and left the room. I wanted to go after her, but I had to be there for Sam, because I reckoned Helen was just sharpening her claws to start on him next.

But it seemed she had someone else in her sights. 'And you can stop looking at me like that Sadie,' she said, sliding into Kate's now vacant chair. 'Sitting there all holier than thou and clinging to your best friend's husband. So, you finally got what you wanted?'

Sadie stiffened.

'Good luck.' Helen took a large gulp of wine, I hadn't even noticed her pouring another, she was adept at this. 'Cheers! His wife's dead, she's not in your way anymore,' she said, holding up her glass.

'She's not in *yours* either,' Sadie replied, cool as a cucumber.

Tim defeatedly flung his napkin on his still full plate. 'Sadie,' he groaned, 'what are you talking about?'

'Oh, I'm sure she and Lauren discussed me all the time, "the mad mother", giving her shit all the time,' Helen said, glaring at Sadie.

Sadie shrugged. 'Everyone knows you two had your problems, I didn't need to discuss it with Lauren. Whatever happened between you, I hope you can live with yourself.'

'That's *enough,* Sadie,' Tim suddenly said.

Now it was her turn to stand up. 'Yes, Tim, that *is* enough!' she said. 'I've had enough of all of you and your dirty little lies,' she snapped, and, turning to Sam said, 'I'm going. I can't take one more minute. I only came here for you. I'll get a taxi.'

Sam looked awkward. 'No, no, I'll drop you back, I said I would.' He stood up, clearly very uncomfortable, and glanced over at Tim apologetically; 'Sorry, can I call you tomorrow?'

'Of course, mate.' Tim wafted his hand at Sam like it was all fine, and I was grateful once more for his kindness.

As they headed out of the room, Helen yelled after them. 'That's right, you go, two love rats leaving a sinking ship!'

'Helen, *Helen...*' Tim was saying, in a vain attempt to shut her up and calm her down. But she was beyond that. She lifted her glass of wine, as if she was about to congratulate him. I was waiting for the sarcastic comment, something terrible about her husband. I cringed, waiting for the remark, wondering at Tim's patience and hating Helen for what she'd become. She held the glass aloft, the wine was spilling slightly because it was so full, and she was so pissed she couldn't control her hand movements – or so I thought. But with one swift movement, she hurled the contents of her glass at him, and he gasped, like she'd just stabbed him with a knife.

'Helen!' I exclaimed, as Tim sat there, his face dripping, his eyes closed in pain and humiliation, while she walked slowly away from the table, leaving just me and Tim, both wounded. Everyone else had left – her work here was done.

'She's just tired,' Tim said quietly, as he wiped his face with a napkin. I could have wept for him.

We sat for a while, staring at nothing, until eventually I reached out and touched his arm. 'Things will get better, Tim, they *will*. I'm sure, given time, she'll come through and you'll be back to where you were – well, as close as that can be without Lauren.' I didn't really believe that myself, but had to offer him a palliative.

He sighed. 'Yeah, I thought that too, but she's been like this for a long time, long before... Lauren. And now I don't know anymore, it's all such a mess. I think me and Helen we've – what is it they say, we've "come to the end of our rainbow".'

My heart went out to him. 'I don't know how you've coped with everything, all the troubles on your shoulders and still you're there for everyone else,' I offered, knowing he was probably right, but feeling sad for them both.

We didn't talk much more, I helped with the dishes, said good-night, and walked the five minutes home, glad to be alone in the cool night air – my head was all over the place.

Letting myself in the house, I went into the kitchen, where I could hear Sam's voice. I tried not to show my displeasure when I saw Sadie sitting at the table with him, their heads together like two teenage lovebirds.

'Mum, are you okay?' Sam said, jumping up when he saw me.

'Yes, I'm fine. I thought you were taking Sadie home?'

'I was, but we just… we wanted to talk to you.'

'Oh?' My heart thumped to the ground as I saw them glance at each other knowingly. I guessed what this might be, but really didn't want to hear it. Sadie could never fill Lauren's shoes, despite desperately wanting to, and I resented her for using Sam in this way, he was lost, vulnerable, and likely to agree to anything.

I slowly took off my coat, looking from one to the other, while Sam suggested I sit down, which I did, reluctantly. He pulled up a chair next to me at the kitchen table. It all felt so formal. I glanced over at Sadie, who was getting up from her chair, and all I could think was, *Christ, is Sadie going to ask me for his hand in marriage?* I wanted to be sick. This was all I needed after everything else; 'shady Sadie' as a daughter-in-law, the cherry on the bloody cake.

'Cup of tea, Georgie?' she asked, civil, pleasant, not like her at all. Funny how things were changing now she'd got her hands on Sam.

I nodded, mumbled 'thank you', and she wandered over to the kettle and turned it on. I was strangely grateful, my mother always made tea in a crisis, and judging by the serious look on Sam's face, this was a crisis.

'Is Sadie pregnant?' I heard myself ask.

Sam looked at me, a mix of horror and bemusement on his face; 'No! What the hell, Mum?' He glanced over at Sadie, who was smirking.

'God, for a moment then, Georgie, you looked like you'd seen a ghost. Don't worry I'm not about to pop your first grandkid.'

'I didn't mean anything, I just—' I lied.

'So, now we've established that no one's pregnant, we want to talk to you… about what's been going on.'

'Okay,' I replied uncertainly.

Sadie brought three mugs of tea to where we were sitting around the table.

'I can't lie, I'm a bit scared,' she said, sitting down.

'Scared of what?' I asked, puzzled.

'Of what might happen if I told anyone.'

She must have seen the wave of doubt that crossed my face, because she hesitated and glanced over at Sam, saying under her breath, 'I don't want to tell her.'

'You *have* to,' he replied. 'Mum has to know – just tell it from the beginning, like you did with me.'

I groaned inwardly, convinced this was this some fictitious drama Sadie had created in an attempt to get Sam's attention. But I couldn't have been more wrong.

CHAPTER THIRTY-EIGHT

Sadie looked from me to Sam, clearly unsure whether to tell me what had been going on. I waited, dreading what she was going to say, but eventually, she took a breath.

'It's difficult to know when to start, but... you remember me telling you about how when we were kids Lauren paid me to take the rap for stuff?'

I nodded, still slightly disbelieving of Sadie's tall stories about Lauren shoplifting and writing on toilet walls. She looked again at Sam, and he nodded for her to continue.

'Well that's how it began, it was like this pact with the devil, you know? I admit, I took the cash, I knew it was wrong, but figured it wouldn't do any harm. It started small, and as we got older, she'd pay me to write her essays, or she'd skip school to meet some guy, so I'd sign in for her. She even paid me to dye her hair the same colour as mine, so if she was somewhere she shouldn't be, we could say it was me. It was fine, it was an arrangement, it suited her to have me around covering for her, and suited me to get money, and we were both okay with it. We were friends, and I liked her. I didn't have to explain anything to anyone, my mum didn't know or care where the money came from, and her parents would have gone apeshit if she'd been drinking underage, or hanging around with guys who did drugs.' She paused, and I wondered if she wanted a reaction, but I didn't flinch. I still wasn't sure about Sadie. I didn't understand why she felt the need to tell me all this again, it wasn't relevant to Lauren's death, the killer had been arrested. Now was the time to stay calm and start moving forward, not the time for Sadie to settle some old score with Lauren. If she thought snitching to Lauren's husband and his mother would endear her to me, she was wrong, I wasn't interested. I was surprised at Sam giving this oxygen, it was uncomfortable to hear her making allegations about Lauren, and sullying her memory when she wasn't around to defend herself.

'When we got to sixth form, my grades were higher than most in my class,' she continued, 'but my mum said we couldn't afford for me to go to university, I had to get a job instead. I was so envious of all the other kids talking about which unis they were choosing and going to open days with their parents.'

'But you went in the end,' I said, reminding her that even if Sam was listening to this like it was new, I was familiar with the narrative. 'I know that Tim and Helen paid your university fees, I never understood why. Were they just being kind?' I asked. This was still sounding suspiciously like some fantasy that Sadie was peddling, where *she* was the princess instead of Lauren.

Sadie shook her head. 'No, the university thing was something else, it wasn't out of kindness.' She paused. 'Lauren had just passed her driving test. I didn't have a hope in hell of affording a driving lesson, let alone passing my test, so I was really chuffed when she took me out for a spin in her new car. We had a great night, went to the pub, and of course Lauren had been drinking. I thought we'd get a taxi and she'd pick up the car the next day, but when we went outside she started heading towards her car and I tried to stop her.

"Oh it's fine," she said, "my dad can get rid of drinking tickets, he does it for Mum all the time." And then on the way home, she got stopped by the police. I was terrified, but she was all cute and charming and thought she could win the officer over, but he was having none of it. So she told him who her dad was and he called Tim and said, "Your daughter's here, she's just been pulled over for drinking and driving." Tim gets on the phone, he's furious and Lauren's looking really worried. Tim can be bloody scary.'

I'm sure if you're a seventeen-year-old in the wrong place at the wrong time, anyone's dad who's a policeman is scary. Tim was probably concerned and wanted to make sure Lauren was okay.

'So Tim drove out to where we were, he had a word with the police that stopped us, but they said they'd already filed the report and it was still going to be processed. He was fucking fuming! And when he drove us home, he was shouting at Lauren and she was crying, it was just awful. But then, he suddenly pulls the car over, parks up in a lay-by and says to me, if I'll take the rap, he'll pay for driving lessons for me. I said no way, I wasn't interested, it wasn't worth me getting a five-year ban, but as Tim said, "A ban wouldn't mean anything to you, Sadie, you can't even drive, love." He was calling me love and telling me how him and Helen thought of me like their own daughter – it was what I'd always wanted to hear, and for a moment I almost agreed. But I thought about it and realised that if he really cared about me he wouldn't be dumping Lauren's crime on me. It didn't matter to him if I had a criminal record, I was nothing to them, and it was then that I realised I only had myself. I didn't have anyone fighting for me, so I had to fight for me, and I refused. But he wouldn't let it go, kept begging me, but the worm had turned and when he realised I wasn't going to give in, he changed.'

'What do you mean?' I asked, leaning forward, wanting to make sure I understood everything, because the way her eyes had now filled with tears made me think this was real.

'He turned nasty, he still kept it hidden under his smile, but I remember thinking how he looked just like a snake. He couldn't hide how much he hated me for saying no to him.

He tried a different tack then, he stopped begging and told me if Lauren was charged with drink driving, not only would her career be ruined, but so would his. I said that wasn't my problem, and that's when he said he could *make* it my problem.' She wrapped her arms around herself and started to rock slowly on the chair.

'Are you okay talking about this?' I asked, concerned by her obvious fear.

'Yeah, yeah, I'm okay. I feel like the more people who know, the safer I am. But I know Tim could do me so much harm.'

'What do you mean?' I asked, still finding it hard to believe, but willing to listen now.

'He said he could get me charged with something, or drugs could be "found" at my house, and Mum would be in trouble too.'

'Really? And did you believe him?'

'Yeah, I did. Then he asked me how much money I wanted. I was beginning to realise I had no choice, so why not make it work for me. If I had a decent amount of money, I might actually be able to go to uni, do medicine, my dream. I felt I owed it to myself, and James too, he was the only one who cared about me. He'd been giving me extra maths lessons in his own time, applying for bursaries and financial support,' she added, and I thought about his kindness. My feelings were so conflicted about the man I'd once thought I might have some kind of future with, then reminded myself of what he'd done.

'Even with James' help, and if he managed to get me some kind of bursary, I knew I'd still have to get a job if I wanted to go to uni. It was a demanding course, and so many kids from poor families fail because they don't have the luxury of concentrating on the academic work, they have to hold down full-time jobs so they can eat too. And I can't lie, I suddenly saw this as the answer to my prayers – so – I'd take the rap if he paid my uni fees and my student rent. I remember Lauren saying her parents had come into an inheritance around that time, so I knew they had the money, and if the Jacksons were going to use me, then I had no problem being paid for that. To be honest, I never thought he'd agree to it, but he was so desperate to keep Lauren clean, and save his job, that he agreed to it.'

I could barely take in what she was telling me, each sentence a fresh blow. If this was all true, then everything I thought I knew about Tim, and Lauren – even Helen – was wrong.

'Did Helen know about this?' I asked.

'God no, she was like Lady Muck. Thought the good old Jacksons were just being kind to Lauren's poor, sad little friend. She blew hot and cold, and seemed to want my eternal gratefulness for having my education paid for, but she didn't have a clue. Lauren said she was too busy with her lover to care what was going on.'

I felt this was slightly unfair of Lauren, but then again if that was her perception, no wonder she was following Tim's lead. She clearly felt she couldn't speak to Helen; in fact, the more I was hearing, it didn't seem like she and Helen had the perfect mother and daughter relationship I'd always imagined they had. And Helen didn't really know her daughter at all.

'So, did Tim keep his promise, did he fund your university course?'

'Yeah, say what you like about Tim, but he was pretty good about money, he always paid up. But then Lauren followed me to Manchester and she seemed to think I existed merely as her dumping ground, and whatever she needed, all she had to do was pay me for it and I'd do it. Away from home she was even worse, treated me like a servant, said I had to do her essays, and wanted me to go drinking with her every night. I couldn't afford to, but she paid, and if I said no, she'd threaten to tell her dad. My own work was getting behind, and I realised this wasn't healthy, and it was no way to achieve what I wanted to. So one day I said no, I wasn't going to do it anymore. That's when she told me her dad could make anyone look guilty of anything, and if he thought I'd upset her, he'd make sure I was thrown off the course. I knew he would too, I was scared of him. That night I went back to my little room and packed my bags. I realised that this payment wasn't a path to my dreams, it would be a toxic cloud forever hanging over me. If I stayed, I would never be free of them, because they didn't see it as a transaction, they were so bloody deluded they were lying to themselves and saw it as an act of kindness.'

This was shocking. 'I can't imagine Lauren being like that, going along with something so... so wrong.'

Sadie shrugged. 'Lauren could be a mean girl, but she wasn't all bad, she just panicked when things went wrong. She'd always call her dad and he thought because he was a bloody policeman he could do anything, that he was above the law. He'd do anything for his precious daughter. I got caught up in all that, and came up against the *other* Lauren, who did what her dad told her – and believed he could make everything better.'

I sighed and tried to get a sense of perspective on all this. Who knew what the dynamic was between the two friends. Perhaps Lauren was capable of being a mean girl, as I was sure Sadie was too. Perhaps as young, confused women they both took chances and were both guilty in different ways of behaving badly? Lauren should have taken responsibility for what she'd done, and should never have treated her friend like that, but Sadie took the money knowing it was wrong. My main concern was what Sadie was saying about Tim, I was finding it very hard to reconcile with the man I'd known for over twenty years.

'So, anyway,' Sam continued. I think he could see the doubts on my face, so took over the story. 'You know I told you about the night Lauren came home late, a couple of weeks before the wedding?'

I nodded.

'It was because she was involved in that hit-and-run.'

'Yes, she was treating that poor girl at the hospital, wasn't she?'

They were both shaking their heads. 'No. She'd just dropped me off and was driving home to the cottage,' Sadie said, then paused before adding, 'but she was tired, she'd had a drink, only one but... in the dark, she didn't see the girl walking along the road. By the time she realised what happened, she just panicked, and kept on driving.'

CHAPTER THIRTY-NINE

'So *Lauren* was the hit-and-run driver?' I asked, in disbelief.

Sam and Sadie both nodded.

'That was when everything changed,' she said. 'It had always been manageable until then, but even Lauren knew that this time it had gone too far, and she was a mess. She called me the next day and said she knew she'd hit someone and was about to stop, but a car was coming up behind on the road and she panicked. She'd hoped and prayed it might be an animal, but was so worried it wasn't, she didn't hang around, just turned the car around and headed to her parents' where she told Tim all about it.

'But while she was talking to Tim, Helen came downstairs and couldn't understand why Lauren was there late at night. So to put her off the scent, they told her Lauren just wanted to talk to her dad because she was having second thoughts about marriage. But Helen saw she had a bruise on her forehead, from hitting her head during the accident, and she got the wrong end of the stick, assuming Sam had hit her. It was a mess, and Helen was convinced Sam had hurt her, even though Lauren told her a million times that he hadn't. But that night, Lauren and Tim were locked in his home office trying to work out what the hell to do.' She paused.

I realised then that might explain Helen's attitude towards Sam and the way she'd implied he was violent. No wonder she thought he took after his father and why she was convinced he'd killed her daughter.

'So what did they do?' I asked.

'Well, I was at home and I got a call from Tim, asking if I was prepared to do what I'd done before? He didn't tell me it was a hit-and-run, just said Lauren had bumped the car and there was a chance the police might call. If they did contact me, I had to say I was driving that night at that time. He said it was nothing, and if it did come to anything, he would "make it go away".'

If I'd had any doubts about her story, this expression confirmed it for me. It was the same expression Tim had used about Sam's charge.

'I refused, but he said he'd make it worth my while.' She looked at me, a shadow of guilt across her face. 'I wanted to go back to uni – and if I could get him to help me, I could go on my own this time. Lauren had a job, a life, a husband, and we were actually getting along. Sam had changed her, made her realise what she was, and she'd become a nicer, kinder person, and I seriously considered helping her as well as getting what I wanted.' She stopped talking, and again looked guilty. 'I'm not proud of that, Georgie,' she added. 'But I swear I had no idea that someone had been hurt, let alone died.'

I shrugged. I wasn't going to offer her absolution; if what she said was true, she'd colluded with both Tim and Lauren in the past, she wasn't blameless.

'But then, the day after Tim made the offer, I saw on the news that there'd been a hit-and-run just a couple of miles from me,' she continued. 'I had this feeling it had something to do with Lauren's "bump" in the car. I didn't want to have anything to do with it, but Lauren knew if Sam found out she'd lose him, he wouldn't put up with anything like that.' She glimpsed over at him and smiled.

'So what happened?' I urged, dying to know where this was all leading.

'Well, Lauren was a mess, she kept calling me all the time, begging me to say it was me, scared to death she'd lose Sam and her job. Tim was the same, saying I owed them, that they'd always looked after me, and always would, but I was like their cleaner, or the woman who Helen paid to do the laundry, I was just another service to Tim, he didn't care about me as a person. Anyway, I told him firmly that I wasn't playing ball and he got really pissed off.'

This was beginning to feel very real, and I could actually see something like this taking place. I knew Tim was a caring husband and father, so caring that he'd probably do *anything* for his wife and daughters.

'Anyway, the girl who Lauren had hit was brought into the hospital and Lauren would go into her room and see her. She said to me this might be her chance to redeem herself and even though she wasn't her patient, she'd get her through it. So after her shifts she'd go and sit with her, talking, holding her hand. Everyone, including the girl's parents, thought she was amazing, this wonderful, caring doctor who gave all this time to their daughter. Little did they know the truth,' she said in a bitter aside.

'What an awful situation...' I said.

'Yeah, and it really got to her. The girl was called Anna and she lived for quite a few weeks, and Lauren became really paranoid, thinking she knew what happened, that she was watching her from her hospital bed, even said Anna sat up, pointed at her and said, "You are my murderer."'

I shivered at the image of this, it was like something from a horror film.

'Yeah, and all in Lauren's mind, because apparently the girl was brought into the hospital in a coma in April, and they switched off her life support in June – she never woke up.'

'I remember reading about it in the newspaper thinking, how sad, she was only in her twenties. I was so angry about the driver,' I added.

'Yeah, well Lauren heard a lot of angry voices at the hospital when the girl died, and she wanted to come clean. She was going to tell Sam, go to the police, but her dad was really putting pressure on her, telling her life wouldn't be worth living, that she'd lose everything, so would he, and there was the fact she was pregnant. She didn't tell Sam or her parents, she had to work out what to do, but the last thing she ever said to me was, "I'm going to put all this right, Sadie."'

'So you *knew* about the pregnancy?' I paused. 'Was the baby Sam's?' I asked, looking straight at my son.

'Yeah, yeah, the baby was mine,' he offered sadly. 'Sadie's explained it all to me, Lauren found out about six weeks after we married, right in the middle of everything when the hit-and-run happened and she was working long hours – or so I thought. But she was staying at the hospital desperately trying to make it up to the victim, praying she'd live. She was in a mess, she knew if she confessed, she'd be arrested, the baby would be born in prison. She knew I'd be devastated and might even end the marriage. Meanwhile her dad would have lost his job and could also end up going to prison. She knew that would kill him, and Helen.' He shook his head. 'God, she was under so much pressure. All the time I knew she was unhappy – I just thought it was because she wanted to end our marriage, that she'd made a mistake.'

Sadie nodded. 'She hated herself, and called herself a murderer, said if she wasn't pregnant she'd have killed herself and put everyone out of their misery.' As she said this, I saw Sam wince, and I put my hand over his. 'Once the girl died, it became manslaughter, even murder, and the police were even more determined to find out who the driver was. Then it turns out the other car that was coming up behind Lauren that night *had* seen the hit-and-run. But the guy had moved to Spain and had no idea what he'd witnessed was so serious. He was back visiting the UK, saw something in the news about the victim's death, realised it was the accident he saw, and went straight to the police. He was able to describe the car and even remembered some of the registration number.'

I gasped. 'So now the police *knew* it was Lauren's car?'

She nodded. 'Yeah, and suddenly Tim started calling again, saying how could I abandon my best friend when she needed my help? He was really playing on my heartstrings and said I had to save Lauren. But to save Lauren meant sacrificing my own future, it was like my life wasn't worth as much as hers, that I had nothing, I was nothing, and a few years in prison would give me something to do. "She's a doctor, she saves lives," he kept saying, and offering me huge amounts of money. I wasn't interested, and I told him so, but still he kept calling or leaving messages on my phone.' She paused a moment, and I saw the fear in her eyes. 'Also, by then Tim had managed to get himself on the hit-and-run case, putting everyone off the scent, and hiding evidence. I had this feeling that I was now in a very vulnerable position, and he might even be able to frame me. I was worried this was heading my way whatever I did.'

I was beginning to realise how hard things really had been for Sadie. She had no support, was emotionally and financially vulnerable, and a sitting target for someone who was willing to take advantage of her situation. I saw now how the Jacksons had never been her benefactors, or her surrogate family as they liked to say; they'd just used her.

'I felt so alone, I was scared and wanted to talk to someone I trusted,' she said. 'So after about a month of harassment from Tim, I called the only person in the world I could rely on – James.'

I flinched slightly at this, poor Sadie being so desperate she had to go for help to someone who turned out to be a murderer.

'James was horrified, at first. I don't even think he believed me, but eventually offered to go to the police with me. But I'd had some minor drug offences from the past, Tim would be ready and waiting for me to go to the police – and he could make things very difficult for me. I'd taken the rap for a previous drinking and driving charge, so I already had a history of driving offences. Anything I told the police would end up being my word against his, and who would you believe, the high-ranking detective and his doctor daughter against someone like me? I might as well have just walked into the station and confessed to the hit-and-run.' Her eyes filled with tears at the memory. 'Anyway, James helped me, and called Lauren to say she had to do the right thing, that she and her dad must stop this now, because it had gone too far.

'He told me she felt ashamed and said she would do the right thing in her own time and wouldn't be told what to do.'

'Oh God!' I said, hitting the heel of my hand on my head. 'That explains a lot. Kate overheard that conversation, and thought James and Lauren had been having an *affair*.'

'Nosy old Kate,' Sadie muttered, with a scowl. 'She's always been the same, picks up bits and pieces and causes all kinds of trouble, such a stirrer, mind you the whole family's messed up.' She sighed.

Putting the conversation in context, without Kate's interpretation, I added, 'It seems Lauren was torturing herself.'

'She didn't want Sam to know anything because she was scared he'd end things with her, she did really love him,' Sadie looked at Sam and smiled.

CHAPTER FORTY

I found it hard to take in what Sam and Sadie were telling me. I'd thought I knew these people. Over the years we'd shared so much, how could I have missed this? But we can never really know what goes on behind closed doors, and inside family relationships. And as it turns out, I didn't know the Jacksons at all.

'They certainly kept her secrets,' I said, almost to myself.

Sam nodded. 'I find it hard to imagine how Lauren could keep all that from me. She'd done something terrible, and not to stop that night was unforgivable, but I wish she'd talked to me. I feel like I somehow failed her, but it was like she was living two lives – the simple, happy one with me, and this other, complicated mess she'd caught herself up in. On the morning of her death, just before I left for work, she'd said we had to spend some time together. I'd agreed, and as we were both off work the following weekend, we'd decided to stay home, and get back to being us again… she told Sadie that was when she was going to tell me about everything, including the baby.'

I could see this upset him, it was heartbreaking. He'd lost his wife and his baby in one tragic event.

'I didn't know any of this when Lauren was alive, I found out from Sadie when she came to see me when I was on remand. I wanted to tell you before, Mum,' he said, but I didn't want to cause problems for you – or Sadie, especially as I was stuck in prison.'

'Yeah, I wanted Sam to know, because I had a feeling it was relevant, that somehow it was tied in with Lauren's death,' Sadie added. 'And there's something else... too.'

'What?' Did I even want to know?

'Tim called me last week. He said he'd just discovered who really killed Lauren, and though the police knew it, they didn't have enough evidence. That's when he said it was James. Of course I was shocked, I didn't believe him at first, but he said James had had inappropriate relationships with some of his students. He now suspected Lauren was one of those students – and that she was going to blow the whistle on him.'

'Did you believe Tim then?' I asked.

She looked uncomfortable. 'I wasn't sure, I didn't know who to believe, and I don't have a very good track record for knowing who to trust. For all I knew, Lauren could have been sleeping with James for years; I know she had a real issue with him in the past few months. I wondered if they'd had a fallout so perhaps it *was* true – that would make sense if she'd decided to come clean about everything in her life?'

I didn't offer my own conclusion on this, which was that Lauren's feelings for James turned to hate when she found out he was her father. She saw him as someone who wanted to take her father's place, and Tim had protected her for so long in so many ways she didn't want another father.

'So what happened? *Did* you help Tim to get what he needed to charge James?' I asked.

She looked pleadingly at me. 'Thing is, I knew Lauren had an issue with James, I just didn't know what it was, so what Tim was telling me could be true, and it could also get Sam out of prison. Tim was so upset, so I asked him what he needed me to do. He told me I had to ask James to come over on the pretext of helping with my CV, and give him a drink using mugs or glasses from the cottage. I was really, really doubtful, but Tim assured me I was helping the police, that I'd be virtually working undercover, nailing Lauren's murderer and also getting Sam out of prison. To be honest, after taking all the blame for Lauren all those years, it wasn't the biggest ask he'd ever made of me. I thought he'd changed, that he wanted to make up for all the bad stuff, save Sam and get the killer, and along with him, I thought I was doing a good thing.'

'So then he took the DNA evidence *back* to the cottage, and *that* was the new evidence that got James arrested?' I asked.

'Yeah. Tim promised me Sam would be released if I did it, and he kept that promise so I felt good, you know, I'd finally done something right in my life. But tonight was weird with Helen and Tim and... and I'm worried.'

'Worried?' I asked.

'Yeah, I have a horrible feeling it might not be James who killed Lauren after all. And tonight, watching them, listening to Helen being vile, I don't know, but I'm worried Tim got me to set James up – what if Tim's covering for someone else?'

'But who?'

'I don't know... but I saw Tim watching me tonight and got this weird feeling, and when Helen yelled at Kate and she stormed off, Tim gave me this look. I was going to say something to Helen, but he sort of shook his head and that's when it hit me, he's worried that I might know who *really* pushed Lauren down the stairs.'

I couldn't take this in. 'But it was James, wasn't it?'

Sadie shook her head. 'I don't know, I thought I was helping to get the right man, but now I think I might have just framed James. Do you remember the night you came over to my flat?' she asked me.

'Yes, James had just left, it all seemed a bit weird,' I said.

'Not really, I asked James over, we had a coffee, he left my flat, then you came over, and later Tim came round for the mugs. We got talking about Lauren and I told him that on the day she died, she'd called me and said she was going to tell the truth about everything. I remember he went white, and said "don't ever discuss this with anyone", and I said I wouldn't. But then I pointed out that Lauren might have told her Mum, because she said she was going to, she said she was planning to meet her mum, tell her everything, then call the police. I think then Tim realised that it might not have been James who was the last person to see Lauren.'

'So, Sadie reckons Helen met up at the cottage, they talked and Lauren told her,' Sam said. 'We think there was some kind of argument... and...'

'And now Tim's planting evidence to cover for Helen?' I filled in the sentence.

I heard Helen's words from earlier in the evening, her guilt at her daughter's death. 'It was my fault, Georgie,' she'd said.

Had Helen killed her own daughter?

CHAPTER FORTY-ONE

We talked until late into the night, and after a few hours' sleep, I woke the following morning still unable to process everything that had been said. As it was so late, Sadie stayed in the spare room and the following morning while we ate breakfast, we decided that before we went to the police with our theory, we would try to get some evidence. I knew that if I could get Helen on her own, take her by surprise, I could find out exactly what happened the night Lauren died. So as soon as I'd gathered my courage, I called Helen.

'Is Tim there?' I asked.

'No, he's working.'

'Okay, I'm coming over,' I said, and before she could respond, I jumped in Sam's car with Sadie. 'I'll go in,' I explained. 'She's on her own, so Tim won't be there to tell her what to say, or speak for her. I'll ask her some questions, and when she starts talking, and I know for sure it's her, I'll text you. So can you then call the police, and tell them Helen Jackson has just confessed to her daughter's murder?' I found this hard to say, but I had to face it.

Sam parked up, and I left them in the car and walked nervously towards the house. Eventually, after a couple of knocks, she opened the door.

I didn't wait for her to invite me in, just walked through,

glancing up the stairs, aware of Kate's feet standing there; she was listening again.

Once in the sitting room, Helen flopped on the sofa, I took a seat, and just looked at her.

'Helen, tell me what happened the night Lauren died?'

'What the hell, Georgie?' she looked away.

'You said you and Lauren were in a bad place when she died and it was all your fault, is that what you were talking about?' I asked. 'Were you trying to tell me something?'

She didn't speak for a while, just stared ahead.

'Look, Helen, I know something happened between you and Lauren the night she died,' I said gently.

She groaned, like an animal in pain. 'Oh, Georgie, I fucked everything up, my life, Lauren's – even Tim's.

'Was it an accident?'

She was sobbing now, and shaking her head.

'I just wanted her to accept that James was her dad and when she refused to accept the idea I just... lost it.' Tears sprang to her eyes, and I wanted to cry with her.

'Oh, Helen, how did it come to this.' I put my arms around her and hugged her until she eventually pulled away.

'I think Tim's covering for you. He asked Sadie to get James' DNA and he planted it at the cottage... you *can't* let James take the rap for this.'

'No, no of course not...' she started, but before she could continue, there was a sudden noise and we both turned as the living room door creaked slowly open. There in the doorway, was Tim, standing in the silence, glaring at both of us.

'You needn't look so shocked for me, Georgie,' he said. 'I knew about James years ago. I saw letters, she left them lying about to hurt me, didn't you, Helen?'

'Perhaps I just wanted you to find out?' she said, wearily.

'I'm a detective. A good one. Nothing gets past me,' was all he said. I found it sad that he felt the need for bravado at a time like this – but even sadder that Helen couldn't at least be sorry about her deceit.

'Instead of listening at doors, why aren't you at work like you're *supposed* to be?' Helen snapped, wiping her eyes, suddenly becoming brittle, defensive.

'I was. I popped back for... Forgot something.' He made a show of gazing around the room, but he hadn't come back for anything, in fact I wondered if he'd ever left for work that morning. I guessed he hung around the house to keep an eye on Helen; he must have known she was on the verge of confessing.

'You do that a lot. Say you're at work when you aren't,' she said, matter-of-factly. 'Like the night Lauren died, you said you were working, and I only found out you weren't when the police turned up,' she hissed.

He walked into the room shaking his head. 'That's it. It's over, Helen, I can't do this anymore,' he started. 'I've spent these last few months fighting to save you.' He looked at me. 'Yes, Georgie's right, I framed your ex-lover, I'm assuming it is *ex* now? After all, you're a bit old for his tastes now, aren't you?'

'You vile bastard!' She almost hissed at him, but he ignored her.

'Yes, I planted his DNA, but only to protect *her*,' he said to me, looking over at Helen, who curled her lip.

'Protect me, from *what*?' She looked at him like he was dirt.

'Darling,' he said in a slightly creepy voice, as he moved towards her. 'Georgie knows now, and how long before the police do? Sam and Sadie are parked around the corner, Georgie obviously didn't feel safe coming here to see you on her own...'

'No, that isn't the reason...' I started, but he wasn't listening.

'Helen, we can get you help, you must have done it under stress, you might not even remember?' he said, still using the gentle but slightly unnerving tone. 'You can't hide it anymore, and neither can I – God knows I've tried. I knew it was you, but I also knew your lover had been calling her too. Is that why you attacked her that night? Were you jealous of your own daughter? Was that it?'

'What the *hell* are you talking about?' she hissed. 'I didn't attack her!'

'You were the last one to see her that night, you went to the cottage, you had a fight and...'

'No, no. When I left the cottage that night, Lauren was angry, and she was hurt, but she was still alive.'

'Helen, give it up, please stop pretending,' he pleaded.

But then she suddenly sat up in her chair. 'Why *could* no one get hold of you on the night she died?' she asked, repeating the question. 'I've always wondered but I don't think I wanted to know.'

'Typical of you, you can never face anything, can you?' he snapped.

'Me? What about you? You couldn't even face seeing our daughter when she'd died, you couldn't even be there to support me, knowing it was what I wanted.'

An idea was beginning to worm its way into my head. 'I thought you'd seen her, Tim, you said her face was a mess, that her limbs were twisted. When did you see her?' I asked.

Helen shot me a look.

'At the hospital,' he replied.

Helen looked from me to Tim. 'But you never saw her. One of your police colleagues had to identify her body,' Helen said, confused.

And suddenly I knew, I just knew.

'I saw the police report, I saw photos...' he tried.

I shook my head. 'No, you told me you'd *seen* her. I remember you describing what you saw, and it wasn't Lauren in the morgue, it was Lauren at the bottom of the stairs. I know, because I saw her that night.'

He made an attempt to shake his head, but I could see he felt defeated.

'Lauren was threatening to tell Helen, Sam, and the police about the hit-and-run. She couldn't live with the lies any longer,' I said, knowing she'd planned to tell Helen that night, but Helen was so caught up with the issue of James being Lauren's father, she'd ended up storming out before Lauren had chance to tell her about the hit-and-run.

'It was *you* not Helen who wanted Lauren to keep quiet,' I said. 'And it was *you* who lost your temper and pushed her down the stairs.'

He turned to me and stared for a long time. I held my breath, unsure how he would react. But then he started nodding, slowly, like an old, old man. He looked at Helen and fell to his knees. 'I loved her so much, you know that. I didn't care that I might not be her biological father, as far as I was concerned she was mine. You have to believe me, love, I never meant for anything to happen,' he said, addressing Helen. 'She just took her phone and ran upstairs, said she was going to call the police and tell them everything, how I'd covered for her, how I'd made things go away. I just didn't want her to wreck her life. She was twenty-six, she could have ended up with ten plus years in prison, she'd go in a young, vibrant woman, and come out middle-aged. She had her life ahead of her, the poor girl had died, never came out of the coma, and telling the police wouldn't bring her back, so why ruin another life? But Lauren just wouldn't listen. She was shouting, yelling, telling me what a bad person I was, a terrible father...' At this, he broke. I saw the tears in his eyes and knew that of all the hurt, losing his daughter's love and respect was, for Tim, the worst thing of all.

He flopped down on the sofa. 'I ran after her, up those treacherous bloody stairs. I was yelling for her to think about what she was doing, and yes, I was angry. If she called the police, we'd both be in trouble, both end up in prison... so I grabbed the phone, she lunged for it and, in my blind temper, I pushed her away.' He gulped. 'I'll never forget the horror on her face as she fell backwards, looking straight at me, the shock in her eyes saying, "Dad, how could you do this?" It was seconds – but it will stay with me for a lifetime.'

And then, he started to cry and I thought he'd never stop.

EPILOGUE

It's late afternoon in September, over a year since Lauren died. Helen and James have invited us over for a late-summer barbecue, it's poignant, because it will probably be the last time we'll ever enjoy in the lovely big garden together. The house that has so many memories, but held so many secrets, is up for sale, and as sad as Helen is to leave, James doesn't feel comfortable living with her in the Jacksons' old home.

'He has nightmares about Tim escaping from prison and banging on our bedroom window in the middle of the night,' Helen told me. 'It's all a bit Heathcliff and Cathy for me, and not Tim's style, passion was never his forte,' she'd said with a smile. Understandably, she can never forgive Tim for what happened, but he'll never leave prison, and as she says, 'A life sentence isn't enough after what he did to my child.' I know she has bad days, but she's finding a kind of happiness with James. I think it was probably meant to be. I often wonder if they had run away together all those years ago, they might have been spared the tragedy of Lauren's death. But as Helen says, there's no point in wondering what might have been; we have to live with what we have, in the here and now. And I think she's happy here and now, she's certainly much calmer these days, and doesn't drink like she used to. I guess she's finally stopped seeking oblivion in alcohol. I know she's conflicted about leaving her home; there are lots of ghosts, some good, some bad, but it was once Lauren's home, where she grew up, where she lived for most of her life.

'When I'm alone, I sometimes think I hear music playing in her bedroom, and I'm sure I hear her laughing,' she said only the other day. But she's reluctantly moving away for a new life with James, where he can sleep at night without imagining Tim's face pressed against his window.

As soon as James was released, Helen wanted to be with him, and I wasn't going to stand in their way. She's loved him for a long time, and it felt right. I didn't have any hold over him, so when she told me how she felt, I said, 'Go for it.' They'd both been through hell and deserved some happiness. And honestly, I'm fine with it, but I did like James, and even now I sometimes catch him looking at me and wonder 'what if?'

But the priority now is to heal, and move forward, and we want Lauren to move with us on that journey. And the past twelve months have been all about her. We've celebrated her birthday, Christmas and wedding anniversary. And today we're setting her free, helping her to leave this house along with Helen and Kate, and earlier we sent off a dozen white balloons. Some of the balloons burst on the brambles clinging like flesh to the prickles, while some sank without trace. But we saw enough of them against that big, blue sky to give us all a little hope for the future, and I hoped Lauren's spirit flew with them, and I remembered the good things about my daughter-in-law. I thought about how much she'd loved my son, how desperately she'd wanted to keep their marriage, and have her baby – and her laughter on their wedding day.

Who knows when her fate was sealed? Was it Helen staying with Tim, who went on to shape who Lauren became? Or was it the day she threw a ball at a neighbour's window, and paid her best friend to take the rap? Whenever that moment was, Lauren was caught up in the Jacksons' secrets, cover-ups and lies. And it was this that had sent her hurtling towards her final end. Taken too soon, at the hand of her father, who loved her, indulged her, enabled her, and rescued her, then sent her tumbling to her death.

We don't always *see* the people we love, or the damage they do. Tim was once a hero to his wife and daughters; Helen herself had once described him as her 'rescuer'. He was always there when they needed him, used his position in the police to cover for the time Helen had drunk too much to drive, and later when Lauren did the same. Helen was right, the fruit doesn't fall far from the tree. Lauren was similar in many ways to her mother, but like Helen, she was a good person, who made bad choices. Lauren knew she'd made mistakes, was ashamed of the cavalier way she'd put her own needs first, and hadn't considered the devastation her behaviour had on others. But making a life with Sam, and discovering she was pregnant, changed her, and she wanted to right those wrongs, she was filled with remorse and determined to change. But when she finally found the courage to make that change and tell the truth, her father tried to stop her, and she paid with her life.

'Everyone saw the lovely, kind, caring Tim,' Helen told me recently. 'But there was always something bubbling underneath. He never hurt us, but it always felt like he might. It was his temper I was afraid of, because deep down I knew that if he ever really lost it, that could be dangerous. And that turned out to be true.'

As for me, the fallout from Lauren's death made me realise how I'd always accepted what people presented to me. I was too trusting, and believed too easily the picture they presented to me. I really thought the Jacksons had all the answers, and I envied what I perceived to be their closeness, their happiness. But that's all it ever was, my perception, and as Helen once said, 'Georgie, you only see what you want to see.'

Now I know that regardless of how close you might feel to someone, everyone has their secrets, and secrets usually lead to lies. Even Kate had her secrets, and just after Tim was arrested, she came to see me, told me something that had been puzzling me for a while.

'On the day Lauren died I drove to the cottage, hoping to hang out there while she was at work,' she said. 'I just wanted some peace from the arguments between Mum and Dad, and it was quiet there. Anyway, while I was there, I went upstairs to her room and looked through her wardrobe because I wanted to borrow something to wear for a party. Then when I saw her wedding dress, I tried it on. I know I probably shouldn't have, and I don't know why, I guess I just wanted to know what it would feel like to be a bride.'

'That's okay, Kate, you mustn't feel bad,' I'd said, feeling sad for the little sister always in Lauren's shadow.

'It *wasn't* okay though, Georgie, because she came home early, and I heard her coming up the stairs, and panicked. I tried to take it off quickly, But I'd put her red lipstick on and as I lifted the dress over my head, it wiped off on the dress. She came into the bedroom and screamed because she didn't know I was there, and I made her jump and then she started telling me off, and as I struggled out of the dress, I knocked over her wedding picture. It smashed. I felt terrible. She... she was crying, Georgie.' Kate was clearly still distressed about this. 'And when she died, all I could think about was how I'd made her cry. It was her last day on earth and I ruined it for her, I still feel so guilty. I even had the dress cleaned after she died, because I wanted to do it for *her*.'

That made sense; it all added up now, but I do worry for Kate, who clearly struggles with guilt surrounding her sister's death.

'Try not to define your relationship by the final hours,' I said. 'It was about years of being sisters, there were happy times, and giggles and lots of love during those years. You can't condense you and Lauren into the last time you met.'

I watch Kate now, in the garden. I think she will find happiness – it could take a while, but, amazingly, I think the one person in the world she really didn't like might just be the key to that happiness, for both Kate and Helen – Sadie, having recently passed her driving test has driven them both here, and, like Helen, she seems more relaxed, more at ease. Without the demands of Lauren and

Tim, she can be herself, and is embraced by Helen and Kate for who she is, not what she can do for them.

I too have, against all the odds, grown fond of Sadie. In the same way I admired the Jacksons for how they presented themselves, I disliked Sadie for her confidence, her rather brash demeanour and lack of basic manners. I knew this was all part of the brittle armour she wore so she didn't get hurt, but I really wasn't sure what was beneath that armour. But turns out she was just another good person making bad choices, the drugs, the sexual moves on her teacher, and taking the bribes of money offered by Tim, were all about survival. Sadie's proved herself to be honest, and trustworthy, everything she told Sam and I about the Jacksons turned out to be true, and I'll never doubt her again.

Sam is still close to Sadie, but says it's too soon after Lauren to be with anyone else. I believe the horror of finding his new wife dead has numbed Sam, she was his first love, his only love – and it will take time before he can give his heart to someone else.

So, in a couple of weeks he's heading for Australia to work as part of an environment recovery project for the bushfires. It's initially a year, and he's excited, I've seen a glint in his eye about this work that I haven't seen for a long time. I watch him now, playing ball with Kate as the rest of us sit chatting at the garden table. Selfishly I'd prefer if he didn't fall in love with a place or a woman on the other side of the world, but he must find his own direction, and be happy. If that happens thousands of miles away, then so be it – his happiness is all that matters.

Sadie wanders over with two glasses of wine, one for me and one for her, and while the others chat around the table, we decide to stroll round the garden.

'I'll miss Sam when he's gone,' she says.

'I know you will, love. Me too,' I reply, aware that her feelings aren't reciprocated.

'I cried at their wedding, you know.' She looks at me as if waiting for my disapproval.

'Really?' I feign surprise.

'Yes. I never told Sam, but I think I was a little bit in love with him. I'd never have acted on it though.'

'No, it must have been hard for you, but his heart always belonged to Lauren.'

'I know, and even though she sometimes made my life difficult, she could also be kind and funny and loyal. Did you know she paid for my prom dress out of her pocket money because I didn't have one?'

'I never knew that,' I say.

'She was fond of you,' Sadie says with a smile. 'We both wished you were our mother when we were younger.' She giggles, then hesitates before she says, 'I think I wanted to marry Sam because it would mean I'd get a nice mum too.' She pauses. 'He's one of the good guys, there aren't too many around here...' she says, with a sad smile.

'I'm sorry, Sadie. Love isn't always like in the films, is it, some of us get left behind,' I say with a sigh, wondering if I'd ever meet anyone again.

'Yeah, you and me are both in the same boat, aren't we? Lauren had Sam and now Helen has James. Are you a bit pissed off about Helen being with James?' She gives me a nudge.

'No,' I say too dramatically, then I laugh, a little embarrassed because what she said had a grain of truth about it.

'Honestly though, I wouldn't blame you if you still have a thing for him. He's pretty special, I was a mess when he dumped me.' She sighs.

'What?' I ask, smiling – is this her little joke?

'Oh don't worry, it didn't overlap you and him, it was years ago,' she says with a reassuring smile.

Years ago? But she's only twenty-seven now!

I look at her, unable to hide the shock on my face.

'Don't you go telling anyone, especially Sam.' She gives me a wink.

I couldn't speak, but Sadie just keeps walking, and talking.

'James said if ever anyone found out, he'd lose his job, so I don't tell people.'

'What... when did this happen?' My legs are about to give way any minute.

'He used to give me a lift home from school; I was only fifteen so we had to be careful.' She gives me a little smile. 'He'd wait outside in his car round the corner, or if he was tutoring me, we'd just walk out together, it was exciting. And his car was lush, and he'd play nineties music – it was really cool.'

'Did you, did you *sleep* with him?' I ask, slowing down the pace, not wanting to believe what I'm hearing.

'Yeah, of course,' she glanced over at me like I was mad. 'I remember the first time he drove to this back road on the way home. He parked the car near some trees so no one could see us, and put his hand on my thigh...' She smiles fondly at the memory and we both gaze over to where James is flipping burgers on the barbecue.

I try to hide the look of sheer horror that must be on my face. All I can think is how he fooled everyone, including me – and now Helen.

'You're not jealous, are you, Georgie?'

Before I can say anything, Helen's voice booms across the garden, 'Let's drink to the Jackmoores, or what's left of us.' She's holding up a magnum of champagne and is calling us all to heel so she can say something important, but I can barely focus on anything.

I don't know how my legs take me to the table, where everyone's gathered, but they do and Helen pours the champagne.

Lifting her glass high, she says, 'To Lauren.'

Everyone repeats this, and takes a sip. The bubbles sting the back of my throat, it tastes like acid.

'Oh, and I have something else to announce,' she says, and she reaches for James.

My heart drops to the ground and bounces around the patio as he steps forward and they hug; I know exactly what's coming.

'James has asked me to be his wife.' She giggles excitedly, and we all murmur congratulations, as she demands another toast. 'So, to new loves, and new lives – from the ashes, we shall rise!'

With shaking hands, I lift my glass and try to smile. Helen is looking up at James adoringly, and my heart is breaking for her. I think about all the Sadies of the next generation, the vulnerable children who are now being used by all kinds of people. And it starts with taking the rap for a broken window, a drunk driver, or a hand on your thigh after school.

I could ignore what Sadie has just told me, I could easily pretend that I didn't hear, tell myself it doesn't matter. Or I can decide it does, and that by speaking up I'm speaking for all those Sadies out there who have no voice, whose mothers don't hear them, whose stepfathers touch them, and when a kind teacher offers them a lift home, they climb happily into his car.

Everyone around me is sipping champagne and wishing James and Helen the best. I have to stop this, because this man, who's touched all our lives, has dark, troubling secrets. And if the Jacksons' lives and Lauren's death have taught me anything, it's that we have to kill the lies and listen to our collective conscience.

Helen's happiness will be smashed, along with this champagne celebration, over in seconds because the truth is so powerful and happiness is so fragile. But this is bigger than one woman's happiness, and I have no choice. So I take a sip for Dutch courage, put down my glass, take my friend aside, brace myself for the storm and say, 'Helen, there's something I have to tell you...'

A LETTER FROM SUE

Thank you so much for choosing to read *The New Wife*. If you enjoyed it, and want to keep up to date with all my latest releases, just sign up at the following link. Your email address will never be shared and you can unsubscribe at any time.

www.bookouture.com/sue-watson

The setting for this book was inspired by a visit to Devon, and Dartmoor, a National Park of vast moorland. It's a place that can deceive you; in spring and summer it's beautiful, dressed in swathes of purple hued heather dotted with baby lambs and wild ponies. But in winter, it's a different place, thick, rising mists, extreme cold and in this bleak, beautiful emptiness lurks the foreboding grey-bricked, 200-year-old Dartmoor prison.

While there, I couldn't help but wonder what it would be like to live in one of the old cottages dotted on the moorland in the shadow of the prison. How would it feel to live somewhere miles away from your nearest neighbour, no street lights, just a blanket of stars, and definitely no Starbucks? And that was it, I was seduced, and just had to set *The New Wife* there, among the good and the bad, the beauty and the darkness.

I'm not the first, and won't be the last, writer to be inspired by this place. Agatha Christie and Sir Arthur Conan Doyle were both beguiled by the brutal, craggy landscape and climate of sudden mists, that hide secrets and people, especially murderers. I do hope I've brought some of this to life for you, especially for those who haven't been to this part of the world. If you are lucky enough to visit Dartmoor, make sure you also visit the spectacular beaches not too far away, because like the characters in the book, Devon has two sides – the one it presents to the world, and a darker, more secret side.

I hope you loved *The New Wife* and if you did, I would be so grateful if you could write a review, it doesn't have to be as long as a sentence – every word counts and is very much appreciated. I love to hear what you think, and it makes such a difference helping new readers to discover one of my books for the first time.

I love hearing from my readers – you can get in touch on my Facebook page, through Twitter, Goodreads or my website.

Thanks,

Sue

www.suewatsonbooks.com

facebook.com/suewatsonbooks
twitter.com/suewatsonwriter

ACKNOWLEDGEMENTS

As always, my huge thanks to the wonderful team at Bookouture who are amazing, and never cease to amaze me with their professionalism, enthusiasm, and brilliant author care.

Thanks to Isobel Akenhead for coming up with the original idea of two childhood sweethearts marrying, and the complications that ensue when one of them is found dead. Thanks also to my editor Helen Jenner, who has run with me on this journey, and whose ideas and insight have shaped the book into one I am proud of.

Special thanks to Jade Craddock, my brilliant copyeditor, who always finds ways to improve my books, even after several edits when I think it's fine – and it really isn't! And huge thanks to Sarah Hardy and Anna Wallace for their brilliant and incisive reads.

My American friend and reader Ann Bresnan has once again excelled herself, and I couldn't be more grateful. Along with good ideas, and a forensic eye, Ann picks up on my English-isms, and points out things that may be lost in translation to my valued readers and friends in the US and Canada.

Finally, I want to thank my family, friends, book bloggers, and readers, who are always with me on my journey. You all, in your own way, contribute to my books, from your own stories. Our chats about life over the internet or coffee are all little treasures for me to take back to my writing nest and store like a magpie. Thanks to all of you for those amazing gems!

Printed in Great Britain
by Amazon